IN THE
HALF
LIGHT

Anthony Lawrence was born in New South Wales in 1957.
He has worked as a stockman, fisherman, truck driver and
teacher of English and Drama. An award-winning poet,
this is his first novel. He lives in Hobart.

IN THE HALF LIGHT

A Novel

ANTHONY LAWRENCE

PICADOR

First published 2000 by Pan Macmillan Australia Pty Limited

This edition published 2002 by Picador
an imprint of Pan Macmillan Ltd
Pan Macmillan, 20 New Wharf Road, London N1 9RR
Basingstoke and Oxford
Associated companies throughout the world
www.panmacmillan.com

ISBN 0 330 48551 2

Copyright © Anthony Lawrence 2000

The right of Anthony Lawrence to be identified as the
author of this work has been asserted by him in accordance
with the Copyright, Designs and Patents Act 1988.

'Pas De Deux For Lovers' by Michael Dransfield, from *Streets of the Long Voyage*,
University of Queensland Press, 1970.
'Year's End' by Richard Wilbur, from *Ceremony and Other Poems*, Harcourt Brace, 1950.
Last Night's Fun by Ciaran Carson, Johnathan Cape/Pimlico.

All reasonable attempts have been made by the author to obtain permission to quote from
material known to be copyright; any copyright holders who believe their copyright to have
been breached are invited to contact Pan Macmillan.

1 3 5 7 9 8 6 4 2

A CIP catalogue record for this book is available from
the British Library.

Printed and bound in Great Britain by
Mackays of Chatham plc, Chatham, Kent

For my son Cormac

Acknowledgments

I WOULD LIKE TO THANK The Literature Fund of the Australia
Council for a three-year New Work Fellowship, and the Asialink
Foundation for a travel grant to stay at the Akiyoshidai
International Artists' village in Yamaguchi Prefecture, Japan,
where this book began.

Thanks to Richard Flanagan for the continuing spark of his
interest in the work, to Kathryn Lomer for the gift of weeks of
uninterrupted writing time, to Tina Neylon for taking me back
to County Cork, and to Dicky Deegan for sharing his
knowledge and playing of Irish Traditional music, especially the
Uilleann pipes. Thanks also to Rita Flaherty, from the Inisheer
Hotel, and constable Denis Lawlor of Galway city police, for
their advice and information on life and death on Inishmore. To
Nancy Schaffner, Sarah Day, Lisa Warner and Craig Archibald
for listening, reading and for being unfiltered, when it mattered.
To Nikki Christer for her support, patience and vision; to
Judith Lukin-Amundsen for helping me to read the scale on the
map of what I'd done; and to Rachael Rose, whose generous
readings and suggestions helped solve the puzzle of these
spindrift pages, I offer special thanks.

In the pub that night, two men debate the Irish word for
the wake of a boat on the ebb tide

Ciaran Carson, *Last Night's Fun*

HEADLIGHTS

M Y FATHER is telling me about his life. It's my life
too, because we're back at the holiday house on
the coast, and my mother is lying on a camp bed, her
dress up around her waist. My father is kneeling beside
her, holding a length of cotton between finger and
thumb. At the end of the cotton is a bottle cork, pierced
with a sewing needle. The cork is hanging, not moving,
like a miniature bell over her swollen stomach. I'm
inside her. I can hear voices. The light is shifting around.
My father is saying If the cork swings clockwise I'll be
a girl. My mother says It will be a girl. How do you
know? my father asks. Women know these things, she
says, and moves around on the bed.

You don't remember that of course, my father says,
looking at the back of his hand. He always does that
when he's unsure of himself. He looks at the back of
his hand a lot. I ask him if the house on the coast is still
there. He doesn't know. He's sure the lagoon is there,
with its ribbon weed, flathead and bream. That's
important. The lagoon was a place I knew well – first

from lit, muffled descriptions and then, in the world, from walking its blackmud borders; from throwing bits of laughter and my name like bright lures over the water.

In a warm red place, I saw gold circles spinning, then black lines and sparks forming spirals behind my eyes. I saw light as a scrim of decaying web. It tracked through my head and down into my arms and legs. My spine was humming with it. With these shapes came the sound of my blood. With the blood, a pulse of fast internal talk. It's my second language. It's the talk no one else can hear.

The cork was wrong. I came widdershins into the world, my brain still releasing its broken lines, wheels and sparks.

Some people speak of memories from the womb: prescriptive, thumb-mouthing dreams. For some it's the vague backdrop of their first two years: the sights, sounds and textures from a wordless dependency. I remember the shapes and colours that veined the inside of my head, but also the way the light would change as I was carried along over the boards of the verandah, its green wooden blinds dividing the day. Now, when I press my closed eyes in the corners near the bridge of my nose, I see similar designs from before birth and from when the world opened. They are the same gold circles that once turned, losing sparks and lines like Catherine wheels in the blood.

What is nameless in childhood, no matter how strange or terrifying, can often be tolerated, even nurtured, because there are no points of reference with which to align fear or danger. My headlights, and the sounds that began to accompany them shortly after I was born, became a source of constant amazement, even pleasure.

Early one morning, at the start of the Christmas holidays, a tiny alarm bell rang, and although I all but ignored it, a warning flashed its weak signal and I became aware of shadows moving around between the layers of gold and silver light.

We lived in a country town, high in the New England Tablelands of New South Wales. In the dark school of childhood I see huge balls of balancing granite, black frosts and snow, tubes of ice clicking from the mouths of taps, and, best of all, a massive black pine across the road that the Willoughby brothers had climbed and claimed as their own with a white flag cracking at the top.

The Willoughby boys were tough. Their slingshots were perfect beige forks, their bows and arrows sleek and deadly. Their snowballs were spiked with gravel. They could spit and hit flying insects.

After weeks of my watching them and of being watched, they crossed the road and stared at me. When I didn't run away, they said We've been watching you, do you want to come on a picnic to the river? I felt proud and happy to be asked, and said yes. We were standing in front of their house. When Mrs Willoughby came out in a dress like a sack full of potatoes, the boys asked if I could come. She said Go home and ask your parents. I ran home, made sure no one was watching, stood before the red brick letterbox, and asked them. I said Can I go on a picnic to the river with the Willoughby boys? then said Thanks into the letter slot, and told them briefly about what I'd been doing all morning, moving from one foot to the other as the headlights came on and voices spoke over one another.

When the Willoughbys dropped me off outside my house late that afternoon, it was dark and I was thick with trouble. A police car pulled away from the driveway. My father came to the window. He said Where have you been we thought you were dead. Then Mr Willoughby's arm came over the front seat and his finger stopped near my face. You said you had permission, the finger said. He never asked us, my father said, his face like a red moon at the glass. Now get out of that car.

In the bathroom, leaning over the sink, I thought I heard the Willoughby boys laughing outside the window as my father removed his belt and went to work.

There are many things the tongue refuses. Telling your Mum and Dad about a letterbox filled with voices is one. Telling yourself you don't care about the beltings or the heat it leaves on your arse and legs is another. But that night, in my room, listening to my parents' talk come and go like a wireless in the wind, I heard My Name and The Police in one sentence. I heard No Pocket Money fall from my father's mouth. My mother said The Willoughby Brothers. Then, as if they sensed I was listening, they spoke softly, conspiratorially. I closed my eyes, waiting to cry. I imagined them sitting up in bed, looking into their rumpled laps as car lights folded over the walls and ceiling. I waited for my name to be spoken again, but it didn't come. So I said my name instead. It sounded strange, as if a reflection had spoken. I said it again, louder this time, and then I heard, from a nearby room, the unmistakable sound of parents lying on their backs in the dark, barely touching, going over and over just what it was they hadn't done.

SAPPHIRES

M UM AND DAD loved to go into the country.
Picnics were their specialty, and any river or creek
with a shifting pebble-bed and a grassy bank was perfect.
   Dad had been taken sapphire hunting when he was
young, and considered himself an expert. He had a
matchbox full of uncut stones that he'd rattle near my
ear. I knew where he kept them, and I'd get them out
when no one was home and spread them on the floor.
I loved the way they had different lights inside them, and
when I put one to my eye, the day had magic in it.

Glimmer. Sheen. The surface of Tenterfield Creek
contains enough sapphires for everyone. We find
fragments of dark blue stone that turn lightsparks into
sapphires that turn back to stone when dry. When we
aren't sieving and throwing mud, we're upstream, at a
deep section, lowering string weighted with cubes of
raw steak from the bank, waiting for yabbies to rise like
twists of angry woodsnags with a vegetable-straining
safety net held under them.

We are harvesting, up to our elbows or waists in a swirl of pebble-layered New England water. Dad's wearing a pale blue shirt that's going dark to the shoulders as the fabric drinks. I'm wearing underpants and a straw hat.

We are playing. The game, if that's what it is, has no name. I'm trying to find the perfect, flat round stone. Several fine specimens are on the bank, dry and lustreless. They failed the test because of a chipped edge or uneven circumference or width. The perfect stone should fit easily into the palm. Its weight should take the hand down, but not too far. It should contain the light of inner minerals. The ultimate test for the perfect stone is its ability to fly and skip over water, leaving stoneprints on dam, lake or river until it settles into a tail-leaving slide. I have thrown several perfect stones. You know them when you hold them. Something goes into your hand. A root of stone enters the skin and grows there.

Dad's game involves bombing tiny green fish with the long blades of stone he's stockpiled on the bank. He whistles as he lets them go, making a sound with saliva that he hopes is like a water tower over the shell of a broken sub.

Mum's upriver with my sister. Their game is called Jump Up Sally, where jumping and hiding feature heavily in the rules.

We've eaten lunch: chicken, watermelon, grapes, cheese, bread rolls. Mum said Don't swim on a full stomach you'll get a cramp and drown. Where we are, the water is so shallow it's below my knees when I stand. Mum's afraid of water. That's because her mother drowned in the Murray when she was little. She watched her go under. When I had baths, she wouldn't leave me alone, even when I was old enough to wash myself. When we were playing under the garden hose, I'd see the curtains opening and closing with concern.

Dad's had enough. He's on the bank, drying himself. I'm cold, but I want to find that stone. I go under and open my eyes. Green and silver fish go in and out of light, like ripples. I can't see very well because the water hurts my eyes, and makes everything blurry. When I surface, without a stone, Dad's no longer on the bank. I get out and listen. I look to where Mum and my sister were playing, and see them standing together. Dad's got his arm around Mum's shoulders. They're standing still, looking at something. When I reach them I see an old house at the edge of the bush, with smoke rising from a redbrick chimney. They can't be interested in that, so I look around for something else. There's nothing but trees, a beaten-up old truck near a fence, and the river going off into the distance.

What are you looking at?

Smoke, my sister's voice rises at the end of the word as if she were offering me a cigarette.

And?

Just smoke.

Mum puts her head on Dad's shoulder.

I watch it too. It fans out at the end of its rising and goes the colour of low clouds.

There must be something more to this than just watching smoke, and I say so.

Mum pulls her cardigan close and moves from foot to foot.

Before you were born, she says, shivering, we'd drive up to the lookout on winter afternoons and watch the night come down. If it was still, like it is now, the smoke-lines would be rising all over the place. Some were grey, some white. She took a big breath and let it go. They were pretty. They were good times.

My sister is already bored with smoke-watching and kicks a stone around. I'm not far behind her. Dad gives Mum a kiss and holds on to her for ages. I wait. They kiss for too long. I look back at the river. Let's get some yabbies, I say, but it doesn't work. They're still kissing, as if no one was watching, as if the smoke had stopped rising.

LARS ACKERMAN

W HEN I HAD the words to contain what I'd seen,
no one seemed to know what I was on about –
or else they feigned ignorance. My parents took my
questions as more evidence that I was indeed a very
strange child. Friends simply lost interest and entered the
leafwalls of cubby houses or else pretended to know
what I meant before running away.

Lars Ackerman understood me. We recognised each
other immediately. I saw him coming from a long way
off. It was as though he had a special smell. Lars saw the
shapes, heard the words. I could tell that he was just like
me, and I needed him.

Invited to play at his house after school, I saw crayon
and pencil drawings on the walls and doors. Mrs
Ackerman sat in a big chair in the kitchen, nodding
behind a panel of cigarette smoke as Lars showed me
around. Sometimes she said things into the air. Her
voice sounded like stones being dropped into water.

The house was a mess: clothes thrown over furniture,
things falling apart, food scraps on the floor. In the
corner, a light globe fizzing under its cover. Each room

was cold and damp. In Lars' room, on the wall behind his bed, I saw the gold shapes. In the bathroom, black lines, red sparks. I told him that I understood. I said Lars we have the headlights. He nodded, his head to one side like a puppy. He traced a shape on the wallpaper and said My horse's tails, they make me do funny things. Then he laughed and ran from the room.

Lars was often in trouble at school, turning his eyelids up to reveal the wet, pink undersides and terrible whites, pissing into bubbler basins, or talking to himself and losing his temper. I had no interest in doing tricks with my eyelids or pissing where people put their mouths, but I did talk to myself and I was often tired and cranky. I never knew I was having these one-way conversations until I was stopped and told. Under a tree at lunchtime, someone tapped me on the shoulder. I remember surfacing, as if from a great depth, with the tatters of words on my lips. The boy said You're talking to yourself. I called him a liar and kicked out. Tears and teachers. I was reminded, again, to control my imagination and temper. Then the phone call home.

That night Mum and Dad sat me down and said Why Do You, What Can We, Don't Do That, There Are You Know, No More Of This James, Understand? I told them through tears that I had a secret friend – Someone from up here, I said, lying, pointing to the side of my head. I knew girls and boys who talked of having them, so it seemed a good thing to say. But it was nothing like that. I just talked. The words appeared, held together by strings and hooks of light.

Some months after my visit to Lars' house, my mother told me that Mrs Ackerman had died. I heard my father say She killed herself. I didn't understand completely. I knew that she was dead, and I was sad, but why would someone, and how, where? Lars didn't come to school for ages. When he did come back he looked terrible. He was pale, there were dark rings under his eyes, and he talked to himself all the time. He'd stopped playing with his eyelids and pissing in public, but now he had new interests. He talked about people I'd never heard of, and one day he showed me some paintings he'd ripped from a book at his uncle's house, where he was living. The paintings were horrible, and they troubled me profoundly: a giant eating a baby, an arm sticking out of its mouth, with blood in the air, men being shot against a wall, their arms outstretched in No! and other men lying down in blood. Lars carried the folded pages in his pocket, and would bring them out in class, or stand at the centre of a small crowd in the playground, holding court with the gruesome images. When he first showed me the paintings, I could feel him watching my face. When I looked up, he was grinning lopsidedly, a saliva bubble gleaming on his tongue.

There's a lot to think about, isn't there, he said, and laughed.

I hid from him all that lunchtime behind the toilet block, and for days avoided him whenever I could.

A few days later Lars was gone. Our teacher talked about a new, special school. The kids said Madhouse. I closed my eyes and said hello to him. I asked him where he was and how he was doing. I saw him moving in and out of focus, his ice-blue eyes and big, blond head looming in the air as my words went into each other like the rain.

STEPHANIE

———

AWAY FROM the balancing globes of granite, the
black frosts and snow; away from the pine tree and
its concealed ladder to the flag; the Willoughby
brothers and their handcrafted arsenal; far from that
small country town, we entered a new life in the
city, where Dad had landed a job. I became a full-
time student of my luminous inner workings. It was
a kind of black entertainment. The day that luminos-
ity was given a name, entertainment went to ground
forever.

In my fourth year of high school, locked into a grid of
suburban streets and gardens, I woke early one morning
and was given instructions.

Having packed a change of clothes into my school
bag, I hurried through breakfast, then walked up the
road past the other kids waiting at the bus stop. I
continued on down through the bush, to the river, and
followed a path through trees crackling with insects up
to the highway, where I walked to the station and
caught a train into the city.

This one day was to be the real beginning of my long apprenticeship to disorder.

I changed into my other clothes in the toilet at Town Hall Station. Leaving that huge room I laughed, and the sound came back at me, amplified by the tiles.

From frequent visits with friends on the weekends and on my own, I knew Sydney well. I'd walk around, see a movie, sit in Hyde Park with the pigeons or get lost in the streets. Usually I'd end up down at the harbour, watching people.

At the Pyrmont fish markets I moved along windows filled with crushed ice and fish, their sea colours gone to a flat, neon gleam. I wanted to sit by the water and eat king prawns and drink lemonade, but I sat up against the side of a building eating peanut butter sandwiches and drinking warm water from a tap in the wall.

On through Chinatown, past the markets up to Central Station, where I entered the main waiting hall with its black metal rafters and huge clock looming overhead. I bought a soft drink and a packet of chips and found a place on a curved, plastic bench. Some of the people around me had suitcases. Some carried large canvas bags over their shoulders.

I hadn't seen her arrive. I was watching the hands on the clock when she started talking. She seemed old, but she could have been twenty. I found it hard to define someone's age, once they were outside the boundary of teenage years. She was wearing a dark blue sweater and blue jeans. Her hair was short, black, and dull in the grainy afternoon light. The strap of her shoulder bag divided her breasts. She was smoking a cigarette that crackled and sparked when she drew on it. She inhaled loudly and blew thick lungfuls into the air above her head. She smoked as she talked. Was she aware of giving voice to this seamless, public flow of words? Listening to her made me feel terrible. It was an old feeling, like the shape of a headache moving slowly into view. She was talking about things I didn't understand, but the fact that she was talking to herself was enough for me. I moved closer. I could smell the cigarette smoke as I knelt to one side of her, watching and listening. She said Wherever you go you need to struggle. Don't think about it, alright? There's a train coming and it's got my name in the window. I can see you.

I wanted to hide when she said that, and a red splinter of light appeared behind my left eye. I tried blinking it away, but it grew. I looked up at the talking woman and her face had a flame licking out the side of it. When I looked again the flame had gone and she was waving her hands in the air. People on the bench were shifting around, rearranging their luggage and not knowing where to look. No one engaged with her. A woman took her daughter by the hand and led her away. I closed my eyes and listened to the woman beside me give meaning to every word I'd ever spoken on my own. She was speaking quickly, with little emotion, it seemed, about the sea. About dolphins and killer waves. Dead sailors. Irish sailors. Her father in a small, white boat off Galway Bay the night his heart blew and he went overboard into phosphorescence down to a bed of weed and sang to her all night and then for days. Still sings to me, she said, looking straight through a little girl that had stopped in front of her to listen, as if she were being told a story.

I wanted to tell her that I knew what she was doing, that it's alright to talk to yourself, but I couldn't. She lit another cigarette. I got up from the bench and walked a few steps and turned to look at her. She was leaning forward, elbows on her knees, tapping ash on the floor.

Fuck the sea anyway, she said.

I went down to the toilet, to wash my face with cold water. My head was going sideways. On the way out, I looked into my eyes, looked away, and then looked back, trying to detect movement. Someone coughed in a cubicle. The sound seemed too loud, even with the tiled toilet's sharp acoustics. Sounds had been getting louder. Bird calls came through traffic. Music on the radio at home gave me headaches. And with this increased sound came an intensifying of the lights in my head.

When I came back into the waiting hall she was gone. She was not among those sitting with their bags or at any of the food stalls. My heart raced. I went to the main entrance. Taxis, someone checking a map. Then I saw her. She was half a block away, head down, moving strangely along the footpath. I followed her.

I was aware of doing the wrong thing. I felt both stupid and guilty, yet I had to watch her. Did I want to meet her? I'm still not sure, although walking up that city street behind her, hanging back as she stumbled and lurched from shop to shop, I was overcome with a sense of something familiar, as if this woman were someone I had known, a long time ago, and had forgotten.

She entered a chemist. I found myself at a cardboard display stand gleaming with scissors, clippers and files. She was at the counter, arms folded, staring at the wall. I went to stand beside her. I leaned forward near her left shoulder, and breathed in. Her sweater and hair smelled of cloves. A man wanted to know if I needed help. I said no and backed away. The woman was handed something in a paper bag. Then she turned and swayed from the shop.

15

The sky was dark. The edges of the buildings looked blunt and dirty, becoming part of the sky. I kept a few paces behind her, stopping to look in windows whenever it seemed she might turn around. She had a terrible limp, her body rocking heavily to the right. It looked painful. I watched her directly and peripherally. Then she was gone. I ran to the next shop and looked inside. An antique shop. No one. My chest was thick. I'd lost her.

Sunlight flared into the street and then faded. It started to rain, lightly at first, then fast became a wall of broken silver, releasing a smell that was part chemical, part natural from the road and sky. I stood in the doorway of the shop, watching traffic, the rainbeads tiny explosions and bubbles on the road. The shop was dark, framed prints lining the walls. There were large empty boxes on the floor, a few ratty chairs, a marble wash-stand with its mirror hanging from one hinge. I could see a pool of light at the far end of the room. I tried the handle of the door but it was locked. I put my face to the viewfinder my cupped hands made and looked deep into the shop. Grey walls. A dirty cone of yellow lamplight. Then a shadow leaned into the wall. When it moved again, a woman's face came into the light, framed by short black hair. She moved forward. A sweater and jeans. Behind me, footsteps, voices, the driving rain. I knocked on the door.

We're closed, she said.

Something brushed my arm. An old man was standing behind me holding a handful of plaited leather bracelets. He offered me one.

Fifty cents, he said.

No thanks.

For your girlfriend.

No.

He stepped back, still proffering the bracelet. Rain dripped from the frayed, filthy hem of his long brown overcoat onto bare feet. His face was a mask of cracked leather. He smiled, shivered, then shook his hair out like a dog. You're a good boy, he said, then he backed away and entered the rain.

The light and the woman were gone. The door was covered with stickers and small posters. Then a name: *P. Riley: Antique Dealer.* I took a pen from my bag and wrote the words on the back of my hand.

Going home on the train I thought about her, saw her again and heard her words, saw her leaning forward at the back of the shop, peering through a gauze of lamplight. I wanted to know the colour of her eyes. Her name.

Through the flashing grey steel girders of the Harbour Bridge, I saw water and boats. I made a circle on the glass with my breath and looked through it. The girders, water and boats vanished. I saw a film of light with air bubbles floating through it. What were they? Did everyone have them? I closed my eyes and saw them again, moving like transparent chains through space.

When I surfaced, the mist circle had gone, the train was in a tunnel, and the people in the carriage were staring at me. I knew then that what I'd seen inside had been turned into words, and the words had been spoken. I stared back at the faces, one by one, until they looked away.

That night I couldn't sleep. My bedroom, a breeding ground for spiders and mould, was dark and damp.

I sat up and turned the bedside light on. I heard, from the bush that merged with the steep back garden, a possum cough and a night bird quip profoundly before it flapped away. I kicked the covers down, stretched out and touched myself.

I'd discovered how to make myself come by accident. Wet dreams didn't count. I'd only had one that I knew of, and that was disappointing, leaving me with damp pyjamas and no memory of the dream that had caused it. The first time it really mattered was during summer holidays. Floating on my back in a stone oceanside pool, one hand gripping the conglomerate poolside, the other waving through the water for balance, I edged along and passed under a thick stream of warm seawater that flowed in each time the swell lapped the poolside. It felt wonderful. I came back and hovered there like a strange, surface-feeding fish. The swell arrived and the water streamed. I was overwhelmed. My body tensed and my headlights went crazy. One more long pulse of seawater, and something came away from deep within me. When I sank into the clear green water and pulled my swimmers down, a cloud of thick white fluid swirled against my thighs.

Lying on cool sheets, the memory of that pool was fantasy enough. I watched, as if from a distance, my hand rise and fall. I saw the words I'd written outside the antique shop. Then I saw the woman's face. Her mouth was opening, her teeth lit with moonlight. I saw the space between her breasts where the strap of her bag had divided them. The letters on the back of my hand blurred and my eyes sparked with water as I leaned back against the end of the bed and painted my belly and chest.

In the morning I feigned sickness. I told Mum I'd been throwing up. I'm staying home today, I said, and went back to bed.

Mum knew I was lying, and said so, but she left me alone in my room.

I lay there listening to the click of dishes being put away; to the vacuum cleaner's drone. Then I slept again.

When I woke and opened the curtains, I saw that Mum's car was gone. It was late morning. A cloudless day. I went upstairs and looked through the telephone book. Then I dialled the number for P. Riley, Antique Dealer. I tried to hear a telephone drilling into the dark air of the shop.

Hello? A woman answered.

Is that P. Riley?

No. That's my father. What do you want?

Are you an antique dealer?

No.

I listened to her breathe.

Who is this? What do you want?

I was at your shop yesterday.

I wasn't open yesterday.

I know, but I was standing outside and I saw you inside the shop.

Who is this?

My name is James.

James what?

James Molloy.

There was a long silence. I saw a shadow with a phone receiver glowing inside it.

I remember. You were looking through the window. What do you want?

I don't know. I mean, I want to talk to you.

Is this some kind of joke?

No, really, I was standing outside your shop and I knew I had to talk to you.

What about?

I don't know.

Listen, I've got no time for games.

A bus or truck went by, changing gears outside her shop.

Are you still there? she asked.

Yes. Can I come and see you?

No. I'm not open.

Are you closing down?

Something like that. Look, I've got to go.

I heard a match scrape and flare. She inhaled. How old are you?

Sixteen.

Why aren't you at school?

I stayed home so I could talk to you.

She laughed, and then she started coughing. Her lungs crackled like grassfire. When she'd stopped coughing she said You tell me what's on your mind, and maybe we can talk some more.

I looked at the words on my hand. The ink had faded, the letters bleeding into skin.

I think you're an interesting person.

How do you know that? We've never met.

I heard you talking.

The words were out, and she fell on them.

Where did you hear me talking?

At Central Station, yesterday. You were talking about the sea, about Ireland.

She hung up. I stood there as if nailed to the floor, the receiver still pressed to my ear. I watched a line of ants moving over the surface of the table. I put the receiver down. Someone was hammering next door. Then I realised I was holding my breath. I exhaled and breathed in deeply, my head reeling.

I showered and dressed quickly. Then I heard Mum's

car coming down the drive. I left the house through the back door and ran to the bus stop.

When I reached the shop I stood to one side of the door and looked in. There was no pool of light, no woman inside its anaemic glow. I saw prints, some lying just inside the window, some stacked on the floor against the wall. One was a landscape with poplar trees lining a narrow road that snaked into low hills. In another, four exotic-looking fish floated one atop the other like a layered, sub-aqueous kite, their Latin names a line of copperplated light beneath their jaws.

I knocked on the door. Knocked again. Stepping back and looking up, I found three small windows, each blinkered with filthy curtains. I picked up a small stone and lobbed it at the glass. It clicked loudly and then rattled down the tin roofing. I considered calling out, but was conscious of people moving past. I looked back through the shopfront glass. As I was staring hard through my reflection, a woman's voice called from above.

Go away!

She had opened one of the windows, her right hand extended fully as she held the latch. Go away now, she said.

It's James.

She looked at me carefully. I know who you are.

I've come into the city to see you, I said, then became aware that a few people had stopped on the sidewalk.

Well, you've seen me now, so you can leave, she said, and closed the window, trapping a flap of curtain. She opened the window again and lifted the flap away.

What did you do? a man asked.

I need to ask you some questions, I shouted.

I thought the curtain moved, but I couldn't see her.

The people were waiting to see what would happen next.

A light came on in the shop. I went to the glass – nothing but empty boxes and their brooding shadows. I hurt my eyes concentrating hard on the shop's every detail, as though she might materialise on the wall, the floorboards. I scanned the ceiling, as if she might be lying there, vaguely luminous, pointing at me as she curled her lip and snarled. The thought hurt me, so I stopped it.

My headlights were active now, and the traffic made the air vibrate and taste like wet metal. I stepped sideways to the door and knocked. Four times. I relaxed my eyes and let the reflection of the street take over. I saw the shapes of people passing. A fire engine flashed over the glass – a fast red box full of warnings. I saw the old man selling leather bracelets pause, look around, move on. Then the door was being unlocked, opened, and I was entering the shop, attended by a wash of lavender light and voices that could have come from a large, tiled, underground room.

She stood behind the door as if it were a shield. When I entered the shop she closed the door, locked it.

Five minutes, she said.

The air smelled of dust and mould. At the end of the room she turned and lowered herself into a chair. There was another chair beside the desk.

She reached over, bending the lamp's segmented stem until light pooled in a clean-edged circle on the desk wood. Then she flipped open a packet of cigarettes, selected one, and held it aloft between finger and thumb. In the half light her features were barely discernible. The cigarette seemed to hang in the air. Then she leaned forward until her face was visible. She drew on her cigarette, formed a small O with her lips, and blew a smoke ring. It shivered from her mouth, rippling away over the table until it hit the base of the lamp, dispersing in a clove-scented swirl.

You don't seem to have a problem calling strangers on the phone and giving them the shits, she said.

I thought you'd talk to me.

And you don't mind standing in the middle of a footpath and calling out in public.

I had to do something, I said.

I tried to see her face, but she had leaned back away from the light. The tip of the cigarette glowed.

She asked me questions. I tried to answer them. She wanted to know more about why I'd followed her. She didn't believe me when I explained that she seemed familiar, like someone returned from a long way off.

Her voice came and went in the smoky lamplight, as if she were covering and uncovering her mouth with a hand. I was aware of traffic at my back and the blue light in front of me. When I moved forward, trying to see her, she leaned away. When I asked her about her father, the one who had drowned in Ireland, she leaned in and looked at me with one eye.

He wasn't in Ireland, he was in Sydney, drunk. He drowned in the bath, she said, using both eyes to inspect the end of a hairstrand.

I saw a man in a black suit lying face-down in bathwater. I left him there and said I talked about dying once. A girl at school told me.

She lowered her head into the edge of the light. Do you think about dying?

Not much, I said. Do you?

All the time.

She stood up. She moved around the table to stand beside me. I could smell her.

Have you told your parents what you've just told me?

You mean talking about death and stuff? Kind of, but they don't understand. Dad just says Get some sleep you'll be alright in the morning.

Have you ever seen a doctor about it?

No. Why, should I? Do I need to see a doctor for talking to myself?

Suddenly I felt trapped in a very small space. The walls came together, their shadows peeling away. The circle of lamplight intensified and licked the desk wood. I stood up and turned around. The room turned with me. I thought I was going to throw up. My heart jack-knifed and kicked around. My hands were going numb. I couldn't breathe properly. Then I fell. I went down slowly, with the ceiling like a low, black cloud stretched over my head. I felt hands on my shoulders, then something warm and wet moving over my forehead.

You're alright, a woman's voice came down to me. You were frightened, that's all. You're safe now. Can you hear me?

Yes. My voice sounded hollow, distant.

Can you sit up?

She helped me back into the chair. That's enough talk for now, she said. Too much talk is bad for the head. I'm sorry for being so rude, on the phone and everything. But I need to protect myself. You know what I mean, don't you?

I think so.

She lit a cigarette. It crackled and threw a spark. I just realised, she said, I haven't told you my name. It's Stephanie.

Stephanie Riley, I said.

It sounds good when you say it, she said. Then she said James. She knelt down beside me. She smelled of cloves and sun-dried washing. I'd like to see you again. She held my hand. Her skin felt papery. We need to have a proper talk. You can call me. But not for a week or so. I want you to try something first.

I looked into her eyes. I couldn't speak.

I want you to write down how you feel each day.

I found some words. You mean about talking to myself?

Yes, but also just in general.

Like a diary?

Well, yes, but more than that. I'd like you to write down everything you can, especially about when you feel strange. Could you do that?

Yes.

Good. When you've done that for, say, eight days, would you call me?

She let go of my hand, got to her feet and went to the door. Look at that, she said.

I went to stand beside her.

The city. Bastard of a thing. She opened the door, held it open.

I moved out onto the step.

Don't forget to write, she said, and laughed.

I laughed too, but it hurt. When I looked out into the street, I heard the door close and the locks being set. I watched her move through the shop. Then the light went off.

As I started up the hill towards the station, something clicked in the base of my skull and a woman's voice came in. Bastard of a thing, she said. She said Clovesmoke. I will see you when you know, she said.

TAKING NOTES

I BLACKENED PAGES. I stayed in my room. And although I went to school every day, in the afternoon I sat at a card table, the curtains drawn, writing furiously in a pool of lamplight. Words. Images. Were they accurate descriptions of feelings? Is it possible to describe such things? Did they have a shape and colour? Texture? When the words wouldn't flow, I went back to the ocean-side pool. The floor of my bedroom was littered with pages and tissues. I tried to remember what the voices were saying, but memory often faltered, leaving me with a veneer of headmusic and fast syllables. So I made things up. I wanted Stephanie to have something, to see what had been going on in my life, whether it was true or a lie. I gave names to voices and placed them in curious locations. At school, in class, I went to the Bahamas or to the Highlands of New Guinea. I went underwater off Bermuda and listened to rainbow-flanked reef-dwellers blow their secret language to one another over the brain coral. I heard a village elder in Mount Hagen describe a touring storm. His words came in wandering lines and he moved through them, his voice thick with rainwater and mud.

A teacher's shadow fell over me as I was writing. I tried to conceal the page. She removed it from under my splayed hands, stood reading, and then announced to the class that she had something important to say. People turned in their seats and waited. My breath held itself. She started. The Bahamas, Bermuda, New Guinea, Reef Fish, Rain, a Parade of Words.

Where is the mathematics in this garbage? she asked.

Someone laughed.

Where is your head, young man?

Someone said On the floor, miss.

Laughter.

I sat in ruins as she walked up and down between the desks, reading my words. I should have ripped the page from her hands. I should have stood up and said Give those pages back, you bitch, you don't know what it means. But I sat in face heat and said No Thing. She put the pages down on the desk and said I want to see you after class, but the bell went off and I followed it, out of range of Come Back Here, James Molloy.

There was trouble. What friends I had in high school were smokers, fighters and teacher-haters. They brought Santana and Rolling Stone album covers to school and talked about Lou Reed. This was true rebellion. I went to their houses after school and listened to Blind Faith and Eric Burdon singing 'Sky Pilot'. One boy, Steve, wore a sleeveless denim jacket with *Hell's Fellas* written on the back with silver studs. Clem, who hated roses and cats, was famous for taking a tomato stake to the heads of prize roses on his way home from school, and for drop-kicking cats over bushes.

We met in the black, early hours and stole milk money from under empty milk bottles. We threw stones at streetlights and said Fuck to cars. We phoned the most hated teachers and said Get stuffed, you couldn't cane a toad, dickhead. We rolled cigarettes and spoke in a private language involving the names of native birds, animals, plants and Monty Python sketches. We understood each other perfectly and laughed ourselves sleepless.

I'd been carrying the notes I was writing for Stephanie in my pocket – a thick, doubled-over wad of soiled and dog-eared weirdness. At the back of the library I took the notes out, reading and adding to them. I had to keep watch – this was not cool behaviour.

My friends accepted my unpredictable monologues. At least they never let on. Once, when I asked Harry Gordon if he'd ever heard me talking to myself, he just looked at me and said Does Raggedy Anne have cotton tits?

Harry was wild. He held the record for the most number of canings in one week before suspension saved his hands. Twenty-four strokes of Pearson's wicked Rangoon stick in five days left his palms and fingers veined with blue and crimson. His thumb was swollen. Bloody broken, he said. Harry was using the suspension to plan his revenge. He said he had Pearson's address, and would start by pouring sugar into his petrol tank. Then he'd kidnap his dog. And just in case Pearson didn't think he was serious, he'd cut its head off and stick it on the school fence. As far as I know, he never acted on his threats, but to hear Harry talk you'd swear he was capable of anything. He'd been raped by an ice cream man when he was twelve – first the lure of the music, then the offer of free ice cream and a ride home in the van. He was driven into the bush and forced to lean over the fridge. Harry said the ice cream man was bald. He said he'd recognise him from ten miles away. Whenever he sees an ice cream van, he always goes up and checks the guy's head. Pearson was bald too. I think that explained a lot.

Harry called himself a rocker. He had long black hair and played pool at the Crystal Palace pool hall in the city. He wallpapered his bedroom with Drum cigarette packets. Harry told me things he never told anyone else. I trust you, he said. You're fucked in the head, but I trust you. One day he said You should start writing things down. When I asked him for examples, he said You know, all the weird stuff. Such as? Such as Leave the dog alone and listen, will you!

And?

And where are the problems I love to touch?

You're full of shit, I said.

Whatever you reckon, Harry said, and punched me in the arm, too hard as usual. Then, as if considering a bleak memory, he said quietly You should've dropped that teacher who took those pages in class.

At the end of eight days I'd written myself out.

GALWAY

SATURDAY MORNING, when everyone was out, I
phoned the shop. I was about to hang up when she
answered. I told her that I'd written things down. I told
her about Harry repeating some things I'd said. She
laughed and said Come to the shop tomorrow. She said
something else that ended with a long wet cough, and
then she hung up. She didn't say what time. I looked into
the telephone receiver and saw her there at the back of
the shop, smoking in lamplight, her fingers resting on the
table, her breasts throwing small shadows onto her blouse.

On the train I was almost sick from nerves. I knew each
station's name, and went through them in my head. No
one stared at me. I must have done it silently. My left
leg was trembling. I put both hands on it, and they
trembled too. An old man walked into the carriage, said
You're all fucked, and went out backwards, bowing to
everyone. A child repeated his words and was slapped
to tears.

I saw backyards with people in them. In a tunnel I
saw my face in the glass and outstared myself. Going

over the bridge I practised what to say to her, but the words came apart. My head hurt. My face was hot and my left leg trembled uncontrollably.

When I knocked on the door of the shop my headlights were on and I was shivering. It was early afternoon. The street was alive with people coming and going from movies and cafes. I knocked again. Then the lamp, a shape in its glow, and the sound of locks being undone.

I followed her into the shop, my heart going mad. The air smelled of cloves and dust and smoke. Music came from somewhere near.

Watch your step, she said, then turned to the left, out of lamp-range. I stumbled after her, climbing narrow stairs. When I entered the room she was beside me saying Coffee, tea, hot chocolate, whisky?

Tea, thanks, and she was gone again.

Sit down, she called from another room.

I chose a big, red armchair and fell into it. My hands were doing their own thing, picking at the chair-cover, scratching, moving through the air. A kettle whistled.

She returned carrying a large wooden tray. She set it down and handed me a mug. She lifted her glass, took a sip, and sighed loudly.

Fifteen-year-old scotch whisky, she said. Liquid gold. You can taste seaweed and the saliva of fishermen in this stuff.

Was she serious? My hands bumped into each other and were still. I remembered the notes and worked them from my pocket. I've got these for you, I said, holding them out to her.

What are they?

The notes I've been doing. On how I feel and everything.

Thank you. I'll read them later. Was it a hard thing to do?

Sometimes. Mostly I couldn't tell if it was real or not.

Just like life. Drink your tea before it gets cold. She took a packet of cigarettes from a bag, selected one and lit it. She angled her head and inhaled deeply.

That's better. She laughed and coughed.

The room was small and bright. Two chairs. A sofa. An old beaten-up cupboard with white cups hanging from rings inside it. The windows I'd called up to, and the ratty curtains hanging in a fog of smoke.

It's a nice place.

No, it's not, but thanks anyway, she said. The music was rising and falling, and she was moving to it.

What kind of music is this?

It's Irish. Irish traditional music.

Are you from Ireland?

In my blood I am, she said, looking through her glass of whisky. Her eye looked like something floating in a jar in the science lab at school.

Where in Ireland?

From Galway. Have you heard of it?

No. Is it nice?

It's beautiful. I've never been there, but I know it's beautiful. Maybe I'll get there. She drank, studied her glass.

Why is it beautiful?

She looked at me. Kept looking at me.

For many reasons. The people mainly. The landscape. The music. The ocean. She raised her glass. The whisky.

But this is from Scotland.

True, but it's all Celtic. It's still got the mood inside it.

How do you know so much about Ireland if you've never been there?

I just know. There's some things that explain themselves. I've seen films, read books, looked at photos, and I know some Irish people. I've just put it all together.

Can I have some whisky?

You're not old enough.

I don't care.

She went out to the other room and came back with a glass that had a band of whisky inside it. She raised her glass and held it forward. May the road rise with you, she said, and tapped my glass with hers.

I said the same thing, and liked the image the words made. Then I drank. It burned my tongue and throat, but I liked this new thing, especially the warmth in my stomach and feet afterwards.

We sat listening to the music, not talking. The light had changed. The room was dark now. She got up, went to the window and lifted a curtain.

It's going to rain, she said. I like the rain, do you?

I don't mind it. I like it on a tin roof. That always sends me to sleep. It's safe.

Yes, it is safe. It's like a big, warm hug.

The music finished.

Would you like a hug, James?

Yes.

She came over and sat in front of me. Then she put her arms around my waist and put her face on my chest. Her hair smelled incredible.

Put your arms around my shoulders, she said.

I watched my arms and hands go out and then down around her. Something came loose in my side and floated there. Something else took hold and started to grow. I moved back in the seat so she wouldn't notice.

What's wrong, are you uncomfortable?

No.

I can hear your heartbeat.

Yes, I said. I could hardly breathe.

Would you like to hear mine?

I couldn't answer.

Stephanie sat up. Let's exchange places, she said.

Kneeling on the floor, looking up at her, I saw her hands coming down to my face. Then they were guiding my face towards her. My body followed.

Put your head here, she pointed to the middle of her chest.

She was so warm. Your heart is loud, I said.

Let's just sit here for a little while and listen. Would that be alright?

Listen to what?

Whatever. It doesn't matter.

I think I might have nodded or said Alright into her chest. Her heartbeat was going into my neck. The light came and went as clouds passed. Then it stayed dark. The room became cold. I pushed up against her. She held me. A car horn lifted away from the street. Then it began to rain.

It fell with no pre-storm drops or gusts of wind. It came in a solid wall that drove pigeons from the ledge outside the windows and glazed the glass with feather shapes and wave shapes. Her apartment had a tin roof. The room roared and sang. I said It's so loud, isn't it. She didn't answer. I said I've never heard anything like this before. She didn't speak or move. I thought she must have fallen asleep, but when I looked up her eyes were open and she was looking at me.

What? I said.

You're a lovely person, she said. Don't stop holding me.

I held her.

James.

What? I almost answered her before she spoke.

When was the last time you were scared? Really scared.

I don't know. I get scared a lot. Maybe when a dog came out while we were stealing milk money. Or when I got stuck while climbing a pipeline over the river.

They were lies, at least, they weren't the worst things, and she knew it.

What else?

When I see and hear things. Lights and voices. They make me really scared.

Yes, she said softly. And what about when you're just lying down, or standing quietly somewhere. Do you ever get scared then?

Maybe. Do you mean like when you think someone is watching you or something?

It could be like that. It could be anything.

Through the sound of the rain I heard something down in the shop – a print falling down, a box being moved?

Did you hear that? I asked.

Hear what?

Down in the shop. I just heard something.

There's nothing there. It's probably my cats. They like to play hide-and-seek.

I pushed away from her and sat up, listening.

Please, James, it's nothing. Relax.

I got up and walked to the stairs. I looked down into the shop. Is there a light down there?

Yes, but you won't need one. There's nothing there.

I started down the stairs, running my hands over the wall for balance.

Standing in the shop, looking out at the wet, grey street, I listened hard, my breathing loud and steady. A group of people walked past, laughing and chatting. I sat down on a box against the wall. Then a small, gold light came on in my head, followed by another. Black lines began to drift, like a parade of rain over the lights.

James there are times the light means nothing
matters you're just tired Harry what happened in
the bush can be a scary place, don't you think
it's weird that currawongs look away from you
can tell if a marsupial is spooked by the way
my name is Mr Pearson and you're
joking aren't you boy what do you mean the night
I first saw Julie in town I thought she
turned around and kissed someone I recognised
him from the well-behaved dickhead club at school
he always gave speeches on assembly and did
I tell you about the way

A light went off and a voice backed away. Another light and another voice replaced them.

James?

Stephanie had come down into the shop and was standing in the dark.

You were right, there was nothing here, I said, waiting for her face and body to come into focus.

No, she said.

What time is it?

It's ... I'm not sure. About five? Do you have to go?

I suppose so.

She came and stood beside me. It's still raining, she said.
We listened.

James, I wanted to tell you so many things. Things
about me and my life. Important things. You heard me
talking that day, at the station. Now we're even.

What do you mean?

I was down here while you were talking to yourself.

I wasn't talking. I was just thinking about stuff. About
school.

You were thinking aloud.

What did I say?

Who are Harry and Julie? Are they friends from school?

Kind of. No. I mean, Harry is. Julie is a girl at school.

Fancy her a bit, do you?

She's got a boyfriend.

From the dickhead club at school?

Did I say that? Yes.

She crushed her cigarette out and placed it on the
skirting board. We watched the last smoke rise and blur.

I don't have to go right now, I said. I could stay a
bit longer.

You won't get into trouble?

Maybe, but it's worth it.

You go back upstairs then. I've got to find something
down here.

She put the big book down on the floor and turned the
light on. It was dark outside now, and the old-looking
light in the room made the day seem tired and extra long.

The book was all photographs of Ireland. We sat on
the floor and she turned the pages, talking about places
and people, about the music. She came to a large folded
piece of paper near the middle of the book. She opened
it and spread it out on the floor. It was a map of Ireland,

with beautiful drawings of crosses and something like knitting designs around the edges. She got up and put some music on. A woman's voice and a guitar. She poured two whiskies and we drank, looking down on Dublin, Cork, Galway, Clare and Donegal. She talked about everything. She knew the names of small towns, and when she said them, the words were filled with music. She looked at me when she said Skibbereen, and I wanted to kiss her. When she said Clonakilty, I did kiss her, on the side of the face. She leaned back, smiled and said, with an Irish accent, You're a bold boy altogether, which sent us into hysterics.

Lying on the floor, on my back, images from the book went around in the air above my head.

What are you thinking about? she asked.

Ireland.

Silence, then cars cutting through the rain.

James, do you have any idea why I was talking to myself that day?

Same as me, I suppose.

Which is? She reached out and found my hand.

We can't help it, I guess. We're different.

Yes, we are. She squeezed my hand. Can I ask you a question?

Traffic. Breathing.

James, have you ever heard of schizophrenia?

Do you have it?

Yes.

Stephanie waited for me to speak. I was holding my breath.

I was diagnosed when I was twenty-one, she said. It was a relief when I knew the reasons.

What were you doing?

Just being very uneven with my family and friends, and

I was hearing things and seeing things a lot. I couldn't tell which was the real world, and it terrified me.

Do you think I have schizophrenia?

No. I'm not saying that. I'd never say that. I just wanted to tell you about me, to try and make sense of a few things for you.

I haven't heard you talking to yourself since that day.

No, that's because I take tablets. They help me. Not always, but they're my safety net. A safety net with holes in it.

They didn't work that day at the train station, did they?

I didn't take them. I was sick of taking them. You get like that. They stop you going over into the other world, but they can also make you feel drowsy and dry out your mouth. Sometimes my eyes go funny and my vision is blurred.

Stephanie touched herself on the neck. When her hand came down, she said James, would you see someone about how you feel?

You mean a doctor?

Yes. But not on your own. I want you to tell your parents. Tell them how you feel, and ask if they'll arrange for you to see someone. Will you do that for me? Will you do it for yourself?

Alright.

Do you promise?

I promise. When?

Soon.

Alright.

And after you've seen someone, will you let me know what they said?

Yes.

Good. She got to her feet. Would you like something to eat?

What?

I don't know. We could go out and get something. Some Chinese, or a hamburger.

A hamburger?

Good idea. Let's go.

We got hamburgers and milkshakes and brought them back to the shop. As we were eating, I asked her my question. I asked about her limp.

We lived in the Blue Mountains when I was young. My Dad loved trains. He took me and my friend Wendy to a big model train exhibition. We didn't want to see the trains, we just wanted to get out and look at boys. Anyway, train-heads from all over were coming to show off their models, to talk about them and swap things.

The place was crowded. People were carrying model trains and books. We went into this huge hall. Dad said Stay beside me or you'll get lost. Get lost, said Wendy, and Dad threw her a filthy look.

After a few displays we were bored. Wendy said Let's get out of here.

We ran through a car park, then across the road to some old, dark buildings with broken windows and steep, grey roofs. Wendy said Let's go over there and look around. I was worried that Dad would already be looking for us, but I said alright.

We went through a torn wire fence and walked over to one of the buildings. There were train tracks out the front of it with weeds growing up between the sleepers and old bits of paper and cigarette butts everywhere. Wendy went over to a door and tried the handle. It was locked. She climbed up on a rusted drum and looked through the window. It's like a barn, she said. She climbed down and went to another door. It was huge, on rollers, and when she pulled on it, the rollers moved and stopped. Give me a hand, she said, and together we pulled on the door until it started moving. We got it open enough to squeeze through and we stepped inside and looked around.

I expected it to be dark and cold, but there was dusty light coming in from skylights set high over the middle of the roof, and it was warm. Wendy started running around, picking up things and throwing stones at the walls. I told her to be quiet or someone will hear us and come. She said No one ever comes in here, and threw a stone at a window. It shattered, and a swallow went off its head, flying back and forth, going from sun to shadow.

To one side of the shed there was a narrow wooden staircase going up to a walkway that ran just below the high windows. Halfway up the wall there was a circular metal rail with big rusty hooks hanging from chains. I asked Wendy if she knew what the hooks were for, and she said For when they bring the babies in to freeze them. I threw a stone at her and went over to the stairs. She told me to be careful.

The stairs had no hand-rail. I went up slowly, each step creaking and puffing with dust. Wendy came up too, looking like someone afraid of heights.

When we reached the wooden walkway, we looked out and over the shed. The swallow had stopped flying and was sitting in a little nest on one of the rafters.

I stepped out onto the wood. It moved. I looked down. I put a foot out to the side and started to turn around. The floor cracked at the edge and broke away. I fell sideways. The light went into my head. I heard my clothes rip and then I stopped falling. Wendy was screaming. I tried to bring myself up but I couldn't do it. I looked for her up there on the landing, but my head was thick and loud, and the swallow was doing circles in my eyes. I said Wendy get me down I'm caught, but she was still screaming and then I saw her running down the stairs into the shed. She shouted I'll get help don't try to move. I said Hurry up and then felt sick. The light was going fast and slow, and it must have been raining because water was dripping from the end of my nose and into my ears. I tried to reach up again, to grab my legs but I still couldn't reach. I wiped my face to get the rain out of my eyes. My hand came away red, and then I screamed too. I screamed until the light changed forever, and the sky came out of my mouth.

The hook had entered me just below the right hip. The weight of my body dragged it deep and it ripped a long gash down to the middle of my thigh. The muscle was torn, and the nerves were damaged terribly. I was in hospital for ages. I thought I was going to lose my leg. Even after weeks of lying around with these huge stitches in my thigh, with people telling me how well I was doing, I was convinced that one morning I'd wake up with one long shape under the sheets and a red stain where the leg had been.

The story of my limp, she said.

It's incredible.

I'm lucky to be here, she rubbed her thigh.

With me? I asked.

You're a cheeky one. She struck a match and looked at me. She looked at me again. It was like she had two or three ways of looking – interested, very interested, and You'd Better Be Listening To Me! It was the last look that I was seeing now.

What are you thinking? she asked.

About your limp, it must be hard to get around easily and things like that. And I suppose people look at you.

That's true, but how do you think it affects me emotionally?

Is it bad?

She laughed. Coughed and laughed. Yes, it's bad.

She straightened and crushed out a cigarette. When her head came up her face had Now I'm Being Serious all over it.

It makes things tough. There are two people in this body, James. More, sometimes. Two people who share the same breath, light, smoke, drink, terrible thoughts and dreaming. One staggers from room to room, shop to shop. One talks to herself while her leg drags and slides. Sometimes I want to kill the cripple and keep the talking idiot. Sometimes it's the other way around.

Her eyes went to water and she said I'm sorry. I should never have said those things. I don't even know you.

I tried to tell her that it was alright, but I said Well let's get to know each other.

Stephanie wiped her eyes and looked at her watch. James, it's late. You've got to go or you'll be in real trouble. I'll be in trouble too, she said.

Will you tell me what you think of my notes? About how I feel and everything?

Of course, she said. I'll read them tonight. Now go home.

At the door she kissed me.

Thanks for telling me about the limp, I said.

She moved me onto the street.

Could I have another kiss? I asked, but she was closing the door.

THE COAST

SCHOOL HOLIDAYS began and Dad said Gerringong. I liked it there, with the long itchy grass around the guest house, the mosquitos at night, and the smell of the stuff that Dad sprayed into my room using a pump with a long handle.

I swam and walked, watched cricket on television. I played billiards with Dad. My sister played elastics or ran through the darkwood rooms. My mother slept and read big books and magazines.

I thought about Stephanie and wondered what she was doing. Did she wear pyjamas to bed? What did her bedroom look like? What was her middle name?

Next day, at the ocean pool, I gave her a middle name. I said it over and over until the warm water opened me and I went out of myself and came back swallowing air.

At the end of the first week I went to the shops and phoned her. It was five o'clock. I thought she'd be home, reading or listening to music. The phone rang out. I stood in the phone booth trying hard not to feel awful. A yellow dog trotted up and lifted its leg on the booth door, which made me feel better. I tried again. The coin dropped, my finger made circles, the phone rang. Out.

It's a hollow feeling when the person you need isn't home. I said I'll try her four more times. After that I'll stop. Four is a great number. Four times four is even better. Sixteen is the king of four.

She wasn't home sixteen times. I went back to the guest house and rolled billiard balls over the green felt. And thought of her.

That night my mother said Can we talk?

This usually meant bad news. I followed her into the dining room.

She started saying how she was worried about me.

Don't worry, I'm alright.

Are you sure? You've been very quiet lately.

I'm fine.

I found some papers on the floor of your room.

I went funny and said What pages?

What do those things mean, James?

I was writing stuff down, that's all.

Why don't you tell me how you're feeling?

I do.

But not really.

What do you want me to say?

You can tell me anything.

I know.

Do you want a cup of tea, or a soft drink?

No.

Who is Stephanie?

The room had wooden panels on the walls. The tables were covered with white sheets. Somewhere nearby, someone was clicking glasses together and singing softly.

James?

What?

Who is Stephanie?

Someone I met.

At school?

No.

Where then?

In the city.

Mum pushed her chair closer to the table and leaned at me. She took my hands in hers. I think you'd better tell me what's going on, she said.

So I told her. I went back and found details. I told her almost everything.

Would you like me to speak to this woman?

No.

I don't think it's good that you're seeing her.

She's nice. She's helping me.

What do you mean? Don't we help you?

Yes, but it's different. She knows things.

What things? James, this is serious.

Things, I said. She's the same as me. She's got the headlights and voices.

When the words came out they were loud and went through the room. Someone stopped singing. A head came around a door and a mouth asked if everything was alright.

Mum said Everything is fine, thank you. But it was not. My head was hurting. Mum was talking fast now, and then through tears she was saying What do you mean headlights and voices? I want to talk to this woman, so you had better tell me her phone number and where she lives. She needs help, telling people those kinds of things. She's dangerous. Who does she think she is?

I got up from the table.

Sit down, James, this is important.

I started to walk away.

Please tell me what else she said.

I reached the door.

We love you don't you know that?

I went outside.

You must know that.

I walked down the road. The night was warm and clear. I walked to the jetty and sat on the end, looking down into black water with bits of moonlight moving round inside it. You must know that. You must know. You must. You.

THE NOTE RETURNED

———

A T HOME I tried to help around the house. Mum and
Dad were watching me. They were being too
nice. My sister stayed out of my way more than usual.
She must have been told that her brother had headlights.

The first day back at school, Harry showed me some
photos he'd found in a park. There were all these nude
girls, doing things. We sat behind a rock near the oval
and looked at where the hair was dark and small. Harry
said I saw my sister once. She looked like her, he said,
pointing at a girl in a photo. You ever seen that? he
asked. No, I said. I thought of Stephanie, and wondered
what she looked like naked. I saw her in her room,
taking her clothes off. She was –

The bell went. Harry put the photos in his school
bag.

You alright? he asked.

I was still sunburnt. In class I peeled the dead skin from
my arms and nose and made a tiny mound on the desk.
A teacher's voice droned on and on. I skinned myself
and thought about Stephanie. She was standing on her

bed, her arms over her head. She was moving from side to side, singing. I went up to her and put my mouth to her stomach. I touched her legs. She put her hands on my head and pulled me close. I touched her pubic hair and a noise went through my fingers. She shivered. I licked her skin. Her body smelled of soap and moss. She said James I've been, and then, Would you just, and then, Oh yes, there, now let me, and then I came back to class with a painful erection and a headlight blinking deep in the back of my skull like a harbour light.

Next day I went into the city, changing from my school uniform into jeans and a pullover. As usual, it was overcast and windy. The weather knew when I was coming to the shop. The clouds got together and told each other. The sun put a mask on and went to sleep.

I stood there knocking and looking in through the glass. I stepped back and checked the windows. Called her name. Threw a small rock. The dirty curtains did not move. I went back and knocked.

Across the road was a cafe where I'd once bought a milk shake. I went in there, bought a drink, and sat by the window. A man sat down beside me and opened a newspaper. He smelled like my dad – aftershave and clean clothes. He lit a cigarette, turned pages.

Bloody rain, don't you hate it, he said.

I said I didn't mind and watched the shop.

Where are you from? he asked, without looking up from the paper.

I looked at his face in the window glass. He had the head of a sheep.

Why aren't you at school?

I said I was waiting for someone.

Girlfriend?

No.

Do you come to the city often?

I said A bit, and he asked me what kinds of things I liked to do.

I thought what kind of question is that, but said nothing.

I've got a place near here, he said. You want to come and listen to music or something?

I looked at him. He was tapping his cigarette into an ash-tray and his hand was shaking. The arm of his coat had ash on it and his tie was crooked.

He said What do you think?

I said I've got to go and walked to the door.

Nice to meet you, he said. I come here every day. Maybe we'll see each other again?

I went out into the rain and crossed the road. On the other side I turned back and he was watching me. He waved. I walked to the shop. It was still dark. Still and dark. I scraped my feet on the mat and looked down. There was something sticking out from under the door. A large yellow envelope. I picked it up and saw my name on it, written in big black letters. I wondered how I'd missed it before. Maybe she had put it there while I was over the road, talking to the man. One end of the envelope was wet. When I pulled on it, the paper came away and I saw some pages inside. They were the pages I'd given her. Disappointment made heat go into my neck. I unfolded the pages, but there was nothing more. My hand went into the envelope. I found something and lifted out a big card. It had a photo of stone walls with seaweed draped over them, and there was an old man wearing a cap looking down at his dog. On the back of the card it said Inishmore, Aran Islands. I opened the card. I found, on both sides, the neatest, smallest handwriting I'd ever seen. I sat down in the doorway, my back against the glass.

Dear James,

I'm sorry I'm not here. I wanted to see you, but there wasn't time. There are some things I'd like you to have. I've left them with Mr Gray, who owns a camera shop just down the road. He's expecting you. I know you will like them. What else can I say? That you have touched me deeply. Go safely. May the road rise with you.

Love and tenderness, Stephanie

I placed the card with the other pages and put them inside my shirt. I looked over at the cafe. The man was gone. I wanted to knock again, to call out.

I went down the street until I found the camera shop. It was closed. I didn't want to leave. I found a piece of paper and wrote a message to Mr Gray, asking him if he knew where Stephanie had gone. I pushed the note under the door and walked away. Then I ran back. I tried to reach the note but my fingers wouldn't fit under the door. Using the pen I managed to scrape it back. I wrote my phone number down, pushed the note under the door again and stood up. A woman was standing near the road, watching me. I almost started to explain what I was doing, but she spoke first.

What are you doing?

Leaving a note for someone.

What kind of note? She took a step towards me and looked at the base of the door.

A note for the owner of the shop.

What does it say?

I felt anger in my head. It's none of your business, I said.

It's my business if you're doing something wrong.

Just fuck off.

I'm going to call the police, she shouted.

I walked.

The next afternoon Harry came home with me after school. We went down into the bush and rolled cigarettes and watched cars pass on the road below. Harry dropped small clay bombs and whistled as they fell. Sometimes we heard a dull thud, sometimes a car braking hard and a door opening and closing. One driver yelled something.

I told Harry about Stephanie, right up to leaving the note for Mr Gray, and he said Yeah, but did you get a root? Then he went serious. Did she talk about going away? he asked.

She talked about Ireland, I said. She wanted to go there.

Then she's gone to Ireland.

No, she would've said.

Harry threw a stick into some ferns. If I wanted to piss off real bad I wouldn't tell anyone.

Maybe.

Did you give her those notes you were making?

Yes.

What did she say?

Nothing much, only that she'd read them. She thanked me.

What for?

For letting her read them.

I don't know about her, Jim, he said. She could be a weirdo.

She's not a weirdo. She's fantastic.

A fantastic weirdo.

Anger jumped up. She's not a weirdo. Don't say that.

Well she sounds like an alcho or something.

Harry must have known it was coming because he stepped away as the punch glanced off the side of his head. He fell backwards into a she-oak and said Fuck. Then we were wrestling. We went over the edge of a small overhang into a sea of ferns and sticks. We crashed through. I landed on a rock. Winded, I looked around and saw Harry lying in a tangle of sticks and ferns, smiling. There was a line of blood over his eye. He said I didn't think you'd ever hit me. Then he climbed away, dusting himself off and giving me his hand. A branch had snapped off, the end of it piercing the skin of my calf.

Back on the ledge, I took my jeans off. It was only a big splinter.

Well, pardner, Harry said, we'd better get that arrow out of your leg. Then he rolled two cigarettes and lit them. I'm sorry, Jim, but really, you don't know her. I didn't mean what I said.

I'm sorry too. Then I said I'm going to try and find her.

Maybe that's not a good idea, said Harry. But I'll help if you want. Don't know where we're going to get the money to go to Ireland, though.

Who is Mr Gray? Mum is standing at the top of the stairs, calling down into my room. Her voice has got broken edges inside it. She calls out again. He phoned while you and Harry were out. Who is he, James?

A man in Sydney. He owns a camera shop.

Now she's coming down the stairs. I'm in bed. It's early, but I'm so tired. She stands on the bottom step and looks at me.

And then? she says. Why this sudden interest in photography?

I'm not interested. He's got something for me.

Yes, I know. Some books.

I don't know why, but I'm angry at Mum for telling me. I wanted to be surprised.

She comes over and sits on the end of the bed. What are the books, James?

I don't know. They're a present from someone.

James! she almost yells my name and her hand whacks the edge of the bed. What's going on?

I met someone.

Yes, that's obvious. Who is it?

I've already told you.

Stephanie?

Yes.

Where did you meet her?

A small hole appeared in the bed between us. I watched it grow. My feet were easing over the edge. Mum didn't see it. Maybe she ignored it. She kept talking.

James look at me when I'm talking to you where did you meet her what's her name I need to know what's happening tell me now mister.

I said Headwords, Stephanie, Antique shop, Written Feelings, Irish Music, Whisky, Galway, Schizophrenia. When I surfaced, the hole was huge and Mum was crying. Her head was lowered and her shoulders were moving up and down in time with Why didn't you tell me this before can't you talk to me?

I said Yes, but I didn't know how. I said Do you think we could see someone about it? About how I feel and everything? Mum said Yes, I think we should, and then the hole got wider and my legs dropped into it. I said Help me and she held my hand. I said I'm falling and she wiped her tears away. I was in up to my chest and Mum was getting off the bed saying Get some sleep, we'll talk in the morning. I said Please get me out of here, but by then I'd gone under, the sheets and blankets coming in on top of me like rough grey water. I went down, going head-first into a terrible sleep, so tired, my headlights blinked and went out like a sparkler.

Dad was never one for big displays of emotion, privately or in public. He kept his life inside. At the dinner table or sitting in church he kept the same steady gaze and spoke of essential things. Coming in from the garden, gleaming with sweat, he breathed heavily, wiped his chest down, and made sure you noticed it. After work, he'd go straight into the bedroom and change. The metallic click and slide of coat-hangers. The brief hello.

It must have been hard for Mum to explain to him that their son needed professional help. Dad stood under a sign that said WHAT DO YOU MEAN HE NEEDS HELP, and Mum waved a banner that said I'M NOT SURE BUT WE'VE GOT TO DO SOMETHING.

They came into my room next morning. Dad was pin-striped, Brylcreemed and aftershaved. Mum was hair-rollered and floral. They looked like an idea of someone else's parents. When they started talking, they were unmistakably mine.

What's all this about? Dad asked before checking his watch. He looked at Mum. Karen?

Mum's name never sounded right, but she responded to it.

I think we need to make an appointment for James to see someone.

Dad said Well, can you tell us why you need to see

a doctor? What kind of doctor? A counsellor or someone like that?

A psychologist, I said. They're called psychologists.

That's right, said Mum.

Don't be ridiculous, Dad said. You don't need a psychologist.

Mum looked sideways at him. I don't see what –

Karen, you can't be serious, Dad said, brushing something from the end of his sleeve. Then he looked at his watch again. It's not a good time to be discussing this.

It's never a good time for you, is it? Mum said.

I think she meant Dad never has a good time. I think Dad thought she meant that too, because he went dark and then said Right, I'll come home early. We'll talk then, alright?

Dad started to climb the stairs but stopped. And who is this bloke in the camera shop, James? he asked.

Later, Mum said to his feet, which were level with her head on the stairs.

Fine, Dad said, and went up.

Mum played with her hair. I pulled the covers up and waited.

Mum threw a sock at me. You're going to be late for school.

Good.

Come on. I'll make some tea.

Thanks.

James, I want you to be honest with us. About everything.

Alright.

So, we'll talk this afternoon?

Yes.

Good. I'll drive you to school, if you want.

Don't worry.
I'd like to. Is that alright?

On the way to school, she said she wasn't happy either, but it wasn't anything to do with me. Well, mostly anyway. I asked her what she meant and she turned the radio off. We stopped at a red light and she began to cry. I didn't know where to look. Is it anything to do with Dad? I asked. She nodded and cried.

The school bell had gone. We sat in the car.

Mum said I don't want you to worry about it.

I said That's alright, and got out of the car, trying hard not to cry myself.

When she'd gone, I walked down the road, and kept walking until I reached the train station.

BOOKS

WHEN MR GRAY gave me the books, he looked at me as if he wanted to say something, then he turned back into the shop. I waited. I looked around at the gleaming cameras and photos of weddings and landscapes on the walls. Mr Gray did not look at me again.

On the train I opened the parcel. There was a huge, hard cover book called *Ireland*, and a small red book called *The Faber Book of Modern Verse*. Stephanie had signed them. Her name looked like a mistake in ink. In the red book there was a piece of paper. It was a poem, in her handwriting.

> *When the day comes apart*
> *birds reel and go.*
> *The light is terrible.*
> *Hold the day together.*
> *You and the birds and the light.*
> *Hold on.*

Had Stephanie written this? Was it her poem? What did

it mean? The poem had been placed beside one by
Richard Wilbur. I read it, to see if it could tell me
something, but all I found were ferns and house lights
and fish moving around under the ice. I found another
poem by Charles Madge, about someone called Grant
who was blocking a pass, whatever that means. I didn't
understand everything, but I liked the way the poems
made me feel – confused, but alive in the body. I got
lost in poetry all the way home.

That night Harry phoned. When I said hello, he started
talking. So where are we going to start looking? I was
thinking maybe she's gone up the coast for a while. Or
down the coast. There's a place we used to go, on holidays. The Royal National Park. There's all these little
shacks. You can get into them easy. We stole some stuff
once – tins of food and a knife. Anyway, that's what
people do. They piss off into places people don't think of.
Or maybe she's still at the shop and doesn't want to see
anyone. Pretending to be gone. I don't know. What do
you think? Anyway, we should start looking now.

I saw a small space and entered it. She left me two
books, Harry.

Didn't you hear what I just said?

Which part?

Everything.

Yes. She left me two books, one about Ireland and a
book of poetry. Modern poetry.

It's all crap. Listen, what do you reckon? About
looking for her?

Do you want to hear a poem?

You aren't listening to me.

Yes I am, but I want to read you a poem.

Who wrote it?

Someone called James Wright.

Who's that?

A poet.

Congratulations, Sherlock. Where's he from?

I don't know.

Go on then.

At the end of the poem, Harry said Where did you find that shit?

In the book Stephanie gave me.

She must have really hated you. What's he on about?

I don't know, but I like it. Do you?

No. I think it's stupid. Harry sighed and said Poetry. Then he said Right, I think we should look for her on Saturday.

In bed that night, I thought about poetry. I said the word out loud. Poetry stayed in the air above my head. Then I said Stephanie. It hovered and then it broke open and turned to black air. I saw her behind my eyes, leaning forward as she spoke and tapped ash onto the ground. I saw her limping up the street, and then she turned around. Go away, she said, stop following me. But it wasn't her voice. It was the voice of the man in the cafe, the man with ash on his sleeve. He said Do you want to come back and listen to music, you lovely boy? Then Dad was coming down the stairs, saying Let's have that talk, James. I told him I was tired. He said I'm sorry I got home late. I said something neither of us heard, and then I saw Stephanie turn away behind my eyes and limp like a huge black and white ground bird dragging an invisible wing.

THE SMELL OF PEOPLE

——·••·——

W E WENT straight to the antique shop. Harry was quiet. I looked at his face as he was leaning forward, staring through the glass. I'd never seen him so serious. He seemed older.

It's so dark, he said. Does she live in there?

No, upstairs.

It'd give me the creeps, having all those empty boxes and bits of crap furniture lying around.

Harry stepped back and knocked on the window. Come on, open up, we know you're in there!

Stop it! I grabbed his arm and pulled him away.

We walked to Central Station. I looked for her in everyone. The light kept changing, and wind swept big leaves and papers before us. In shadow I held my breath. In sunlight I watched myself pass in shopfront glass. I said her name four times, silently. Harry stopped walking and asked me why I was saying her name.

In a park below the station, Harry threw his pie-crust and made a pigeon cloud. They flapped and went over each other. Then seagulls came down like bits of smoke. The pigeons stepped aside and let them in.

There must be more seagulls in the city than on the sea, Harry said, and threw a rock. I hate the bastards. I saw someone take a gull's head once. The stupid thing got tangled in the line, trying to steal a man's bait. The man reeled it in and popped its head off with his thumb. Harry mimed a lighter jumping into flame. A line of blood went into the air. The man laughed and threw it back like a small fish.

As Harry went on about gulls and fishing, I looked around the park. There were people in suits and dresses, standing or lying about on the grass, eating and drinking. There were children circling their mothers. Gold and brown leaves were blowing everywhere. A little girl made a leaf mound and dived into it.

Harry had stopped talking. He'd walked away down the path and was standing, hands on his hips. When I reached him he said This place gives me the shits.

The park?

No, the city. It's mad. It gets into people and makes them do weird things.

A truck backfired and Harry jumped. He pulled out his tobacco and rolled a cigarette. What do you think, Jim?

About what?

About the city, about Stephanie. Anything.

I don't know. Maybe she *has* gone down to that place with the shacks. The place where you used to go. Where is it again?

The Royal National Park. Era Beach. Burning Palms.

Harry flicked his unsmoked cigarette into the grass. No, she wouldn't go down there, he said.

Why not?

It's not her scene. Too weird. Too open. She sounds like someone who needs a dark hole to hide in when things get tough.

In the waiting hall at Central Station I showed Harry the seat where Stephanie had sat talking to herself and dropping ash. I sat on the exact place, and tried to feel what she'd felt: the cool, moulded plastic, the texture of the cement floor. Overhead, the big clock made a dark shape in the air.

Well, just because we're sitting on the same seat, doesn't mean she's going to walk up and say Here I am, ha ha you couldn't find me.

She wouldn't say that.

Let's go and check out a few places, Harry said, moving his bum around on the seat the way a dog drags its arse on the grass.

We asked faces behind desks in every hotel from Central to Wynyard Station. They must have thought we were mad. Harry loved it. He put on a voice, and spoke around his cigarette. One man said You're too young to smoke and this is not a movie. Harry said You're too old to be alive, dickhead, and we ran from his shouting. In another place, when the woman behind the desk laughed and told us to leave, Harry said Listen doll, open your book and give us the names or I'll plant one on ya. She thought it was great, but still wouldn't open her book and check the names.

Then we got serious. At a hotel near Circular Quay we waited outside until someone left the building through the guests' door and we ran through it. We stood on a square of old, smelly red carpet at the base of a narrow staircase. Harry went up first. As I climbed,

I thought of Stephanie inside the old train building, looking down before she fell.

Upstairs was dark and old and smelled of dust and smoke and some kind of perfume. The door numbers were faded. Some were broken. The floor creaked as we moved along it. I was holding my breath again. I caught myself doing it more and more. I exhaled loudly. Breathe, Harry said, and elbowed me in the guts.

At the end of a long corridor, someone came out of a room and nearly knocked into us. The man slammed the door of his room and went into another room across the hall. He slammed that door, too. Music was coming from somewhere, and a woman was singing badly. Then she started shouting. Then she broke something. A toilet flushed, a door opened, and the man was standing in front of us. He had long brown hair and was wearing a blue singlet. His shorts were too big and they were falling down exposing his belly.

What are you staring at? he said. He took a step closer.

Harry said We're looking for Stephanie.

The man wanted to know who the fuck Stephanie was.

Harry said She's lost, have you seen her?

Clive you spilled my wine, you cunt, a woman shouted.

The man said Who sent you?

Harry said Mr Smith, and you'd better watch it, Clive, because he knows where you are.

You're lying, Clive said.

No I'm not, Harry said. Mr Smith is angry. I'd watch it if I were you.

Clive came for us, his arms swinging. We easily outran him, taking the stairs in a few jumps and then looking up at him. He was kneeling down at the top of the stairs, crying. He moved the hair from his face and said Please don't tell on me. Promise?

Promise, said Harry.

We went out into the street.

Who is Mr Smith?

The doctor from 'Lost in Space'.

I feel sorry for that bloke.

Yeah, said Harry. Where to next?

Circular Quay. Ferries churning dark green water to milk. Gangplanks and the smell of people. Hamburgers and soft drinks. We weren't really looking for her. We were walking around in a fog of vague intentions, talking about where she might be and what she'd be doing, but mostly we talked about sex and the best way to speak to girls; about fast bowling and Let it Bleed. Harry knew something about all these things, but he knew a lot about girls. I'd heard him in the playground, making fun of Jenny Stevens. She didn't seem to mind. She laughed and pushed him. When I tried it, with Julie, she went away in her head and said I have to go now. I asked Harry how he did it, and he said the secret was not to try too hard. Just don't think about it, that's the trick.

We were sitting on the train platform, watching trains and people. Rats were moving about over the tracks like shadows that had dropped from the wall. They stopped to sniff things, then skittered away into holes or under ledges, moving from side to side. I was about to ask Harry what he meant by not trying too hard, when a train came in, a scream went over us, and a woman ran past with her hands at her mouth, saying Oh No, Oh No. A small crowd had gathered at the front of the train, and people were looking down onto the tracks.

The driver was still sitting in his seat. His face had Terrible Things inside it. Then he got up and climbed down onto the platform, where he walked away from the crowd and stood against a wall and lit a cigarette. Someone shouted Do Something. Harry said Someone's gone under the train.

My body found itself in two parts, and they went in different directions. One side went over to the crowd and looked down and saw the red shirt face eyes help me I can't help me, and the other side went a few steps from the bench and felt sick my neck clicks don't look stay there. When the parts came back together, I heard a whistle go to the end of its sound. It came off the wall the rats had entered and repeated itself around the station. Harry said Shit this is awful. I said There's nothing we can do, is there? Harry said no, and I said the same, and then we walked away. My shoes weren't working. I couldn't feel the ground. Some men pushed through carrying blankets and a stretcher. I heard myself breathing. I didn't like the sound, and the more I heard the harder each breath became. I said Harry I can't breathe, but he couldn't hear me, he was pushing through people, leaving the platform, saying There must be so much blood.

Blood. Trainlights. Windscreen flash. The spark from a chrome whistle. The light in gutterwater. Headlights. Lightheads. Highleads. Help me I can't see you. Molloy you're fucked. Can you hear me? Stephanie's curtains. The end of her cigarette in a dark room. Where are you? I'm anywhere you want me to be over here and there. Why didn't you wait for me? I waited years for you and then I went to ruins darling, save me. I had to go. Thanks for the books. Go into them. Headfirst with the headlights on. Enter the heart of poetry. What will I find? You will find yourself and then you will find me. Where? We are waiting in the spaces between words. We are hanging like rainbeads on the undersides of branches and wires. Between what is said and what is dreamed. Between the ribcage and the pulsing chambers. There are windows inside every good poem. Sometimes they are hard to find. The view is half-heard music. Listen with your body. Which window will I open? You will know it when you find it. For now, remember that when breathing stops, the hands and lips throw shadows. Watch yourself mouthing a twist of silence and fear. They have many masks. Wear them and remember me.

Breathe.

I looked up. Harry was kneeling over me.

You've been away again, haven't you.

Away, yes.

Breathe.

I breathed and saw my left leg moving up and down. As soon as I noticed it, it stopped.

Where did you go? I mean, you were really gone.

Yes.

Where? What happens?

It was something about books and windows. Stephanie was telling me stuff about how to find her and everything.

So where is she? Come on, Jim, this might be it.

She's inside a window.

Oh great. Which one? Can you point it out to me? We're in the city, for fuck's sake.

It's not that kind of window. Really, I can't explain it. It's a window inside poetry.

I knew when you read me that thing on the phone that poetry was going to be no good for you.

I got up and walked away. I said Please don't ask me any more about it. How can I explain when I don't understand myself? I was getting angry. Just don't ask me, alright?

Yeah sure, Harry said. Next time you go to Ga–Ga Land don't expect me to send out a search party. Then he said he was sorry. He didn't mean it. I said Don't worry, and we sat on the grass watching ferries come and go.

I didn't want to ask about what had happened on the station, but I couldn't help it. Harry said when I was out of it an ambulance and police cars arrived. People came running. The street was a siren, he said. Then he went serious. Did you go off because of that? The accident and everything? I think so, yes, I said. My head was throbbing. Jesus, Harry said and rolled a smoke.

HELP

————

WE ENTERED a red brick building. It could have been the front office at school. It had the same kind of smell. The same kind of woman sat at the desk, wearing glasses that made her eyes swim around.

We sat in the waiting room. Dad slapped the arm of his chair. I'm sure this man is very good, he said. Then he stood up. He looked like a big kid, his hands all over the place. We'll get through this nonsense, he said, as one of his hands found my head and started throwing my hair about. Mum held my hand until I couldn't stand it any more. About two seconds. Then a woman came out and said my name. I put my hand up like an idiot, and the woman said Dr Finlay will see you now. Harry would've said Well that's good, wouldn't want a blind quack checking you out!

Dr Finlay looked like a maths teacher or a scientist. He had a beard but no moustache. It seemed weird, like half-mowed lawn. We sat on chairs and waited. Dr Finlay said So, James, how can we help you today? I knew he was going to say something like that. I almost said Are you going to help me tomorrow, too, but Mum jumped in.

Doctor, James, Voices, Things, Strange, Secrets, Normal, Worried, How, Father, Mother, Trouble, School, Good Boy, Cruel, Why?

Dr Finlay nodded.

Dad said Doctor, is there a name for what my son has got?

Dr Finlay said Your son hasn't got anything.

Dad said Cough, fair enough, well, you know what I mean.

Dr Finlay said Of course, but we prefer not to label people here, Mr Molloy.

I thought about soup cans and pencil cases.

Mum said Can you tell us anything, jigsaw features?

Mum said Can you tell us anything, Doctor? It's just that we're so worried.

Dr Finlay said Depression.

Dad said Does my son look depressed to you?

Mum said It's deceptive.

Dr Finlay said That's right, it is. It's the invisible illness.

Illness? Dad said the word, then Mum repeated it. I felt the shape of it in my mouth and turned it over with my tongue. It had blunt edges, and tasted bitter. Illness? I said, and Dr Finlay went on about how names aren't important, it's just that some people are affected profoundly by depression, and we have to help them with counselling and drugs, sometimes –

Mum stood up. She was shaking. The curls were bobbing at the sides of her head. She shook a finger in front of Dr Finlay's naked lip. Reckless, We, Better, Stupid, Dare, Practise, James, Illness My Arse, Come On, and she was leaving the room and we were following her.

In the car on the way home, I closed my eyes and saw Dr Finlay's top lip shining. When it moved, a word came out. The word was *Illness*. It moved slowly into the air. Then I saw another word inside it. When *Illness* opened, *Pain* came out and trembled like a moth drying its wings.

Stop the car, I said.

In the gutter I tried to get rid of the words. I opened my eyes and mouth and burned the cement with my lunch.

At school, I felt that Harry was avoiding me. I didn't know why, but I could feel it. He wasn't hiding, he was distant. His voice had No Interest in it. When I spoke to him, he responded but his words were empty. I said Do you want to come home after school?

What for, to listen to poetry?

No, just to talk and maybe listen to music.

I'm sick of 'Tea for the Tillerman', he said, and looked at me.

A wedge-tailed eagle had looked at me the same way once, at the zoo. Its eyebrows lifted and its eyes went zoom into my head. Its eyes could see blood from a great distance. My blood ran away when that eagle looked at me. My blood had fur and feathers on it, and it scattered.

After scaring me with his eyes, Harry said So I guess you've given up on the idea of finding Stephanie? Maybe you made the whole thing up. Anyway, I don't think that now. Not really. I just think you might need help.

Help. I left the word turning between us, and walked away. Harry said I'm sorry, Jim, but I kept walking. I thought There's no need to be scared of me because I talk and see lights, but the words died out and I was in the toilet, becoming terribly alone.

I saw Dr Finlay once more, and he saw me. Mum apologised for being so rude the last time. She said We're so worried and I didn't know what to do I'm sorry but I was frightened. Dr Finlay said Never mind, and then he turned to me and said How Are You, Enough Sleep? Getting Along? Difficult Time.

Somewhere in the middle of his words I heard Psychiatrist Friend Of Mine. Dad said Are you sure that's necessary? Mum said Whatever is best for James. I sat there like someone at a tennis match, watching my name go back and forth.

After that visit to Dr Finlay's, lying on my bed, I understood. No one could help me. I waited for the room to go dark. I listened to the bush. When it was safe, I told Stephanie what was happening in my life, and she said No matter what you tell people, they will always have their own ideas about what you should be doing. Listen, but don't believe everything. Wait for the words your heart can trust.

Sleep found me waiting.

SHRINK

———

THE PSYCHIATRIST'S name was Dr Lap. His office was in the city, upstairs in a darkstone building with windows like squares of muddy water. I went with Mum. Dad had something to do, like not go to the shrink with his son. He didn't understand. Coming with us wouldn't have helped him understand any more.

There was a lift, but we took the stairs. They were dirty and windy and smelled of cat's piss. Someone had written and drawn things on the walls. They could have been the walls at Lars' house.

In the waiting room there were black-and-white photos of racing cars and one of a man holding a big silver cup in the air. He had a vine around his neck and he was smiling. Under the photo it said *Cyril Lap, Champion Driver, 1948.* I pissed myself laughing and Mum said Stop it, you're embarrassing me. When I showed her the photo and said his name out loud, she laughed too. A man wearing fat trousers and a wide blue tie came out of his office and stopped. Mum bit her laugh off and said Are you Doctor Lap? He nodded. He must have wondered which one of us needed help.

Dr Lap asked lots of questions. He wanted me to tell him about the voices, about how I felt when I heard them. I tried to explain. He leaned forward and rested his chin on his hands. He nodded. He said Do you ever see things? Things that aren't there? Imaginary things? I wanted to say I know what imagination is, dickhead, but I went on, again, about the headlights, though I never called them that. Dr Lap's whole body nodded. I told him about Stephanie, about hearing her speak, the times we met, her tablets, her suggestion that I write things down. When I'd finished speaking, I wished I'd never opened my mouth. I was yabbering. I'd let too much go and I felt hollowed out.

Do you still see Stephanie?

I shook my head. I'd had enough.

Is she a good friend?

I looked around the room.

Mum hit me on the arm and said James, Dr Lap just –

I don't see her any more, I said coldly. She's gone away.

The words were for Mum. Then I closed myself down.

What kind of tablets did she take, James? Dr Lap's silver pen hovered over his notepad. He waited. Mum waited. There should have been a big wallclock chipping edges from the day, but all I heard was them waiting.

Dr Lap shifted in his seat, wrote on the pad, and said Possible Treatment and Medication. I felt Mum's hand growing into my shoulder. I couldn't speak. Dr Lap rustled out of his chair and walked around. He said There are many people in the world who are different. It doesn't make them bad or weird. Just different. The chemicals in their brains make them this way. It's just something that happens. It's no one's fault. Think of yourself as someone special. Treatment can help you. Would you like to try?

Mum said Yes please, Dr Lap, and I started laughing. His name was a riot.

Dr Lap overheated and said Very well. He pulled over to his desk and scribbled something on a pad, ripped off a sheet and gave it to Mum. She read the note. Kept reading it.

I'd like to see you again in a couple of weeks, Dr Lap said.

Mum made a time.

At home Mum opened the bottle of tablets and gave me one. I swallowed it with lemonade, then went down to my room and waited for something to happen. There was a bitter taste on my tongue. I lay back on the bed and wondered what feeling better would be like. Dr Lap said it might take a few days for the pills to work. I watched the ceiling and listened to my pulse come and go inside the pillow. The sheets were cool, my body heavy. I was very tired. Soon I was going under. The last thing I heard was a bone in my wrist clicking as I turned over and let my breath go into the wall.

CAVES

———

ALL MY LIFE I've been drawn to caves. They seem to amplify the sound of a thought being made in the confines of the head. My earliest memory of them finds me aching all over, sniffing and delirious, my face in Dad's neck as he carried me through the Jenolan Caves. It must have been hard for him, to be amazed while lugging a sick bundle through the spotlit guts of the earth, but he told me things, and held me up to see the boneframe of a wallaby printed into the side of a sweating wall.

Colours in that cave are still behind my eyes: beige and bone-white, ochre and burgundy where drips fed each other to make a meeting of calcified tongues. Below a high narrow bridge, water the colour of the eye on a peacock's fan went deep and slow. Someone flicked a coin into it. A woman said You could paint with that. I wanted to go from the bridge, headfirst in a slow-motion dive, out into a great, stained cathedral of light.

There were caves I found in the hills while Dad played cricket; cool, shallow mouths with grey sand floors and spiders weaving overhead.

At home, a red blanket over a card table made a cave

I was allowed to sleep in. I'd stay in my pyjamas for days, hiding with a flashlight and a book, warm and dreaming, in the womb again.

In Sydney, a red-rock cave above the Lane Cove River was a place to hear your voice break into pieces and come back at you, bright with powdery dust and nonsense. The walk to the cave was just as mysterious. I found luminous orange fungus on fallen logs, used condoms, and once a headless bearded dragon. I played rock music under that bloody overhang with friends, dancing and jamming, a stick with tin foil wrapped around the end for a microphone, air guitars, and always someone far below, on the other side of the creek, an audience of one making crowd-sounds with their breath and clapping.

In winter we'd go in convoy into the Blue Mountains to stay at a cottage near Porters Pass, in Blackheath. We called it Bleakheath, because it was always misty and dark and very cold. The cottage had belonged to a friend's grandmother, a woman who'd been famous for walking the streets in a long, dark blue overcoat, making currawong calls and creaking like a gang-gang cockatoo when it rained. We took over the rooms, playing cards and Scrabble, making pyramids out of beer cans against the verandah wall. Our favourite place was a cave below a dripping overhang, on Porters Pass. We'd stay in there all day sometimes, playing guitar and singing, telling stories by a fire. Jack, bird-call expert, would make the sounds of an old woman blowing through the Blackheath backstreets, his voice coming back at us from a distant cliff wall. One day we all signed our names on a sheet of paper. We dated it, folded the sheet into a jam jar, and buried it under a small cairn of stones at the back of the cave. Years later, Jack said he'd found the cairn kicked over, the jar gone. In its place someone had left a photo of a dead hairtail – a long, slender-bodied chrome-plated fish with huge teeth. On the photo were the words: *Trace, Glen, Darce & Gatto*. Jack said he'd never heard of these people, and that he'd been troubled by this curious replacement of our names ever since.

I can't recall the exact moment when the need to leave came on me with a presence as strange and troubling as a week full of headlights. I'd never put much faith in omens, but on a humid, edgy afternoon, something worked into my guts and sent me reeling into the bush.

I crabbed to the edge of a low overhang and dropped through a cool wave of ferns and found the cave I'd heard about from a man called Spook.

Spook lived up the street in a run-down, split-level house with gutted cars in the yard. Sometimes when I walked past, Spook would be sitting high on his verandah, smoking and hacking up something to spit, or he'd be at the wheel of a rusted-out car with fins, staring through the screen like a skeleton. When I'd finally had the courage to talk to him, I went up to the window and said Hello Spook. He jumped, slapped the wheel, and said Don't ever call me that. Then he said I know where you live, mate, which frightened me. His eyes were sockets with wet balls pushed into them, and his lips were bleeding slugs. He said You live near the cave, don't you. When I asked him which cave, he adjusted the rear-vision mirror and stared at me through its cracked silver.

The cave where they were murdered, he said, lovingly.

I went out backwards from the yard that day, tripping over tyres and bits of metal. When I reached the road I ran. Spook's weird looks weren't the only reason for his name.

The cave was deep and cold, with moss and leaves

sucking at my shoes. The ferns and small spiky trees spilling down over its entrance made the light uneven. A car passed on the road below. The cave swallowed the ripping sound of its tyres.

The sand at the base of the cavewall was pocked with tiny craters. I picked up a brown ant and dropped it into one. As it tried to climb out, its frantic legs made the sand slide, and it fell down to the centre of the crater. A pair of grey pincers surfaced, grabbed the ant, and dragged it under. Its feelers were the last to go.

Ant lion. Bulb-bodied predator of dark, sandy places. When aeroplanes go over, the drone makes ant lions toss sand in the air. I lifted out a palmful of sand and filtered it through my fingers until the ant lion lay on my hand, the ant still between its pincers. I put my mouth above it and made a low, droning sound. The ant lion wasn't fooled. It didn't move. I put it down on the sand and went further into the cave, walking doubled over until I reached a cold wall, wet with seepage. It smelled of mould and turned earth, like an old book opened on a rainy day. I struck a match. The cavewall came to life with thin lines of trickling water, orange fungus and slime. In the next matchflare I saw names carved into a dry section over my head: *Vivian, David, Robert, Mel*. Above these, in a dribble of white paint, *Spook*.

I collected sticks and leaves and made a fire. In its cold light the names danced and bled at the edges. There were newspapers and magazines scattered around the cave's edge, a small suitcase filled with stones and plastic bottles, a handbag with a broken strap, a pair of torn underpants, a shirt, a buckled sheet of tin. Under the tin I found a large black plastic bag tied with a belt. When the belt slipped away, the bag fell open and a dog's head dropped onto my foot. Its lips were pulled back into a yellow snarl, its teeth threw blunt sparks in the firelight. The tablets I'd been taking dissolved into useless powder. My blood showed through the skin on the backs of my hands. My tongue clacked in a white film of saliva. The dog's head turned and found me listening:

They hated me because I never chewed their balls or returned them slick with mouthbubbles and fun. I liked a good stripe of sun near an open door, and the sound of a cat tearing barkstrips as I came for it. And I hated my name. Prince. What gets into these people? They fed me pebbles of dried bloodbone and kicked me out of the way. I started chasing my tail. They put an ice cream container around my head and called me flowerpot. I went from my tail to cars. I saw myself in a polished door once. A white plastic collar with eyes looking back at me. I bit turning rubber and lost a few teeth. Then someone booted me. I went for the leg and found it. I tasted blood and liked it. They came for me with a rope. They said Walk, but I put the nails in and wouldn't go. They dragged me down through trees to a dark place where I saw a fist rise and fall with a metal bar inside it.

Walking back to the house, I found a large rock, sat down and swallowed a tablet. I said I want you to work. Come on. I was sure I felt something then – a word or a puzzle of song that haunts your head until you remember it. I was smoking and concentrating badly on whatever came along into my head when I heard a muffled, scraping sound. I turned, thinking bird or leaf on stone. I saw a dark green wall of bracken and a leaning fence. Smoke. Think. Scrape. The sound lifted away and died between my knees. I leaned forward. A snake's eyes tipped me off balance and I fell over. I crawled away and waited for my breath to reach me. The snake was curled and pressed up under the lip of the rock like a whip of shadow with

Go Away printed into it. I crawled closer, feeling around for a stick. It was a big black snake, a red band lighting its underside. Before I could move again, its head came around and its tongue forked the air. Its eyes were bits of light in the tight-fitting dark. I looked into them. Let me see. Let me hear.

The sun is over and the stone is warm. My spine is wavelight. My hollowpoints are loaded. Stay. What is my name? I come from a globe of yolk and a twisted coupling. Smell me. Reach out and know the depth of sorrow. That's enough. Now back off and wait for the puncture wound of love. I will find you a mouse for company and a hole for sleep. I can smell the earth change. I can smell your blood through the feet you wear to warn me. Be still. Listen. There is a bird on my tail. It can wait a morning for my eyes to move. Then it drops. The scar on my side is a beak-dagger wound where the Watcher cracked me into rock and let me go. I flicked away. I was young. My blood glued leaves together. I went to ground more than ever. The watcher went over all day, the smear of blue sky under its wings like an invitation to come out. Its eyes became wider with each pass until I could look into its head. I saw lizards turning into bloodlines and my own kind attempting difficult knots with their bodies. I made a spiral and bled into the centre of it.

The snake unwound itself from the dark and moved out slowly, watching me. Its language had gone deep into my chest and legs. I was not afraid. I was grounded with a shock of recognition. As the snake entered a green cross-thatching of ferns, its tail vanishing like the end of a serious thought, I felt myself drawn to the need for absence.

LEAVING

THAT NIGHT, with the taste of snake and dogwords in the cave of my mouth, I packed clothes into a canvas bag and filled another with cans of food and packets of soup.

I had fifty dollars from the milk money Harry and I had pinched on our early morning raids through the suburbs. I knew where I was going, but not for how long. I picked up the bottle of tablets, then put them down again. I wrote a short letter and left it on the bed. It said *Don't worry I'll be fine*, but I knew how pathetic that would sound. It would take two minutes for Mum to go off her brain, and a while longer for Dad to say What now? I already felt sick about them finding the note, and almost ripped it up. I left it there on the pillow. I tried to think of a good reason to stay. Their worry wasn't good enough. I had to go. The faces Mum and Dad would make in the morning and the words they were going to speak were already taking shape in the air. I sat on the bed and thought about Stephanie. I saw her face. It was enough to get me going. I opened the window and stepped out into a cool morning. I walked up the drive, past a blacked-out room where two people had around three hours of sleep before their hearts and voices came for me.

INTO THE TREES

———

W HEN I REACHED the highway, I walked with my
hand out, trailing one finger like a surface lure. I'd
been hitching rides since I was twelve, when a friend
showed me, with great pride, how to get around without
paying fares. We'd never pay on trains. Jumping the
tracks was too easy, despite the station guard with his neat
uniform, red face and whistle. But hitching a ride was different. It involved real risk and cunning. At first I'd felt
self-conscious, knowing every driver was checking me
out, my face full of Pick Me Up. But soon I was engaging
their stares, and I learned where to stand, choosing longer
straight sections of road. I'd thumbed rides all over
Sydney, and once went to a country town for the day, for
fun, to see if I could make it there and back before dark.

The only time I was afraid was when, in a white truck
with a man wearing filthy clothes, a man who chain-
smoked and did not speak, even when I asked him
questions, I saw something move, and when I looked
down he had exposed himself. It was the first adult
erection I'd seen. He said Would you like some of this.
I told him to let me out, and he did. I watched the

truck until it was lost to the traffic, then I walked to the nearest bus stop and went home. This was before I knew Harry. It gave me a small idea of what he must have felt, just before he was driven into the bush in the back of the ice cream van.

The highway was quiet. The morning rush hour was still a while off. Paper trucks gunned past, a few cars gleamed, slowed, drove on. I walked, feeling air pass over my outstretched hand.

The first car to stop was not my idea of a ride. Two cops got out and put their hats on. Name, age, address? I told them anything. What you're doing is stupid, Richard, the older-looking cop said into his notebook. Do your parents? Where are you? Why? I promised to stop hitching and go home. They weren't convinced. They suggested I get into their car. We'll take you home, the younger one said. I said No thanks and started walking. I could feel the coplights of their eyes on my back.

If we see you hitching again this morning there'll be trouble, a voice said before a car door clipped it off at the root.

There's already trouble, I said to myself.

They drove by slowly, leaning forward and glaring at me through the passenger window. They looked stupid and too serious, like teachers in uniforms. I sat on a bus-stop seat and rolled a smoke. They cruised by again, still leaning forward, their bodies saying Don't you fuck with us.

I smoked and pretended I hadn't seen them.

After two short rides, one with a homebound cleaner, the other with a man who started crying as he told the story of his marriage bust-up, I decided to catch a train the rest of the way. The walking and waiting had taken me deep into peak-hour traffic. No one had time for a young bloke shouldering a canvas bag lumpy with Godknows what. Every passing face was dark with the unbreakable promise of another day's work, and whatever bullshit was leaking from the dash during drivetime radio.

On the train I watched suburbs come and go through a rocking window. I could hear what was happening at home. Mum'd be on the phone to the cops. The cops would put out a call, and a car would answer that they'd seen me in the pre-dawn dark. Then Mum would be in my room, hunting for clues. Finally she'd be in a chair, sighing and going through The Reasons. I didn't know them all myself.

I stepped off the train into a cold, bright morning. To the south, over a blunt horizon of blue hills and smoky gums, a cold front was steaming in with its freight of rounded thunderheads.

I went through what Harry had told me about the Royal National Park, about the shacks at Era Beach and Burning Palms. Beaches with names *that* good had to be worth visiting. He had described the way in – how they'd mostly follow the track, and other times bash through the scrub, making their own trails. I'd often daydreamed of walking in there, my pack rattling with fishing gear.

I looked at the map in my head and tried to follow it. I saw a narrow road, a car park, a track down into the scrub and, finally, after a lot of walking, a wide green valley. I folded the map with my eyes and started walking.

Trees on both sides of the road made a dark screen. I walked on the edge, the tall dry grass bristling and

catching on my legs. Parrots washed the spaces between
the trees with blue and crimson light. A noisy myna
flicked from branch to branch, following me, letting me
know I was under investigation. A kookaburra swung
up on a thick rope of air and dipped its head at me.

I once saw a boy from school shoot a kookaburra with
an air rifle. I was at his house. Currawongs were
swooping into the rain. Rainbow lorikeets clowned
overhead. We were shooting at tin cans on the end of
tomato stakes in the garden. The boy swivelled around
and, without warning, aimed the gun high, paused and
fired. A rainbow lorikeet dropped like a paint-stained rag
into the grass. He reloaded quickly, searched the trees,
took aim and fired again. A kookaburra jumped and
settled. I thought he'd missed. The bird turned its head
and looked down at us. Blood was dripping from the end
of its beak. It didn't move. I shouted as the boy levered
the barrel down to reload. Fuck off, he said, snapped the
rifle closed and took aim. I ran and kicked him in the side.
He went down, the gun cartwheeling. He went for it,
stood, spat and aimed at me. A grey tangle flapped down
between us. The kookaburra lay on the ground. The boy
lowered his gun. I put my hands under its wings and lifted
it away to the side of the garden. Wet leaves and soil will
always smell of shot birds.

A truck with men in the back roared past, throwing a
wake of white dust and laughter. They were wearing
blue overalls. Shovels and rakes were racked against the
truck's cab. One of them shouted something the wind
removed, and they were gone. I stopped and listened.
Birds, insects, leaves.

I've always heard the bush. Beyond the day-
announcing calls and chimes of birds, the amount of

wind it takes to give voice to leaves and grass, beyond
the obvious there were other sounds. Now I can say
these sounds were like the workings of the body,
especially at night: a valve opening and closing, a
bloodline flowing from head to foot and back. But when
young, sitting in a cold globe of shade under some
onion-skinned boulder high over a cricket field as Dad
ran in to bowl, I'd put my ear to the stone and listen.
Someone clapped or appealed, a bat cracked a ball to
the fence, but these were outside what I heard at the
heart of a balancing rock – a voice or fragment of song,
a pulse from the earth. I'd tried to hear these things at
home, but the bedroom wall had the movements of
people inside it, and the floor returned a hum of
electrical wiring.

I walked into the trees and put my ear to the smooth
cool bark of a gum. Once I'd heard water dripping.
Another time a high limb creaking when there was no
wind. This time I heard instructions. I heard *Keep
walking, don't worry about directions*, so I entered the trees,
stepping over fallen branches into the travelling shadow
of my body.

In a clearing I sat down and ate a sandwich, drank
water from a flask. There was a sour taste in my mouth.
My left leg was shaking again. It had been going off
every few hours, and the bones in my knee were aching.
I lay back in the spiky grass. The myna bird was leaning
from a low branch directly overhead. Its eyes were
shining from its mask of dark feathers, and its beak was
opening and closing as if it were tasting something.

*You are new. Your face is haunting. Rise and go. The trees
are not yours. Where are you? I say song and fly alarm, now
go. The bright yellow eye will find you. Open your arms and*

leave what you know. Your name is closed to me. Others will come. The leaf wall will blow and others will say their alarms behind you. Breathe and be tall. Go.

I heard the leaves, and over them the dying drone of an aeroplane. A car gleamed red through the trees. Clouds bloomed and scattered. The myna bird entered a shadow. Its thin branch vibrated and stopped. My head was thick. I stood and swayed. I whistled. Nearby, behind the trees, a small animal moved and paused, moved again. I followed the sound, my hands parting branches and scratchy flowerstems.

THE SHACK

———

T HE TREES BECAME more evenly and widely spaced
as I stepped over sharp grey pockets of stone,
through sparks of wildflowers, onto a large flat shelf of
granite. I'd been walking and stumbling with no sense
of time, the map in my head blacked out and useless.
My face and hands were stinging with cuts and
thornpoints. I saw a large, open section of grassland. The
sight of this uncluttered expanse after so much bush-
bashing made me feel strange. For a moment I couldn't
move. My left leg went off like a drunk dancer, and I
had to sit down.

I checked the trees. I expected the myna bird to
reappear, to let me know that I had to keep moving. I
hadn't seen it since the clearing, but its voice was still
in me.

I entered a valley, with palms and thick clumps of broad-
leafed grass scattered over it. It seemed out of place,
considering the terrain I'd come from. I walked down,
aware of the freedom in my legs after so much short-
stepping and slipping over rocks and leaves.

The valley was bowl-shaped, bordered high on the left with a thick stand of gums. To the right it dropped away suddenly and I saw, beyond its ragged green edge, a band of ocean, cloud-smeared and calm.

The shacks were just as strange as I'd imagined them. Most were very small, one-room jobs with dirty windows and doors that looked like they'd been opened with boots instead of keys. Some were made from sheets of tin and boards, some from packing crates and whatever could be thrown together: rocks, driftwood, plastic bottles, polystyrene floats, hessian sacks filled with sand and clumps of weed-spiked mud rammed into any available space. There were also two shacks made from beer bottles and tins. These shacks were the same size, though some distance apart. I looked through their windows, hoping to see something familiar, something from Harry's words, but the dusty shelving, old kettles, fruit boxes and camp beds told me nothing. My face in the webbed, rain-smeared glass told me more than I wanted to know, and I turned away.

I left my bags behind the water tank of the first bottle shack and went off to explore the valley.

It was a relief to have no weight on my back. I stepped lightly away from the shacks, down the green slope of the valley's seaward edge. As I walked, the ocean revealed itself in bright layers, as if the scene were a scroll being drawn towards me. A gull surfaced from below the cliff edge and hovered there, riding the updraught before angling away. A mast seemed to grow from the grass and gleamed until the boat appeared, its blue decking a grid of fish traps and wires.

I sat on the edge and looked down. Another gull floated up and wavered at the end of a length of cold air before sliding away. The cliff was knotted with tree roots and knuckles of tough yellow grass. Rockslides had scarred the face, ending in brown and yellow mounds of rubble like grounded comets, their tails pointing back to the base of the cliff. Some of the larger rocks had tumbled into tidal pools. A long way out, on a calm sea, fishing boats moved slowly, with gulls attending their wake-lines. On the beach to the left, a lone fisherman stood knee-deep in the foam, his long beach rod a tapering black line overhead. He was walking slowly, feeding and retrieving line as he went, his head fixed in concentration.

I followed the edge until I found a path. It was more a deep erosion line, snaking left and right down the cliff, but the tree roots made good hand-holds as I crabbed over shifting soil.

At the base of the cliff I looked up and scared myself. It was a passage more dangerous than I'd imagined.

I sat on a fallen boulder and watched the fisherman. He was half-hidden by a dark rise of stone where the drop-off met the beach, and he was leaning back, his rod fully loaded as he walked up and down, looking at the rod tip and then out into the water, where waves were breaking and creaming over a distant sand bar. Then the rod went limp. He cursed and started reeling in the line. He kicked at the water. When the end of the line came in, he studied it closely and shook his head. Then he stood, without moving, staring out to sea.

I picked my way carefully over a rockspill, keeping close to the base of the cliff. When the sweep of beach came into view he was gone. It didn't make sense. At the far end of the beach was a headland with a long, low point jutting into the sea. The point widened into a high collar of stone and shrubs that he couldn't have climbed in the time it took me to walk down to the beach. Behind where he'd been fishing, the cliff was a near-vertical wall, veined with seams and gullshit. A wave boomed and its towering spray fanned over me. It felt good to be wet. I climbed down to the beach.

There were footprints in the sand going back up the beach, but they ended at the cliff. Above me there were small horizontal ridges and cracks, and higher still a protruding lip of rock that threw a curved, blunt shadow on the wall.

It was now late afternoon. When I climbed to the top of the cliff, going a longer, safer way over the headland spine, the sun had already entered the bush, leaving a dirty pink smear above the treeline. Wind ripped into me, turning my clothes to bindings of ice.

Bottles and tins. I chose the shack with the most bottles and worked on the door latch with the screwdriver blade in my pocket knife until it dropped away and the door moaned open. There was just enough light to see what a bad choice I'd made. The place was a riot of rat-chewed newspapers, empty baked bean and spaghetti tins, chop bones, old hurricane lanterns and a truckload of dust and sand. The camp bed was like a sinking boat in a lake of garbage. I waded over and cleared the wreckage, flinging tin cups and magazines into the walls. The clean-up would have to wait. There were sheets on the bed, but they'd never been washed. Dark stains bled into the fabric. The pillow looked like it had been rubbed into a fire-blackened tree. I found two blankets on top of a leaning cupboard. When I lifted them down, something shot off into the wall and skittered around on the floor. I lit a lantern and rolled a smoke. I sat on the edge of the bed and made a rabbit head on the wall with my hands. The flame twisted. The rabbit died.

Lying under the sheets in dry clothes, I watched the dull flame of the lantern and heard the bush come alive. I tried to see animals and birds in each branch-crack or disturbance of leaves, but only one shape emerged. It was a silhouette of two people in a house in the suburbs. Their voices were muffled as they moved through the rooms, joined at the head and heart with worry. I raised the lantern glass and blew the shack into darkness and a terrible sleep.

STORMLIGHT

I T TOOK ME half the day to clean the shack, and even
then it looked like shit. I fought off the urge to look
properly through the window of the other bottle-and-
tin place, in case it was tidy. But cleaning gave me
something to do and, besides, the shack had a water
tank. The water came in a trickle slow as rust, with a
similar colour, and it had bits of leaves and mosquito
wrigglers in it, but it tasted alright if you closed your
eyes and didn't think too much.

In the cupboard I found a rickety pyramid of baked
beans and spaghetti cans. I opened one and forked out
a mouthful of beans. They tasted like soft metal.

As I sat out on the grass after a lunch of beans and a
cupful of drowned insects, a helicopter came whipping
over the sea. It slowed and wheeled around to hang its
clatter over the edge of the headland. It tipped forward
and came inland. I bolted for the shack, watching
through the window as it hovered, turned, and went
back out to sea. I knelt there looking through the
cleaned glass, but it didn't return.

I lay on the bed, reading magazines and listening for the helicopter, but the sea was the only engine, and it was roaring.

Late in the afternoon, I stood outside the shack with the blankets over my shoulders, watching the undersides of storm clouds change from grey to dark green and purple, like new bruises, their edges blunt and rolling. Lightning flickered and forked, connecting them with threads of silver, and thunder went through and over them like a net of sound that came back from the headland with birds and the smell of rain inside it. The cloudbank stretched from headland to scrub and far out to sea. At its centre, a thunderhead was bleeding dark lines of rain, drawing light from the sea and sky, growing in size until it had taken every cloud into its form. Its cargo of rain found land long before it was overhead. It fell in a cold, angled wall. I stood in the doorway, watching the hills and trees dissolve. The tin roof sang into my bones. Lines of rain found every hair-thin crack or unsealed nail hole. On the floor, puddles formed and spread. The windows fogged over. I moved the bed from a steady drip and covered the magazines with a canvas sheet. A bell of thunder broke open and the shack went sideways. I found a dry place under the window and watched the violent parade of rain and leaves paint out the grass until the whole valley was gone to a scrim of water with no spaces between the rainbeads.

I woke to a black room and driving rain. When I stepped down, the floor was under water. I tried to find the lantern, but must have moved it when the rain began. I rolled a cigarette and looked around the shack in match light. It took four matches to find the lantern under a stack of wet newspapers, but the wick was sodden. I went back to bed and sat up, hugging my knees and trying to think of the words to a song Mum used to sing when it rained.

We'd sit before a water-feathered window, and she'd go on like a girl, making faces and using her fingers to describe the storm. She said her mother had been taught the song by *her* mother. Although she'd died when I was young, I could still see my grandmother sewing in a dark room with a radio on the table beside her, the old music wavering in time with her needle-lifting hand.

I couldn't remember the words, but the tune came easily. My fingers made the shape of the rain, and I hummed as the night went into itself and stayed there. Then I felt stupid and put my hands down. The song went out in my throat.

In a dream, a telephone rings but you can't answer it. You need to run down the hall, but your legs won't move. In this dream, someone was knocking on a door. I waited for them to leave, but the knocking went on, getting louder. When I woke the knocking had stopped, but a voice had replaced it.

Are you alright? a man's voice came through the door wood.

I couldn't speak. My heart stalled, flipped over and started beating again. I saw a faint glow through the window, and then a wandering beam of flashlight came through the glass, blinding me.

Could you open the door?

What do you want?

Just to say hello. Thought you might have drowned. It's fucking wet out here. I've got some hot coffee. Thought you might like some.

I tried to find the door, but the flashlight had left a

flare of yellow behind my eyes, and it was all I could see. I found a handle and opened the cupboard. I crashed into a box and fell over.

If you want to wreck the place, that's fine, but I'm the one that's drowning out here. The man knocked again and I followed the sound to the door.

He was leaning up against the door frame in a long yellow raincoat with a dripping hood. He turned the flashlight into his face and I wished he hadn't. He became one of the monsters we'd made as kids, under the card table and blanket, telling ghost stories and pretending to be scared. This time it worked. The man didn't need a story. He lowered the light, said I'm friendly, and moved past me into the room.

A GUIDE TO
AUSTRALIAN FISH

———

H E TOOK OFF his raincoat and cracked it violently.
He could have been killing a large yellow bird.
When he turned around, his flashlight wandered through
the shack, isolating wet bundles, dripping angles.

Make yourself at home, he said. He pulled up a fruit
box, put the flashlight between his knees, and worked
at the wick on the lantern. Wet as buggery, he said. Any
more lanterns?

I went to the cupboard. Can you shine the light in here?

The beam found two lanterns wrapped in a grease-
stained towel. I handed them to him and he inspected
them closely.

This one's fucked. He placed it gently on the floor.
This one's not much better, he said, sniffing the glass
and testing the wick. But it'll have to do. He flipped
the top on a silver lighter and a flame leapt after he rolled
his thumb. The lantern glowing, he placed it on the
floor between us and started talking.

First off, this is not your shack, and you've got a real
hide breaking in. Second, I don't give a shit where
you've come from or what you've done.

I started to say something, but his hand came up and whatever was in my mouth disappeared.

Thing is, you just don't do that kind of thing around here. Anywhere really, but especially around here. But you know that already. I just wanted to say what's in my head, understand? Now, seeing as it's pissing down, and most likely will be for some time, you're welcome to stay. Until it stops raining. Right?

Then his voice softened. His body relaxed. He said he built one of the other shacks ten years ago.

Carried most of the building materials down through the bush and brought some in by boat. A lot of hard work went into making these places. People think Oh yeah, funny little joint made of bottles and shit, but they mean a lot to the people who built them. You can't build any more, either, and you can't sell them. You can hand them down to your family, but you can't sell them. I know people who'd love to buy one of these places.

As he spoke, about the shacks and the people who made them, his hands described each detail carefully. In the moving light I could see that his fingers and knuckles were scarred. His face was long, and there was a scar coming down from his hairline that wormed over his right eye. His nose went off at an angle halfway down the bridge. I couldn't help looking at it as he spoke.

My nose has been broke lots of times, he said, replacing a wet strand of hair that kept falling across his eyes. Everyone looks at it. I'm kind of used to it.

Before I could ask if he meant his nose or people looking at it, he said Both, and then asked for a cigarette. He seemed surprised when I handed him the pouch of tobacco.

Roll your own man, eh? You can't be all bad. He

made a trumpet that looked like it had weeds growing out of the end of it. He rolled his thumb and the flame bent towards him as he drew on the smoke. Name's Colin. You?

James.

You like fishing, James?

Yes, but I've not done much.

I could tell you were interested. He sat up straight and stretched. The cigarette threw a spark when his hands came down. You were watching me yesterday.

That was you on the beach?

Yep. Got bit off by a small shark. Thought it was a mulloway at first. They're beautiful big surf-hunters and reef-gliders. But when I couldn't feel the beat of that paddle tail or the head shaking down the line, I started to wonder. Didn't have to wonder for long, though. Noah's bloody arks. They're fine as long as they don't find my bait, he said, and laughed. It sounded like a straw broom on a path.

So where did you go? After you stopped fishing?

Into the cave, to watch you.

I didn't see a cave.

I know that.

Where is it?

In the rock. He smiled and pinched the end of his cigarette. There's lots of caves around here.

Would you show me?

Maybe. Why?

I like caves.

Give me a better reason.

I tried to think of one. Because you can feel different in them, I said, then felt stupid for saying it.

That's a good reason, he said. Maybe I'll show you my favourite.

Do you live here? In your shack?

Sometimes. I stay in the cave, too, when I feel like it.

But don't you have a job or anything?

I'm on a pension.

The rain continued. We sat without talking, watching the flame behind its cone of burned glass. It was good to have company. Colin was a tough man, but I felt safe. He'd seen and done a lot, that was obvious. His experience had given him a strength of spirit that was in the way he moved his hands, in his eyes when he spoke.

Thought you might like to take a look at this, he said, reaching into a canvas shoulder bag. He lifted out a small, thick book and brought it forward into the light. *A Guide to Australian Fish*. He turned the book over in his hands. You want to know about mulloway or Noahs, bream or hairtail, beakies or pigs? Read this. He offered it to me with a gesture that would've been at home in a shrine.

You can borrow it, but if you treat that book like you did this shack, I'll cut your balls off and throw them to the gulls. Got it?

Got it.

Right. I'm going back to bed. He looked at his watch. Jesus wept, it'll be light soon. Maybe I'll just make some coffee and wait for the rain to stop. You want some?

We walked up the hill to his shack. It was the last one before the line of scrub.

The walls were mostly flour and sugar bags and tin cans.

They're filled with sand and mud, he said, opening the door. These walls have got half a beach in them.

102

The shack was bright, clean and warm. A kerosene heater glowed in one corner. There were bookshelves filled with paperbacks and magazines. A hat-stand stood near the door, dark coats and woollen beanies hanging from the pegs. His bed was along one wall, under a window. It was clean, well-made, and the pillow was huge and soft. It made me sleepy looking at it. A small red rug covered part of the boarded floor. A fishing net looped down from the ceiling, its orange corks like painted light globes.

He pulled up a straightbacked chair with a pale blue cushion on it. There you go, champ. Did you bring the fishing book with you?

No. I left it.

Doesn't matter. I can show you without it.

I didn't ask what it was he wanted to show me. I knew I'd find out soon enough.

He poured water from a large plastic bottle into a dented saucepan, then put fire to a small gas ring. This done, he sighed, and sat down slowly on the edge of his bed. Rain thrummed on the roof.

Now, let's hear it, he said.

What?

His eyes were somewhere over my head. I waited, thinking Hear what? The rain? The wind?

What are you doing here?

I had to leave home for a while.

He scratched the side of his face. We all have to do that sometimes.

Colin got up and lifted a curtain from the front of a stack of boxes. He took down two mugs, opened a jar and spooned coffee into them. Black coffee's all we're having, he said, and poured the water. He handed me a mug. Pass that tobacco will you.

I gave him the pouch.

Listen, James, everyone gets dark and bleak. When I go under, I go fishing. It's the best way to beat the black tide. Get out on the beach or the rocks or your boat and chuck a line in.

What's the black tide?

The pits. The abyss. The spirit's lowest ebb. I know all about it, mate. The black tide comes in and takes you with it. It's the undertow of your heart, the rip in your head.

So, when the black tide comes, you just go fishing? That's all?

That's it. Well, almost. You've got to choose the right time. And try to use fresh or live bait.

When's the best time?

Knowing the phase of the moon's a good start. Right now's perfect for mulloway. New moon. People say the full moon's best. Bugger that. If you were a big fish, would you be hunting mullet or tailor in the surf zone with the moon all over you? Nah, you'd be gliding through the gutter with your headlights off.

I laughed.

What's so funny?

Headlights. That's what I call what happens in my head when things go weird.

When's the last time it happened?

It comes and goes. Some days there's just a flicker of lights. I looked directly into Colin's face. I hear voices, too.

Shit a brick, you have got it bad, cob. Then he leaned forward. I've heard them too.

What do you mean?

Just what I said. I've heard voices. Maybe not the same way you have, but everyone's different.

What did they say?

They told me to use fresh bait or I'd come home without raising a scale.

Anger went through me. I stood up. I thought you were serious, I said, and went for the door.

Come on, James. Colin was up and standing beside me. I'm sorry. It was a stupid thing to say. I'm just trying to make sense of it, you know? He offered me his hand. Friends?

My hand went into his and disappeared. His skin was rough as bark.

No more jokes, I promise. Finish your coffee.

He opened the door, then turned around quickly. Shit, it's stopped raining. Know what this means?

What?

It means bugger the coffee, the tide's rising, and there's a mulloway down there with your name on it. Coming?

THE GUTTER

———•◦•———

C OLIN GAVE ME a woollen beanie and a huge coat
to wear until we reached the beach. He put a
head lantern over his raincoat hood. Outside the shack
he adjusted the beam until it threw a wide pool of
light.

You take these. He handed me the torch and tackle
bag.

We set off down the slope, Colin leading, rods on
his shoulder, the pool of lanternlight bobbing and
wavering.

As we neared the edge of the cliff, I told him I'd
gone down that way while he was fishing.

You're not the first person to want to know what it
feels like to be a mountain goat, he said. And you
wouldn't be the first to die trying.

We stepped onto the sand after taking a safe track
halfway down the side of the headland. I hadn't seen it
from the beach.

There's a shorter way, Colin said, stopping for breath.
But I wouldn't try it in the dark.

A pale line of grey light appeared on the horizon as if the day were coming through under a heavy curtain. You could almost hear the clouds raging overhead, and although there was no rain, the wind ate through our clothing as we knelt in the sand.

Colin took some fish pieces from a bag. Tailor fillets, he said. Prime mulloway bait.

I watched as he rigged the rods, tied knots and bit the ends from them, attached hooks and threaded the fillets on.

Those are big baits, I said.

Colin said a mulloway could eat four of them and not even know they were in his gob, then he walked down into the water, waded out a few paces and whipped a cast out into the surf. When he came back he handed me the rod. I've just put that bait into the gutter, he said. It's a deeper section of water between sandbars. Mulloway come through looking for tucker. Now, first things first. You can learn how to cast later. For now I want you to get a feel of the rod and the line.

He showed me where to put my finger, to feel for bites, how to hold the rod, and how to pump and wind a fish in. It was a lot to remember, and I stood there going through the list as Colin cast out and walked back to stand a few yards from me.

If you feel the bait moving, don't stand there like a goose, walk with it. Keep it light. A mulloway likes fresh bait and one that's not pretending to be a rock.

The bait moved and I moved with it. Colin was some way down the beach, moving sideways and staring up at his rod, then out to sea, just as he'd done when I'd first seen him.

The crack in the horizon had widened, and light was

pouring through. With it came a wall of cold wind that ripped the crests from waves and frosted my eyes. Colin was walking back up the beach, rod in hand. I looked at my line and saw that it angled sharply to the right.

This current's a bastard, Colin said. Too strong. He clicked his tongue and looked out to sea. Pity. Thought we were in with a big chance. Never mind. We'll give it a shot later. Bring your line in.

We sat huddled in the cold grey light, watching the sea and drinking coffee from a thermos. Colin put a splash of whisky into my mug. It tasted of Stephanie's room, and I longed to see her again. Colin must have noticed because he elbowed me and said What's up?

I'm thinking of someone, I said, and Colin nodded.

What's her name?

Stephanie.

Maybe you should be getting back, eh?

I can't see her. She's gone.

In what way is she gone? Away? On holiday?

I don't know. She gave me some books and wrote a letter, and then she went away.

Colin studied his coffee. I've done that, he said.

I waited for him to go on. A gull cried overhead and the wind threw sand in my face.

I went off when I was younger than you, he said. I was ten. Ran away to a friend's house in the country. Mind you, we were already living in the country, but it's the running that's important in this story. Must have only been a few miles. Felt like a world. I stayed in this big, run-down barn with bits of sky in the roof and a loft that had mice nesting in it. I loved it up there. My friend brought me bread and cake and milk with the cream on top. After school he'd climb up and tell me what was happening. The town was mad. Coppers up and down the streets, talking to people and dragging the river, Mums and Dads giving lectures to kids, strangers getting the eye. My friend said the cops had been to see him three times in two days, saying Did Colin talk about anything, anything at all? My friend reckoned it was terrible trying not to laugh and give the game away. Can't believe I did that stuff. People sick with worry and all.

Why did you run away?

The old man was a prick. He'd get pissed and beat the crap out of Mum, then he'd come for me with his belt or a stick, whatever he could find. Bastard hit me over the back of the head with a pick handle once. Had to get stitches.

You must have really copped it when you went home.

I was lucky. The old man died the night I went home. I was in bed asleep, having climbed through a window. They found him out back of the pub. A lump the size of a sparrow's egg on his head, that's all. When I walked into the kitchen next morning, Mum was asleep in a chair. She nearly died as well when she saw me, then she picked me up, turned me around and near busted my ribs. I can still smell her perfume. After she'd settled down and let me go, I told her where I'd been and why I went there, and she told me about Dad. I said I was glad. I said he was a bastard. First she got angry, then she started crying. She nodded her head as she cried. I still don't know if she was agreeing with me, or if that's just the way some women cry.

Colin took a deep breath and poured coffee into our mugs. He uncapped the whisky.

You want some more of this?

I said yes, and he tipped the bottle.

They'll be looking for you too, you know. That chopper? The one that came over yesterday? Might have been for you. Your Mum and Dad will be shitting themselves right now. You might even be on the news. To go missing, whether you make it through or not, is only a small part of the picture. It's the ones you leave, they're the real missing persons in the end. Their lives go to shit. They lose something from inside and out. They can't sleep. If someone gets nabbed and murdered, they're okay, they're gone. The pain they went through doesn't warrant much thinking about, but it's over, you get me? The loved ones want a sign. A shallow grave is better than a life of guessing. I don't want to scare you. No, bugger it, maybe I *do* want to scare you. Your Mum and Dad are thinking about that grave in the bush right now, James. I can hear them. Their brains are as loud as the ratchet on my reel. They're not thinking you're on some beach with an old codger fishing for mulloway and drinking coffee, they're thinking blood and loneliness. Their hearts are big as blowfish right now. You better believe it. I'm going to town tomorrow. You can come with me.

I said I'd think about it, and Colin said Well don't think too long because I'm leaving early.

We walked back to the shacks in a silence broken only by the rattle of fishing rods and the bright sound of reels and tackle in the bag. Colin's stories had made me feel awful, though he was only trying to help.

When we reached the shack, Colin put his hand on the wall and spoke to the glass and tin. You're a good bloke, James. There's a lot on your mind, and you need to work it out, but for now I think you should go home. He slapped the wall and pushed himself away. When he looked at me, a spark of green light came off a bottle and lit his face. So when I come round in the morning you'll be ready? I nodded. Colin smiled and turned away.

What were you going to show me in the shack?

He stopped. Remind me in the morning, he said, without turning around. And don't forget that *Guide to Australian Fish*.

What are you going to do now?

Whatever needs doing, he said. And I suggest you do the same.

MISTER MULLOWAY

⸺◆⸺

I WAS OUTSIDE the shack when I saw Colin come striding down the hill. He started talking as he came.

Some bastard's trashed the truck. Put a rock through the window and pinched the cassette player and a fishing reel. And just in case I didn't notice they slashed a couple of tyres. Animals.

He stopped a few yards from the shack, rubbed his face and continued.

Happens around here sometimes. The main car park's the one that usually gets done over, that's why I park in a clearing. Can't see the truck from the road. Someone knew it was there.

He turned and looked back up the hill. Fuck. Have to walk to the ranger's station, get someone out. He sat on his heels. Got a ciggie?

We rolled up and smoked.

I went up to the truck to get that reel for you. I'm sorry, mate.

Never mind.

Well, looks like you've got another day up your sleeve. Can't say I'm happy about it. There'll already be lots of questions flying around out there. Thing is, I could answer them. I'm involved, and I'm not doing anything about it. I don't like that feeling. I should've driven you back last night.

I can take care of myself.

That's not the point. You oughta be with your family. I know you reckon they don't understand, but they're trying. It's the best they can do.

Colin sat with his hands hanging fingertips-down between his legs, a line of smoke rising like a seam against his coat. He was looking at something on the grass.

You said to remind you. About showing me something.

He looked up. Did I? Remind me again.

Something to do with fishing?

He put the cigarette under the toe of his boot, pressed it into the grass and stood up.

That's right. A smile opened his face. Feeling strong?

Maybe. Why?

Wait here, Colin said, and went up to his shack.

He returned with a long rod and a silver-plated reel. He whipped the rod through the air. I knew that sound. I'd heard it many times in some master's office at school. One for backtalking. Two for swearing. Four for smoking. Six for a combination of these and whatever it was the pricks imagined I'd done.

Have you ever seen anything like this?

Colin was holding the rod, turning it over in his hands. This is my favourite. Made it myself. It's a fast taper, carbon-fibre number that'll turn a mulloway's head before he knows he's been hooked. It's a big rod, but it's light. Here, feel it.

I held the rod the way he'd shown me on the beach.

113

The tip bounced as I tested the weight. Colin pointed to a red and blue pattern rising above the grip. It looked like lots of connected triangles that got smaller as the rod thinned out.

It's called a chevron pattern. Did it myself. See? Each one of those lines is a strand of special binding thread. Took me a month.

It was amazing. The pattern glowed in the weak morning light.

I love that rod. Took it to bed once. My wife thought I'd really gone mad that time. She gave me shit for weeks.

Where is she now?

Colin turned the rod, kept turning it. She's dead. He flicked the rod and waited for the tip to stop vibrating. Died five years ago. Cancer. Bastard of a thing. Lump in the breast. It was right through her in the end. At least I know where she is.

As if expecting me to ask, he said She's buried up the coast, in the town where she was born. I go there sometimes, just to say hello.

He picked up the reel and screwed it onto the rod. It was like a small silver barrel with an open space on top where the line went on.

These reels are hard to use. Take lots of practice. They're called overheads because the line goes through the runners over the top of the rod. You have to use your thumb to control the way the line comes off the reel. Too much pressure and you're fishing in the sand, not enough and the line gets ahead of itself, coming off in big loops that make a tangled mess. A bird's nest. That reel in the truck was an overhead. I was going to teach you how to use it, out here on the grass.

I held the rod as he started threading line through the runners. The reel clicked like a crab on wet stone.

When he'd pulled it through the last runner, he made a loop in the end.

Right. Give me the rod and hold this. Wrap the line around your hand. He took the rod. I held the line.

What's your name?

James.

James what?

James Molloy.

Wrong. It's Mr Mulloway, and you're about to know what it feels like to be taken from the drink by a twenty-pound line. Ready?

Ready.

Good. I've just cast out and there's a dirty big tailor fillet wafting around in the wash. It's dark. Black. A new moon. You're hungry. You've come into the gutter for dinner. You're a big, lazy bastard who doesn't like to use up too much energy. But when you have to, you can bolt like a quarter-horse with fins. Right now you're cruising. Your radar's on. You turn. Your big paddle tail throws you onto the scent. You glide over the bait. It's moving, but it's not freaking out. You turn and make another pass. Then you swing around, pick up the bait and hold it between your lips. You bite down slowly. Now you move off.

I saw myself with a big slab of tailor in my mouth.

Well go on, bloody move!

I walked off holding the line. It came easily from the rod.

Now drop the bait.

I almost spat I was so involved.

Now pick it up again and go. You mulloway can be fussy eaters.

I moved away.

Faster.

I started jogging.

Now swallow the bait and bolt!

I swallowed hard and ran.

Faster! Head for that palm tree up there.

I'd run about twenty paces when the line went tight and cut into my hand.

Keep going!

It hurts!

Of course it bloody hurts. How'd you like to find a hook in your gob as you sat down for dinner. Now run.

I ran. Backwards and forwards, sideways and in circles. The line burned into my hand and I heard it crackling, under pressure, as it left the reel. Then I found myself being drawn towards Colin, who was pumping and winding me back to the shack, using the rod to take my weight and bring me forward, then lowering the tip and winding like crazy.

How are you feeling?

Fucked.

Good, now one more run and you'll be buggered.

I'm buggered already.

You're not lying down on a sandbar or in the shallows grunting yet.

Yes I am, you just can't hear me.

Run!

I made a short run and took the line around the water tank.

What are you doing? Get out in the open.

I've just taken you under the jetty and wrapped the line around a pylon.

But we're on the beach.

I'm a mulloway, and I don't want to die. I saw this jetty pylon at the end of the beach and went around it. Sorry, but I'm free.

Fair enough.

Colin came over and put out his hand. Give us your fin, he said, and started laughing. You make a good mulloway.

Thanks. Wouldn't want to try it out for real though.

So what do you think of the rod?

I looked at my hand. The line had cut deep into my wrist and the mound below my thumb, but the skin wasn't broken. I said I think it's brilliant.

Colin saw the line-cuts. I could pull stumps with this rod, he said.

SPLINTERING LIKE BAITFISH

AFTER COLIN LEFT for the ranger's station, I packed my bag with a few tins of beans and a flask of water and walked to the scrub that marked the beginning of the headland. I'd seen a few eagles circling up that way, and there was a bright rock that lit up a small piece of the hill. From the shacks, the rock looked like a round window filled with light in the side of a huge dark building.

As I entered the trees, the rock became the exposed sandstone wall of a shallow cave, and it was higher than I'd thought.

I climbed slowly, using rocks and clumps of grass to lever myself from ledge to ledge. Down in the valley, the shacks and their attendant stands of palms looked like a set from some movie about a tropical village the people had abandoned years ago. Gulls cried up over the cliff edge. On the horizon, a tanker connected sea and sky.

As I watched the tanker, trying to see if it was moving, a large shadow folded over the grass below. A hang-glider was cruising. The rider's legs were tucked into a bag that swung from side to side, and the hands went out to grip a bar. It was flying low, making a large, slow spiral. Then another glider appeared, much higher, making the same slow shape in the dark blue air. I thought of my view of the land and sea. It seemed so small compared with what lay below them. When the first glider reached a point that seemed to be level with the cliff, it turned and soared sharply out over the sea, climbing higher as the body bag swung out and the hands gripped the bar. The other glider was gone when I looked up, claimed by the trees and sun.

The cave was shallow, but only at the gently sloping roof section, which is what I'd seen from below. Towards the base it went down into the hill, dropping to darkness. I threw a stone, expecting the well or mine-shaft sound of your own breathing as you wait and wait for the distant splash or crack. I heard nothing.

Leaving my bag at the entrance, I walked in as far as I could, then got down on my hands and knees and crawled into shadow that fast became a narrow, down-ward path into stone-smelling half light. Then my head butted hard into rock. I could feel the lump already beginning to form.

The light from the cavemouth was a pale sheen on the rock above my head. I felt around on both sides, hoping to find a new passage. I wanted to go deep into the side of the hill, to feel the weight of absolute darkness.

In the brief flare of a match, the cavewall danced and a moth the colour of the stone flew into my hand. Another match found spiders and a seam of white stone. I rolled and lit a cigarette. In its glow, the insects and seam started moving. My head was throbbing. I smoked and watched the cave come alive. I saw a pair of underpants in the powdered rock beside me. A beetle emerged from the sleeve of a torn blue shirt and waved its feelers. A light was coming on. I saw the letters of a name beginning to form on the stone. I tried to stop it by kicking out, but my foot ripped open a plastic garbage bag and a dog's head dropped into my lap, its tongue blistered with ants and beetles. I tried burning them off with the end of my cigarette, but they were moving too quickly, carrying off beads of flesh and entering the ground. The light was blazing. The word SPOOK flashed on the wall. I got onto my hands and knees and leapt forward towards the entrance. I hit the wall again and this time, when I felt my head, the lump was wet. It flooded my face, warmed my neck and chest. Water poured into the cave. I drank it, tasting myself. I heard waves, the sound sand makes as it shifts beneath them. I heard a new moon polishing itself behind the clouds. Then something bumped into my ribs, just behind my right shoulder. I turned to find a huge mulloway hovering and shunting against me. It knocked me off balance and I went over. It came at me again. It had a strong, sweet smell, and it watched me closely, nudging and butting, leaking a line of bubbles that broke on the cave roof. I stroked its back. Its scales were like silver coins. Then it backed away and opened its mouth. Its teeth were short, white, conical points. It groaned and coughed. Prawn heads bristled from its mouth. A dark lava of fish remains slipped into the warm current and swirled away. A tailor fillet with a big rusting hook in the skin flapped and settled against my arm, followed by a thatching of bones and shell grit. When the parade of half-digested food had stopped, the mulloway pressed its mouth against the side of my head:

Don't leave. Feast with me. You have come for the tidewater table. Dream and swallow what I offer your opening mouth.

Are the headlights on for you? Give me your line-holding hand. Smell my undersides. Drink the slime I carry for the worms. The perfume of my blood will stain your head. Is there hatred in your casting arm? In your knife? Have you seen me cruising with my love? We can float and feed at the depths of our choosing. You must try it. Would you like to try it now? Here is a scale and here is a tooth. Here is the sound of my gutter-cruising death.

When it had stopped talking I saw, emerging from its throat, a familiar face. The eyes were wide with surprise or terror, and the mouth was opening and closing as if it were trying to say something. I reached out to touch the face, but the mulloway backed off and turned. With a beat of its tail it started moving slowly towards the daylight. I followed it, crawling, the tail beating a current of cavewater into my face. When it reached the entrance, it nosed my bag aside as if it were distasteful food and dived over the edge. I looked down and saw a bright disturbance among ferns and hill flowers. Water rushed past, nearly taking me over the edge. I held my bag and lay on my stomach as the foul tide of prawns and fish guts blew over, making a waterfall that someone climbing the side of the hill would surely have mistaken for the runoff from a killing shed in full production. When the water had soaked into the sand, I gathered sticks and bark and made a fire. As the flames grew, heating my face, a terrible pain filled my head. I dragged a large branch onto the fire and lay back, my thoughts splintering like baitfish.

I sat up and found lights on the black ocean below. I heard small waves licking the base of the hill, and then a voice with my name inside it floated up to the cave.

I answered it and lay back, listening to the sound of sticks being broken, small trees being parted.

I looked up beyond the edge of the cave roof. Stars were wheeling over in blue lines. A planet turned and glowed. Then the sun appeared.

Jesus Christ, what happened to you? the sun said, then it clicked and died.

Two voices came off the stone above me. One said We saw the fire, the other said You look like shit. Then I was sitting up, a hand beneath each arm. Don't try to talk. My hair was parted. A voice took a breath. Stitches, it said. The other voice agreed, and then said Do you know who this is?

I saw a dark shape.

It's Harry, Jim. I thought you might have come down here, after what I'd told you about this place. I'm surprised you didn't come here earlier. I saw Colin at the shacks. Soon as he asked if I'd seen a young bloke around here, I knew.

You've got a good mate here, Colin said.

I knew you were coming, Harry.

Heard me thinking about you from the train, eh?

I saw you inside a mulloway's mouth.

Jesus Christ, Colin said. What have I done?

THE MISSING

WHEN I WOKE they were staring at me, the lanternlight giving them different faces. There was something around my head.

Do you feel as silly as you look? Harry said.

You don't look so good yourself.

At least I'm not wearing a pair of underpants on my head.

I reached up and felt a strip of damp material.

Colin whacked Harry in the arm. It's a bit of singlet, James, don't listen to him. At first we thought you'd need some stitches in that wound, but it's not so bad. Looks like you're growing a horn though. That lump's a beauty. He slapped his knees. Where's the tobacco?

I don't know. In my coat?

No. Checked there.

My bag?

No. I checked there, Harry said.

Must have left it up on the hill. I closed my eyes, saw the cave, and looked away from it. Shit, that was weird up there.

Tell us about it some time, said Colin. Just rest for now.

What time is it? I asked, trying to see through the window. Someone had draped a couple of hessian bags over the glass.

It's late morning, said Colin. You've been sleeping and chatting away all night. Here, drink this. He passed me a mug. The coffee tasted wonderful.

I'd like a smoke too, Harry said. I ran out yesterday.

What was I saying, in my sleep?

You wouldn't wanna know, Harry said.

Lots of things, Colin said. Mostly just words. They weren't connected. But you did talk about Stephanie, that girl you mentioned, and there was talk about fishing.

I love fishing. That mulloway in the cave was a ripper.

Colin and Harry looked at each other.

You also said some very strange things, Colin said.

Harry laughed. So what's new?

Here, I wrote something down. You said *Like frozen-over lakes whose ice is thin, and still allows some stirring down within.* What's *that* about?

It's from a poem. 'Year's End', by Richard Wilbur. It's in the book Stephanie gave me. It's in my bag.

Colin went to the bag, lifted out the book. Let's see. He found the poem. Here, Harry, you read it.

I can't read poetry. I don't understand it for a start, and besides, why don't poets talk normally? They sound like they're pissed.

Colin tapped the book. Come on, it'll be good for you. A bit of culture. He sat back and closed his eyes.

Harry looked at the book, then held it away from him, at arm's length, as if it were going to leap up and whack him in the head. He looked at Colin, then at me. I'm going to have to do this, aren't I?

Yep, said Colin, without moving or opening his eyes.

So Harry began. Year's End, he said, and then, in a whisper, This is stupid.

Read, said Colin.

Harry read each line slowly at first, hesitating over each word, then he picked up the pace, reading with more confidence. When he finished, he closed the book and rubbed his hand over the cover. That's not bad, he said. Wouldn't want to make a habit of it, though.

We sat in silence. Colin shifted in his chair and said The pictures in that poem are really good. I like the bit about the dog lying down in the ashes.

Harry said Yeah, and the bells in the snow.

I said I liked the lights of the houses. Then I stopped thinking about the poem and came back to the shack. So what's going to happen now?

Colin sat up. Harry did the same. We're taking you home, Colin said, dreamily. Truck's fixed.

What about Mum and Dad? They must be so pissed off.

I've seen them, said Harry. They called my place the night you left. My olds went off at me, thought I was involved. Then your mum and dad came over. I didn't know anything, but they wouldn't believe me. They started talking about the cops and everything. Your mum called them. They phoned back later and said a car had seen a young bloke hitching on the highway.

Harry told me more than I wanted to know. He said Mum and Dad had gone to the police, who had come to school next day and he was called to see the Principal. The cops showed him a poster with people's faces on it. Missing Persons, they said. They asked him what he knew. They said Your friend could be one these people, pointing to the faces on the poster. One of The Missing. Harry told them everything he knew, which was bugger all. He told them about Stephanie, because at first he thought I might have gone in search of her, for real this time, but he didn't believe it. The cops wanted details. They went to her shop. They checked around. They came back and said If you remember anything at all, call us. People at school were telling stories. Harry laughed when he told how, in one story, I'd been kidnapped and taken up the coast to a farm. In another I'd gone to New Zealand with some religious nuts. None of the stories he told was anywhere near as strange as what had happened, though, and when he finished talking he went serious and sat back in his chair. You're a bit of a celebrity, Jim.

I lay in bed, sleeping and waking, wearing a bloody headband in a shack that was travelling in time between light and dark.

Colin and Harry were like Mum and Dad when I was young and sick, bringing me drinks and food, making sure I was warm, although I can't recall Mum or Dad ever saying fuck it when they dropped something.

Colin had already phoned home and told them I was safe. Mum said they were on their way, but Colin suggested they wait until we got there.

Driving through Sydney, I felt as though I'd been away for years. People, streets and buildings were unfamiliar. The three of us sat pushed up in the truck's cab, not talking as the suburbs folded away. I looked across at Colin, his face pale green in the light, his nose looking more bent than usual. Harry drummed his fingers on the dash and whistled quietly.

Nearing home, Colin drove slowly and said Whatever happens when we get there, keep your cool. You know there'll be shit flying out of the fan.

When we stopped, the house was lit up like a shop. Just after we'd slammed the truck doors, Mum and Dad came up the drive. The fan was spinning, and there was nowhere to hide as the shit went through the air.

After phone calls to the cops and to Harry's mum and dad, after tears and tea and cake, after questions that remained unanswered, Dad poured Colin a mugful of his best whisky and then sat down and started shaking his head.

We stood up on the road. Colin said goodbye. Dad went up and hugged him. Mum hugged everyone and then stood holding herself as Colin opened the door of the truck. He reached in and came out holding a small black bag.

You're not getting this unless you promise to practise your arse off until you've *got* it.

I opened the bag and lifted out the silver overhead reel. Its sideplates flashed in the streetlight as I turned it in my hands.

Colin got into the truck and kicked it over. He slammed the door and leaned from the window. Take care of yourself, James. You've got a wonderful family and a bloody good friend in Harry here.

The truck idled badly. He looked through the windscreen then back at me.

I'm a missing person too, he said. Then he pulled away.

I watched his tail-lights until he turned the corner, and I saw them all night as I lay awake, only vaguely sensing the importance of what had happened, as Harry snored and thrashed on the floor beside the bed and a night bird wanted to know where I had been.

A BOOKSHOP IN THE RAIN

T HE NEXT FEW days were thrown together with
endless questions and long, dream-filled nights and
afternoons of sleep. There were grey and blue lines
under my eyes. I'd lost weight. I stayed in my room as
much as possible, but Mum and Dad made me go with
them to the shops, to their games of tennis. They
watched me constantly, even when we weren't in the
same room.

I decided not to finish school. Dad went on about a
career, and Mum said A career's not that important. Not
right now. Mum knew a thing or two about life. Dad
said What about the services? The army or navy? See
the world. Mum said God you're pathetic. I said I just
want to feel better. Dad slapped his arm as if something
had bitten him and said I know son, I know.

I got a job working with a friend of a friend of Dad
who had a gardening business. How Barry Davis was
anyone's friend was beyond me. The man never stopped
talking. I worked in the farthest part of the garden to
get away from him, but even when he was up a tree

trimming branches or under a bush, his tongue kept working. He talked about horse racing, dentists, spiders, oral sex, America, beer, death, sunburn, money. Maybe if someone else had talked about these things they might have been interesting, but this man's voice had only one tone and level: flat and loud. I was glad whenever I had to use a lawn mower.

I lasted a month. Barry Davis talked me out of the job. Then I went on the dole, much to Dad's disgust.

You're letting the side down, you know, doing this, he said, much more than once.

By then I had my licence, and I was taking the tablets every day, so Mum let me drive her bashed-up Morris Minor. I liked its little wing indicators and smell. I'd go for drives to the beach, park looking over the sea, and write – I'd started writing poems and stories – or else I'd go to a national park and walk, taking notes on birds.

One overcast, windy morning, saying I was going to the beach to do some writing, I drove through the city and out onto the highway. I had no plan, but I wanted to be somewhere well beyond the feel and smell of the city, though not too far from home.

I drove for two hours and found a small town just off the Southern Highway. It had a cafe and a petrol station, a souvenir shop and a tennis court at the end of the buildings with weeds stitching the sand together and big holes in the fence.

It was dark now. Clouds had lowered themselves into the pines on a nearby hill. When it started to rain, a cockatoo went out of its head, flying low and letting rip a single, piercing screech that stayed in the air long seconds after it had flown, its crest a yellow flame.

I followed a narrow road behind the tennis court and found a small building that could have been a country church, its two small windows glowing behind a screen of willows.

The rain was cold, but falling lightly. As I neared the house, I saw movement behind a window and instinctively moved to one side, to avoid detection. I was angry with myself, and said so. When I looked again I saw a face pressed to the glass, then it was gone.

Out the front was a sign whose paint had peeled and blistered: *The Pines Bookshop*. It was a weekday, and only early afternoon, but it felt like a bad time to be knocking. A dog barked and dragged its chain against the kennel.

I knocked. A voice came from deep in the house, and then footsteps on floorboards. When the door opened, a young woman looked at me through the wire screen. She said I'm sorry, we're closed this afternoon.

I said something like What kinds of books do you sell, and she said All kinds. Then she opened the screen door and stepped out on the verandah.

Do you live around here?

No. In Sydney.

You came out here to buy some books from us?

I found you by accident.

That's the best way to find things, she said, and looked past me into the yard.

When are you open again?

Tomorrow.

She took a slow, deep breath. I guess it's alright if you want to come in, she said. There's lots of books on the floor in the front room. I'm sorting through them. Mum and Dad want me to finish by this afternoon, so you can't stay long, alright?

That's alright.

She opened the door and held it for me.

This was a church once, she said, as we went down a hallway lined with old photos of people and horses. Over the years, people have changed it so much you'd never know, looking inside.

We came to a large, open-plan space at the back of the house.

My name's Tina, by the way.

I'm James.

She stood before a tall bookshelf against the far wall.

This is where the altar was. I like this space. Maybe it's because the prayers are still here, floating around. It feels calm, don't you think?

I guess so.

Listen, I'll leave you to it. Don't be long. Is that alright?

Yes.

Just call out when you're ready.

I moved along the shelves, letting my eyes go in and out of focus, half listening to the rain that was now falling heavily, when a word had me turning and reaching for the spine it was printed on. *Schizophrenia.* I said each syllable out loud. Five sounds from a doctor's office. I sat against the wall, under one of the dripping windows I'd seen from the road, and opened the book. It was a paperback, and although it had never been read − its pages were clean and tightly packed − it smelled like it had passed through many hands. I inhaled its mossy odour and thumbed through each section: *Diagnosis, Family Care* and *Case Studies* a grey blur in the fan of pages. I went to the door and called Tina's name. I wanted to leave, to read what I'd found in private.

Tina appeared and looked at the book in my hand.

Some light reading then? Why the interest?

I met someone who is schizophrenic. We're friends. I thought reading about it might help me to understand her better.

Tina put her head back and studied the ceiling. Her throat was long and smooth, with a small globe of light under her jaw. She was wearing a black coat, red T-shirt and blue jeans. Her riding boots were cracked and mud-smeared. When she looked down again, her hair fell in two thick panels against the side of her face.

Oh, hi, Dad, Tina looked past me.

A big man was in the doorway, with no air between his shoulders and the frame.

What are you doing, Tina?

Dad, this is James.

Your mother wants a hand.

Tina didn't move.

Well, go on then.

See you, Tina said, from the hallway.

Found a book then, James? the man said quietly.

Yes.

He looked at it, then reached and took it from my hands. Opened it.

Two dollars, he said. Does that sound fair?

Yes. Thanks. I paid him.

He walked heavily to a shelf. Here's a ripper. Ever read *Gulliver's Travels*?

I said that I had, but he reminded me anyway.

About all these little people, Liverpublicans, savage little pricks who tie string around this giant bloke and shoot him with arrows and blowgun darts. They only felt like pins and needles in his arms and legs though.

He reached for another book. *Moby Dick*? he held it high.

I said I had to be going. He followed me out of the room and down the hall.

This used to be a church. You wouldn't know it, though, eh?

Tina appeared and stood beside him. She looked lovely in the dull glow of the hall lantern. Her hair had light inside it.

I went to the door.

You know where we are, she said.

The dog barked and dragged its chain. Settle! the man shouted into the rain-wired dark. The dog settled.

Want a garbage bag to put over your clothes, son?

No thanks.

Umbrella then, you can bring it back any time. We trust you and we need the business.

I looked past him into the house. Tina was holding her hands and watching me.

Drive carefully, the man said. That highway's got more black spots than a migraine.

I walked out through the gate and down the muddy road. I heard a crunching sound, and then Tina ran up beside me.

I'll walk out with you.

At the car it started raining heavily again. I opened the door.

Cool car. Is it yours?

No, it's Mum's.

She wiped rain from her face and said Want to do something some time?

Like what?

Go riding?

I can't ride.

It's alright, my horse is a lamb.

When?

This weekend?

I'm not sure. Can I call?

I guess. Do you have a pen?

No. But I can look it up. The Pines Bookshop, right?

Yes. Good then. She waved and stepped back from the car. I saw her running back down the road as I drove away.

Driving home, the windscreen of the old Morrie fogged over the prints my wiping hand had made. I saw farmhouses glow and fade. I saw trucks flaring up in the mirror, and then their streaming tail-lights as they churned away, throwing water. I saw a beautiful girl getting drenched as she said goodbye, and then I saw her walking back into the house, where she would enter a dark room walled with books.

SCHIZOPHRENIA

―•◦•―

T HE TABLETS WERE working. They made me a little
drowsy, and my mouth was often dry, but the
headlights hadn't been on since the day up in the cave
above the shacks, and no one had said they'd heard me
talking.

I'd seen Dr Lap again, and he asked me all the
questions: How Are You, Is Everything, That's Good,
Let's See . . .

I told him what I could, but not about what was
happening at home. If Mum hadn't been sitting beside
me I might have said something. The need to speak
about it was growing wild in me.

They were fighting all the time. Sometimes it began
with a hard word that went blindly from room to room
like a trapped bird no one can catch. Sometimes they'd
sit watching television, not speaking, anger dividing
them in flickering blue light.

Dad would come home from work, get changed, and
go down to dig in the garden. Mum would sit reading
or sewing while the pressure cooker tapped and hissed

on the stove. I used to run and jump near the cooker to make it blow its top and throw a steamcurtain over the room. I thought about doing it again, for fun, to shake the place out of its sadness, but then dropped that idea when I saw Mum looking down into the garden, her face like a grey mask.

It had been almost a week, and the only words they'd exchanged were about Mum's car needing something done to it. Even then, the words ended in rising shouts and the sound of them walking away from each other.

One night, lying in bed, I listened as their voices grew from talk to shouts to screaming. A glass shattered against a wall. I tried to block out what was happening upstairs by thinking about Tina, but the words quickly replaced the image of her face and hair and forced her out of the room. I got out of bed and put a record on, turning it up until the music had buried their fighting. Then Mum was at the top of the stairs yelling Turn that music down, before stomping back into the war.

In the morning, Dad threw open the curtains and said This is what the day looks like, James, just in case you're wondering.

He was still going on about the dole, and how it was a crime to waste my time and it would no more occur to him to stay in bed after 8 a.m. than fly to the moon even when I'm sick I go to work you're better off up and dressed and being responsible it's no good feeling sorry for yourself you're . . .

I lay there watching him talk, the words coming from a red space like the mouth of a puppet.

You're not doing yourself or anyone else any favours you know we're doing all we can James now you've got to do something positive come upstairs come on son.

He adjusted the knot on his tie and stood there waiting. His aftershave floated over me. Then he took a deep breath and held it. I heard a floorboard click and settle upstairs. Dad let the breath go in a long thin stream, then he turned and left. Mum said something under her breath when he reached the top of the stairs. He said something back, and then she shouted Give the boy a break for Godsake, and went away. Dad followed her, shouting At least I'm showing some concern. What have you done since James came home?

Oh you're a real saint, aren't you, Mum yelled. You didn't even bother coming when we went to the doctor's. Your own son's in serious trouble and a meeting is more important. Don't you talk to me about concern.

On they went, banging and stomping from room to room. Cups rattled when they packed down in the kitchen. A door clicked shut at the end of the house, and Dad screamed You're not making things any better, you know. He hammered the wood with his fist.

The house seemed to be waiting as the sounds of anger and hurt passed through it. Then the front door slammed, a car engine coughed and revved violently, and Dad roared away to work.

I sat up and found a day blown through with clouds and changing light.

I knocked on Mum's door. I heard her move. I asked if there was anything I could do, and she said No, I'm fine. I'll be right in a minute. It sounded like she was speaking into a blanket. I had a shower and thought about Tina. I saw her leaving the book room, her hair like a tapering shadow down her back. I put my forehead against the tiled wall to let the water fall on my neck. I always did this when I had things to consider.

It made me relaxed and sleepy, and daydreams came easily.

When Tina faded into the steam, the book I'd bought replaced her. I saw its cover emerging slowly, its one-word title growing in size until it covered the space between my downcast eyes and the swirling at my feet.

I'd read two chapters. Even after reading of how the world is full of people with this illness, I felt so alone. I kept the book under the bed in a paper bag, like a magazine I wanted to hide. But I needed to open it again now.

Before going down to my room, I turned to see Mum with her head down, passing the receiver from hand to hand as she talked in a low, inaudible line of words.

I went into the bush, found a large sunny rock, and started reading.

The chapters I'd seen in the bookshop startled me as they hadn't done then. Now I found others. When I said them out loud, they sounded like something a specialist might say, speaking from some big book in his head: *What Is Mental Illness? You Are Not Alone. Causes. Treatments. Co-Existing Disorders.* I chose *It's Not Your Fault*, and read what I already knew – that laziness is not a part of it; that it's not like lung cancer or due to a poor upbringing; that it can arrive, as if it were a traveller, at any time, any age.

A kookaburra angled in between two sick-looking gums, and with a smoky flutter settled on a branch overhead, where it eyed me, then looked away. I returned to the book, but couldn't concentrate. When I looked up, the kookaburra hopped and twisted around on the branch. It shook itself and stared down into the bush. I stretched out on the rock and closed my eyes.

When I woke, the kookaburra was still there, watching, and my name was being called through the trees.

THE ROCK FISH

———

H ARRY HAD PHONED while I was in the bush
reading. When I called he asked if I wanted to go
fishing on Sunday. His dad had the rods and gear, and
said he could take the Holden. I said I thought I had
other plans, but Harry went off, saying Don't be a
dickhead, this is your big chance to teach me how to
fish.

He picked me up in his dad's Holden and handed me
a map of the Central Coast. Harry's dad had marked a
few spots, and said to make sure we kept to them.

Dad reckons we could catch some tailor from the
beach this afternoon. The tides are right. Harry thumped
the wheel. Whacko.

It was mid-morning when we set out, the rods
strapped to the roof-racks, the big-boned Holden
blowing along.

We took the old Pacific Highway, the radio going
full blast, the windows down, smoking and singing, a
rod tip waving around madly in the wind where it
overshot the roof, the plastic containers full of sinkers

and hooks keeping rhythm in the back. I checked the map as Harry drove. The beaches looked like wading pools and the headlands were tiny mounds of pebbles spilling into the sea.

At Avoca, Harry bought a bag full of frozen pilchards and I bought a whole fresh mullet, remembering what Colin had said about catching mulloway.

Having chosen one of the headlands – not one that Harry's dad had marked – we used the map and asked directions and finally found the entrance to the rocks and water. It was a dirt track that entered the trees below a dark green water tower, high on a hill that gave us brief flashes of the ocean as we climbed it.

We followed the base of the cliff around to the right over a wide flat shelf of smooth stone strewn with tendrils of bleached weed and rock pools agog with slime. The edge of the shelf was at sea-level, and would surely be underwater in a big swell. But the sea was rising and falling slowly, and little waves were breaking with a muted slap and whisper against the shelf face.

A small boat motored past with rods set out the back, the lines shining into the wake. Harry waved and said Ahoy there, but two men sat swaddled in yellow rain gear and did not respond.

Reaching twin black coal seams in the rockshelf, we stopped to check the map. Its detail wasn't enough to give our exact location. The black seams entered the sea like slip-rails, the surge flooding the channel between them with belts of kelp and foam. They entered the cliff behind us and climbed sharply until they disappeared into shale.

I was walking ahead, about to climb a small rise, when Harry called out. He was standing before a large grey rock. When I reached him, I found the rock was two large, smooth pieces, like fleshy lips joined at the base by a thin wafer of stone. At the centre, a grey, mottled groove curved up to a small dark globe, then joined with the two outside pieces to form a canopy before entering the wall of the cliff.

Remind you of something? Harry was smiling and touching one of the outside layers.

I looked hard, trying to find something in the shapes.

Harry reached in and touched the small dark globe of stone, then rubbed it with his palm. He looked up at the cliff. I was thinking maybe the headland would start moaning, he said.

When I understood what shape the rocks were making, and what Harry had done, I felt stupid, childlike.

Harry put the rods down and lay at the centre of the groove, arms up, thrown open over the smooth edges. Imagine being able to lie down in one, he said, and sighed. Then he narrowed his eyes and said You still haven't worked it out, have you?

Of course I have.

What then?

It's a woman's vagina.

Shit, James, I'm glad to hear it. Thought for a minute you had no idea.

He turned over, pushed himself up, and put his face to the dark globe.

Hmmm. Tastes great.

Yeah, right, you'd know all about it.

Matter of fact, I do.

When?

A few times, with Jenny Stevens.

You're kidding.

I'm not. He sat up and stepped away from the rock. Have you done it?

I wanted to say yes. I wanted desperately to say yes. I said no, and realised I had the beginnings of an erection. I moved the tackle bag around to the front so Harry wouldn't notice. It wasn't that I was embarrassed about the swelling in my jeans, it was how weird it would seem to be turned on by talking about a rock.

Have you ever seen one for real? Harry asked, and I wished he hadn't.

No.

They're incredible. Lots of hair, and the lips are kind of crinkled. They're pressed together at first. You have to open them to see everything. It's like unwrapping a present.

Now I really had something to hide. I was sure the bag was being pushed away from me. I adjusted it and turned side-on. I looked up past the black seams. The cliff was layered and bright where the sandstone was exposed. Guess we'd better be going then, I said.

Harry leaned forward and patted one of the outside layers.

Labia, he said. Isn't that a great word.

The headland was scarred deeply where great slabs of sandstone had slipped away, and the shelf was littered with smashed boulders, the rubble diminishing in size and volume as it spread from the base.

Harry toed a fallen rock the size of a soccer ball. Wonder how often this happens?

We ran as fast as the gear would allow until we reached a boulder on the far side of the shelf.

We moved through a maze of giant stones, their shadows wide and cold, though the day was hot and we were sweating. The stones reminded me of the ones I'd explored while Dad was playing cricket, and I had to fight off the urge to lay my ear to them.

Close to the edge of the cliff, we came to a boulder with a large metal plaque bolted into it. It had a man's name, and the dates of his birth and death. Below these details it said *Fished his way to Heaven*.

There were others. We found seven plaques before we stopped looking. Most had little phrases below them, and all were written for young men who had died fishing. Their names went into my head. I repeated them. Behind me, I could hear Harry saying something, but I couldn't turn around. I wanted to feel the weight of their names and how they died. I wanted the moment to last because I could almost hear them as they went over head-first into the swell where they trod water or bled away into the run-off with their mates above them going mad with panic throwing ropes or tackle boxes Jesus Christ someone going in after them and going under in heavy clothes the whole place insane one dead and one about to die and a red crab blowing bubbles on a shell-spiked wall and a gull making another pass above the red fan spreading quickly.

I turned around and Harry's face swam into view. His mouth was working like a landed bream's, and I heard We've got to keep to the track and You look shithouse. When his mouth stopped and his eyes calmed down, he said Do you want to stop for a while and have a smoke? You were off and running, weren't you, Jim. In your head, I mean.

I started describing what I'd seen, but it was useless. The words failed. My teeth came together. Let's just get out of here, I said.

We walked on in silence. The signs and names

hovered in front of me. I was underground in this high place filled with the details of death. It was like a seaside graveyard where the headstones had fallen into place.

We were in a sheltered cove, surrounded by cliffs and boulders that took the sun and cast it back at us. There was no shade, and we were burning. Harry made two hats from a sheet of cardboard he'd found where we left the gear. They looked ridiculous, but they kept the sun from our faces.

We unpacked the gear. I was feeling better, though my left leg was shaking and my mouth was dry. Slowly, frame by curious frame, I showed Harry how to set up his rod and reel. His reel was a threadline, and he told me his Dad had already shown him how to use it. But as for the basics, he was hopeless, losing the end of the line as he fed it through the runners, stepping on tackle boxes and rods, and trying to tie knots with his teeth.

Better stick to using your mouth on things you know well, I said.

You're just jealous, Harry said, and dropped his rod.

You're right.

We fished without success until shadows fell over us. The wind had picked up, and it was getting cold. The swell had been rising steadily for a couple of hours, and now broad waves rolled in and broke under a tongue-shaped rock, throwing white plumes. We chose another place, higher and further back from the water.

I'd been practising with the overhead reel on a school oval near home, and was now able to cast a fair distance without line coming off in a great tangle. I loved the sound and feel of the line spinning under the ball of my thumb, adding pressure at the end of the line's arc.

I cast into a tight curve of foaming swell, where currentlines forked out into open water. As the large mullet fillet sank from view, I felt several light taps through the line, then a solid thump. The line snapped tight and the rod bucked, the tip curving down. I'd set the drag on the reel, and line crackled as the fish ploughed off to the right towards a low ragged cluster of rocks.

Harry was behind me, offering all kinds of advice, from *Don't muck around bring it in*, to *Ease off a bit or you'll lose him*. I went through Colin's instructions, pumping and winding and giving the fish its head when it wanted to run.

I moved along the rockface. I was losing line fast. The fish was still deep, but it had turned away from the point and was heading straight out to sea.

I'm going to lose him! I yelled at Harry, who was now standing on the other side of the cove, trying to follow the seaward passage of the line.

Bullshit! he shouted back. *Just hang on!*

That's all I could do. I could see the silver gleam of the reel drum through gaps in the line.

When the end came, I fell back, staggering, landing hard but safely on my arse. The reel was empty. Somewhere there was a big fish with half a mile of line trailing from its mouth.

We packed up in a full swathe of cold shadow. It was high tide, and waves were breaking over most of the ledges.

Walking out, we stopped at Labia Rock, as Harry had christened it, and stared as if in wonder before some ancient stone shrine. Without Harry's anatomical commentary, it didn't have quite the same appeal, but it was amazing all the same.

It was wonderful to be outside. I liked being with Harry. He made no demands on me. I could say and do more or less what I wanted. To say that he understood me completely was going too far, yet he had seen and done more than most people of his age that I knew. I wanted more days like this: to be with someone I liked, to have fun, to be physical instead of living in the changeable blood of the head.

When I got home, Mum opened the door and there was Darkness pouring out of her. She moved ahead of me through the house and in the lounge room she sat in a chair and looked at the wall. All my plans to tell her about the day went to ground and stayed there.

The house was very quiet, and I said so.

Yes, Mum said. Your sister is staying with a friend.

Where's Dad?

She didn't answer. I saw her crying before she started. It was coming from deep inside her. Her whole body was priming itself to let go with tears, and when they came they flooded her face. She sobbed and doubled over in the chair, rocking herself, her arms around her knees. She tried to say something, but a tiny animal sound came out instead, and she tried to speak again, but she was finding it hard to breathe. I went to her and put my arms on her shoulders. She rocked back and forth, and managed to say that she was sorry, and her tears fell over my hands as she moved her head from side to side, saying Sorry, and then I held her as I'd want to be held myself, as I'd always wanted to be held, with my whole body, and I cried too, with a pain I only imagined I had known.

TWO MEETINGS

———•————

D AD HAD LEFT home. Mum said they'd tried to talk
things through, but they just couldn't be together
any more. I said You've only been fighting for a few
days, but Mum told me they'd been apart, emotionally,
for years. We kept it bottled up, she said. Strangers
under the same roof. What you heard was everything
we've been hiding inside. It had nowhere to go but out,
in those terrible words. I'm sorry you had to hear them.

We sat through a full moon's rising, its light all over
us. I'd never sat so still for so long, drinking mugs of
tea and listening to her say what was in her heart. It
scared and pleased me.

Some time in the morning, drained of tears and
words, Mum got up and went to bed. I went too, but
lay there thinking about Dad. He was living at his
brother's house, which I thought a good thing, as they
were close and shared lots of interests. I presumed, out
of ignorance and hope, that he'd only be gone for a few
days until they sorted things out. I got dressed and went
to sit in the garden. I went back over years, trying to
remember how Mum and Dad had been with each

other. I saw them at the picnic by the river, the day they held each other and watched the smoke rise from the farmhouse chimney. I saw them holding hands one Christmas. And later that afternoon, going to their room, I saw them lying asleep in each other's arms. I hadn't seen them laugh together over something silly or hold each other for a long time. Everything Mum had said made sense, though I didn't want it to.

Next morning, when she went out, I phoned Dad's brother's place. He said Dad had already left for work, and he was worried about him.

He's drinking too much, he said, and not eating properly. He's talking about your mother all the time, I don't know what to say.

I'll come over and see him, I said.

I think you should wait a few days.

No. I want to see him now.

There was silence, then I heard muffled words and my auntie came on the phone.

Your dad's in trouble, but he just needs time, she said.

Tell him I'm going to call tonight. I hung up.

I called from a phone box. Dad sounded awful. We arranged to meet at the oval where I used to play cricket.

I've been trying, really I have, he said.

I know, Dad.

I still love her, you know. Would you tell her that? Would you tell her I still . . .

My uncle said something in the background, and then he was on the phone saying He's got to go now. He'll be alright.

When I got to the oval next day I was late. I'd missed a train, forgetting how far it was from the station. Dad was in the players' pavilion, pacing the boards and smoking. He hadn't had a cigarette for years. He looked bad. His face was grey, and it wasn't just the failing light. He lit another cigarette from the one he'd been smoking. When I asked for one he handed me the pack and sat down heavily on a bench.

For the second time in two days I listened as someone opened themselves and let me hear the sound of their insides breaking. I wondered if I'd hear his blood like old water inside a tree if I put my ear to his chest.

The words came and went. As he spoke, a sprinkler came on, hissing then stuttering loudly as it fired water in a long arc over the grass. The jet of water seemed to be coming from the side of his head, as if all the pressure inside his skull were being released.

He drove me home, and sat looking past me at the light in the bedroom.

Did you tell Mum that I still love her?

Yes, I lied.

He looked at his watch. Turned the radio on. Turned it off. Lit a cigarette. Offered me one.

How long have you been smoking, James?

I don't know. Four years.

Bloody idiot. How's Harry?

He's good. We went fishing up the coast.

Catch anything?

I lost a big fish. Harry caught the land but couldn't land it.

Dad almost laughed and drew heavily on his cigarette. We should've gone fishing years ago, he said.

We still can. Let's go soon.

The light in the bedroom went off. Dad kept

watching the window. For a moment I felt like a cop casing someone's house.

Guess I'd better be going then, I said.

Yes. Dad's hands found the wheel. He took his seat belt off, leaned across and gave me a big hug. I love you too, you know. You know that, don't you?

Yes.

His clothes made a whispering sound as he squeezed me again, and his face was hot as sunburn. It was the closest I'd been to him since I was little, and I only knew that from old black-and-white photos of him holding me and smiling.

When I walked in, Mum said You've seen your father haven't you?

I thought she must have been looking through the window when the light went off, but she said His aftershave is on you. And who's been smoking?

Both of us.

Well that's just bloody brilliant, she said, and went into the kitchen where she started stirring something with a wooden spoon. He gave up smoking more than ten years ago. And when did you start?

Don't go on, Mum.

James, you'll throttle your lungs and die horribly. Is that what you want?

I'll smoke if I fucking well want to, I said, and went down to my room.

When I came up there was a plate of food on the table with a sheet of tin foil over it. I called out. I went to her room and knocked.

I'm getting changed.

I ate dinner watching some show about timber wolves in America. A wolf was lying on her back as the cubs

150

jumped all over her. One of them played too hard and was bitten on the back of the neck. Then it showed a river bordered by huge trees with yellow leaves. The narrator sounded like someone with a wolf's head up his arse as he went on about the Grand Beauty Of Nature.

Mum and I were like lost people in another country, passing each other as if there was nothing to say. There was so much to say it was choking us.

At dinner I said Have you spoken to Dad?

Mum hit the edge of her plate with the knife as she put it down.

Oh? And what did he say?

Mum stopped chewing and didn't look at me.

I went on, knowing how hurtful I was being. I said Really? That's interesting. So I guess you two have kissed and made up and have been going to movies and smooching in the back row?

Mum was quick. She flipped her plate over and left the table in one movement. I sat there with meat and vegetables all over me. There was gravy in my hair. Red wine bloodied the tablecloth. I watched it spreading as Mum started the car and drove away.

Next morning I apologised. Mum apologised too for throwing her dinner at me, and said We're both saying things we don't mean.

My sister came home, and Mum brightened up.

I walked in from reel-casting practice on the oval and found flowers all over the house. Every room had more colour in it than the side of a Spangled Emperor's face. Mum went around arranging them, standing back to assess her work, moving in again, humming and touching. Even my room had a great big bunch of something that looked as though it had been stolen from a war memorial.

We were all talking again. My sister had written some poems and Mum made her read them. One was about a dragonfly, and it was a shocker. I said it was great, and she said Really? and she read another one. I said it could do with some work, and she said How about this one? There was no stopping her. From uncertainty to a confidence overkill in one session. After about six nature poems, Mum came to the rescue with a pavlova that filled a plate as big as a hubcap. We demolished it, pressing the meringue crumbs to our fingertips.

I saw Dad again, this time up the road at the primary school. It was my suggestion. I wanted to show him where I practised the casting.

We walked through the playground. It was dusk. Dad said he'd taken a week off work and had moved out of his brother's house to a hotel in the city where he could try to figure things out.

A circus of currawongs dropped into a black pine behind us and started wolf-whistling and carrying on like smart alecs. We sat on the grass and watched them.

I like currawongs, Dad said. They're cheeky buggers. They've got killer beaks and eyes, but they're playful. We used to have chickens when we were kids. One day we let them out in the yard, just to peck around for a while. We thought they'd be fine because the yard was fenced off and there were no bushes they could hide in. There were about ten of them and they ran around at first, then they stepped slowly and studied the grass. We went inside. I looked through the window and saw currawongs strutting about on the lawn. One had a chicken in its beak. It shook its head and flew away. By the time we got down there, half the chicks were either missing or dead, stabbed through by those long black beaks. I hated currawongs for years, and would try to kill them with rocks on the way home from school. Then I used slingshots and brought down a few.

Dad lit a smoke and watched the flame moving up the matchstick.

So what made you change your mind?

I think I realised that we can't stop things happening just because we don't like them. Not with the natural world, anyway. We see gazelles being torn down by leopards and we think it's terrible. The gazelle has got big soft eyes and a pretty face, but the leopard doesn't see that. It sees dinner moving through the grass.

I shook a cigarette from the pack.

You shouldn't be smoking.

I know. People keep telling me. And you shouldn't have started again.

I know. People keep telling me. And you shouldn't be such a smartarse.

The currawongs left the pine in a whistling, angling mess of wings and went over the school buildings, dragging night behind them.

We lay back on the grass. Dad told me again how much he loved Mum, and I told him all about mulloway and how I was going to catch one.

We talked about the stars, how you can almost sense how far away they are, but then the feeling vanishes as fast as it arrived. We talked about cricket and wedge-tailed eagles and fishing, but behind it all was Mum's face and voice. I looked at Dad as he lay back on the grass. His whole body was focused on being with her again. His pain was like a faint outline of light.

Mum's hurting too, you know, I said.

Dad didn't answer. He sat up and armed his knees.

I'm sure she's thinking about you, Dad.

Well she can think all she likes, but it won't bring us back together.

It might, after a while.

I don't think so. He stood up. I've written lots of letters but can't send them. I dial the number and put the phone down before it can even start ringing. God I'm pathetic.

Maybe you should go away for a while.

I've thought about it. Where would I go? Being on my own would be terrible right now, I think.

Not if you went somewhere nice, like up the coast.

I'll think about it.

He walked off a few paces and turned around. Maybe you're right. A few days up at Sawtell or Coffs. Want to come?

Maybe. I'm not sure.

Have a think about it. I reckon I'll go on the weekend. Here's the number of the hotel. I've written my room number on the back.

He gave me a card.

Just ask at reception and they'll put you through.

As we walked back through the grounds, a security guard spoke from behind his flashlight, wanting to know what we were doing.

Trying to solve a few puzzles, old son, like how do you tell a currawong to put a chicken down, and when love dies, where does it go?

The guard had the light-beam trained on Dad's face.

And if you want to know any more you can turn that bloody thing off or else get it out of my face.

The guard angled the beam onto his shoes and said there had been some kids breaking windows and he was only doing his job. Dad said Fair enough, and then he said We might be kids at heart, but windows aren't our style.

As we walked away, the flashlight speared between us and shivered over the grass.

That night, something changed in me. It was a small thing. It came at me and entered my head and neck, angling down to coil inside my gut. It was a feeling. There were no lights, no words or voices. I liked the feeling, and marvelled as it travelled through my body, coming to rest at the centre of my chest. I wanted to give the feeling a name, but I couldn't find one. I killed the light, parted the curtains and looked out at the trees. Then a name arrived. It took shape on the back of my tongue. I went to the wall mirror and looked at myself. The name sounded like Responsibility, but I wasn't sure. I said the word anyway. It went around the room, covering all levels until it re-entered my mouth and fed me, and fed me until I slept.

TINA

On Friday afternoon, when Mum had gone to tennis, taking my sister with her, I phoned The Pines Bookshop. Tina's father answered and I hung up. When I phoned again, he said Who is this? before I had a chance to speak.

It's James Molloy. I came out last week and bought a book.

The lad with the book on schizophrenia?

Yes.

How are you, James?

I'm good. Is Tina there?

Would you like to speak with her?

Yes please.

Can I ask what it's about?

I just wanted to say hello.

Hang on.

I heard heavy footsteps. A screen door opened and slapped shut.

Tina!

I listened to my breathing shy away from the mouthpiece. The footsteps returned, and at the end of them he said She's on her way. She was feeding the horse. So, how's the book?

It's interesting.

That's good.

Tina said Thanks, Dad, and came on the phone. There was silence for a few seconds, and I saw her waiting until her father had left the room.

Hi, she said softly.

High tide.

What?

It had slipped out. I said high tide, it means hi.

Tina laughed. So what do you say when you're leaving?

I thought about it. Seaweed, I said.

That's great. How come you didn't say seaweed when you left here?

I just made it up.

Really? Can I use them?

Yeah. So what are you doing?

Right now? Standing in dirty, horse-smelling clothes talking to you.

What about later? What are you doing this weekend?

Standing in horse shit, mucking out the stable and grooming Trooper. He's a palomino gelding. Fifteen hands. He lost half his tail a few days ago. Caught it in a fence and shredded that beautiful blond flame.

The receiver knocked against something as she changed hands.

Sorry, you still there?

Yes.

So, do you want to come and get shitty?

Why, what have you done?

Do you want to come and help me muck out? I'll make you some lunch. And Dad's got some bottles of blackberry wine under the house. It's lovely, and he doesn't know how many he's got. He doesn't drink. Not any more. He's on the wagon. He likes to make wine though. Gives it away as presents, and opens bottles when people come.

I saw bottles without labels stacked in the dark. I could smell the fruit, see the stains on my hands when I used to pick them with Mum and Dad, eating too many and trying to tell thorn-blood from the juice.

So what do you think?

Sounds good, except I've got this thing about walking behind horses. Dad was kicked in the head when he was young, lost most of his front teeth. He tells everyone that it happened playing rugby, though.

That'd be right. Personally, I'd consider it quite an honour to say that a horse had knocked my teeth out. It's better than some boofhead's boot in your gob. Besides, if you have to walk behind a horse, you don't give them any room. Hug their flanks. Press up close to them and move confidently. A horse will lash out if it's cranky or spooked. Best to let them know where you are and why you're there.

Tina had a warm, lovely voice. I was thrilled to be able to talk to a girl this way. She made it easy. There were no games inside her words. Harry would be proud of me.

You haven't answered me. Are you coming or not?

Her father's voice went past like static on the wind. Tina said Sorry, Dad, what was that?

She groaned and said Dad just reminded me to feed the chickens and water the plants, as if I need reminding. One more time. Yes or no?

Yes.

Good. Mum and Dad are going to a book fair in Sydney tomorrow morning. I have to help them get things packed up and everything, so it's best if you come out later. Just before lunch?

Alright. Do I need to bring anything?

Have you got any shit-proof boots or shoes?

After I'd put the phone down I realised that I didn't know if I'd be able to have the car. Tina's place wasn't on a bus or train route. I went down into the bush and tried to think of a good story to tell Mum when she came home.

I said I had to go to Harry's to plan a fishing trip.

Do it on the phone, Mum said.

We can't. We need the maps and everything.

I'm sorry, James, but it will have to wait.

Mum told my sister to leave the room, which was a very bad sign. She said What's going on? You're not planning a fishing trip, are you?

No.

Did you and Harry go fishing last week?

Of course we did.

Why should I believe you?

Because we did. Phone Harry and ask him.

So tell me why you need the car.

I was in deep. Telling her meant I had to say that I'd driven the car out of Sydney when I said I was going to the beach to write. I was cornered. I sat down and told her everything.

When I'd finished, Mum said You're not having the car. Then she said I hope you don't lie to this young woman the way you've lied to me.

I left while it was still dark, before the trains started running. It took five rides to get to the Southern Highway, and it was eight o'clock when I stood at the side of the road, angry with myself and not avoiding the feeling.

A truck stopped and the driver said he was going as far as Goulburn. I jumped in and started thanking him. He said Steady on, it's only a ride, and we bucked away into the Saturday morning stream of sport-bound kids and shoppers.

What's in Goulburn? he asked. Bloody dump if you ask me.

I'm only going as far as Bowral.

Easy done, he said, and pulled out the makings for a cigarette. Smoke? he offered me the packet.

I hadn't bought any since before leaving for the shacks, and I accepted the grease-smeared pouch with relish.

As we smoked, he told me about his life on the road.

Used to do the long hauls. Brisbane to Sydney, Sydney Melbourne, that kind of thing. Gets hard on the wife but. She used to come along. Got jack of country music and truckstop food after a while. Then we busted up. Guess who she ended up with?

He shifted back in his seat and waited for me to answer. When no answer came, he said Another truckie. Can you believe it? Sucker for punishment. I know the bloke as well. Thought about givin' him a new haircut with a wheel brace, but didn't. You ever busted up with anyone?

No. I thought of telling him about Mum and Dad, but he was off again.

Worst part is what happens to the kids. Got four. They took it bad. They're with her. I hate the thought of that mongrel bein' their father. But what can you do? I see 'em on the weekend. Good kids. Growin' up quick. Love 'em.

You're still their father, I said.

That's right. He ran a hand through his hair. That's bloody right. Can't never take that away from me.

Before I got out, he gave me some tobacco, a few papers and a box of matches. Watch your back, he said.

I'd made it there in just under five hours. I walked past the small shop and looked down the road, past the tennis court. A station wagon was parked out front of the bookshop, and people were moving around it. I bought a can of drink and crossed the road.

In a small park, behind some swings, I sat on a mound of grass where I could watch the house and car. I thought I saw Tina through a gauze of willow leaves, and said hello to her.

I had chosen a pair of old sandshoes with rips in the canvas. I'd wanted to wear the riding boots that Dad had left as spider traps under the house, but the leather was so hard they hurt my feet just standing in them.

A police car pulled up at the shop, and two uniforms went in. When they came out with white paper bags and drinks, one of them stopped and said something, then they looked at me. They put the bags and drinks into the car and crossed the road. I rolled a smoke and pretended I hadn't seen them.

Morning, said a voice that could only have come from a cop.

Morning, I said, picking a strand of tobacco from my mouth. They were looking for something to do on a Saturday morning, and they'd found it. One had a big belly and was wearing sunglasses. The other had a face like a greyhound. I didn't like greyhounds.

You from around here? Greyhound snapped.

No.

Didn't think so. Where are you from?

Sydney.

Where in Sydney?

Waterfall. It's in the Royal National Park.

I know where it is. What are you doing here?

They could have been teachers. I was enjoying myself.

Smoking and talking to you.

A comedian, Belly said and looked around.

Greyhound got down on his haunches and said Listen, you little prick, when I ask you a question I expect a straight answer, got it? He stood up. What's your name?

Mark Brown.

So you live in Sydney and you're out here sitting in a park at the side the road.

I smoked and found a sudden interest in the rips in my sandshoes.

Greyhound pawed my leg with his polished boot. I was talking to you.

I didn't hear my name, I said.

Belly walked off and crossed the road. He opened the door of the car and got on the two-way. Greyhound said We'll find out what's what. You just sit tight. Smartarse.

The station wagon pulled out of the dirt road and drove by slowly. I lowered my head until my neck hurt.

Belly came back and shook his head.

Greyhound took a deep breath and spoke as he let it go. Seems you're not on the books, Mr Brown.

Only a matter of time, Belly said.

How'd you get here?

I got a ride.

Who with?

My friend Tom. He's from Parramatta, sells radios and stereos from the back of his truck. If you see him, you should pull him over and get something. He'd do you blokes a good deal.

Greyhound sniffed. He looked ready to shake or

scratch himself. Instead, he stepped on a stick, slowly, until it broke. The gesture wasn't lost on me.

The two-way in their car started crackling. Belly walked off, but Greyhound didn't want to leave. I felt sure that if we'd been alone, in the right place, he'd have started swinging.

As they drove away, I rolled another cigarette and waited. They went about a mile down the road and turned. As they came by again, the temptation to wave was almost overpowering, but the rips in my sandshoes had already proved useful, so I used them again.

I smoked and waited. When it seemed a third pass was beyond even these two shitheads, I went to find Tina.

She was walking towards the house carrying a small cane basket. When she saw me she smiled and put the basket down gently on the lawn.

Why didn't you drive up to the house? She looked down the road.

I didn't drive. I couldn't get the car so I hitched.

Really? Don't you think it's dangerous?

I suppose it could be. It's more dangerous around here, I reckon. I just had a run-in with two cops.

Tina laughed and said Were they like fatty and skinny?

More like bulldog and greyhound.

That's them. They've just been transferred here. No one likes them.

I can understand that.

Tina picked up the basket. It was filled with eggs. Oh well, you got here safely. It's good to see you, she touched my arm. Come on, I need a hand at the stables.

We went into a small shed. Tina rattled and banged around, and came out holding two pitchforks. The handles were long and smooth, the curved prongs smeared and spiked with flecks of straw. She led the way through a small swing gate into a yard that reeked of horse. The stable was empty.

Where's your horse? Trooper?

Out the back, in the holding paddock. Ever tried to muck out a stable with a horse inside it?

Tina was holding the pitchfork lengthwise at waist-level. Right, use the fork in one easy motion, she said. As she leaned into the downward swing, I saw a birthmark like a tiny brown wing just below her hairline. She lifted out a forkful of straw and tossed it into a broken-backed wheelbarrow she'd parked in the mud. Easy, isn't it?

We forked and laughed and barrowed. We scraped old manure away from the stable floor and put down a bed of thick, new, earth-smelling straw. We sweated and scratched at our dusty arms and necks.

After shovelling shit and hosing down the stableyard stones, we leaned on the handles and surveyed our work.

Reckon there might be a job for you out here, Tina said. I think you've got what it takes.

I don't think your dad likes me.

Gordon? He's all bluff. He hasn't said anything. Anyway, I'm still his little girl.

She put a finger to the side of her mouth, angled her head and laughed. They don't really know me, though. They think I'm an angel.

Aren't you?

A black one. Come on, let's put these tools away and clean up. Hungry?

I could eat a horse, I said.

I followed her out of the yard with straw all over me.

Tina put ham, bread, a container of potato salad, a great wedge of cheese and a bottle of olives into a wicker basket she'd lined with blue cloth.

Now for the best part, she said. She picked a length of straw from my hair. Let's go and choose a bottle.

The cellar was at the back of the house, its entrance hidden by the low, sweeping branch of a peppercorn. Wooden steps went into the dark.

As I stood beside her in the cool, damp cellar air, the smell of clay and the scent of her recently washed hair had me reeling. I wanted to hold her, and she must have sensed something because she moved away quickly and stood at a wall of bottle-ends gleaming in the half light.

She removed a bottle and studied the label. Not old enough, she said, and passed it to me.

My image of Gordon's wines had been wrong. He *had* labelled them, meticulously. There was a small panel of textured white paper with *The Pines* in emerald green script at the top, and under this was a drawing of a pine tree with the bottling date printed in spidery hand-writing through the mid-section of the trunk.

Dad had hundreds of these labels printed. He writes the dates in himself. She held the bottle out to one side to catch the light from the stairway. This is better. She rubbed the bottle against her jumper. Think one will be enough?

How strong is it?

She turned it over slowly and weighed it in her hands. She smiled through her hair. One's enough.

It was early afternoon when we reached the creek, which was trying to be a river with both narrow and wide sections and deep pools where the water ran quietly with leaves and swirls. Willows lined the banks. Where it turned in the distance, a great gum cranked out over the current, its main branch strung with a rope, knotted at varying lengths for handholds.

We spread a blanket on the grass and unpacked the basket. The food looked wonderful. I didn't know where to start.

Tina tore the end off the loaf and handed it to me. She grabbed a fistful of olives and dropped some into my hand. The oil dripped through my fingers.

Did you bring a knife? I asked, holding the wedge of cheese.

Just break some off. I don't believe in using knives at picnics.

I broke off a chunk, pushed it into the bread and used the crust to wipe oil from my hands.

Now you've got it. Tina took a big bite from her ragged-looking sandwich and chewed loudly. I did the same.

A cicada burred the air and hesitated. A dragonfly sipped at the reflection of a cloud.

I watched her hands as she described the shapes of her words in the air. Her fingers were long and tanned, the nails short and lined with dirt. I liked that they were lined with dirt. On the middle finger of her right hand she wore a silver horseshoe ring. She noticed my interest, held her hand up and said You should always have the ends of the horseshoe facing outwards, away from you, if you're wearing a ring. If you've got a real one on your wall or door, you should have the shoe ends facing up, to catch your luck like a cup. She slid the ring over the first joint, then pushed it back again. I reached out to touch it and she asked if I was happy.

Why do you ask?

Because you have . . . I don't know. There's a bit of

sadness in you. I saw it the day you left here, and today, too, while we were mucking out.

What does it look like?

It doesn't really look like anything. It's a feeling. It's as though what's inside you has come out and covered you.

She touched my shoulder. It's not a bad thing, but I'm aware of it. It's there, so I wanted to ask you.

Is it there now?

Yes. I'm sorry. I shouldn't have said anything. She reached over and lifted the bottle. Let's drink, she said.

Want me to open it?

I'm sorry, James.

Here, let me do it. I took the corkscrew and started turning. When the cork emerged it was stained black with red edges.

Tina held the glasses and I filled them.

Before you taste it, hold your glass up to the light.

The sun hovered in the darkest red I'd seen. I saw Tina's hand moving towards me through the wine, and then she touched my glass with hers and said Here's to all kinds of feelings.

The wine swam on the back of my tongue, and when I swallowed, all the blackberries I'd ever picked were in that one delicious mouthful. I tasted the black ones that fall when you touch them, and behind those a faint sour taste from the berry whose one red side is hidden. I closed my eyes and drank again. I could feel the alcohol working inside me, getting ready to spread to my arms and legs before swimming into my head, and staying there.

Now you look happy.

When I opened my eyes, rising slowly as if from a great, clear depth, Tina was smiling and resting the edge of the wineglass on her chin, her face angled into the air. I'd noticed her doing this a couple of times, and each time I found something new to look at on her neck.

I feel happy. This wine is the best thing I've ever tasted.

I know.

What's the secret?

Dad won't say. But I know he spends ages making it. He got the recipes, for this wine and others, from an old book about some place in England. He says that one of the chapters is about witchcraft.

That makes sense. I think you'd need some kind of spell to make something this good.

Oh look! Tina pointed to the creek with her glass.

I saw willows, moving water.

There. On that snag branch.

A green and blue bird with a sharp beak sat on the end of the branch.

A love dart, Tina said, putting her wineglass down and getting onto her hands and knees. A Sacred Kingfisher. They're my favourite birds. They're so fast and they leave the colour of their wings in the air when they've gone.

Why a love dart?

Watch and see, she said, easing herself down onto her stomach.

The kingfisher shook itself, its feathers settling as if the breeze had combed them down. When it flew off, it left a streak of blue light between the vibrating branch and the willow it entered.

A love dart straight to the heart, Tina said. Would you pass me my wine?

I filled our glasses and lay down beside her.

So what kinds of birds do you like?

All kinds of eagles and hawks, I said, thinking of nothing but the heat and smell that was rising from her clothes. I like crows and currawongs too.

Light went through her hair when she turned to look at me.

Kingfishers?

Especially kingfishers, I said.

Tina tipped her glass and drank deeply.

The branch the kingfisher had left seemed to be moving slightly, but there was no wind, so I blamed the spell of the wine.

I felt Tina move, and when I turned to her, her face was as close as my skin. She pressed her mouth to mine. I had to keep from falling down. A warm flood of blackberry wine poured over my tongue and her tongue followed it. Then I *did* fall down, into and over myself, and she went with me, giving me more wine, tracing the outline of my teeth with her tongue, the weight of her body on my chest and legs and the taste of her mouth in the dark red flow as I drank and tried to breathe, then gave up breathing and gave my tongue to her. I lay on my back as she moved over me, my hands under her sweater, pulling her close, her weight pressing me into the earth, her hair around our faces making overcast light, the smell of her neck and her breath ripe with fruit in my head and mouth, and then she sat up.

The light was harsh, and I didn't know which way I was facing until I found the branch in the water. Tina was sitting behind me, brushing leaves from her sweater.

The wine, she said.

The love dart, I said, and sat up, the weight of her body still on me. There was some wine left, so I held the bottle out.

No thanks.

I drank from the bottle. I collected the food we'd scattered or crushed and put it into the basket. Tina was playing with her ring. A cloud passed over the sun. As she darkened, she said For someone who looks sad a lot of the time your kisses are happy little creatures.

Walking back to the house, our shadows leaned out in the grass before us, looking tired and worn, connecting and separating like people who had travelled far, and were now unsure of where to go, and what to do with themselves once they got there.

When we reached the garden I put the basket down, and because I couldn't think of anything else to say, I said I should be going.

Tina sat on the step and said Yes.

So this is what happens after people cuddle and share their wine, I said, sitting beside her. They don't talk to each other?

I don't know what to say. Before, I couldn't shut up. Now it's like my brain's gone to sleep.

Are you embarrassed or something?

Not at all. No, I loved what we did.

What then?

I was going through things on the way back. I broke up with someone a couple of months ago. I guess I still think about him.

Do you love him?

Do you know what love is? Have you felt it?

I think so.

What happened?

She went away. I don't know where she is.

Have you heard from her?

No.

Tina took a boot off and shook out a stone. Ciaran asked me if I loved him one night and I said yes, and as soon as I'd said it I knew I shouldn't have.

It's an easy thing to say.

Yes, but it shouldn't be. It carries a lot of other things along with it.

Such as?

Such as trust and respect and things like that. She looked into her boot. I trusted and respected him. But I didn't love him.

How do we know anyway?

I think it's beyond the words we have for things. I've been in love. I thought a piece of my side was missing. She put her boot on and stood up. She stamped the ground, as if removing it had altered its shape. Ciaran was my Drama teacher at high school. I was in year twelve. He wasn't married or anything, but he was thirteen years older than me, and when we were found out, people treated him like shit. He got threatening phone calls and letters. My God, it's as if he made me fall in love with him. Mum and Dad went silent on me for ages. You don't plan to fall in love. And when it happens you're a criminal. I felt so sorry for him. He was a good man. He *is* a good man. He lives down the South Coast now. Runs a fishing charter boat out of Bermagui.

Did he love you?

Desperately. I used to watch him standing down by the river, when I was up in my room. He'd just come by and wait for me to appear. We'd watch each other for ages.

Tina sighed and said So, my first real love and the world throws a bomb at me. I'll never forget him. He taught me about plays and poetry, and I taught him how to get his hands dirty, and enjoy it. She sat down again. Why did you love ... did you tell me her name?

Stephanie. Because we understood each other.

In what way?

I heard Mum saying I hope you don't lie to this young woman ...

Stephanie is schizophrenic. She's the one I mentioned when I bought the book. I met her in town one day when I'd taken off from school. She was talking to herself. I listened to her. Then I followed her home.

Jesus, James.

I know. It sounds weird. Please, just listen.

I told her the story, glad to be telling it, hoping she'd understand. She did.

She sounds wonderful. Are you sure there's no way of contacting her?

I'm sure.

How about you? Are you alright?

Yes. I take tablets. They help.

It was getting dark. The roofs of the stable and small sheds were grey outlines.

I've got to feed the chooks. Want to come?

Are they dangerous?

Very. She leaned over and put her arms around me. Her breath still smelled of the wine.

The seed flew from our hands in a white spray. The chooks flapped and pecked. Tina dumped a container of vegetable scraps onto the dirt.

That lot should keep them happy for a while. We let them out too. They love it. I like watching chooks, the way they check out the ground with one eye as if trying to decide if there's anything worth eating down there.

We watched them feeding.

You don't have to go.

It's a pain in the bum trying to hitch when it's dark. Every driver thinks you're a maniac.

Are you?

Maybe.

I mean you can stay. Mum and Dad won't be back till tomorrow. They're staying with friends. Other book-heads. The fair goes for two days. They've got a stall. It's their big weekend away.

I'll have to call. Let Mum know what I'm doing.

Don't tell her too much, Tina said and kissed my neck. A small flame licked up under my jaw and my teeth caught fire.

When I phoned, Mum said You just be careful. Then she said Do you want me to come and get you tomorrow? I said I'd be fine, and she told me that Dad had sent her some flowers and that she was feeling awful.

I don't know what to do, she said.

He sent you a love dart.

Tina put her head around the corner. What are you talking about, James?

When I put the phone down, Tina said Can you tell me now?

Dad sent Mum some flowers, you eavesdropper.

If you use one of my sayings, of course I'm going to listen. You should have seen my ears. They went up like Trooper's. She threw me a towel and robe. You need a shower.

After I'd showered, I sat in the lounge room listening to music and drinking coffee. I lay down on the sofa and closed my eyes. Then the lights went out and there was a faint tap on my chest.

Here's something for you to read, Tina said.

I could see the faint outline of her body.

Don't turn the light on for a couple of minutes, she said, and was gone.

I waited, concentrating on my breathing, listening for sounds of her. I was holding a cool sheet of paper. After counting to ninety, I turned the light on.

Dear James,

   After you've read this, wait five minutes then go down the hall. The door is the last one on the left, before the book room. Knock twice and enter. Don't speak.

I counted the first minute out loud, then walked around the room. I walked, counted.

At the end of the hall I saw light flickering in the glazed panel of the door. I knocked twice and went in.

The room was divided by a large piece of material, fixed to the wall at both ends by thumb tacks. On my side of the screen, directly at its centre, a high-backed chair threw a grid of thin shadows. I could see Tina's outline through the material. She was sitting in a chair. She looked like a black-and-white negative. In each corner, large candles were leaking slender flames. The air smelled of vanilla. I sat in the chair. Waited. Then Tina moved. She reached up, the shapes of her hands like hawkshadows. My hands moved to them, and when we touched, her fingers opened and she lowered her hands to the bottom of the screen. It started to rise. I saw her bare feet, then a dark green hem. At the top of her skirt, around her waist, a wide black band. Then a white shirt, which darkened with the ends of her hair. When the screen had moved past her face, she lifted it over her head like a veil and let it fall. I pushed my chair back and knelt before her. I kissed her eyes closed and

174

lowered my face. I found a button and sucked it. It tasted like a coin. Tina put her fingers into my hair and drew me close. My hands went under the hem of her crushed green skirt, and I touched the rough hair on her legs. She put her hands on my arms as though asking me to stop, but then she stood and led me to a bed in the corner. She sat on the edge and put her face to my belly. She opened the front of my robe and held me. The horseshoe ring gleamed. She pressed me to the side of her face, then took me into her mouth, her tongue swirling under the head as she milked me. I watched her. Her eyes were closed. I saw her cheek fill with the shape of me and then she stopped moving her hand and her tongue flicked slowly from side to side. I felt a wave draw back inside me. My hands were lost in her hair. Her tongue slowed and the wave flattened out. When she took me from her mouth, a strand of clear fluid looped and settled on her lip. She caught it like a webstrand on her finger and licked it away. I could barely stand. I wanted her to keep sucking me, yet I was glad she'd stopped. I knelt before her again and my hands made a ripple under her skirt. She lay down on the bed, her arms thrown back. I watched the skirt rise and saw fine dark hairs on her calves and thighs. My hands travelled over the cool plates of her knees and my mouth followed them, a shock of taste going the length of my tongue as her skin responded with a seamless ripple of risen flesh as if she were cold or afraid, and I warmed her, rising to cover her body, then to unbutton and lay open her shirt, her nipples hardening and darkening as my teeth raked their undersides, then I was licking her breasts and easing them in turn into my mouth, the wet and the hard trying to reach each other, with hunger a pulse in the root of my tongue I pushed down to her belly and traced a dark line from navel to the pale blue edge of her underwear like a tideline between the skin I knew existed and the triangle of hair I had dreamed of since oceanwater had teased and emptied me, the cotton peeling away down her thighs and coming free where the dark was lit with a gleam like wet petals, her scent that of all the animals I had ever wanted to touch, my mouth understanding what to do, its instruction in the craving that flowed through mouth and chest, in the way she arched her back and lowered herself, brushing my chin then easing away, I opened her with my opening mouth and licked her slowly, through two waves of sea-tasting skin, the hair thinning to fine lines at the sides of my tongue as I swallowed what her body made and entered her with my fingers, to the knuckles, feathering over a texture like oil, licking up to the globe I knew from the stone by the sea, and finding it, eating her where her sighs and the brief touch of a hand indicated, my fingers drawn deep, my face in a pure concentration of wet hair and the flower shape of her, blooming as she lifted away from the bed and cried something I'd tried to imagine so often, and I answered her with a sound of my own until she was breathing loudly and I was lying beside her, my hand in her hand.

To sleep beside a woman after making love for the first time. To share her breathing and to listen to her body move. This was the greatest thing I had known. I kissed her shoulder as she slept. I took strands of her hair into my mouth and sucked them. I licked her right nipple when she turned over and flipped her hand onto my chest. I did not sleep. Morning came and I was aching to be inside her body again. Sleepily, she moved over and on top of me. She reached down and guided me into her, and then she moved backwards and forwards, up and down. I went with her, my body responding to every gesture. When she lowered her head and started licking my nipples, I came and came and saw the room turn inside out.

Sitting outside in the sun, drinking coffee, Tina kept looking at me and laughing. I asked her what was going on. She laughed again.

When you have an orgasm, your eyes go different colours.

I said she was imagining things, and she said No, there were red and blue lights going off behind your eyes when you were coming.

In the bathroom, while Tina was feeding the chooks, I masturbated quickly and looked into the mirror, to study my eyes as I came. The lights I saw were different. The blues were like sapphire, the whites without any hint of redness. I had never seen them so clear.

WAITING

——•————

T HE MAN AT reception said Dad's phone was
engaged. I asked if he'd seen him. The man said
If I knew what he looked like I might be able to tell
you. And besides, it's really not our —

I hung up before I could say Fuck off, and walked to
the station.

It was 9 a.m. when I entered the hotel. There were two
men at the reception desk. As I waited for the lift I felt
sure they were watching me, but when I turned around,
one was writing and the other was talking on the phone.

I knocked on Dad's door. A cleaner walked past
pushing a trolley. I knocked again.

He's gone out, the cleaner said. I saw him leave about
an hour ago.

I stood in the lobby, trying to decide what to do.
People were coming and going, sitting around in
armchairs near potted trees, drinking and smoking,
talking quietly. The only vacant seat was beside a
woman who looked as if she'd been hypnotised, her fur
coat bristling with fluorescent light, her blue hair piled

high. I sat down and reached for a magazine. The woman's perfume was overpowering. Turning a page, I saw her hand on the armrest. The veins were standing out and the skin was dry. She had a ring on every finger.

I put the magazine down and looked out the door.

Waiting is a terrible thing, the woman said. It's all we do. Are you waiting?

Yes. My father's gone out for a while.

My father went out forty years ago, she said. Then she leaned over and angled her face at me. Does your father live in the hotel?

Not really. He's staying here at the moment.

I understand, she said.

Are you waiting? I asked. Her eyes were almost lost in folds of powdered skin, her eyebrows dark pencil lines.

Of course, she said. I'm an authority. There are different kinds of waiting. At the moment I'm waiting for my heart to slow down. I have a complaint. It trips over and throws a tantrum. Last night I waited here, in this very chair, for an old friend.

She moved, touching her hair with an open palm.

But these are standard forms of waiting, she said. Waiting to move. Waiting for the rain to stop. Waiting to shuffle off.

She turned in her chair, her head moving with the rest of her body as if she had no neck. What is your most potent memory involving waiting?

I saw a mulloway leaving a cave. I felt the warmth of Tina's body, lying beside the creek. I saw the first sparks from my headlights in a warm red place.

Waiting to be born, I said.

Bravo. Indeed. May I ask your name?

James.

James ... ?

Molloy.

My name is Emily Cynthia Winterbottom. My late husband's medieval ancestry gave me a name I am proud of. Those poor people waited at the bottom of a hill for the sun to reach them. It rarely did. I live in a house that gets the full flare of the morning sun. I wait for it. Especially in winter.

She smoothed the pleats in her dress. She sighed.

Your father, she said, then shook her head, as if she'd said something she regretted. Your father. Do you take care of him?

I said yes, then realised I had never thought of taking care of Dad.

Good boy. We need our children's love.

A group of people entered the lobby. One man left the group and went to the elevator.

There's my dad.

Don't keep him waiting, she said.

Dad was getting into the elevator as I ran over. He gave me a hug as the door closed and we went up to his floor without talking.

His room was a mess.

If I'd known you were coming I'd have cleaned the place up. Why didn't you call? What happened about our fishing trip?

I'm sorry, Dad. I know. I met someone. I went to her place for the weekend, and I kept thinking about how I should have phoned.

That's alright. It's good to see you. Tell me about her.

Her name's Tina. She lives at Bowral.

Is that it?

She's great. I like her a lot. I'd like to see her more often.

Then do. He went to the window.

I sent Mum some flowers, he said.

I know. She told me.

What did she say?

She said she likes them and doesn't know what to do.

Put them in a vase, I guess, Dad said.

I threw a sock at him. So what have you been doing? During the day and everything?

I walk around. Go to the Botanical Gardens, China-town. On Saturday I went to Paddy's Market. The nights are bad. I get so restless. Here, I bought this for you.

He went to his suitcase and pulled out a plastic box about the size of a thick paperback. It rattled when he passed it to me.

Thought you might need a tackle box. There's hooks, sinkers and swivels in there.

Thanks. We can use it when we go.

You're on. Right, what'll we do? See a movie? Go for a walk?

We don't have to do anything. We could just stay here.

No. I'm sick of the place. I'm aware of all the other people that have been in here. He looked around. And I can't keep the place clean. Even hanging up my clothes is a mongrel.

That's alright. Don't worry about it.

I'm lonely, James.

I know.

Dad went into the bathroom. I look like shit, he said.

When we entered the lobby, Emily Winterbottom was still there. I waved to her as we went past, but she didn't see me.

Who's that? Dad asked.

A waiter, I said, and then regretted saying it. I might as well have made a joke about her name.

REPTILES AND FISH

T HE HOTEL WAS near Circular Quay, so we walked
around looking at the ferries. It was a fine, clear day,
though humid. We were sweating, and soon had dark
patches under our arms. Dad walked quickly, whereas
he'd always been slow. Mum was forever telling him not
to dawdle. He hadn't shaved for days, and his face was
dark with brown and grey bristles. His shirt was creased
and had come out of his trousers at the back. He didn't
tuck it in. As we walked I felt like doing it for him.

We found ourselves approaching the Opera House.
Its peaks had bits of sky on them, and boats planed over
its harbour-facing windows.

I hated it at first, Dad said. But now I think it's
beautiful.

I've always liked it, I said. When I was young I
thought they had concerts up inside those shells. I
couldn't figure out how they'd do it, though. All these
people up in the roof, singing their guts out.

Dad said What do you mean? They *do* have them in
the roof. The actors are suspended by invisible ropes,
and they fly around like big fairies.

We laughed ourselves stupid and walked on through tour groups, past a crowd watching two jugglers, out beyond the shadow of a gleaming tiled bonnet, until we reached a sandstone wall.

Are you going to introduce me to your friend? Dad asked, finding the shirt tail and tucking it in.

I saw Tina lying in the faint light of early morning. I saw the horseshoe ring as her hand opened on my chest.

James?

Dad was looking at me with his eyebrows raised.

Did you hear what I said? I asked if you're going to introduce me to Tina.

Yes. Maybe she'll come fishing with us. I'll ask her.

You can't ask a young woman to go fishing. What kind of date is that?

She asked me to muck out a stable. She's into all kinds of things. She likes to get her hands dirty.

I'm not sure I should ask you any more about that.

I'm not sure you should either. But you can if you like.

You really like her then?

Yes.

Why?

She's lovely. She's fun to be with, and we talk about anything.

That's important, Dad said. Being able to talk is wonderful. Have you met her parents?

I've met her dad. You'd like him.

Then will you invite them out for dinner? You and Tina, your old dad, and her parents. What do you think?

Sounds great.

Dad took a deep breath, and I felt sure he was going to talk about Mum, but he said You can talk to me, can't you?

Yes. I watched Dad's shadow moving over the path.

I can talk with you now more than ever before, I said.
I know. I feel that too.

Dad, I care about you. You know that, don't you?

He stopped. He turned and looked at me. Of course
I do. He started crying. He didn't try to stop it. He put
his arms around my shoulders and sobbed. I felt
uncomfortable at first, wondering if people were
watching, and then I hugged him. He said You do.
Then he said it again. I hugged him harder, and his
breath came in hot flushes over my face. He relaxed his
grip and straightened up. He wiped his eyes. I hope you
know the same about me, he said. I love you, James.

I know, I said, and felt a wave of sadness go through
me. It was a mixture of my growing love for Tina and
the terrible times that Mum and Dad were moving
through.

Dad looked around and said Let's go into the
Gardens.

I hadn't been to the Botanical Gardens for years. The
last time was with Dad and his brother, who knew all
the proper names for the trees and would say them like
he was tasting something nice. When I reminded him,
Dad said My brother knows the proper names for
everything – rocks, birds, flowers, clouds, shells, dirt.
He's got a photographic memory, but that's not the only
reason. He loves everything to do with the earth.

Some kids were playing under a huge Moreton Bay
fig. They were so small against the folds at the base of
its trunk, which looked like the foot of a brontosaurus.
One little girl in a red dress was standing alone, watching
the others. As we came near I could see she was crying.
In one hand she held a plastic bucket, in the other a
small green spade. She looked like she'd been suddenly

transported to the gardens from the beach. Dad went up to her and knelt down.

What's wrong, sweetheart?

She cried and wouldn't look at him.

Are you lost?

I saw a man walking quickly towards us through the group of kids.

What's your problem, mate? he said as he shoved Dad out of the way and took the girl by the hand.

Dad stood up and said There's no problem, I was just worried about her. She's crying.

The man was wearing a T-shirt with a goanna on the front of it, and his black shorts were falling down.

She doesn't need your help. Piss off.

There's no need to be such a prick, Dad said. I was only trying to help.

The little girl ran off and stood watching us.

What did you say? The man took a step forward.

Come on, Dad. I took his arm and tried to lead him away.

I said I was only trying to help.

Before that. What did you call me?

Jesus Christ, said Dad.

No, you called me a prick.

My Dad was being helpful, I said. Just forget it.

Fuck off, Rin Tin Tin, the man said, then turned his head and spat into the grass.

Dad offered the man his hand. Come on, he said, let's shake and forget the whole thing.

I saw a man with a dribble of spit on his chin make a fist and get ready to use it. Behind him, a little girl in a red dress was holding a bucket and spade. When I looked at the man again, all I could see was a goanna. You're a cunt, the goanna said, so I punched it as hard as I could. It fell down and started moaning. I hit it again, swinging into the side of its big, balding head, but it didn't run away. I kicked it. It felt like a bag of mud with small sticks breaking inside it. You've broken my fucking ribs, the goanna said. Then I was being dragged away. When I'd stopped kicking, Dad was beside me, urging me along, saying Just keep walking. I looked back and saw a man kneeling on the grass, holding his chest, his face wet and red in the shade of a massive tree.

I don't know whether to thank you or call you a bloody idiot, Dad said, as we walked up George Street.

Do both then, I said.

Seriously though, James, I thought you were going to kill him.

He was going to hit you.

Maybe. Anyway, thanks. I hope he'll be alright.

Until someone else thumps him, I said.

I realised where we were when Dad started talking about a camera he was thinking of buying. We were two or three blocks from the antique shop, and I was in between feeling sick and excited.

You're very quiet, Dad said.

Stephanie's shop is just up here, I said, and quickened my pace.

Stephanie?

The woman I met, that day in Sydney. Bloody hell, Dad, don't you remember?

I think so.

She was the one who helped me, who told me about —

Now I remember. Do you want to go another way?

No. I want to see the shop.

I hardly recognised it. There was a *For Sale* sign on the window, surrounded by posters and handbills. The boxes and prints were gone. I saw where Stephanie had sat in lamplight, and I tried to see into the corner, to the bottom of the staircase, but it was too dark.

Let's go. What a depressing place, Dad said.

I just want to check something. I stepped back and looked up. The curtains were still there. A pair of pigeons strutted and preened themselves on the roof. I wanted to call out, to throw a stone. I felt empty and my chest was hurting.

What are you doing, son? Dad was looking around nervously. Then he said You shouldn't come near this place. Remembering is one thing, but it's not good to get so involved.

It's too late for that, I said, with a taste like metal in my mouth. I didn't have words for what I felt about Stephanie and Tina. One had gone. One had entered my life. Confusion had tied a knot in my head and thinking about it pulled the knot tight.

Why don't we go to the fish markets? I said. I wanted to get away from having to think about Stephanie.

Dad said That place stinks, but I was already on my way.

I made Dad stop at every window, telling him the names of the fish. He was impressed, comparing me with his brother.

How did you learn all those names?

From a book. Colin, the man who drove me home from the shacks lent it to me. It tells you everything.

I told him about nannygai and snapper and bream and mullet. I went through deepwater, estuary and reef dwellers. I explained why some fish have big, chunky scales and why others are streamlined, with tail-forks.

After we'd walked around the entire market, Dad said Don't suppose you feel like some fish and chips?

I don't mind a bit of shark, I said.

Flake in Melbourne, Dad showed his knowledge.

Barramundi in some places, too, I said. Chuck some sauce on it and serve it to the tourists, who's going to know?

Don't worry about coming up, Dad said as we stood in the hotel lobby. He gave me a hug and rubbed me raw with his bristles. I know I keep asking, but would you tell Mum that I love her? I want to come home.

Alright.

Thanks, mate.

When Dad walked off to the lift, I almost ran from the hotel.

At the shop I tore the *For Sale* sign down. It ripped, and kept ripping until it was in pieces.

WORK

———

WITH THE SHAPES and sounds of the Aran Islands constantly in my head, I went looking for a job. Whether it was because of how I still felt about Stephanie, and the fact that she was missing and might be there, or because the books she'd given me had planted the ghostlight of the need to experience the place, I wasn't sure, but I didn't care what kind of work I did, as long as I found a job soon and as long as there was a ticket to Ireland at the end of it.

I went to the job office and looked at cards arranged in job type and location. There was a mountain of work for plumbers, cabinet makers, sheet metal workers and sparkies. Truck drivers and front-end loader operators were also in demand.

I found a board that should have had Odds & Sods written at the top of it. Here was my big break. Fruit pickers, labourers, gardeners and kitchen hands were being called to the front lines of shithouse pay and conditions. I wrote down some details, took a number, and sat there looking miserable with all the other punters.

I lied about my experience, and the woman supported my claims as she spoke on the phone to someone called John and Rudi arranging interview times.

John was the head gardener at a private girls' school near Sydney Harbour. He sat me down in a salami-smelling office that looked like a cubbyhouse some kids with no imagination had thrown together from boards and painted-over windows. John told me how he demanded punctuality, responsibility, courtesy, and real application. I didn't need a day on the job to know that John would be impossible to work for.

The kitchen was a different story. The restaurant was part of a large hotel, and the chef's name was Rudi, an Austrian who fairly waltzed me around between the tables and stoves, explaining everything and introducing me to the cooks. My main job would be washing up, but I'd be expected to help garnish salads and other meals when they were busy. Rudi gave me an apron and pair of rubber gloves and said Alright, you can start, we're going to be busy tonight.

The split shift was a bastard. I'd come in each morning at ten, work through a pile of saucepans, strainers, icing bags, pots, ladles and whisks, then help the cooks get ready for lunch. I'd finish around two, and tie on the apron again at six, finishing with a hose in my hand between ten and midnight. The restaurant owner would often bring us cold beers, and we'd drink fast, washing the steam and grease from our throats.

The restaurant was too far away to go home during the afternoon break, so I went to parks and read poems or walked through the streets, making up stories about the people who lived there. Sometimes I'd stay at work and sleep in the change room, stretched out on a bench.

One of the cooks christened me Stiff after he saw me asleep with the tablecloth over my head.

I was saving money. I worked on public holidays and most weekends. I saw Tina when I could, and we made love in the bush or in the car, parked far away on headlands over the beach. She came all the way to the restaurant one night with Gordon and Eileen, and Rudi made them a special dessert with fruit and liqueur, and sent a message that I had spent all afternoon preparing it for them, and see what a good student of food I had become.

One of the cooks resigned. I heard Rudi talking to him in the office. There were raised voices. A hand slapped the tablewood.

His replacement was a bloke up from Melbourne. He opened his red toolbox full of knives, selected one, and stood there sharpening it. He walked around with his head tipped back and sniffed all the time. I asked him how long he'd had the nose bleed, and he said Can I enquire as to the meaning of that statement?

His name was Roger, but I called him the Rat. It soon caught on. He was the ground beneath jokes at smoko. When he'd come out to sniff the air and look around, we'd stop talking and bust ourselves trying not to laugh.

The Rat liked to give me orders and tell me the best way to scrub a frypan. He'd roll up his sleeves and give a big demonstration, his voice too loud. I told him his methods were rooted, and this only made him sniff loudly. You're an unfiltered little heathen, he'd say. I thanked him and bowed. The Rat thought that if you wore an apron you must be a moron.

Do you understand? he'd say, at least twice, showing me where to place a sprig of parsley.

On a Sunday afternoon I came in to find the Rat stirring a big pot full of something with a layer of scum bubbling on the surface. I didn't like being alone with him. He gave me the creeps. He sniffed and started giving me orders. I put up with him and waited for Rudi to arrive.

I was scraping trays when the phone rang. The Rat said There's a call for you don't be long.

It was Dad. He said he'd spoken to Mum, and they were going to meet. His voice had a quality I hadn't heard for weeks. He spoke quietly, brightly.

We're going to be a family again, he said.

The Rat said Come on you've got work to do. You're not getting paid to be on the telephone.

I said I had to go.

I'm so happy, Dad said. See you soon.

When I came out of the office, the Rat was writing something into a small note pad. He flipped it closed and said You're being watched.

Ten minutes later the phone rang again. The Rat answered it and said No, he's busy, and put the phone down.

Who was that? I stood at the office door with soapy water dripping from my gloves.

One personal call is more than enough when there's work to do.

Who was on the phone?

The Rat ignored me and went into the cold room. I followed him.

I need to know who it was. It could've been my father. There are things happening at home.

Congratulations, the Rat sniffed in the cold air. Here, take this and put it on my table. He pushed a large bucket of peeled potatoes across the floor with his shoe.

I said he could take it himself, and pushed it back at him. Then I went into the office and phoned Dad's number at the hotel.

Behind me, the Rat said Do you have a hearing problem?

Dad said Hello? and a hand appeared and pushed down on the cradle, disconnecting me.

I'm calling my father, I said, and started to dial the number again.

No, you're not. The Rat pulled me around by the shoulder.

I asked him as politely as I could if he'd like to go and fuck himself, and turned again to the phone.

The Rat pulled me away from the phone. I will not be spoken to like that, he shouted.

I lined him up against the office wall and gave him a proper nose bleed. He minced off into a corner saying You beast through his cupped hands as he slid down onto the floor.

When Rudi arrived, he followed the blood trail out into the change room. He came back, said We need to talk, and went into his office.

I told him what had happened. He tapped the side of his head with a pencil and said I see. The Rat came in with red flowers all over his white tunic.

Why hasn't this animal been asked to leave the premises? the Rat snapped.

Rudi told him to get out. The Rat ran through the kitchen, rattling things and talking to himself.

You can't hit people, James. He could have you up for assault.

I was about to explain, but decided talk was useless.

Go and have a smoke, Rudi said, and went out to talk to the Rat.

When he came outside, he said I'm sorry but I'm going to have to let you go.

I know, I said. Then I went and told the Rat a few

things I'd been meaning to say since he started. He backed away into a stove and dabbed at his nose.

I spent the rest of the day in a local park, watching people.

I told Mum they'd cut back on staff. She made all the right concerned noises, then settled down and said she'd spoken to Dad, and they'd arranged to meet. I acted surprised and asked when.

This Friday, at the Lane Cove River. There's a place where we used to go. It's lovely, she said. The only arguments we used to have in those days were about where to put the blanket down.

She asked how things were going with Tina. I said fine, although I hardly saw her.

Are you serious about her?

Yes.

Are you in love?

No.

Are you sure?

No, but it's too easy to say the word.

Mum said You've been doing some growing up lately, haven't you.

I don't know about that. I might love her, I said, but I want to spend more time with her.

You're being careful, aren't you.

Being careful. Opening the car door for her? Driving safely? Not swearing? Wearing condoms? Yes, I'm being careful, I said. But Tina's not a fancy kind of girl. She's down to earth.

I'd like to meet her. Will you invite her for dinner? When?

Mum thought about it and said What about next weekend? You're not working now and, besides, this meeting with your father is on my mind all the time. I'll be more relaxed after the picnic. I *hope* I'm more relaxed afterwards. Is that okay?

Alright.

I don't know what to wear when I meet him. What should I wear?

I don't think Dad's going to mind what you wear. He wants to see you, not your clothes.

Mum wrapped me up in a big hug. Maybe things will work out, she said. He's been trying so hard.

I hope so, I said from the depths of her clothes.

When she let me go, she said You're still taking your tablets, aren't you?

Yes.

Good. She looked at her watch. I have to go shopping. Thought I'd make some things for the picnic. Do you want to come?

On the picnic?

Shopping, you dill.

No thanks.

Right then. Think you could vacuum the house while I'm out?

I reckon I could manage that.

Have a think about getting another job, too. The newspaper is on the table.

I cleaned the house, then took the paper out onto the lawn.

The drivers and tradesmen were still being hunted down. So were the gardeners and pot scrubbers. Then I found Wanted: ushers and snack bar attendants for new cinema complex.

When I phoned, a man with a voice like fast-flowing creekwater wanted to know my experience.

I said Usher, Projectionist, Theatre Cleaner, Actor,

Popcorn Popper. I've never worked in a cinema before, I said, but I'm keen to learn. I like films, and I enjoy working with people.

The creek hit a deep spot and slowed down. Would you like to come in for an interview?

Creekwater turned out to be a fat, bald man wearing a crimson coat and black trousers. His bow-tie looked like a dead flower. He must have had a bath in perfume, and his fingernails were perfect. Apart from looking like he'd just jumped ship midway through a circus tour, there was something strange in his attitude towards me. He sat behind a desk you could land a plane on, asking questions about school, family, and previous work experience. His eyes were like searchlights, wandering all over me. At first I thought this might have been a nervous habit, but Creekwater wanted me. His mouth was alive with Come here, sweet boy.

He stood up and said I'm interviewing people all afternoon. Thank you for coming in. We'll call if you've been successful. Any questions?

Are you going to stop gawking at me you dickhead? I hope to hear from you, I said.

The job was a breeze. Take tickets, tear them in two, give half to the punter, go into the theatre, paint the aisles and a few people with torchlight, then watch the movie. I stayed out of Creekwater's way as much as possible, which was difficult as he stood at a high place near the stairs, surveying his staff, rocking on his feet. When I had to be near him, when he wanted to speak with me, I found the carpet very interesting.

Apart from the odd drunk who felt the need to give a commentary on the film, or kids who turned the art of rolling Jaffas down the aisle into bloodsport by lobbing marbles or coins into the air, there was little to do. I saw *Jabberwocky*, *The Goodbye Girl*, *Newsfront* and others so many times I could reel off great chunks of dialogue, which I used on Harry and Tina.

There was a woman who came every Friday. She didn't care what was showing. She just asked for a ticket and went in.

There was a man with bright red hair who had *Glory* tattooed on the knuckles of his right hand. He had some kind of accent, and he'd sit smoking in the foyer until the movie started. Then he'd get up, check his watch, and go in. I asked him why he waited so long before going in, and he said It's the mystery.

I wrote poems sitting on the stairs. I found the voices and shifting light helped me concentrate. I also wrote letters, which I never posted. I wrote to Tina, Harry, Stephanie and Colin. I wrote to myself. I used the dialogue from films, things Creekwater had said. I'd been writing at home, too, putting each finished poem into a special folder. Sometimes I read poems to Mum while she was cutting out the pattern for a dress, or while she was out in the yard. I read one to my sister. She said You're sick, and ran away. I'd showed a couple of them to Tina. She handed them back to me, saying They're good. I asked her to say more, but she couldn't. I sensed she was being nice about the fact that they were terrible. That was alright. I just needed her to know I was writing, and that it was important.

After I'd been working at the cinema for two months, hoping I'd let Creekwater know that I was extremely interested in women, he overspilled his banks.

James, you are doing a lovely job, good boy.

I tried to say thanks.

You know, I was wondering if you would like to have a drink with me after work. There is a gorgeous bar just down from the cinema.

I tried to say no thanks.

We could have a quiet chat there.

His eyes had already taken my shirt off and were now busy with my belt.

I don't drink.

Coffee then?

It makes my heart race.

Oh well, in that case I don't suppose you would like a blow job?

What's a blow job?

I want to suck your cock.

Why is it called a blow job?

Creekwater fidgeted and said I don't really know.

I mean, if you suck, why say blow?

I don't know. Fidget, bow-tie adjustment. So, what do you say?

I've got a girlfriend.

I was wondering. Men do it better, you know.

If you say so.

I really would love to do that for you.

No thanks.

Will you think about it?

Not often.

Creekwater walked away. He kept his distance for a week. Then he said he wanted to see me, after work in his office.

I knocked and went in. He was standing beside his table, masturbating.

Don't leave, he said, mid-throttle. Please.

He must have thought I'd blow the whistle on him, because he said I could take a few days off, with full pay. You deserve a break, he said. I couldn't disagree.

I found a cheap flat near the city. Being close to work was fine, but the place was a dump. It was a room under a big, darkstone house. It smelled of cat's piss and mould. The windows were broken. It was furnished, but the lounge and chairs were broken and damp, the bed lopsided. Tina came up from Bowral on the weekends, and together we cleaned and repaired things, but the smells remained and there was still a terrible absence of light.

Dad came home. Everyone was nervous. Whenever I went over for dinner, they'd talk to each other in ways I hadn't heard, but there was still some sadness in the air. I could see it. They were quiet, calm, and when they talked they listened to each other. They held hands a lot. We drank good wine and stayed on at the table after we'd eaten. I'd been to friends' houses where this happened, and I liked it. It was strange to discuss more than work, the television dark in the corner. But something was wrong. It might have been that way because I was there and they couldn't relax. I saw a barrier between them. I could see Emily Winterbottom nodding her head, saying, discreetly They are waiting for each other. I was waiting for them too, and for myself. I wanted clear signs, but the scene was muddy, and a moulting brush was being used to paint it.

On a Sunday afternoon, after we'd been for a long walk around the bay, I asked Tina again if she'd move in with me. The first time I mentioned it she'd said it wasn't possible. There's too much to do at home, James. There's my horse, Mum and Dad, the bookshop, work, money. Now, lying on the bed, talking as lines of grey light divided us, she kissed my neck and said she could think of nothing better than getting colds from the damp and smelling cat's piss when she woke. We made love in the bathroom, which had the most light. Standing under a hot veil of water, taking her weight with my hands, I pressed into her and said My love through black strings of fragrant hair.

THE SPACES
BETWEEN THINGS

T INA FOUND A WAY through her parents' objections
and moved into the flat. Mum and Dad came over
with a load of second-hand furniture and helped us clean
the walls and floors. Soon, the place seemed to have
more light, and the cat's piss faded to the tolerable odour
of mould.

We had a house-warming party. It was good to meet
Tina's friends from Bowral, and Harry came with Jenny
Stevens, who seemed much older than I'd remembered
from school. She poured me a drink, took me aside and
said I always thought you were a bit of a lout at school.
I told her she was not far off the mark, and that I'd
always thought she was a snob.

I'm still in therapy for it, she said.

We played records and danced in the small, globestrung room. I got drunk and made a speech. Harry
interrupted me constantly and flicked whipped cream
into my hair.

Some time well into the night, after all but Harry and
Jenny had gone home, Tina said Who wants to go and
cut some rushes at the bay?

We walked to a small park overlooking the water. We found a place on the grass beneath a Moreton Bay fig and wrapped ourselves in blankets. Jenny opened a bottle of wine and told us how she used to come here when she was little.

Once for a Sunday school picnic, and a few times with friends, she said. There used to be a boatshed just down from here. If it was low tide, we'd wade out to the front and sit on the wood, watching the water. We used to imagine we were waiting for a boat to come and take us away.

After a couple of bottles and stories, Harry and Jenny fell asleep. Tina and I sat up between the folds of the tree and watched the bay. Small boats motored quietly over black water. It was so dark, the bay could have been a contained bowl of sky, the boats small aircraft coming in to land, their lights mirrored on a wet tarmac. I counted the shapes of blacked-out houses, stacked high between pockets of trees on the other shore.

Tina moved against me under her blanket.

I haven't seen the sun rise for years, she said. Think we can make it?

There's no way I can sleep now.

I can't see you very well, she said, but I can see enough to know that you don't look sad. I haven't seen it for ages.

I haven't felt it for ages.

Do you love me?

Yes.

I think you do too.

The blanket made a hood over her head.

I can't decide if you look like a monk or a devil, I said, putting my arm around her and bringing her close.

A star slipped its moorings and flared.

Seen any love darts lately? I asked.

Only in the shower, she said.

A light came on in a house below the hill. Someone moved past the window. Tina unzipped me. I watched a square of yellow light until my eyes went to water and Tina was saying Would a monk do that?

When first light washed over the bay, Harry and Jenny woke and went home. The water was lined with the wakes of five or six small boats. A ferry appeared around the point and nosed into the wharf.

I'm going to find a job today, Tina said and stretched out on the grass.

Whatever you do, don't work in a cinema.

What about a waitress in a coffee shop?

As long as you wear your apron to bed.

Or a stripper? There's always work at the Pink Panther.

How do you know?

Haven't I told you about my other life?

You could always try the bookshops.

No thanks. I'm booked out.

We lay back and looked up through the branches of the fig.

What do you see mostly, branches or sky? Tina said.

Sky.

Me too. It's what we look for. The spaces between things.

We held each other without talking. The sound of someone hammering came over the water.

An elderly couple came past walking their dog. The woman nodded and said something under her breath. The man tugged the dog away from our blankets.

I have to go home for a couple of days, Tina said. I

need to put Trooper into agistment. Poor bugger. He hates it. The people are good to him though. They're friends of Mum and Dad. She looked up at me. Her face was pale, her hair everywhere. First though, I'm going to find some work.

We were exhausted and thick-headed from the wine. Tina went into every cafe and record store from Rushcutters Bay to Kings Cross. In Darlinghurst she went into a bar and came out with a job.

I start next week, she said, beaming. I've never pulled a beer in my life.

Do they know that?

Not exactly. The man said he'd show me the ropes though.

I'll bet he did.

He seems nice. She turned and looked at the door of the bar. There are some interesting people in there, she said. It should be fun.

Tina went home to Bowral. I returned to the cinema. As I was leaving work that first day back, Creekwater was watching me from the stairs. I went to him and asked politely if he'd had the carpet in his office cleaned.

That night, in the flat, I walked around trying to relax. I put a record on, made coffee, played the only chord I knew on Tina's guitar, looked out the window, and finally went to bed early where I smelled Tina's hair on the pillows and couldn't sleep. I ran a bath and lay there thinking about love, and what it meant. I had no words for it, and each thought dissolved into steam. Love was in the surge and flush of blood as it toured my body. It was in the image of a young woman standing in a dark wine cellar, selecting a bottle, and then behind a screen of material in a bedroom lit by four candles. I wanted to know more. I was so raw with what had happened between us sexually that it occupied my thoughts almost constantly. I saw myself in the arms of a woman deep in a ratty chair, my head pressed into her chest, listening to her heart. Stephanie must have felt my erection. Had she not gone away, would we have made our way to her bed? I felt guilty then, and thought of Tina again. Love. I didn't get it. How do you know? Does sex have to be a big part of it? My body took over. It said yes, and my hand splashed in and out of the water. The sea poured in through a hole in a pool wall and I positioned myself there, floating until I broke open and lifted myself out of the water as a hot, salt-sweet splash hit my neck and another found my open mouth. Then I went to bed, where I slept badly, tasting myself each time I woke.

THE COLOUR OF PAIN

————

WHEN I WALKED into the flat the phone was
ringing. It stopped as I reached for it. I was on
edge. A bad day at work: a fistfight between some
sharpies and rockers on the steps outside the cinema,
and a drunk throwing up on a pinball machine. I got
changed and rolled a smoke. Sitting on the steps, I closed
my eyes and saw someone with razored hair wearing
braces and boots get a hammering from a rocker. Then
the phone rang again. When I picked up the receiver,
a woman's voice had the colour of pain inside it.

James, this is Eileen Sewell. Tina's mother.

The colour was coming through the perforations of
the mouthpiece.

Breathe.

James, I'm afraid I have some very sad news.

Breathe. No.

I'm sorry. Static. Breathe. James. Tina was . . .

James, hello, son. This is Gordon.

Tina was kicked in the head by her horse as she was
trying to settle him in at the new stable. Trooper's

weight behind his foot as he lashed out in confusion or fear at being moved, and Tina behind him, thrown clear into the straw.

I swallowed Gordon's voice and it went through me like an X-ray, printing my heartbeat to the wall.

If there's anything we can do, he said, and then Will you be alright? We can come and see you, you know, when everything . . .

The air had been drawn into the receiver. The room turned around and was still. I said something and Gordon said something else. I put the phone down. Tina's voice arrived with lines from one of her favourite poems: *what to do and where away to go?*

I stayed there with the night all around me on the step with a beer smoking in the bath and a telephone drained of colour beside the bed you know it's alright with the smell of my darling's hair on the pillow and not far from here the cutters are working the shape of the bay without speaking, harvesting rushes.

day is so deep already with involvement.

VOICES IN THE HALF LIGHT

W ITH TINA'S DEATH on permanent replay, I took
time off work and did not sleep for two days.
I'd left my medication in the flat. I did not want a
bandage over the time I needed, although I knew the
dangers involved in not taking the pills. Danger was
already alive and well and kicking in my blood.

Mum and Dad wanted me to come home, but I
stayed in the city, in a room over a pub near Wynyard
Station. At night I watched the street from a small
window or walked around the harbour. During the day
I went to the fish markets, or Chinatown. I walked,
losing parts of myself all over Sydney. I dropped a beer
bottle and cut myself trying to find the pieces. A suit
and tie removed me from my deep fascination with a
sidewalk blood smear and suggested I go home. I
wanted to tell him what had happened. I wanted to
remember everything and know nothing. Tina.

The funeral was held in a small cemetery near Tina's
home. I got there early. Dad drove. He dropped me off
and went to the pub.

Pines. A pair of magpies beaking the grass. Too many flowers, wild and on the graves. I sat against an old wooden fence where I could see the cemetery gates, and waited. I was exhausted. Pine needles fell in different colours, painting my hands and shoes, the black material of one of Dad's old suits. A magpie sang the broken light of someone laughing. My heart was moving around, filling and draining like a caught blowfish. When I tried to find my pulse, my fingertips burred with a dull vibration.

Headlights entered the cemetery, followed by more headlights, moving in a slow line towards me. I felt stranded. I moved behind the trunk of a pine and watched the cars. I saw Tina's coffin behind long windows with sky and branches passing over them. Hightide. In the back seat of the car behind her, Eileen and Gordon, sitting up like shadows. The cars made a circle on a wide grassed area. They could have been parked at a country football match. When everyone had come together, standing close in a dark wall of arms and legs, I walked over and stood to one side.

The coffin was lying over the grave. Green mats had been placed to hide scarred earth. Eileen and Gordon were in each other's arms. The minister was talking. Tina. He was telling a story. It was not about a horse. I heard Love of Life and Generosity, Who Are We To Question, and This Day Has Given Her. Two sets of orange footprints on the green mats. I looked around. Windscreen flash through my left eye as Tina was lowered into the grave. I saw yellow clay swirls and the passing of roots, bright beetles nudging stones aside. My chest opening. A hand came to rest on my shoulder. I was under ground. The sky was glass. A blue lightspear overhead. A kingfisher dived and was caught in my hair.

I tried to free it. A shadow moved beside me. The shadow said Are you alright? I could not answer it. People were leaving. Eileen and Gordon were not leaving. I was somewhere in between, and then the fine string like rubbed web that had been holding my body and head together came apart, and I saw my feet leave the grass. I was running. Out through a maze of parked cars. To the fence where I had waited. The sky and the pines and the kingfisher caught by its wing. Then a road and the sound of cars passing. The day coming apart and reforming, the edges not meeting. I looked through the spaces between sunlight and cloud and saw a black suit by the roadside. It tripped and fell. It sat up with bloodlines jumping from the side of the face it had grown from the cuttings of pine shadows, gravel. I came back through the day and it closed behind me. A car had stopped. A man and a woman were helping me up from the ground. Gordon's hands and Eileen's tears, the love dart coming free to flap in the tight half-circle our bodies made. Where it lifted away, it left a blue smear on Eileen's brow. She wiped her face and studied her hand before placing it to her mouth.

Time lowered itself into my head and stayed there, turning. I was taken to the Pines Bookshop. Gordon went back to the cemetery and found Dad, who'd left the pub and come looking for me.

When I woke, Eileen was holding my hand. She looked awful. Shadows and grief had smeared blue make-up over her cheeks and under her eyes.

Dad was in the background, talking quietly with Gordon, who kept looking over at me, his big body moving backwards and forwards, his hands with nowhere to go.

My headlights were on. Voices answered each other and went from room to room, bringing news of the world. Lars Ackerman walked up to the bed and said About time you came back. I've been looking for you. Harry shook his head and sighed. Why didn't you tell me you were lonely? Nice clothes, by the way. Colin sat in the corner, polishing a fishing reel with a cloth, singing quietly to himself. Stephanie looked in through the window and smiled. She breathed on the glass and fingered my initials into the fog. All night I looked for Tina, but couldn't find her. In the morning Dad drove me home. I was aware of the noise of the engine, the odd word or line of song from the radio. Passing a small farm on the outskirts of Sydney, I saw a young woman riding her horse along the fenceline, on the other side of the road. Her dog was running behind the horse, its tongue flapping. She did not look at us as we passed. I looked at Dad. He was watching her in the rear-view mirror. Then he looked at me. I thought he was going to say something, but he looked into the mirror again, then back at the road.

BEDLAM

THINGS CHANGE IN the telling and the living. What happened after Tina's funeral is composed of dreamthreads and the fabric of what the mind allows, after suffering. The hole that had once opened on my bed opened again, this time on every surface I occupied. Earth, water, street. I was freefalling, catching at ropes of comfort thrown to me by family and friends. They tried to go with me, but pulled out as the speed increased. I fell through a soft, clicking rain of capsules, catching them on my tongue and breaking them open. They had no effect. I spread my arms and angled away through a thousand scenes, watching my family watching me, their eyes over the edge of the abyss, their mouths grained with silence.

After falling for days, I came to a place where the light was harsh and constant. Far below, people moved slowly. I fell among them. They scattered when I arrived. I swerved through corridors, my hands out before me, raking walls and floors. I saw myself in a blister of speed in a metal mirror and screeched at the image. When I landed, I was caught by two men and tamed with strange water. I looked up. The hole had closed. My hair was ruffled, my eyes running. I was put to bed in a white room and given a mouthful of comforting words by a woman who knew my name. My window was a blacked-out cage, wired and sightless. Then the woman left. I slept for so long that when I woke she had become much older. She held out a glass and said Choke on this, hawk-pretender. She said Hello James, you look much better, and helped me sit up. Her shadow on the wall had blue light inside it. After she'd gone, I looked through the window. The view and the light had returned. I saw a garden and a dark green bench, a group of people in dressing gowns smoking and talking with their heads together. I got out of bed and went into the bathroom. In the mirror I saw a wound on the side of my head, and then a black car with its cargo of dead love passing over my eyes. I put a hand to my head. My hair went into a wind-lifted crest, and when I called for help, my voice was hunting.

Mum and Dad came with flowers, books, a cassette player and a stack of music. They came with news from the Other Side. I'd been thinking about Gordon and Eileen, of the terrible space in their lives, and their pain. I was worried about them. They'd come to me in a dream: Eileen appeared at my side holding a horse's tail in one hand and a book in the other. You should learn how to ride, she said. Then Gordon walked up and put his huge hands on Eileen's shoulders. When you're ready, son, he said. I told Dad about the dream and asked if he'd call them, to see how they were. He said he'd already spoken with them, and that they'd said they were coming to see me, when they could. As Dad spoke, I saw them at the bookshop, holding hands. I saw them passing Tina's room, looking through the glazed panel of her closed door. When the door opened, Dad touched my arm, bringing me back, saying They send you their love. Harry and Jenny came and told jokes and stories. It was only my face that laughed. I lay there as people sat beside the bed on those first few days, watching their mouths open and close. Later on we walked in the grounds, the concrete like sponge rubber. I was aware of the texture and weight of my tongue. I could feel where it entered the back of my throat. The chains of light bubbles over my eyes were thick and grey, as if I were looking through a microscope. My voice surfaced trailing a streamer of hurt and confusion.

The drugs were doing their slow, blood-fed work, leaving a wastelight of false confidence to lever itself into the makings of a smile the chronically normal would surely see as being evil. The tablets were tiny anchors and blunt hooks that made their way through my body, emerging from the soles of my feet and taking me down in a slow spiral to the bottom of a deep and ill-lit pool. I got used to being there. I learned how to breathe underwater. I finned and rolled through dark and light, making faces at the glass when people came. Out of the pool, I was heavy and had trouble walking. In the recreation room I watched television and tried to follow movement over the screen. Table tennis was a riot of slow-motion knock knock fuck roll tap give me the ball are you crazy? The room was soft-edged and monitored. A circle of armchairs faced the television. There were talkers and starers, dreamers and dribblers, swearers and silence-protectors. There were weepers, whisperers, geniuses and monsters. Which one of these people had I become?

Sitting outside in the sun, days, weeks or months after I'd been admitted, someone I'd never seen came over carrying a guitar. His long grey beard had twists of bright orange hair running through it. His glasses were tied around his head with string. He sat down and offered me a cigarette.

He lit our smokes. My name's Eric.

I introduced myself.

I've just come down from the bad ward. He twisted a peg on the guitar and squinted around a smokeline that was rising into his eyes. Things were getting tough in there. I was doing time with the mindless ones for a month before they saw the afterglow and set me free.

What's the bad ward?

The place where the difficult cases go. You know, the old padded-room trip. He removed the cigarette from his mouth and let a curl of smoke drift into his nose. Do I look like a difficult case?

No.

Liar liar brains on fire.

Play a song.

I'll play one if I want to. Don't ever tell me what to do. I hate that shit. Never again, understand me? What do you want to hear?

I don't care.

Eric's fingers moved up and down the neck, picking a beautiful melody. He played with his head lowered as if he were looking for something on the other side of the light-grained guitar body, one brown, ankle-high boot tapping in time. When he finished, he lifted his head and a stick of ash broke over his sleeve.

How long have you been here, James?

I'm not sure.

Gets like that. Listen, take a tip. Record the days. They'll try to get away on you, but you've got to keep an eye on them. You with me? The days have incredible powers of concentration and cunning. They'll try to outfox you, especially when you're sleeping. What kind of drugs are they giving you? Doesn't matter. We could do a swap if you like. Makes things interesting. Get to walk different roads for a while. See different things. Are you a voice man? I am. The broadcaster and receiver of sublime information. Mind you, I can turn them off whenever I want. Hello, Eric, are you there? Just joking. Watch the days. They can accumulate so fast, you wake up one morning and the bastards are gathered at the window, shouting curses and spells at you. I'm not kidding. Do you play guitar?

One chord.

Other days the cunts are afraid to come out, and you get stuck in limbo. I lost nine days and I made Stella, she's my favourite nurse, go and find them. She came back with a big plastic bag full of time and tipped it over the bed. Shit a brick. Have you ever had nine days in bed with you? Amazing. Listen, I've got to go. They're letting me out of here this afternoon, and I have to go and clean my teeth and polish my shoes. You know the stuff. Bebop a shingle, James.

Eric got up and held the guitar by the neck like a stiff waterbird.

Give my regards to your loved ones, he said, and walked.

I saw Eric again the next morning. He was in the rec room, reading a magazine. When I said hello, he held the magazine in front of his face. I watched him for days. The night he knocked on my door and said Have you got any spare days for a silly old fuck, I stopped watching him and started avoiding him.

People came and went. Sunlight stank. The polished linoleum drank my image and gave it back with a ball of caged neon at the centre of my chest like a moon seen through door wire or the exposed heart of a mute, mechanical man. I staggered and danced. I fell upon myself in a time of weeping that moved through all the phases of the body's tides. Shift. Sweep. I heard every organ from my brain to liver flexing their coils and wet baggage as I turned over in sleep or walked the walk of the tired down paths into wafers of sun in yards the birds avoided. Then I stopped listening and began to recover. At first I thought it was an impression of recovery, so I listened again and walked until I was certain. I walked for three years, in and out of the gates of that watchful stack of buildings, looking back constantly, hearing my name and seeing Tina's face in every tailwind. I'd put on weight, and Eric had taught me to play the guitar in exchange for a little time, which I gave enthusiastically.

On weekend homevisits I watched television or sat out in the garden, returning to the same place in a novel I'd been trying to finish for ages, watching ants hurry over the page. Sometimes Harry came over and we'd go down into the bush and sit on the stone where I'd seen the black snake. We talked about everything but how shithouse I looked and how much time I'd lost, though I never mentioned Eric.

Harry visited. He'd been working as a stonemason's apprentice, and wanted to start his own business.

The dead need markers and roofs and the living like to waste money, he said.

He spoke of the north coast, of fishing, and of how he and Jenny were thinking of getting married. He asked me to be the best man, and I started crying. I was nearly twenty years old, and I wanted to go away. I wanted the headlights to go out and the voices to stop. I cried and rocked on a large warm stone, and when Harry's arm went over my shoulders I cried for him as well, and couldn't stop, and the bush went around us bright with parrots and flowering gumnuts, and Harry said You've got to get yourself out of that place and back into the world, Jim.

FOR THE TIME OF YOUR LIFE

O NE BLEAK, rainy Sunday afternoon, sitting in the television room watching a movie, I sensed that someone was standing beside me. I ignored them. I didn't want to talk or move.

There's a lot to think about, isn't there? said a slow, deep voice. I looked up to find a man looming over me. His head was big, his eyes ice-blue, and his hands were large and veined.

As I got out of my chair he grabbed me around the chest and said We're brothers. His breath smelled awful and his hair was greasy on my face. I managed to pull myself free, and took a few steps backwards, my heart fighting the slow drain of the morning's medication.

Don't you recognise me? he said thickly.

I looked into his face and I saw a boy about to turn his eyelids up to reveal the whites. I saw a dribbling friend, a boy who had gone from the world for years.

How did you know I was here? I asked.

I didn't know. I've just come in. Last night. And now I've found you. He stopped, took a breath. I've been away, but you know . . . He looked around, then stepped close.

I had to come back, he whispered. I always come back. I haven't been here for ages. I've been up the coast. The hospitals up there are fucked. I like this place.

We went out into the garden. Lars Ackerman told me of how he'd been in and out of hospitals since leaving school. When his mother died, none of the family wanted to have him.

A ward of the state, he said, and dribbled. He looked around the yard. Oh, yes, I've been having a ball. Then he leaned over and said, in a different voice, I am about to enter the realm of crime and punishment. When I asked him what he meant, he pointed to a crow that was hopping over the grass. The yellow eye will tell you everything, he said.

We went to his room. There were drawings and paintings on the bed – some in frames, some on canvas and textured paper. There were some very fine nudes and barren landscapes. There were also some vibrant pastel works containing the lines and sparks and horses' tails I'd seen on the walls of his bedroom at home. Seeing these shocked me, and Lars was quick to recognise my reaction because he took my hand and said quietly You know about these, don't you, James. I have to do them. Sometimes I stop for a while. He pointed to a nude woman sitting on a rock in the water. I do these. Then he picked up a pastel and traced red lines to a centre of black and silver swirls. But I always come back.

Lars told me he had thousands of paintings and drawings. He'd arranged with a cousin to leave them at her house, whenever he was out of circulation.

So what's the diagnosis, James? What label are you wearing?

They think I have schizophrenia, I said. I hadn't

spoken the word for ages, and the sound of it twisted something in my guts.

Anyone can see you're marked for greatness, Lars said. I'm bi. Bi-focal, bi-polar, bi-God.

I didn't know what to say then. Lars swept the artwork from the bed and sat down.

Come on, tell me your story, he said. He patted the bedspread and crossed his legs. Make it a long one. There's fuck-all to do here today.

I went quickly through the years.

Lars held out his hand and said So, you're a poet. That's fucking brilliant. Show me your work.

I said I didn't have anything to show him.

Show me your work, James.

I forced myself off the bed and went to get the folder of poems.

I woke to screaming. People were running in the corridor. We were told to stay in our rooms. I ducked out and down the corridor. There was Lars holding part of the steel frame he'd ripped from a trolley. The trolley was on its side, food items and cutlery surrounding it. He had blood on his shirt, and he was grinning. I could see a leg protruding from a doorway behind him. Lars kicked the leg and screamed. He swung the bar and danced in a circle. He spat and sang. A male nurse tried to take the bar away and Lars cracked him over the side of the head. He went down in a blood line and writhed on the ground. Within minutes, hospital security staff came running. They went in fast, and Lars was taken down. He kicked and swore. His eyebrow had been opened and blood flowed freely down his cheek, spreading through the fabric of his shirt. It took four men to restrain him as he was injected. He went limp.

His right eye rolled back and a line of saliva gleamed on his jaw.

The nurses he had belted with the steel bar were taken to general with deep lacerations on their heads. Lars was spirited away.

Next morning, I saw a nurse removing the paintings from Lars' room. When I asked about him, I was told he'd been taken to another place.

High-security number, the nurse said.

I asked about his paintings.

The nurse looked down at them and said they were being collected by a family member.

Have you seen them? he asked.

I said that I had.

What do you think?

I told him that I liked them, especially the abstract swirls.

He's quite well known, actually. He sells his work. The word's getting around. He might be famous, one day.

As the nurse walked off with a flapping bundle, he said Most likely after he's dead, which mightn't be too far away.

Lars had produced a large body of very fine work, on medication, over years of stress. He had transformed his life into paintings and drawings of beauty and strangeness. I thought about him constantly, over the days after he was taken away. When I enquired as to his whereabouts, I was offered No Information. I wanted to contact him, to tell him how much seeing him again had meant to me. Lying in the dark I saw his eyes, heard his voice, felt his big hands on my shoulders. Lars had inspired me to return to writing, to make something important and lasting from the torn gauze of my days.

Three years. It felt like many more. The day I went home with no weekend pass hanging like a sentence overhead, I entered the bush, walked deep into the cave, and laughed. It hurt my ribs and I loved it. I got a stitch and threw stones at trees. The spell had been broken. Something had come free in me.

I was still on medication. I knew that extended time without my headlight-drugs would be dangerous. I swallowed them daily and entered a new life, still bound to the earth by a synthetic dependency, but on the earth nevertheless.

At the hospital I'd had no thoughts of money. But now, driving one day with Dad, he mentioned my savings and said perhaps I should go on a holiday. Bali, he said, or Perth. Fishing, relaxing in the sun. I couldn't think that far ahead. Lying around at home was the best holiday I'd had in years. I said Why don't we all go away, like we used to. I looked out the window and saw a seagull dividing a dark wall of trees. What about Gerringong? We could play billiards and hang out at the beach.

Dad slapped the wheel. Glad I thought of it, he said.

We went to Gerringong and stayed at the old darkwood guest house. We walked, fished, and slept our way through two weeks of beautiful weather. I returned home feeling good. I was losing weight. I felt confident and calm.

Six months after leaving the hospital, on a pension, I was ready to leave home again. I had to go. Mum and Dad were worried. They gave me a long, spoken list of reasons why it was a bad thing to do, but I was determined. I'd been reading Irish poets and losing myself again in the book Stephanie had given me. I was spending hours in the library, working through books on the Aran Islands, Dublin and Galway. I'd saved enough for the air ticket, but didn't have the money to stay more than a few weeks. When I said I was going to Ireland, Mum laughed and Dad went to bed.

Next day I withdrew my money, went to a travel agent, and organised a passport.

I put the tickets down on the kitchen table and said I'm going to Ireland. I was expecting the response, and it came: Not Ready. How Will You. Wait Until. This Is. When You're. Don't Bother.

After the protests had died away, we sat around talking about Ireland. The night went on around four people who were really talking and listening, with interest and love, to each other.

Two days later, after dinner, Mum and Dad said they needed to talk with me privately. We went down to my room.

Dad was holding an envelope. Mum was holding her arms.

It's just that we didn't want your sister to hear this. It wouldn't be fair, Mum said.

Dad handed me the envelope. I thought Hospital Report Doctor's Orders Danger. I opened the envelope and lifted out a piece of paper. I turned it over and found a cheque for three thousand dollars.

For Ireland, Dad said.

For the time of your life, Mum said, and started laughing and crying at the same time.

THE WIDE VALLEY

—————

I ARRIVED IN Cork city after hitchhiking down the coast from Dublin, where I'd been doing the tourist thing. I'd been to Sandy Cove, to see the James Joyce museum, to St Stephen's Green, where I lay on the grass, eating lunch and thinking about how lucky I was to be out in the world.

I had loved Dublin. It had both warmth and austerity, and the pubs were brilliant. In one, I'd seen a student rugby team pack a scrum down in the middle of the floor. The hooker fed a pint glass into the scrum and they stamped it to splinters. In another, a music session began in the early afternoon with a man on guitar and a woman on fiddle. By midnight, the large, circular table was overspilling with people playing every kind of instrument.

But I was told by a woman I'd met in the park that there might be a better chance of finding work in Cork. She told me a little about the city.

So now, on the last ride down to Cork, I sat on the back boards of a flatbed truck between two chained black dogs, who watched me carefully and gave me the lip-curl every time I moved. The driver and his companion laughed and talked all the way into Cork, drinking something from a small glass flask. Watching them gave me a thirst. I walked along the river and found a pub. Four pints of Guinness and a conversation about bass fishing later, I went looking for a bed and found a room above The Wide Valley, a pub with thick, circular glass tiles on its street-facing windows and a huge open fireplace.

That evening I walked under the interlocking branches of great amber-trunked trees that shed rainballs and a pasting of saw-edged leaves. On the river, swans curved and floated out into arcs of bridgelight. A warehouse fell into itself, its windows rocked in, leaking the cold ash of squatter's fires.

Approaching the city, on the other side of a bluestone wall, I found a spillway fanning loud and fast from the foundations of what could have been a factory or slaughterhouse, the water bloody with rust or entrails.

With the rain a trickle of ice down my back, I hung draped over the top of the wall, watching the flow, trying to determine its source and reason for being there.

You'll not be the first to go over, a voice croaked from the path behind me.

I worked myself up and back and dropped to find a man in yellow raingear. He was holding the handle of a small trolley he'd stacked with sodden newspapers and bits of wiring bundled together with string.

They won't be pulling my bones out of that foul sea, he said, and chuckled. His teeth were sharp and staggered. His tongue laboured like a small dark fish at the stained wires of a baitcage. You'll be warmin' yeself at a fire and forget the whole thing, he said. Don't allow no sadness past the gates of warmth, I tell ye. Hear that?

Thank you, yes.

Haven't got some coins?

I felt for some change and gave him what I had. He held one up to the streetlight and said I thank ye. You'd best be movin' on. He stepped forward and the cart jolted after him like a miniature train carriage startled from its sleep of cold connections.

I followed him for several minutes, but then crossed the road and sought the shelter of a line of shops that led to the pub. Water pooled on the worn path between shops. The wind threw a beer can end over end into the road.

Lying in the bath, I went under and heard the creaking of skin on porcelain, then the old man's voice removing me from the wall, away from a pleated bloodfall of foundation water.

After a week of walking and drinking, I met a man called Finbar late one night in The Wide Valley. He told me about his brother in Melbourne, and said he'd try to fix me up with a job at the council, where he worked on the road gang, *laying pipes, smoking and doing bollocks.*

I started the following week, doing road maintenance with men whose voices were musical and warm. I inherited certain things. I learned how to fix gas leaks in old piping, how to manage time in a roadside tent with mugs of tea and biscuits as the rain delayed another session of standing around beside holes and tools. I learned how to throw a stone underarm down some country road after work, using a whipping action that stops short at the hip and sends a rock further than I could throw it conventionally.

I loved working with these people, and I loved the light we almost laboured under: the light, the rain, the light and the heavy rain. The low skies that grafted the taste and smell of poetry to the bones.

REEL

O N A BLOWING, white-capped Saturday afternoon,
I caught a bus to Kinsale. The harbour was thick
with yachts, their mastwires cracking thinly in the wind.
I drank coffee in a small shop with pictures of boats and
old houses on the walls. Shelves stacked with Irish
sweaters and hand-woven landscapes for the tourist
trade. The smell of lanolin like a farm memory in the
air.

Climbing a steep path above the harbour, I watched
a yacht come in, its sails down, leaving a pale wakeline
as it turned towards its mooring. The day was cloudless,
cold. At the end of the path a low, greystone building
backed into the side of the hill. When I reached it,
walking around to the front, I heard voices and saw
people sitting at rough-hewn tables, drinking pints and
eating food from wicker baskets. I went in and ordered
a pint.

The far wall of the pub was bright with a long
aquarium. It sat like a band of caught, late-afternoon sun,
apparitional with fish no Irish water could contain. I
went over with my pint and found a world of luminous

red and blue fighting fish, sea horses, strings of bubble-veined seagrass, castles with bulbous eyes peering from their gaudy battlements. Some fish were transparent, their skeletons gleaming, their tiny organs like jewels in the heart of an opened watch. I drained a creamy collar from the Guinness and moved along, finding a curious warmth in this neon tank for the exotic and the bizarre.

Someone fed the jukebox. Someone else applauded the choice. I returned to the bar and finished the Guinness quickly. I ordered another and drank it off. Four pints later I was drunk and happy to be that way. I bought a pack of cigarettes and went outside. The wooden table was empty. I sat down and sipped at the pint, aware of the need to take it easy. In the bin, Eric had passed me his philosophy on drinking: Throw the first few back, then imbibe with a dreamer's pace. I had not consciously followed his suggestion, but it seemed right, under the circumstances, which were nameless and beyond definition.

Dusk came down and night attended it. I was smashed. At a table in a back room, in with a group of men up from Skibbereen, I sat, listened, laughed and learned. I was happy to talk about Australia, but their stories of fishing for salmon and Atlantic bass, hunting, entering and leaving some farm cellar with a bottle under wraps ... these stories took me deep into the night and a load of trouble. They were seasoned drinkers. At first I'd tried to keep up, but when I fell back – stray traveller on the road with hand raised in mute farewell – they continued around a glitter of foam-webbed empty glasses, their accents coming off the sea.

Then there was a car ride. Streetlights filling and emptying the window. A guitar on the stereo.

When the car came to rest, doors opened, arms and legs angled out and away, and I looked up to see a house lit like the stern of a boat in port, people standing at a globestrung railing, glasses pooled with light held at chest level.

I followed my drunk companions into the house, down a corridor warm with the smell of bodies and coats and smoke from a fire somewhere. In the kitchen I was handed a glass with a slice of clove-studded lemon swimming in hot amber.

You look terrible, a woman said. I'm not sure you need this.

What is it?

A hot toddy. Whiskey. Bushmills. She sipped her drink and said You've fallen in with a band of serious boozers.

I know.

Where are you from?

Australia. Sydney.

I have family there. You've probably heard that a lot.

Her face twinned and came back together. I looked down into the glass. My hand was shaking.

What are you doing in Ireland?

I'm not sure yet. Look, is there a place I can lie down?

Sure. Come on.

I followed her back into the hall and up some stairs.

She knocked on a door and went in. It was a small room with coats and handbags on a bed under the window. She gathered them up and patted the bedspread. Have a sleep. I'll come up in an hour or so. It's going to be a grand party, you shouldn't miss it. Besides, you can't stay here. Fair enough?

Fair enough.

Good then. She turned back the bedspread. You Aussies have a reputation for the drink, you know.

I took off my shoes and sat on the bed.

But I'm sure you've heard the same about the Irish,

she said, and looked out the door. There's a bathroom just around the corner. If you need to be sick or whatever. Fine.

She went out and closed the door gently.

I got under the covers and rode the bed to sleep as music pulsed through the floor and muted light from the window made a fan that flickered on the wall above my head.

He shook my shoulder and said It's your round, fella. I tried to see him, but the light had faded to black that swam as the jukebox pumped in the corner and dancers hit the boards. He shook me again and I looked up to find a woman leaning over me.

You've been asleep for a couple of hours, she said. How are you feeling?

I sat up and looked around. Where am I?

At the party. How's your head?

I put a hand to my brow. It's still there.

Only just, I'd say, she said and stepped back. They're breaking out the instruments. There's going to be a bit of a session. Like to come down?

I'll just freshen up.

Grand. See you downstairs.

I went into the bathroom and turned on the light. The neon tube over the sink flickered and stalled, flickered and came on. The face that looked back at me had dark circles under its eyes. I said hello, and the face turned away. When it looked back, it said You're a fucking idiot, and then hands were palming icy water over the eyes and hair.

As I went down the stairs, I heard a skirmish of music coming from outside.

The house was all but empty. I went into the kitchen.

I saw flames licking through its curtained, yard-facing windows and the shapes of people. Outside, a large crowd was milling around, their faces burnished and shadowed as the fire twisted. Against the wall of the house I saw a group of musicians tuning their instruments. Two were lounging in folding chairs, the others were standing. I walked around to a place under the low edge of a black-hemmed tree and tried to find the woman who'd shown me the bed. She was standing in a small group off to one side. As she listened to another woman talk, her head moved up and down and a hand appeared to replace a strand of hair. When she spoke, her hands moved into the firelit air, describing words. The other woman said something and she laughed, loudly, throwing her head back. Flamelight caught on the underside of her jaw.

The players started and the music leapt from their hands and bodies. Someone whooped. A dark-skinned man sat with his hands inside the leather straps on the ends of a concertina, its bellows folding and unfolding like an oriental lantern fleshed with sound. He was smiling broadly, moving his head from side to side. Another man played the guitar, fingers moving over the frets, the other hand a wristed blur. A woman stood between them, her fiddle and bow married in a shifting light of angles and precision, her hair divided by the fiddle body, one length hanging below the cradled wood like a misplaced shadow, the other behind her back. She rocked as she played, and her hair threw lines of gold. Standing beside her, a man played a flute, his fingers dancing atop a dark bar of polished wood. In the cold air, flushed with pockets of warmth from the leaping fire, my head cleared and I went into the music, returning to Stephanie's room above the shop, seeing her face as a piper's drone went around us and over the traffic noise and heavy rain. I watched alternately the players and the woman who was now standing alone, her eyes closed, a coat about her shoulders with the collar turned up. I went to stand beside her.

You look a whole lot better, she said. She nodded to the players. They're great, don't you think?

Yes. I love this music. What is it that they're playing?

It's a reel. I don't know the technicalities, but I know one when I hear it. It's all to do with the tempo, beat, things like that. Do you play?

No. I tried the guitar once.

Irish traditional music is a curious world, she said, smiling. A tune can have many names, many voices. Two fiddlers from different parts of the country will play the same tune and change it because of their playing style. It's wonderful. Goes for most things, I suppose. Singing, talking, dancing. She put her head back and pulled the coat tight around her shoulders. Drinking, poetry, body language, she said.

The players started into another tune.

Is this a reel? I asked, watching sparks die out high above the fire.

Yes. You won't hear a waltz tonight. I wouldn't mind though. I like mazurkas. I go to sleep to them.

Mazurka?

Polish waltz.

She nodded towards the band and said See your man on the flute?

I saw a man smiling and shaking his head as he played.

He's a curious crowd of people, she said. An eccentric. People find him a bit confronting, but I like him. Had a crush on him actually, a couple of years ago. His name is Paddy. He can be like a lamb one minute, and a lion the next. I've seen him laughing and crying at the same time. It went on for ages.

Sounds like you should get to know him.

I haven't the energy for a man like him. He'd wear me out, she said, and laughed.

A couple had broken away from the crowd and were dancing near the fence. The woman was holding the hem of her long black skirt. The man was backing in and around her. Then they formed other shapes, other histories of dance and song, eyes on and for each other, smiling, moving to the raw, tight sound that seemed directed at them.

Do you want a drink? I asked.

My name's Sheena.

What?

My name's Sheena. And yes, I'd love a drink. There's a bottle of Bushmills in the kitchen. It's in a brown paper bag in the cupboard under the sink. It wouldn't last five seconds otherwise. Could you bring a couple of glasses?

I turned away, then turned back to ask if she wanted a hot toddy, but she was skywatching with her eyes closed.

As I returned with the bottle and glasses, the players stopped and stood by their instruments. Passing them, I looked over at the fiddler. She held my gaze and then turned away.

Sheena started telling me about her life. As she spoke, I watched a woman standing near the house, talking with friends.

I came back to hear Sheena say that she worked as a librarian in Cork city, and that she'd only been there a few months.

I'm from Galway originally, she said. My marriage ended, and I had friends in Cork, so . . . She held her glass up to the firelight. So here I am, she said, wistfully, and drank.

I want to go to Galway, I said. I mean I have to go to Galway. I'll go soon.

Why do you have to go there?

To find out why someone recommended it.

An Australian?

Yes.

Galway is beautiful. The city's grand, but it's the countryside I love. It's got a Galway smell.

What's that?

Sheena thought for a moment and said It's like haybales with the sea inside them.

Have you been to the Aran Islands?

Of course. We used to go there with friends, especially over Christmas. We'd go other times as well, to practise our Irish and just wind down. There's a little cottage up the hill from the harbour on Inishmore. Your man who owns the place is a chef. Well, he's a cottage manager now, but the man can cook. Big tables with crisp white linen tablecloths and silver candles and bowls of incredible food. A banquet. We'd walk during the day, or sit around reading if it was raining. On Inishmore you can sit around reading a lot. And at night there was this wonderful food.

You had a banquet every night?

No! She laughed. On Christmas Day. Well, actually, on Boxing Day too, and sometimes the day after, if he was feeling good or had enough booze in him.

A half-familiar face from Skibbereen staggered over and said How's about ye? He loomed at me, red-faced and tweedy, and said We thought you'd gone back to Australia. He turned to Sheena and said So, you're takin' good care of the boy?

Go away, John, Sheena said playfully, and shoved him in the arm.

Just makin' sure youse are havin' a good time. Even convicts need a break from all that rock breakin' and lashin'. He winked and staggered off.

John's a darling, but a pain in the underside when he's drunk, Sheena said, watching him go through the crowd, a bottle raised in his fist like a flameless lantern.

I'll go to the Aran Islands, I said.

Do. And when you go, say hello to Mark. Tell him Sheena said hi, and remind him not to drink too much.

Would that do any good?

Of course not, but he'd expect it of me.

The music started again.

Do you dance? Sheena asked.

No.

No you don't dance, or no you don't feel like it right now.

I don't dance.

Sheena shrugged the coat from her shoulders. Would you hold this? She walked to the other side of the fire where John was highlighting some drunken point with the bottle, swaying and jabbing the air. Sheena took his arm down and removed the bottle. She gave it to someone and led him away onto a clear patch of grass.

Touch that drink and you're a dead man, John shouted over his shoulder as he was trapped into a loose embrace and danced between the fence and a standing wall of clothes. Sheena was moving freely, her legs kicking, feet scuffing the grass. John was all at sea, down the face of a wave of music and rolling on the swell the bad weather in his head was making, his arms and legs at odds with each other. Sheena laughed when he attempted to tap-dance along the half-bricked edge of a garden plot, and feigned mock horror when he crashed into a bush and struggled, feet in the air, trying to free himself. A few people applauded. Someone shouted Give that man a crash helmet!

People started to leave. I was talking to some students from Cork University when Sheena came up and said she was going and asked if I needed a ride.

As we walked into the kitchen, a woman turned for the door and brushed past me. It was the fiddler from the band. Her hair was dark red in the house lights, and she smelled like woodsmoke and something else I couldn't name.

You're a bit taken with her, aren't you?

I don't even know her.

What difference did that ever make? she laughed and lifted the car keys from her bag. Besides, she's spoken for. Your man on the guitar? That's her fella.

What's her name?

Sarah Carmichael. You want me to ask her for her number? Like, there's this Australian fella over there wants your number, but he's too shy to ask himself.

No, thanks anyway.

Sheena flipped her car keys in and out of her hand. You coming then?

Outside The Wide Valley, the small car idling in the icy morning, we sat without talking. A man stumbled past, hands in pockets, head down into the wind.

So, Sheena said, using the back of her hand to clear the windscreen.

Do you want to come up for a while? I said.

No. Thanks. Well, yes I do, but I know myself too well, and I'm trying to deal with a few things. So yes and no, is that alright?

I thanked her for the night and got out of the car. She wound her window down and said If you can find the Cork city library, you can find me. Her words were pale blue plumes in the air.

THE CAFE LORCA

A WAKE TO THE BELLS of Shandon tolling hollow to
believers and kneelers all over the city. Other bells
followed them, a rope-driven arrangement of metal
demands from Cork to Monkstown, Cobh, Kinsale, all
the parishes roused into service.

Awake, still heavy to the bones from a day and a night
of drink, I sat on the edge of the bed and listened to
the bells. Parting the curtains, I saw families in their best
clothes move in unspeaking knots along the street.
Church-going a serious affair. A man pedalled past on a
bicycle lifted from another century, its black-iron frame
distorted in wheeling shadow on the road. In a window
opposite, someone whipped two curtains together.

I showered, found some clean clothes, and went out
for breakfast.

Following the river, I paused to watch seagulls crane
their necks territorially and dive for whatever the dark
current offered. Swans drifted into the great shadow of
a warehouse, their red beaks like spikes of ceramic, their
feathers the light where a clean window once opened
onto the day.

I walked with no plan or direction. At a bench where the river turned sharply under a cast-iron bridge, I sat and rolled a cigarette. Smoking and dreaming, I felt the sun beginning to melt the flakes of ice in my blood. Though relaxed, I was vaguely troubled by a feeling like regret, though more intense, more physical.

Beside the river, an old woman was feeding pigeons. They knew her, and made a coat of grey and white wings around her legs, waist and shoulders. One sat on her head as she palmed wheat like a bee swarm, brief and grounded. A dog approached and the pigeons scattered, only to re-form, burble and strut, their urgency a muscled wingpuzzle on the grass.

Beyond the rise and fall of birds and the shawled woman, a tall building, its beigestone wall holding her face and the wings in sharp relief. I crossed the bridge, its blunt spikes burning my hand, the night's cold still in the metal. To a green wooden gate, sentry to a lane – narrow pass in shadow permanent and steel blue like a sick vein magnified in fitful sleep. The gate opened with a groundbird's cry and clicked shut after I'd gone a few paces. Startled, I turned back, expecting the form of another entrant, building-curious or thick with robbery. A pigeon flapped and fell over the river. The gate slats gave its flight the frames of a drawing seen through the thumbing of page ends. I went on, keeping close to the wall, a husk of cold air grazing the back of my hand. At the end of the lane I found a huge door braced with brass hinges like gold crowns stripped of their jewels, hammered out and nailed into the future. Three worn steps led to the door, their centres worn to a curve from the traffic of a nameless trade. Taped to the wood, a poster: *The Plough and the Stars*, Granary Theatre. That trade. That shape the structure standing water's edge in the barge days and still cold the grains the leavings of mice and black waterbeads from a sealed beam weeping audience stained and acoustically fine. I tried to write the date of the performance into my notebook, but words fell short of themselves. I went through the gate, carrier of fatigue or terrible chance that had weathered the small links in the chainmail of my medication. I had been taking the damn tablets why this falling? A standing wave of panic broke above me, but I was moving fast and its fanlines ebbed at the base of the riverwall. The woman and the pigeons were gone. So was my hunger. The light was intense when I looked at the river and no less so when I deliberately studied my hands and sat on the bench and said This is illusion it will pass, but my heart accelerated and my left leg beat a retreat with no visible movement into the earth. I started running. My feet were below me looking strange, my shoes in the dust a blur. A tree dissolved somewhere near. A woman opened a door and closed it when she saw me. My neck was humming. A red line planted a fish hook behind my left eye and the line snapped tight. I was hauled up where a flatbed truck sat idling roadside blowing blue feathers of light from its pipe. I found the driver and said something like Can you help me? or Where am I? He mouthed a word and tugged his cap and pulled away, looking back over his arm like a track-inspecting engineer. I went to earth and stayed there, trying to focus on my hands, which were shaking. Thoughts came and went out like wet touchpaper. Things I recognised became alien and grievous. An approaching dog smiled. Did I ask it for directions or assistance? What I remember of this head and body-claiming blackness is a doppelgänger feasting on itself in a room full of mirrors. I was James Molloy and anyone I did or did not want to be. I was sitting roadside in Ireland nursing a psychotic episode. I'd like to think I called it off like a savage black dog, because some time later I found myself outside the Cafe Lorca. I was exhausted. Ordinary man out walking on a Sunday morning. Pleasant dander by the river. Good old constitutional before a pint and roast. Wretched scenes internal. Serotonin faultline. Voice breaching lipwall, thanks I'm fine, just a stitch.

At a table by the window, spooning green velvet soup with fierce concentration, I looked past the tree-webbed shape of my head in the glass and watched people, thinking too much about them – the knowledge that each face has been seen before, in various forms, and that it will be seen again. I concentrated on a wedge of soda bread, willing such thoughts away. When the glass contained nothing but light, I sat back and waited.

Why had the black tide overtaken me like that? I'd been responsible with my tablets, not missing a beat. Was it simply anxiety that had floored me by the river? In that beautiful place? Does terror have a non-expiring lease in every landscape?

I had a half-bottle of Paddy in my day pack. I unscrewed it and started drinking. Alcohol can be the perfect drug to send anxiety packing. After three or four decent hits, my hands settled into a steady vibration and my heart slowed down.

I was calm and glowing from the whiskey. Three women had arrived and were sitting at the next table. Over coffee I learned that Bernadette, Sharon and Ruth were nurses. They met each week at the cafe, to listen to music and to *Pass the time and a bottle*, as Bernadette put it. When the bottle they were passing came my way, it was under brown wraps. I drank. When I'd recovered, Bernadette was watching me over the shelf of her tabled arm like a child waiting for drama. It was a real tongue-and-throat-burner. Satisfied, she laughed and said My uncle is a good man for the secret water.

Your man's got a still in Wicklow, said Ruth, too quietly.

Poteen, Sharon said.

The bottle went into a bag, the cups were taken away, and someone started playing a guitar. Someone else sang. People arrived in small groups, as if on cue, and soon a session was under way. Sharon was there for her brother, a musician who came in carrying his guitar. He wore a huge blue overcoat, his hair knotted and wild on his shoulders. Bottles with brand names went around, gleaming from hand to hand. Bernadette sipped on her poteen, tipping her head back like a pigeon drinking. When she lowered her head, she sucked air through her teeth and smiled. A button accordion wheezed and angled brightly through a reel. A bodhran player kept a subtle beat in a corner.

The session had been going for an hour when the woman I'd seen at the party in Kinsale entered the cafe carrying her fiddle case. She stood against a wall and folded her arms. She looked different in daylight. Her hair seemed lighter, the red streaks not as obvious. Her face was pale, and when she turned side-on, her nose was large, almost Romanesque. She was wearing a dark red pullover and black skirt. Her leather boots were criss-crossed with green laces.

Sharon touched my arm and said Do you know her?

Yes. Well, no I don't know her. I've seen her play. Do you know the name of the band?

They're called Lapwing.

Are they playing today?

Bernadette leaned over and said They're brilliant.

Bernadette's a walking talking guide to Cork music, aren't you, Bern.

It's a small place, Bernadette said.

The music stopped and people got up to order coffee or step outside for air.

Her name is Sarah, Sharon said. Sarah Carmichael.

I was about to say that I already knew her name, but there didn't seem any point.

Would you like an introduction? Bernadette said. If you do, then you'll be needing a shot of this, for courage. She lifted the bottle from her bag.

I need confidence, not a sledgehammer, I said.

Suit yourself. Bernadette lowered her arm and the bottle slipped away like a sea burial.

Sarah is her own girl, if you know what I mean, she said. She also likes a drink. And she's got a man. He plays bouzouki and guitar in the band.

I've heard some things about her, I said. But really, gossip leaves me cold.

Bernadette took a hit of whiskey. Gossip is essential, she said. We learn about people that way. Sure, things get inflated, but there's always some truth in it. It's our job to sort through the shite and find the honesty. Ruth's a grand one for the gossip, aren't you, Ruth.

Bernadette! Sharon sat back and looked at her friend.

I'm sorry, Bernadette said.

Ruth said You're one to talk. Give me that bottle. Then she turned to me and said Sarah is a hard one to know.

How do you people know so much about her?

She's famous, said Ruth.

For her playing?

For everything, Bernadette said.

By the time evening had turned the windowglass into a wall-length mirror, Sarah Carmichael had still not opened her fiddle case. She was sitting with a group of musicians near the counter, listening quietly and smoking constantly. When the others got up to play, she leaned back in her chair, her elbow on the table, the cigarette leaking a blue line from her angled wrist. At the end of a song, she crushed out her smoke and looked around. When she found me looking at her, she sat up straight and reached for another cigarette. Bernadette and Ruth were at a loud table, where other bagged bottles were being assessed for their fire. Sharon told me about her work at the hospital; about how she'd had meningitis as a child; about her Munster-representing, hurling-playing uncle who was a legend in his time. I heard a line of broken talk, my concentration on a woman sitting raptor-like at a smoky table.

I should go, Sharon said. You're not listening.

I'm sorry.

I don't mind that you're interested in Sarah. You've joined a long line. But you're being bloody-minded and very rude. You hardly looked at me the whole time I was speaking.

She picked up her coat and bag.

I'm sorry. Don't go.

You don't mean that. If Sarah Carmichael gave you ten seconds of her time, which I doubt she would, you'd be all over her. Your eyes would be falling out of your head.

She walked over to Bernadette and Ruth and then she left. Bernadette swayed over and said What did you say?

Nothing. I wasn't listening.

Sharon's the best listener I know. I guess she expects other people to be like her. She looked over at Sarah. That's the trouble, isn't it, she said.

Yes.

Trouble with a capital S, she said, and stopped a laugh.

Bernadette got halfway to her table, mouthed something I couldn't understand, and pointed at Sarah behind the raised shield of her hand.

Sharon's brother played a couple of songs. His voice was deep and powerful, his playing fine. When he finished, he sat down and lifted a bottle from his coat. Sarah came to his table and leaned on the edge, her face close to his. He nodded. She said something else and then she turned away and went upstairs. A few minutes later Sharon's brother got up and followed her. I looked over at Bernadette. She was watching me. She tipped her head in the direction of the stairs, pushed her lips forward and shrugged. I finished my cigarette and went upstairs.

They were standing at the far end of the upstairs dining room. When I entered, Sharon's brother said So, there you go. Sarah smiled and said Yes. He said I'll see you. Sarah nodded. He left her and walked past me. Sarah picked up a magazine and started leafing through it. I approached her and words turned away.

Why have you been watching me? she said, looking at the magazine.

I've been watching everyone, I said. It sounded stupid.

Yes, but you've been watching me a lot.

Because I want to talk to you.

I'd had a similar conversation years before. The shape of it was clear. Stephanie holding the telephone and breathing as I tried to speak.

I saw you at the party in Kinsale, I said.

Yes. You were watching me there, too. I saw you

watching me twice. That was enough. I didn't have to find your eyes again to know where they were looking. Same as tonight. She put the magazine down on the table. So what's going on?

Below, someone started singing, unaccompanied. Sarah closed her eyes and sighed.

We listened. I watched her face. I looked at her neck. She was wearing a gold necklace with a Celtic cross hanging from it. It was beautiful, with ropework done in silver. When she opened her eyes she said You're doing it again. It's very disturbing, you know, to realise you're being watched. Especially when a man is staring at your breasts.

I wasn't looking at your breasts. I was admiring your cross.

She touched it. What's your name?

James.

James, I've a couple of things to tell you. One is that there's someone in my life. Second thing is I'm not really into being cornered like this. There's something else, too.

I waited. Breathe. I waited.

It doesn't matter, she said.

Tell me.

She looked at her fingers. Find someone else to look at, alright? She went to the stairs. I saw a wave of black material slip from the top step.

When I came down into the cafe she was gone. My table was occupied. I ordered a coffee and stood against the bookshelf, where Sarah had been when she arrived.

Sharon's brother came over.

Do you want a drink? I've some whiskey.

No thanks.

Suit yourself. He pulled a half-bottle of Bushmills

from his coat pocket and took a hit. At the end of a long sigh, he capped the bottle and said Did you speak with Sarah while you were upstairs?

I found a silence and went into it.

It's just that she said you were staring at her. You see, she's going out with a good friend of mine. Do you get the picture?

I said that I did.

I mean, I don't give a shit one way or the other, when it comes down to it. All's fair in love and bollocks. But she felt the need to speak to me. She feels put out, do you know what I mean? A bit oppressed or something. I know that sounds heavy, and maybe it is. But women don't like to be gawked at by a stranger. Not at any time, from what I believe. Am I making sense?

It's just that I was –

She's not one for being fucked around. Can I make it any clearer?

No.

Good man yourself. Listen, there's loads of single girls around.

It's alright.

I know it's alright, I just want to tell you that Sarah's spoken to me and now I'm speaking to you. Do I sound drunk?

No. Are you?

I'm fucked.

It doesn't seem to affect your playing or singing.

I'll take that as a compliment. Fine then. Good man.

He offered me his hand. I accepted it and he squeezed my fingers hard.

Remember what I've said just now, he said calmly, then returned to his table.

I felt uncomfortable and stupid, and was rescued by Bernadette, who came to tell me that she'd heard Sarah's band were doing a gig in Clonmel.

You could just get yourself over there, she said. A kind of happy accident.

I told her I'd been warned off.

He's all bluff and bother, she said. Besides, Clonmel's gorgeous. You could be sightseeing.

Courting, said Ruth, behind her.

Touring and hooring, said Bernadette.

LAPWING

I'D ALREADY BEEN going away for weekends, catching buses or hitch-hiking out into rural Cork. To Bantry Bay, Skibbereen, some of the tiny, backstreet-and-water parishes. I phoned Sheena at the library and we arranged to meet and drive out of Cork for a picnic.

We found a place by a small deep river, upstream from where some men in waders were fishing. As we watched them cast and retrieve, so pensive at their work, Sheena gave voice to what I'd been feeling for weeks.

Cork's a great city, she said, tracing the outline of her ear with a grass blade. But you know, it can get to me. Like, if you see the same people all the time, and those people do the same things, it gets deadly boring. Sometimes I want to leave for good, but when that thought gets too real, I back off.

What do you love about Cork? I asked, selecting a grass blade for myself.

I love the people, mostly, and the great music in the pubs. I love the river, even when it's bloody and reeking. I love the buildings, especially some of the churches. Have you been up to the Shandon Bells?

I said that I had, and she said her cousin had thrown a model glider from there one windy day and that the plane had soared out of sight, right across the city.

What do you love? Sheena asked.

Much the same as you. I love talking and drinking with people. And I love the back streets, getting lost at night in some part of the city I haven't been in before.

I wouldn't dare do that, Sheena said. Not just because I hate being lost, but it's dangerous.

I'd never thought of Cork being dangerous. Apart from the odd brawl outside a pub, I'd never seen or heard anything that I'd consider being threatening.

People do get killed, she said. She pulled her knees to her chest. Do you feel like reading me a poem?

I read, from memory, a poem about listening to a novelist talk about his life.

Sheena recognised the novelist, and said He's a desperate man.

We lay down on the blanket. I felt Sheena's hand on my arm. Then she was turning and pressing her mouth to my neck. I sat up.

What's wrong?

I couldn't tell her that another woman's name was lying just under my skin. I said I'm sorry, it's not you, and Sheena moved away over the blanket and said If it's not me then you're hallucinating. Then she gathered the picnic items and put them into a plastic bag. She drank off her wine.

I looked over at the fishermen. One was kneeling, attending to what looked like a transparent funnel that curved from shoreline to water. The other was casting, the line whipping back and forth, gold in the late sun. When I turned back, Sheena had gone. She was sitting in the car, up on the road. When I got in she said nothing. As we drove back to Cork I said I'm sorry.

There's no need to apologise, just write a poem about it, she said, and straightened her arms against the wheel.

With the name Clonmel in my head I barely spoke at work. We were laying a new gas line through the city. The old, heavy metal cylinders with their bandaged leaks and festering oxidisation were being removed, replaced by bright yellow pipes which lined the roads for miles like bars of stalled sunlight.

Finbar was in fine form at work, hitting me behind the knees as I struggled with the end of a pipe, or throwing clods of earth that broke against my boots and back. I tried to respond, swearing and returning mudballs and gravel, but a woman's voice was doing aerial tricks in my gut. I saw the outline of her wonderful nose in a leaden sky, her hair in a weave of grass on the verge.

After work, Finbar and I went for a pint at The Wide Valley, which became several pints and a slow walk up past the barracks in a fine misty rain. We sat under a moss-quilted wall and looked out over the city.

You can be a right black sod, Finbar tipped a bottle and drank.

At work? I know. I'm sick of gas pipes and your jokes.

No, I mean a lot of the time.

The city lights seemed to grow and fade from view, giving the darkstone buildings a glazed, distant look. A woman's voice went out on the wind.

What do you think of Clonmel?

Finbar spat and wiped his mouth. I don't think of Clonmel. Bastard of a place.

Seriously.

I am being serious.

What's wrong with it?

The place is full of maniacs. I got run over in Clonmel.

You mean you were lying under a truck, pissed.

I was the bollocks! I was crossing the road and wham! Bastard took my legs away.

Were you hurt?

No, I got up and blessed the traffic. Of course I was hurt. Broke my leg. Haven't been back since.

I'm going there tomorrow night.

You be careful.

I'll try. I'm going to hear a band.

What band?

Lapwing.

Fine band.

Do you know Sarah Carmichael?

The fiddler? I know her.

What do you think?

Of the woman or the fiddling?

The woman.

Is that it? Are you in love?

Don't be stupid.

Come on, you've got the auld hot flushes, haven't you.

I think she's interesting.

Finbar got up and stretched. Have you told her that?

I've not had much of a chance to tell her anything.

I'd say that's good. I'd say you need to find someone else to speak to.

No one seems to like her very much. That just makes me more determined to get to know her.

No, you're on the wrong track. She's got problems.

We've all got problems, I said. Anyway, what are

they? What's all this bullshit I keep hearing about Sarah? Why is everyone so against her?

Finbar threw the bottle over. There's no need to get angry, he said, stepping down into the road. You'll be right, Jim. He rubbed his hands and blew into them. He turned and looked out over the city. I'm going.

What problems, Finbar?

Finbar shrugged. He came back to the kerb and sat down.

She's a champion boozer. I'll tell you that for nothin', he said.

You're the one to talk.

Fair enough, but I'm not in lust with myself, am I. I'm not chasing myself around the city like an eejit.

Finbar changed his tone. That was out of line, he said. Sorry.

He looked at me over his bottle, which was stalled below his mouth. I said sorry, alright?

Alright.

Anyway, yeah, she's a boozer.

He tipped the bottle and drank, wiped his mouth. She's also a ball-tearer. She went out with a friend of mine a couple of years back and treated him like a dog. I'm serious. She used to order him around something fierce. I used to bloody well cringe to see them out together. I told him. I said That girl is busting your balls.

What did he say?

He told me to feck off, of course.

So is that it? She's a boozer and she treated your friend badly?

Well yeah. Isn't that enough?

No, it's not.

Well, there is something else. People say she lies and can't be trusted.

I stood up. What proof do you have of that? I asked, loudly.

None. But the people who told me swear it's true.

It's gossip. It's talk. What the fuck is wrong with people that they have to go around bad-mouthing someone like that?

You asked.

And you're telling me shit, Finbar. Have you got anything else to say? Something that might make sense?

Finbar corked the bottle and got to his feet. He stepped down to the road and suddenly turned and hurled the bottle against the wall behind me.

You're being a right bastard, he shouted. You ask me to tell you things I didn't really want to say because I thought they might hurt you. Then I tell you, and you act like a fucking idiot, blaming me. Thanks.

He walked off, swinging his arms. He picked up a stone and threw it into the ground.

I watched until he was a black rag in a streetlight, then I went down to the river and watched the swans drifting and feeding into the dawn.

CLONMEL

S TANDING ROADSIDE, hitch-hiking late on Friday afternoon, buffeted by a cold, wet wind, a small van pulled over and a red-faced man got out and said Are you coming?

The van reeked of paint and turpentine. The man draped himself over the wheel as he drove, his face near the wiper-smeared glass. He looked like a captain in the wheelhouse of a small boat, afraid of the weather and the swell.

When I offered him a drink, he said I've got my own, and reached under the seat. A hip flask surfaced and threw a spark of blue light. He drank, replaced the bottle, returned to his watch.

Our talk covered house painting, whiskey, the Pope, cigarettes and sex. It ended with whiskey, and as I stepped out of the van he said My life is a cargo of hurt.

I repeated what he'd said as I walked into Clonmel, a groundsheet of small black birds flapping overhead, following me, then falling back to settle into the branches of a dusky tree.

The stage was lit with blue and green light. Five chairs were arranged in a half-circle in the glow. In front of the chairs, leaning into their stands, a guitar, bouzouki. A concertina lay on the floorboards, throwing a blunt blue shadow.

I looked around. Sarah was sitting at a table near the bar, her arms folded, the side of her face divided by strands of hair. A woman was leaning in close, talking to her. Sarah was not responding. She looked around, towards the door. Instinctively I turned around too. When I looked back she was cutting the air in front of her face with the blade of her hand and shaking her head. The woman beside her nodded.

The band went on stage. Sarah sat down and placed her fiddle across her knees. A man stepped to the microphone. We're going to play some old favourites and a couple of new tunes that Sarah has written, he said, and smiled at her. Sarah did not look up. The man said We'll start with 'Braids and Thistles', and when he sat down he counted the band in and they ripped into a reel, their bodies moving with each shift and repetition of the notes, which rose and fell, soared and skimmed. Sarah's cradled fiddle made dark shapes that seemed to hang in the air. The bow was a vein of strung light, angled and fast.

Each instrument fed into and off the others, a weaving of tight, lyrical sound. I closed my eyes, trying to isolate each one: the bright fan and swoon of the concertina, fingers quickstepping over the bouzouki frets, the flute's long, mellow notes combined with breath-spurts and windings, and Sarah's fiddle, like a thread stitching the heart of the reel together.

Sitting there in the back, I went deep into every note.

I loved this music. Since I'd arrived in Ireland, its rhythms had become a major focus in my thinking and dreaming.

When she stood up and introduced a song, Sarah's voice sounded tired. When she started singing, that tiredness dropped away into longing. She had a beautiful voice, and she sang in Irish, the words entering and leaving each other, trailing mystery, grace.

The song over, she sat down to loud, long applause. The man on her right, the bouzouki player, leaned across and said something to her. When he lifted his head, I could see that whatever was said had troubled her deeply. She held the fiddle in her lap. She turned it over and seemed to be studying the woodgrains. Then she straightened. She looked at the man, and her mouth was tight. The others watched. Sarah stood up, walked to the side of the stage and packed her fiddle and bow into the case. Then she returned and stood in a blue wash of light, facing the room.

I'm sorry, but that's it for me tonight, she said. Some things are beyond a joke, especially when the joke teller is a walking punchline. Then she gathered her skirts and walked to the bar.

A murmur went around the room. The concertina player got up. As he passed the bouzouki player he lowered his head and said something under his breath, then joined Sarah at the bar.

A Mary Black song came over the speakers. People went to the bar, leaving a wide space around Sarah and the man who was comforting her. I poured a whiskey and felt like two people: one wanting to go and say that it's alright, the other wanting to leave. I stayed at the table, watching. Sarah threw back two small glasses, then went to a table and put her coat on. She steadied herself and looked up at the stage. There was only one man sitting there, like someone stranded on a badly-lit station.

Michael, Sarah said, lifting hair from under her collar with the back of her hand.

Michael shielded his eyes and looked down.

Fuck you forever, she said, and walked out of the club. People followed. She told them to leave her alone. She said it again. People came back in, talking quietly.

I went outside. Sarah was leaning against the passenger door of a white Bedford van, drinking from a bottle and smoking. When she saw me, she looked away.

Don't say a bloody word, she said.

Can I have a drink then?

She straightened and looked at me closely. Jesus, she said. What are you doing here?

I came out to hear you play.

Then you've wasted your time.

I liked what I heard.

Then you've got no taste, she said. It's the worst we've ever played. She was looking at the ground. I'm sorry, she said. That was mean. Thank you. She lifted the bottle, drank deeply. It's been a bad time. Here, have a drink.

I went to her and took the bottle from her hand.

Who the fuck are you?

I turned around to see the bouzouki player standing in the doorway. I ignored him and drank.

I asked you a question, he said, his voice much nearer now.

Go away, Michael, you pathetic article, Sarah said. Go back to your little spotlight and masturbate, for all I care. You wanker. She reached up behind her neck.

When her hands came down they were holding the gold necklace, the cross turning. She threw the necklace at Michael's feet. You know where you can shove this, she shouted, and opened the van door, placing her fiddle case into the back.

Give me those keys, Sarah.

Sarah went around to the driver's side and opened the door.

Michael followed her and grabbed her arm. Sarah shook herself free and said Don't touch me, you fucker.

Michael turned and stared at me. I looked at Sarah. She was indicating with her head for me to get in. I moved towards the van. Michael was onto me quickly. He swung me around and pushed me into the wall.

Who in the name of fuck are you? he shouted, his face in mine.

I tried to push past him. He got me in a headlock and then he punched me in the face. His fist slammed into my nose and it opened. The stage spotlights went on in my head and I was pouring blood over my shirt and the footpath. I tried to see where I was, and Michael hit me again, this time in the back of the head. I tasted the wet pavement. It was salty and cold. Above me, two voices went in and out of focus and volume. When I got to my feet, Sarah was pushing me towards the open door of the van and screaming at Michael. I closed the door as a bottle flew past the windscreen. I was bleeding all over the place.

The van lurched forward.

Put your head back and pinch the bridge of your nose, Sarah said.

I tipped my head back and looked over at her. She was driving fast, her face set hard in concentration.

Where are we going?

Back to Cork.

What about the others?

They'll be fine. Keep pinching your nose.

Driving into Cork, Sarah said So I guess you're wondering what's going to happen now.

Regarding?

Now. Here. Cork. Two strangers.

Yes, are you? We could go somewhere and have a coffee, I said.

Sarah pulled the van over. I tried to hear her breathing over the idling engine.

Whiskey then? I said.

I don't have any. Not with me, anyway. I saw the last of it go flying past the window.

I pulled the bottle from my pocket.

Good man, she said. My bar or yours?

VOICES

———

S TANDING BESIDE her as she opened a small gate set
into a stone wall, I could smell her hair and what I
hoped was her body.

She led the way down a narrow path between
overgrown flower beds. At the entrance to her house,
she said Just for a drink, alright?

Passing through a glassed-in entrance, Sarah paused
and touched my arm. The gesture surprised me, and, as
if sensing this, she withdrew her hand and said I'm not
sure why I'm here with you. But I guess I'll find out.

The lounge room was gloomy under the gold eye
of the single bulb. The carpet was worn and frayed at
the edges, the curtains brown and stained. I offered
Sarah the bottle but she waved it away, saying There's
a bottle of Paddy in the cupboard. Let's have hot
toddies.

While she put the kettle on and prepared the glasses,
I looked through her bookshelves. Novels, poetry, art
and music. I chose a book of poems by Michael
Longley and sat in a deep red armchair, its arm rests
worn smooth to a gleam of pale fabric. I opened the

book but couldn't concentrate. The room was like a replica of the one above Stephanie's shop. When Sarah returned with two steaming glasses, the familiar scene changed to intense *déjà vu*. A low, bright cloud of smell, sight and touch drifted over and into me, swirling there.

Sarah arranged two large cushions on the floor and lay on her side. She raised her glass. Here's to a long and much-needed absence of aggression and ego, she said. We touched glasses. Sarah shook her head. This is just too easy, isn't it.

Are we supposed to be uncomfortable? Look at our hands? Talk about the weather? We can do those things, if you'd prefer.

No, we can't.

What then?

This is fine.

I caught myself looking at my hands.

Tomorrow should be warm and sunny, Sarah said.

We laughed and spilled our drinks. Sarah opened a packet of cigarettes and offered me one. She pushed a huge cut-glass ashtray over the floor.

So, she said.

Do you own this house?

No, I rent it. I never think about owning anything. Though I long for security. To have something stable, solid. Dreams. I feel like I'm always moving on, that I'll always be on the move.

Does Michael feel the same way?

You're not getting off that lightly.

Meaning?

Meaning I'm tired of talking, especially about that shite. And anyway, you're the one who wanted to talk. So talk to me. I'm waiting. She traced the edge of the ashtray. Her claddagh ring clicked on the glass.

Which of the three symbols on your ring do you most believe in?

She held up her hand. Love, friendship, loyalty, she said. All three are difficult to find and maintain. Though all three are possible. Which do I most believe in? I'd like to say love. I'll say love. And you?

All three. But yes, love.

And have you ever been in love? Completely and without borders?

Yes.

And?

She died. Her name was Tina. She was kicked in the head by her horse.

That's horrible.

I opened and closed the book of poems. You must have been in love with Michael.

Michael has a good heart, when he opens up enough for it to work properly. She studied her glass. I said I wasn't going to talk about him.

It's alright.

No. I'd rather not. I'd prefer to listen to you.

She went to the mantelpiece and lit a large yellow candle.

Lying with her head on one of the cushions, her hair like two dark wings on the floor, she said You're a thousand miles away.

More like thirteen thousand.

Thinking about Tina?

Yes.

So you still miss her?

Yes. Sometimes. I was missing her just then.

Sarah shifted under a blanket. She stretched and

sighed. Oh God, I'm so pissed. Her eyes looked red and swollen in the candlelight.

Mind if I share some of the blanket? I'm cold.

As long as it's the blanket you're after. Come on then. She smoothed the carpet with her palm. Come on in.

We talked about what had happened in Clonmel. Sarah spoke about the others in the band, about how they'd got together, her favourite gigs and the towns they'd visited. The gig in Clonmel was supposed to have been a warm-up for a short tour of the west coast, culminating in a three-day stopover on Inishmore, one of the Aran Islands.

Things have been really fucked up now, she said. It's not as if we're rich people who can do and go where we like. We'd all taken time off work for that trip.

You can still go, I said. It will be hard, being with Michael, but you've got to think of the band.

I can't see it happening. Can you imagine? Jesus. I don't want to be in the same space as that bastard.

Sarah pulled the blanket up over her face and sighed. But you're right, she said. We should still go. Oh well, if things fall apart on the road, there's always my work here.

What do you do?

I have two jobs. I work in a bakery, three mornings a week, and I teach violin some evenings. I don't have much money. If you're digging for gold, the seams are barren.

Sarah found my hand. Our fingers laced and warm, she said So, why me? You're a persistent article.

You have presence.

Oh come on, James. You can do better than that. A park bench can have presence.

No really, it's you. You stand out.

Like a park bench?

There were loads of women at that party. I talked with some of them. I was amazed by you.

Because I happen to be a musician.

No. Well, that's great. But it's you. I can't define it. Try.

I saw firelight, tasted booze, heard music and talk. When I turned to look at Sarah her eyes were closed. I touched her hair. It's like you were so confident. I'm not talking about the music. You seemed confident in yourself, and at the same time you were kind of withdrawn, and watchful.

I like to be watchful.

Did you notice me?

I noticed a man staring at me. You made me feel uncomfortable. I've told you that.

And now?

Now I'm so drunk and tired my head is reeling. Would you hold me? Talk to me?

I told her what I could, but everything I said seemed like frames from an out-of-focus movie. I went over old ground, wanting to define my feelings for Tina, and her death. When it came to the time in the hospital, I swallowed my tongue and stopped talking. When I told her about why I needed to speak with her, fatigue or fear set snares in my head and nearly every word was taken. I did say that I could appreciate her playing and her love of music. I concluded with a long sentence about thinking that we might have a lot in common, which left a wide space between us, there on the floor, one which I couldn't fill, no matter how quickly I tried to cover it with thoughts of more smoke and whiskey. Sarah was quiet. I asked if she'd like a back-rub, but she didn't speak or move. It was then that I realised she'd been asleep the whole time I was talking.

I woke to a stripe of pale sunlight dividing the blanket. Sarah was asleep, breathing slowly, deeply. I watched her. The candle was a wick in a yellow spillage on the mantelpiece. In the kitchen I found the makings for coffee. I also found bottles of whiskey, bourbon, vodka and wine. Empty bottles stacked in the corner. A carton of cigarettes beside a packet of tea.

I sat in the armchair, drinking coffee, watching the stripe of light flare and fade. The light went out and I heard the rain begin. It swept over the tin roof, then stopped, started again. I found a sheet of paper and a pen, wrote her a message and left it on the floor beside her head.

Standing on the road, I watched isolated weavings of rain blow over the city. Up on Sundays Well, the parapets of a hospital came and went in smokelines of cloud, like evenly spaced dark hills. Three ravens went sideways overhead. The city was a grid of soil colours and sky colours, alluvial industry either side of the dark river, which was ferrying its gulls and blood to the sea. A shaft of sun lit the domed fish on Shandon. No bells rang. A raven came down and said something like Raucous, yes, a throatfeather hardens me. I heard Sarah move in her sleep. My headlights blew a globe and fizzed out to the sound of boots on wet gravel on a high place between touring walls of rain.

TROLLING FOR
LOCAL KNOWLEDGE

————

LIVING OVER THE Wide Valley had its benefits. I could trip up and down the stairs for a pint, meet some interesting people, and there was often music on tap. But the walls closed in.

For the first two days after Clonmel, Sarah and I did not see each other. She said she wanted time to sort things out in her head, to put what had happened with Michael into perspective. This soon changed. Michael was phoning constantly, throwing rocks onto her roof and waiting for her outside the house when she left for the bakery. He would follow her down the road, abusing her and taking her roughly by the arm. Sarah called the guards, and they went to see him. It did little good. The night he handed a note to a young girl who had arrived for a violin lesson, saying Give this to the fiddle-playing bitch, Sarah knew things were out of control. In the letter, Michael had warned her that if she kept seeing me he was going to *Do a dance on your man's fucking head*. And then one night he phoned her. He said Do you know what this is? Sarah told me she'd heard the receiver being placed on a hard surface, then a sound like wires breaking under tension. Michael picked up the receiver and said I've just jumped on my bouzouki and ripped its veins out. That instrument's had a name for years, though I've never told anyone. Its name was Sarah. Did you hear what happened to her?

Sarah was furious and scared. She came to the pub. We'd sit by the window, watching the city close down, drinking and smoking as small stripes and globes of neon burned through the curtains.

One night, as she sat on my lap, her head on my shoulder, she took a deep breath and thanked me for the note I'd left on her floor.

It was then that I realised how serious and kind you are, she said. Did you know that women see kindness as a very attractive quality in a man? But it's more than that. What I see when I look at you, when I'm with you, is a man who is both vulnerable and strong. Do you think that's true?

I closed one eye and watched a bar of neon blink and die. I said You might be right, and pulled her close.

I'm still learning about you of course, she said. But this student likes what she's discovering.

Michael stopped phoning and coming over to her house. He'd not been to the pub, and we were able to relax there. I thought it strange that he hadn't been making life hard for me. I expected him to round a corner or enter the bar, my name in his fist. We wondered what had happened. Sarah was confused, saying it wasn't like Michael to give up so easily. I sensed her tension. Michael's presence was still there, though spectre-like, influencing her waking and sleeping thoughts.

I'd walk with her to the bakery, and meet her for

coffee after work. On the nights when students came for their lessons, I'd stay at her house. I could hear Michael sometimes then, yelling from up on the road, his words distorted, though their intentions were amplified and clear.

During the hours I spent alone, after work, I'd sit at the desk and tinker with poems or read novels. I'd walk the streets, as this was when some of the best images and lines arrived.

I'd been sending poems to magazines and newspapers since arriving in Cork. I'd go through the various magazines in Ireland and England, as well as some in Australia, placing poems into envelopes, and doing drawings below the addresses: fish, birds, whatever came to mind. I'd had several poems published, and I kept a journal of names, dates and titles. With success came many rejections, and although it hurt, it gave me tangible proof that what I was doing was important, that the work was at least reaching people, even if they sent the poems back with a photocopied *no* or brief invitation to try again. Sharing this with someone else for the first time, I felt both supported and inspired. Sarah would make suggestions on various poems, and offer forms of abuse we could send to the rejecting editors.

I'd told Finbar about seeing the fishermen at Ballymine, and he said his brother was a keen angler. He said He goes beach fishing in Kerry for Atlantic bass, and fly fishing for trout in the rivers and streams around Cork. When I asked him if his brother would take me, Finbar said He'll calf-rope you and throw you to the ground, if you're keen. He loves it. I'll get him to call you.

Finbar's brother's name was Ted. He taught me how

to false-cast and lay the line out over water where trout were mouthing rings in the shifting mirror. We caught few fish, but it was during these weekend trips that I began to associate fishing with writing poetry. The mystery. The physical casting of lures for the silver flash.

Sarah came with us one afternoon after work. We fished a deep section of river just out of the city. Ted and Sarah shared a bottle, and finished it quickly. Ted was too smashed to drive and Sarah seemed no better. Still, she insisted on driving. When I tried to take the keys from her she flew into a rage. Driving home, she almost rolled the car on a bend, trying to avoid a cow that loomed at us from a low, roadside fence, its head and shoulders coming through the wire.

I'd bought my own fly rod and reel, a pair of waders, a small redwood box full of flies. I read books. Sarah and I went camping and fishing. We talked to men and women at the bars of the pubs we stayed in, trolling for local knowledge.

Sarah loved most aspects of fishing – the environment, the craft involved, and the colours of the fish. She hated me killing them, though never objected when I cooked them up in her kitchen and served them with a bottle of something white and cold.

I loved being with her, and we were affectionate in public – something I'd never been totally comfortable with. Tina used to ask me to hold her hand as we walked down the street, and I was never big on cuddling as we sat in a park or on the beach. Now I enjoyed putting my arm around this woman's waist, holding her hand as we walked to a restaurant or pub. And I was thrilled that Sarah enjoyed me doing these things. Sometimes I ached for Tina, for the times I was unable to return her spontaneous displays of emotion. I felt as though I had been away from myself for a long time, and in some ways I had. I'd been out of circulation and practice. I'd forgotten how to touch and be touched. To let go, to open the heart, requires courage. I craved it now.

I was ready to learn, and yet I was afraid of exposing myself completely. My tablets were the white stones that mapped the path out of the forest. Sarah had never seen them. I was on my own. Although I hadn't had an episode of weirdness since that day by the river in Cork, I was waiting. I knew that I had the capacity for causing pain, to myself and others, and that unreliability was a mark on the horizon. It came and went with the swell. I swallowed pills to keep it in the distance. I wanted Sarah to know what I feared, though telling her was impossible, at least while the stones were visible. The burden of withholding knowledge is a terrible weight. It can lie dormant for years. When it surfaces, the terrain of the head and heart can rupture. Is that what caused my headlights? My inability to confront what was too hard or frightening?

BLACKMORE HOUSE

⬥

R ETURNING FROM A long walk one night, I found
an unsigned note pinned to the door of my room
at the pub:

> *I know who you are. You think you know about me.*
> *Stay away from Sarah. In fact, why don't you fuck off back to*
> *Australia. Convict.*

I fisted the note and went down to the pub, to feed it
to the flames.

As my Guinness was settling, someone tapped me on
the shoulder. I turned around to see Michael.

So did you get my telegram? He was standing in a
slight crouch, hands at his sides. He looked terrible. His
hair was knotted, his clothes creased and stained, as if
he'd been eating and sleeping in them since Clonmel.

Yes.

Right then. So why are you still here?

I live here.

You do the fuck.

I looked back at the bar. The pint had settled. The

barman was watching me, his hands caught in a gnarl of white apron.

Your pint's ready, he said, you'd best be drinking it. Then he stepped forward, leaned on the bar and looked at Michael. And I suggest you take whatever's troubling you out into the street. I don't want any drama here.

Then kick this fucker out, Michael said, pointing at me. He's the trouble, not me.

If you don't leave, I'll call the guards. The barman was untying his apron.

Call them. I've done nothing wrong.

Breathing quickly, my heart racing, I turned my back and reached for the pint.

You think you're a clever lad, don't you. Michael was speaking slowly, loudly.

I sipped my pint.

This man stole my girlfriend, Michael said to the room.

A couple got up from their table and left.

If you don't leave now, I'm calling the guards. The barman moved to the telephone.

This man is a liar and a thief, Michael said.

The barman was on the phone, watching Michael as he spoke.

Anything to say for yourself, before I kick the shit out of you?

The barman replaced the receiver and said You can stay or leave, it's your call. The guards are on their way.

I turned around, my back pressed hard into the barwood.

Michael shifted his weight and leaned forward, waving an accusatory finger in the air. You've been warned. Three times. Once with blood, once with ink, and now with words. Back off. Leave Sarah alone. If you want more blood, I can arrange it. He straightened

274

and retrieved his finger. He looked at the barman. And you can go and fuck yourself too, eagle-features. Then he walked in a small circle, addressing people at their tables. A bit of light entertainment is it? Glad to oblige. His face came around slowly, and he held me in one eye, his face angled away. In fact, I'd be happy to arrange more blood for you, convict. He pulled up his collar and moved quickly out of the pub.

Drink your pint, the barman said.

My hand was shaking. I put the glass down. How long will it take the guards to get here?

I didn't call them. A bit of theatre.

It worked.

To tell the truth, I quite liked that part about blood, ink and words. Think I might use it.

Someone near the fire laughed.

You've been causing trouble then?

Apparently, I said, and looked out through the door at the street. I saw leaves, the coat of someone walking fast, but no man crouching low, a snarl on his face. But when I turned to the bar and drained half my pint, I saw him clearly and I saw blood slipping back to ripple and settle in the glass.

I went straight to Sarah's house. I heard her voice from outside the wall gate. She was trying to explain, as clearly and as economically as possible, the most appropriate way for Michael to fuck off. Michael echoed Sarah's sentiments, though with far more volume and less brevity, then I heard him stomping up the path. I found the dark side of a curve in the wall. Michael walked to the edge of the road. He moved to the Bedford van and started muttering to himself. Then he peered into the driver's window. He said Sarah, and then he said No fucking way. He came towards the wall, parted the grass near where I was hiding, and lifted something from the grass. Standing back from the driver's window, his arm whipped forwards and the glass shattered. He spat through the jagged window frame. No fucking way, he said, and staggered off. Then he came back. He stood at the gate. You can shove your fucking band, he shouted. You and those other spineless losers.

The house lights were off. I went to the door and said It's James.

A curtain moved and settled. Sarah opened the door and fell against me.

I'm going to kill that fucker, she said.

I never thought a threat would get to me: a bloody nose, a punch in the back of the head and a stand-off in a pub are black situations, but tolerable. What troubled me most was the unpredictability. A rock through a van window could grow into a fist, a knife, a gun, and Sarah was at the centre of these bleak possibilities. Whatever I did or said affected her.

The next afternoon, having been told at the bakery that Sarah had left early, and that she'd see me later, I returned to my room and waited.

I woke to knocking, then Sarah's voice. For fuck's sake, James, open the door.

She had a bruise on her forehead and her blouse was torn. She went to the window and stood to one side, parted the curtains and looked down into the street.

Michael did that to you, didn't he.

Yes. Listen, James, I've got to go away. I think you should too.

I'm calling the guards. I went to the door.

No, don't, please.

Why are you protecting that bastard?

I'm not. I just don't want to involve the guards.

He's going to kill someone. I went to Sarah and touched her face. What happened?

Michael left a letter for me at work. He said he wanted to talk, to apologise for being so awful. We met in a cafe down the street.

Sarah looked at the torn edges of her blouse. She said At first, he was quiet and calm. He took my hand and said how sorry he was. He asked me what I was doing. He said Are you in love with James? I didn't answer him. He repeated the question, and squeezed my hand, too hard. I couldn't speak. Then he started shouting at me. I told him to go away, and he kicked the table. Then he back-handed me over the face and ripped my clothes. I threw an ashtray at him. It hit him in the head. He fell down. Jesus . . .

Sarah sat on the bed and started sobbing. I wrapped her up and kissed her hair.

I need to go away now. Will you come?

Yes. Of course.

I'll call the lads from the band.

Where's Michael?

Bleeding in hell. I don't know. I don't care.

He's probably waiting downstairs.

No. I think I really hurt him.

I went to the window. Cars. Leaves. A fan of pigeons from the ledge. So where do you want to go?

My sister is the caretaker of a country estate. It's called Blackmore House, a heritage-listed place outside Cork. It's out of season now. No tourists. She's in Clare, visiting friends. I told her everything on the phone. She wants me to go there for a couple of days. I'd like you to come. Will you?

Yes. I'll have to do something about work.

We need to go tonight. We can stay there before we head up the coast. The boys can make arrangements, I'm sure.

I'll call Finbar. He'll have the right lie to tell the boss.

James.

What?

I can trust you, can't I?

Yes.

Sarah reached into her shoulder bag, lifted out a bottle of Paddy.

You want some?

No thanks.

She uncapped the bottle and drank. Drank again. Her eyes fogged over and she said I just need some time away from all this.

Then maybe I shouldn't be coming. I'm a part of the whole mess.

No, I want you to come. I feel safe with you. I meant away from Michael. Away from Cork. I'm so rattled.

I understand what fear is, I said. I was shaking. Sarah touched my hand. She was about to say something, but then came to me and kissed me on the mouth, softly.

Will you tell me what you mean by that, some time?

I said that I would, and then I went around the room, throwing clothes and books into a bag.

Standing in the door frame, we peered like shy children into the street. Then we ran and got into the van. Closing the door, I felt as though I was entering another country. Sarah pulled away from the kerb and said It's going to be alright.

I wasn't so sure.

We drove out through Cork, following the river, cold air blowing through the broken window. I watched the brown reflections of warehouses grow into oily water. We did not speak.

Turning into a narrow road bordered by a high, moss-furred wall, Sarah looked at me, the bruise like a shadow on her face, and said Everything's going to be fine.

I said nothing as a pair of massive gates, like the wings of some impossible bird, filled the windscreen. Sarah slid a card through a slot in a metal box. The gates opened. We drove through, the shapes of trees and the flickering light of a strange country all around us, crowding the cabin of the van like thoughts discarded long ago, now returning to darken the body and the head.

The road narrowed into a ribbon of grey gravel as we left the dark trees. At the end, where the road made a wide loop, Blackmore House went into the sky, its darkstone levels broken by lit windows and a huge door. It was a serious-looking building, with a lane running down its side to a series of small, connected sheds with grey, angular roofs. Sarah drove to the front door and turned the engine off.

I haven't been here for a couple of years, she said. It used to make me feel strange. I got lost once, in the rooms below the main house. I had dreams about those rooms for ages.

We got out and stood beside the van, looking up at the big windows with their curtain sashes and elaborate frames.

Sarah took a few steps back and looked around. I hope I feel better about the place now, she said, and walked to a large ceramic pot beside the door. She tipped it to one side and held up a ring shining with keys.

The entrance to the house was cold and huge. Marble pillars gleamed in the light of flame-shaped lanterns fixed to the walls. A headless mannequin wearing a dress veined with sequins stood to one side of a whitestone staircase. I went for the bags while Sarah found and turned on more lights and opened the upstairs rooms.

In the kitchen we lit candles and opened a bottle of wine. A small web-bordered window held a darkening view of cedars and garden plots bordered by pale stones. Sarah stood beside me, giving a brief history of the place: big families, horse-breeding, game-hunting and eating, winters to die for, tapestry-weaving, parties that lasted for days.

There are rooms under here that haven't been opened for fifty years or more, she said, holding herself. I've found and opened some of them. They give me the creeps. They smell like a long and terrible absence.

FEAR

FINBAR TOLD THE people at work that I'd had a kind of emotional trauma. They suggested I take a week off – more if needed. When I phoned him he asked me to give his regards to Sarah. He said I guess you know what you're doing. When I disagreed with him, he laughed and said I'll have a few pints in your memory.

Blackmore House. One grand, brooding structure planned and stacked around what was once a hunting lodge, the lodge itself blacked out at the centre, its heart caked with the dried blood of deer and pheasant, the shit of horses, foxes, hounds, spilled wine and the dust of four hundred years. Small rooms opening onto corridors that led to other small rooms, their tables and mirrors draped with dust, their chairs backed into corners, the beds made too perfectly. A Georgian residence at the heart of rural Cork. Doric columns in the porch; hollow, polished mosaic-covered Ionic columns in the hall; Corinthian in the great dining room. Four storeys of mould and imagination, the fourth storey hidden in the roof. Sloping window embrasures and a puzzle of doors concealed by being placed flush with the walls. Symbolic plasterwork: the egg and the dart – life and death; the flame and the tongue – sex and speech. Some ceilings painted elaborately, others plain. The walls of the ground floor reception rooms hung with tapestries of hunting, the arts, funerals and birth. Outside, labyrinthine walks through trees and waist-high flower beds, stone walls snaking nowhere, birds concealed overhead singing the day alive with bell notes and flute notes, the light changing into many shades of cold, windy green.

The first night in the house I couldn't sleep. I listened to the rooms shift around on their blood and bone foundations.

In the morning we emerged and sat in silence over cups of tea in a kitchen warmed by a small black stove, looking out at the overcast day, smoking constantly. I had a bath, dressed in my warmest clothes, unpacked my camera and went for a walk. Sarah had to make phone calls, write letters.

Standing under the green-black terraced branches of a Lebanese cedar, I looked up at the small kitchen window. I thought I saw Sarah move away from the glass, but it could have been cloudshadow, birdwing, the passage of an insecure thought.

I followed a narrow, leaf-stitched path until it ended at a high demesne wall. Climbing the wall, its protruding knobs of stone broke away like earth and each fingerhold smelled of decay. At the top I found a sweeping view of fields and a cross in the distance, the church hidden by a windbreak of sprawling, dark green trees. Sheep with electric blue symbols stamped into their wool grazed close by. A cowbell rang and stopped. Ravens read poetry and heckled each other.

Walking back to the house, I stopped to pinch the flame of a daisy from a briar weave. Past tree boles and the cloudy gables of the creamery, into a stand of yew trees and then ash-dark, brooding bog oaks, thinking of the labourers, grooms and gardeners that once walked and worked here.

With generations of dead laughter and weeping at my back, I climbed a huge cedar at the edge of a clearing and sat in a smooth fork, watching the house. Sarah came out from the far side of the house carrying a basket. She walked towards me, stopped and looked around. She placed the basket gently on the leafcarpet and said So, are you going to say hello or have you turned to wood? Then she looked up, to the left. Her head came around and then she smiled. I wasn't sure which branch you'd become, she said.

How did you know where I was?

Intuition. So, have you taken loads of photos?

Some. You were watching me, weren't you.

No. I was at the stables, smelling the ghosts of horses. When I came out onto the path into these trees I sensed you were here.

Bullshit.

It's true, James. Please, believe me.

Her face was serious.

I believe you.

No you don't. You think I was spying on you.

Want to come up?

You think I was watching you, don't you?

No, I don't. Come on, climb up. The view is amazing.

Sarah came to stand at the base of the tree. She placed her hand on the bark, leaned heavily and looked up.

I steadied the camera on a branch and fired off two shots.

Sarah threw a small stick into the tree. Do you love me? she asked.

Tina's face swam in a glass of blackberry wine. A dark drop fell from her tongue onto mine. A love dart divided the air between us.

I'm not sure. I think so, yes. Do you love me?

Yes.

How can you be sure?

Sarah rubbed the bark slowly and looked away. I trust my fear, she said, and pushed away from the trunk. She walked backwards a few paces and said I think you should climb down.

When I reached her she said I want you to see the shape of my fear, and I'd like to see yours. She led me away towards the house. Do you know how to reveal it?

I was about to say something, anything, but Sarah turned and removed whatever was surfacing with a kiss.

We made it as far as the staircase. On cold stone I saw the shape of Sarah's fear and surrendered to it. She made a warm tent from her coat and dress, kneeled, unzipped me, and lowered herself down. Sliding back and forth, she rubbed herself against me, her pubic hair like sparks on my belly. I looked over her shoulder at a tapestry dark with a harvest scene. Sarah said my name, sat up and moved hard against me, pushing down with her palms into my chest. The muscles inside her spasmed and I let go with her name, with handfuls of material and a harvest scene breaking open in my head. She lay on me, with all her weight. On steep stone lightening and darkening with cloudshadow and flarings of sun, we kissed and breathed into each other.

When Sarah sat up she was crying, silently. I didn't know what to say, so I held my words and wrapped her up with my arms and legs and spoke with my body, saying Sleep is what we need now, and later we can trust our fear again.

A LOVE POEM AND A
GRAVEYARD FOR ANIMALS

———

LYING IN A huge bed, sheet lightning taking X-rays of Sarah's face and posting them on the wall, thunder locating every loose board or sheet of iron in the house, we held each other and made love, slept, made love again. Rain all morning. I got out of bed and watched the storm throw a lavender film over the fields beyond the house, turning the branches of the Lebanese cedar by the road into porcelain flowstones.

In the kitchen I made a fire and a pot of tea and sat down to write. Working into the makings of dawn, the words came slowly, the tablewood vanishing under a cloth of blackened pages. I wanted to have the poem ready for Sarah when she woke.

She came out in her dressing gown trailing threads of sleep and whiskey. When she'd settled over a cup of tea and a cigarette, I read her the poem. She said how much she liked it by sitting astride me and arranging her hair around our faces.

What do you know about me? she asked, her words a soft vibration against my neck. You know that I play the fiddle, that I smell good, that I love taking you into my mouth. What else? You haven't asked about my family, about my other life, before we met.

I protested that we *had* spoken about those things, but Sarah said We've only scratched the surface of each other's feelings. If we're going to know each other properly, we have to know everything. Don't you think? Let's make a promise to talk more, about ordinary things.

I promised. She was right. It was as if the details of our lives had been making tight circles in the air around our heads, entering our skin occasionally and moving there, but not going any deeper. Were we afraid to open out completely?

We kissed and held each other as a fresh wave of rain swept over the roof.

Late Sunday morning. A deep fog over the grounds. The rain constant. Wide pools of water bubbling on the driveway.

Sean and Padraigh arrived in a pickup truck. We saw them coming from the kitchen window. They came weaving over the narrow entrance road, taking the apex of each corner with fantails of vergewater and mud.

A familiar tune flourished and died as doors were opened and closed. Sarah went down to meet them. Coming up the stairs, she said You know, we don't sound too bad.

John arrived with a cold, rain-driving wind. He hammered and called our names. I opened the door to a large man with a cardboard box overspilling with vegetables cradled in his arms. He was unshaven and wild-eyed, rain dripping from his misshapen black hat, his collar turned up hugely. He gave me the box.

There's others in the van. I'll get them, he said. You

go up. He looked past me into the house. Jaysus, what century am I in?

After lunch, we went out into a day cast over with low, dark cloud and intermittent rain, John leading, sweeping aside branches and shrubs with a gnarled length of wood.

Passing behind a screen of thorns, Sarah stopped and went into a dense groundcover of pale yellow creepers and flowers. She asked us to join her. Parting twists of dripping colour, she said Here's one, and we made a tight circle around her. A small white stone glowed from the earth. Carved into it were the words: *David – Silence Becomes You – 4.12.1822.*

Sean knelt down. Jesus, you mean babies were buried out here?

No. It's the grave for a pet. There's loads of them around here. There's even one for a horse, out behind the old creamery. Its name was Rembrandt. Can you believe that?

I'm prepared to believe anything this place throws at me, John said.

We looked around, finding the stones with our hands and feet, calling out names and dates, trying to guess what kinds of animals were underfoot. Sarah said that people used to come at night, to disinter the animals and steal the expensive red cloth they were buried in.

Cat snatchers, John said, and whacked a tree with his stick. I'll sort the bastards out. Nothing worse than a cat snatcher. They take them back to their rooms and perform evil experiments. They graft rat heads onto them, then bring them back to life with a solution of poteen and electricity.

Be hard to snatch a horse, Padraigh said.

No problem, John said and sliced through the air with

his stick. They just chop the buggers into pieces, load them onto the cart, haul them away, then stitch cow heads or bums onto them. Animal puzzles.

The rain stopped and the fog started lifting. Anaemic sunlight went through the trees in lines. We walked into a sunken garden. Sarah had brought her camera, and asked us to arrange ourselves at the garden's centre. We knelt or squatted. Sarah directed our positions until John started swearing and hitting the ground with his stick. I liked being close to these men – the smell of their clothes and bodies, their breath, their warmth and honesty. Sarah took two photos, then Padraigh took one of her. I took some of them together: two men smiling, a woman laughing, another man somewhere in between.

While the others spent the afternoon going through songs and tunes, getting ready for the tour, I went for a long walk, out along the estate road and over a high stone wall that obscured a view of the distant harbour. I was feeling tense. Whether it was the weirdness of the animal graveyard, or being with Sarah in a place as bleak as Blackmore House, I didn't know.

As I went down the road, I could hear music. I tried to isolate Sarah's fiddle, but it was lost to thick stone walls and a house-bound wind.

FOX FISH

———

T AKING TWO fishing rods and a box of tackle that I'd found in the livery stable, Sarah and I went off to explore some local water.

Outside a small town where an oracle of old men had been smoking and talking, we saw a fox hunt in progress. The red coats and hard hats flashed through a line of willows at the riverside. We stopped the car and got out to watch. Sarah told me how much she despised fox hunts, saying they were nothing more than torture disguised as games for the filthy rich.

As the lead riders came splashing through a shallow section of the river below where we were standing, a woman on a big bay horse came off and landed heavily in the water. Her horse ran a few yards and stopped, where it snorted and scraped at the water. The woman was soaked. She rubbed her thigh and limped over to the horse. Taking the reins, she looked up at us and smiled feebly.

Swimming is a much better sport, don't you think? Sarah said to her.

The woman mounted up and turned the horse's head.

As she led it away through the willows, she looked back at us.

That was a bit unnecessary, don't you think?

I think it's unnecessary to chase a fox and let dogs rip its head off, she said quickly, and walked back to the car.

We drove in silence until I said Where do you think we should fish?

Sarah stared ahead and said You decide.

I suggested we stop where the river curved sharply away from the road, winding out through a field with tall black trees along its bank. I could see a narrow track leading off from the road.

You're not still angry about the fox hunt are you?

I am, she said. I hate that shite.

There's no reason to let it ruin our day though. Come on. I put my arm around her waist.

It's just that I get so upset. When I was little, up in the north of Cork, I saw the hounds going over a hill with the fox running ahead of them. After the fox and hounds and riders had gone over the hill, there was a terrible sound of barking and horns blowing, and I closed my eyes and saw the blood flying as the fox came apart. I've never been able to get it out of my head.

We chose a place where the river ran deep and slow. The reflections of trees were like an ink stain spreading over the flow.

I selected a fly and cast out to the middle. It landed and shivered. I stripped it back, slowly.

Sarah had fished with fly gear before, when we went with Ted. She found the combination of stripping line and casting difficult, yet she managed to send the fly out, though not where she intended. There were no rising rings from trout that we could see, so random placement seemed as good as anything.

I cast out again. The line whipped and sailed high, settling into a map of reflected branches.

Sarah sent hers out downstream. It floated back, entered a small eddy, then went out wide. There was an explosion of water, and the line went tight. I grabbed the net and stood beside her. She worked the fish well, giving it line when it powered away, then bringing it back. I could see the fish, though not clearly. It was about ten yards out, side-on and using the current to its advantage. As it neared the bank, I saw that it was a large brown trout. Through the cloud and leaf-printed water I could see its beautiful markings – the tiny dark globes on the slabs of its sides, the fins wavering, the tail beating. I lowered the net behind it and scooped it up. It left the water meshed and dripping, throwing a fan of silver.

My lips were going numb as I placed the netted fish on the bank and stepped away. Then my fingers began to spark at the ends with what felt like static electricity.

It's incredible, Sarah said, and knelt beside the gasping fish.

I walked away a few paces and looked up into the trees. The spaces between the branches held a puzzle of dark blue. A bird angled down and sang.

I heard Sarah say something behind me. I talked to myself, quickly. I said Not now. A thought replaced a thought and I tried to follow it. I felt a touch on my arm and I jumped.

Are you alright? Sarah was beside me.

I said nothing and walked back to kneel down beside the fish.

Is there anything I can do? Let's go back to the house, alright?

I don't want this to happen, I said, and the fish said You think you've got problems.

James? Sarah's voice came from the trees overhead. Her shadow had branch-ends forking out of it.

Take your time, the fish said. I think I've got a couple of minutes before the air does its work.

Sarah was beside me, but her presence was a blur. My thoughts were entering and fighting each other.

Just put me back and fuck off, the fish said, and kicked in the net.

I picked up the net and walked to the water's edge.

Sarah was saying something. I heard Catch and Should we? I heard Best one ever.

I lowered the net into the water. The trout left it slowly, then finned away in a swirl of mud. A line of bubbles broke where it went deep. The bubbles had words inside them.

The bank is a secret place. I know the cover of dreams. I felt a pulse in the mounds of your releasing hands. You have trouble. The hook is mine. I will remember you. Think on this when you cast and kill. The scale is a mirror. Where are you going now, traveller?

Driving back to the house, Sarah talked to me, quietly. She told me that she understood, that she'd seen and heard Padraigh go through something similar a couple of times.

It happened during a gig once. He just stopped playing and was completely out of it. I went to him and held his hand. His pulse was very fast. When I looked into his eyes, I knew that he was somewhere else. His body was there, but that's it.

She turned to me. The best people are always the weirdest, she said, through a failed attempt at a smile.

I tried to respond, but my language came as a line of bubbles that surfaced and drifted along the windscreen, breaking open to leave a smear of mud and syllables of fear on the speeding glass.

THE WEST COAST OF IRELAND

A WHITE VAN stacked with musical instruments and five people on the road around Bantry Bay with John's black jokes, Sean sleeping, Padraigh opening out with stories and poems, Sarah loving it all, taking hits from a half-bottle of Bushmills, her eyes in the rear-view mirror alive with being on the road, on the move.

After what had happened at the river, Sarah was attentive and calm. She didn't ask questions, though I longed to tell her everything – whatever that means. Honesty, when under pressure, can be a hard code to break. When together, away from the others, which was a rare thing, we sat quietly and held each other. The air around us became warm and clear. I watched myself. I slept as much as I could, and walked when I had the chance, sometimes alone, but mostly with Sarah, holding her hand and loving the rhythm our matching strides made on the road.

At pubs in Glengarriff, Castletownbere, Lauragh and Kenmare, we drank and laughed and slept. Around the Ring of Kerry, to Dingle, where John and Sean pulled on wetsuits and swam with a dolphin, diving and rolling.

Sarah, Padraigh and I sat on high warm stones and drank, the sun a long, soaking welcome after days of rain and damp.

That night, in the pub at Dingle, the band played brilliantly. Sarah was in fine form, telling stories, singing and playing her heart out. Sean let rip on the bouzouki. Padraigh played the flute with a quiet passion, standing tall and looking relaxed. John's box fanned and threw lyrical shapes, his head lowered, hair in black strings over his working hands.

Next day, raw with hangovers, we left Dingle early in the morning and drove on to Killimer, where we bought supplies and had a picnic by the River Shannon.

Padraigh had been quiet all morning. I sat beside him, and had tried to talk, mentioning various styles of buildings, cattle, sheep. He sat slightly hunched over, murmuring replies or else putting his head down on a folded coat.

Sarah and John were deep in talk about session etiquette, passing a bottle back and forth. Sarah had been drinking heavily. I'd said nothing, though the need to say something was with me constantly. Sean was sleeping.

Padraigh got up from the grass. He stretched and looked around, rolled and lit a cigarette, then walked off. I waited until he'd gone around a point bristling with rushes, then followed him.

He was down by the water, near where a small boy was floating a ship in the shallows.

Padraigh picked up a stone and tried to skim it out over the water mirror. The stone flipped over and sank immediately. He tried again, this time the stone cut a groove three yards in front of him. Fuck it, he said, and reached for another.

The boy waded out, grabbed his boat and ran away up the hill, where he sat down, holding the boat to his chest, watching a man by the water, throwing stones. I could hear Padraigh talking to himself. Sometimes there is . . . What do I have to do? This is bullshit.

I was about to go to him when a white paper bag blew over the grass in front of him. He ran and jumped on it, picked it up and stuffed it into his coat pocket. He looked down and picked up something else I couldn't see. He put this into his pocket too, and went on. Every few yards he'd stop and pick something from the grass. Then he went to the water's edge and walked slowly, head down, pausing as if to observe some object visible only to himself, then moving on again.

I'd followed him a mile or more. We'd come to a series of small, run-down jetties with missing planks and rusted ladders going into the flow. Some had small skiffs roped to the ladders. Padraigh sat down at the end of the last jetty and took his shoes off. He reached into his coat pocket and took out a handful of white things, which he arranged on the boards beside him. A gull floated over. Padraigh watched it go, then raised a hand quickly and waved as the bird angled back over the river. He looked towards me. I was perhaps twenty yards away, between two staked saplings. I turned my face, and when I looked back he was standing and pocketing his white collection. I was about to move, when he walked off the jetty and came in my direction. I lay back and put my arm across my face as he went past. When I looked over he was walking quickly, hands in his pockets, kicking at the grass.

Sarah and John were asleep, coats over their faces. Sean was lying on his back beside them, reading. I couldn't see Padraigh. When I asked, Sean pointed up to the van. He's in a mood. Best leave him be.

On to Kilkee, in Clare, then up to stay with Sean's brother who owned a pub in Milltown Malbay, where the band were to play the following night. For this gig they were being joined by Frankie Power, a piper from Ennis.

A couple of hours before the gig, Padraigh went missing. He hadn't told anyone where he was going, and no one had seen him leave. One moment he was having a pint, the next he was gone. We split up and walked around the town.

An hour later, at the bar, Sarah was on the verge of tears. John was furious. Sean and his brother talked of calling the guards. I went out to the van, to get a bottle for Sarah, and found Padraigh asleep under a blanket on the back seat. I roused him and told him that people were worried, that we'd been looking for him. He turned on his side and stared at me. How can you find a man that doesn't exist? he said, and went back under the blanket. I noticed a plastic bag near his feet. I opened it and found a tangled mess of white string, bits of weed, paper shreds, ice cream sticks, bark splinters, white flowers, the shell of a beetle.

Sarah, John and Sean worked hard to lure him from the van, and when they came in, Padraigh could have been sleep-walking, his legs barely moving, eyes vacant and glazed. John walked past me and said I don't know how the fuck this man is going to play tonight. Sean took Padraigh into the toilet to freshen him up. Sarah ordered whiskies and we sat around a table, smoking and not talking. I said Sarah, maybe you're drinking too much. She said James, why don't you keep your fucking thoughts to yourself.

Sean came to the table alone. Padraigh was at the bar, nursing a steaming glass. I went to him, ordered the same.

Where did you go, Padraigh?

I was walking.

Do you want to talk about it?

The walking?

If you like. About anything really.

Fuck off.

You're the second person to tell me that tonight.

Then maybe you need telling. Padraigh sat back and down. He seemed to go further into his clothes. Who are you anyway?

It was a fair question. I'm not sure, I said, and meant it.

What do you want?

That's a bit general, isn't it? Can you be more specific?

I thought I told you to fuck off.

That's more like it. Alright. I want to be with Sarah. Padraigh laughed and slurped his drink.

I want to drink this hot whiskey. I want you all to have a great time tonight, I said.

I'm not playing shite with those lunatics.

John put his hand over Padraigh's eyes and said Can you guess who this is, Paddy boy?

You can fuck off too, Padraigh said.

That's my man, said John, and came around to my side. How's it goin'? he asked softly.

Before I could answer, he said You'd best be layin' off about the drink, with Sarah. She's a bit fragile, like.

We're all a bit fragile, aren't we?

That's true enough. Listen, I agree, she's been putting the drink away something fierce. Has been for ages. I

said something myself, once. Twice, actually. As you can
see, it's done a lot of good. Anyway, Jim, please, keep
a lid on it for tonight, for a while.

Alright . . .

John stepped back, whacked my shoulder and said
theatrically That's my man! He leaned over the bar,
raised his hand. Some more of those hot amber demons,
if you please!

Frankie Power arrived carrying a fine-grained, well-
travelled wooden case. Padraigh and I had joined the
others. There were warm greetings, and when Sarah
introduced me, she put her arm around my waist. I'm
sorry for shouting, she said.

Sean asked to see the pipes. Frankie placed his case
on the table and threw the brass locks. When he opened
it, it was as if some dismembered wood spider of massive
proportions had been laid to rest on velvet, its legs –
some missing – were arranged lengthwise over a furred
abdomen, its undersides plated with silver tongue-
shapes. Below these, a white mandala: current-breaker,
spider-eye. Chanters, bellows, regulators, drone. Frankie
lifted these curious pieces from the case, chose a chanter
and affixed it to the air bag, putting the spider back
together.

Before he played, he took the reed from the chanter
and held it up to the light. I saw a V-shape in the
polished wedge of cane. Frankie put the reed to his lips
and sucked in, making a short, high rasping sound. The
reed has a crow in it, he said. That's good. Then he sat
down, strapped on the bellows, put his arm through a
sling, and started to play. People stopped talking and
came over. The bar lights held him there, lifting and
lowering the chanter as his fingers worked the holes. An

old sound. A history of weeping and love letters scratched into parchment leaked from the pipes. Sarah was rocking, smiling. John and Sean were leaning forward, watching Frankie's hands. Padraigh was sitting up, one hand around his pint, looking over Frankie's head. When the last notes trailed away, Frankie said This crow is strong and free, and unshouldered the bellows. The applause was loud and sustained.

Frankie Power joined the band for a set of reels, then led them away into a slow air. He completed the night playing solo: an air called 'Boys on the Tide', and a hornpipe he named 'Light in Connemara'. The pipes an extension of his body, the drone and back-of-the-throat ache and lament of all the players and variations on themes and tunes that went into his wonderful playing.

There were posters for this gig and others on the pub doors and walls – towns, dates, and a woman's face in silhouette, with the word *Lapwing* growing out of her hair.

A RIDER WITH NEWS

———•◦•◦•———

T RAVELLING UP the west coast, I was roadie and occasional mediator in arguments mild and fierce. We were making our way through sessions and gigs to Inishmore, the largest of the Aran Islands, where the band had arranged to play a couple of sets with musicians from Inishmore as well as Inishmaan and Inisheer, the two smaller islands.

That Sarah was an alcoholic took time to reach me. Hard drinking can be passed on as a common thing, prompting a word or two of warning or advice from a friend. Often the response is defensive, dismissive. I'd not said anything about her drinking since that time in the pub at Milltown Malbay. I hadn't told Sarah why I took tablets. When she asked, while we were driving – she'd seen me take them in the rear-view mirror – I said I had a headache. From that moment on I became careful, watchful, swallowing them in the bathroom, or some distance from the others, when we were on the road. It was the same as hiding bottles. My secret was a burden, but I could not let it go. I was afraid to tell her. Schizophrenic. What would she make of that word?

Lying in bed, your lover turns to you and says I've
something to tell you don't be scared I should have told
you ages ago will you try to understand? You can feel
her body tense, hear her head begin to reel. I am a
schizophrenic. The room darkens and the bedclothes
gather themselves into a cold line dividing two people,
one who has unburdened himself, the other wondering
who the hell this is beside her, this man, this rider with
terrible news.

MERCY

PADRAIGH HAD stopped talking, though he spoke with his flute. If anything, his playing was getting better. Each session and gig he let it rip. We still spoke to him as if he were going to respond. We continued, around a room or in the van, telling stories and sharing news with a man sitting bolt upright or sleeping long stretches, his breathing uneven and loud.

Standing behind a wall at the Cliffs of Moher, overlooking a sea with wind-ripped troughs and furrows in slate-grey water, seafoam blowing up the cliff face to fly like suds over our heads, I decided to tell Sarah. I didn't know what words to use, or how to string them together. She was leaning against me, her long mohair scarf wrapped around our necks and shoulders. She'd just asked if I was happy. I told her that I loved her, and she kissed me and said I wish you'd say it more often. I've been aching for you to tell me. I love you too. Let's tell each other whenever we feel like it, okay? We can never hear it enough. James, I'm just so on edge.

I started speaking. Sarah moved away to look at me

and the scarf went with her, unravelling until it flapped and sailed out over the path. She reeled it in and looked at me.

I wanted to tell you before, but I couldn't, I said, aware of how thin my voice was sounding.

Sarah didn't speak or move. She held the scarf and waited. When I didn't continue, she shrugged and angled her head, still waiting.

I told her about my illness. I covered years in a few sentences. Voices, Lars, Headlights, Doctors, Tablets, Hospital, Ireland.

Sarah turned to the wall and looked over. She said Jesus, James, and then she said So what happened at the river was part of it then? It wasn't an isolated thing? It's been happening for years?

Yes.

Why didn't you tell me? We're this far down the road and you haven't said a thing. I don't believe this.

There were no words within miles of my mouth.

Sarah slapped the lichen-patched wall and leaned hard into it. Her feet came off the ground and she tipped herself over until the blood went into her face. I went to her and put my hands on her waist, but she pulled away from me. When she came back over and stood up, she put her hands to her face. What I need to know is how this has changed things between us, she said. I need to know that very soon. Now, in fact.

I'm sorry. I know I should have told you before.

Sarah laughed. At least, her voice had the sound of laughter in it. Then she said James, please, you have to tell me everything. She turned back to the wall and looked over. I thought you were learning how to trust your fear.

I was. I am.

Sarah threw the scarf into a mud puddle, lifted her skirts and climbed over the wall. There was a ledge about four feet wide outside the wall, ending in a ragged, weed-lined drop-off. She faced the ocean and pressed herself hard into the stone. Are you coming? she said.

What do you mean?

Just climb over the wall, James. I need you to stand beside me.

I moved and had no sense of moving. I climbed over the dripping stone and stood beside her. A wave boomed and sent a foamcloud over our heads, into our faces.

How much do you trust me? Sarah said, her voice breaking.

I looked at her and couldn't tell if the water was from the sea or her eyes.

I told her that I trusted her with my life, which may have been true.

A good answer, she said, and took my hand. She stepped away from the wall and lowered herself down. I went with her. She let go of my hand and lay down on her stomach, her head out over the edge.

I lay beside her and looked down. Vertigo sent wavespirals into my head and chest and I was upside down rightwayup breathing help me.

Sarah was talking. I found her voice and stayed with it. But her body was moving out further over the edge. I moved with her. When our ribs were pressed into the mud, our arms hanging free in wind blasts and icy spray, Sarah said It's this easy to come close to death. And it's this easy to step away.

I started to say something, but she said I'm angry and very sad that you felt you couldn't tell me this before,

James. Is there anything else? Do you want to dredge your heart for more details? Now's the time.

I said I had no more to say, and Sarah said Well, I'll leave you if you're lying to me. Then she pushed herself back from the edge and sat up. I stayed there, the cold mud coming through my shirt, my face numb.

When I made it back to the wall, Sarah was walking down the hill towards the car park, her scarf trailing like the end of a backward glance.

From the cliffs we drove inland to Lisdoonvarna, site of Ireland's most famous folk festival.

In Riordan's pub, at the end of a hornpipe, Padraigh lifted his flute into the air and, threading it between his fingers as a band leader might revolve a baton, yelled Mercy! then he settled back into his chair and stared at the floor. Someone at the bar echoed him, and the place erupted with laughter. John leaned over and said something to Padraigh, but he did not respond or move. Sarah announced a new tune, and Padraigh went into it, playing beautifully as if nothing had happened.

Sitting at the bar, a log fire throwing amber light on the wall, we sat talking quietly with the locals. I was sitting next to Padraigh when a young woman approached him, sat down and said I love the way you play. He looked at her. She said How long have you been playing? Padraigh turned back to the bar, lifted his pint and drank slowly. He wiped a line of cream from his mouth with the back of his hand. The woman said Did I say something wrong?

I motioned for her to come away, and when we were standing at the fire I told her that Padraigh had stopped talking, that it might be a good idea if she didn't push him. She looked over at Padraigh and said That's fine,

I don't mind if he doesn't talk, then returned to the bar.

She bought a drink, touched her glass to Padraigh's pint, and said Here's to you, Mr flute player. Padraigh stared at a wall of bottles. The woman said My name is Gloria. I play mandolin. She leaned in close. I heard her say into Padraigh's hair Do you want to come back home? I live just down the road. Padraigh didn't move. She said It's okay, I live alone. We can just listen to music and drink if you like. Padraigh drained his pint, stood up and walked to the door, where he stood running his fingers through his hair. The woman went to join him.

Sarah moved quickly. She caught Gloria by the arm and drew her aside. They had words. Sarah motioned with a sweep of her arm to the others sitting at the bar, and then nodded towards Padraigh. Gloria said I think he's old enough to make up his own mind, and she went to him. Sarah was stranded. Everyone was watching now. Gloria opened the door, took Padraigh by the hand, and led him outside.

Sarah followed them. She shouted that we were leaving for Galway first thing in the morning, and to make sure that Padraigh was here. When she returned, she moved slowly back to the bar. I don't like this, she said. Sean got up. He said I'm going to follow them, to see where she lives. The barman said No need, I can tell you, and he sketched a map on a napkin. He assured us that Gloria was responsible, that Padraigh was in good hands. John said Maybe a good shagging is what the boy needs.

We were sitting in the small dining room next morning, drinking strong tea. Sean was deep into a description of salmon fishing when Padraigh came in. He sat down, rolled a smoke, and reached for a cup. He slurped loudly at his tea. I saw a scribble of white string lighting the pocket of his trousers. Glances were exchanged. Sean picked up his story: As kids, we'd lean out over Salmon Weir Bridge and watch fish finning in the lights on their way to Lough Corrib.

Padraigh said This toast is cold. Can we get some more?

As if the room had been holding its breath for years and was now ready to exhale, there was a palpable shift in mood and sound. We laughed.

Will youse stop that God-awful noise and get more toast, Padraigh said. You're a bunch of kids altogether.

John said Good to hear you again, Paddy boy.

Padraigh said You've not heard anything yet, and blew a perfect smoke ring over the table.

GALWAY

I 'D BEEN FEELING tense since we'd left Lisdoonvarna. Sarah had noticed this, and mentioned it. I dismissed it as a headache, and returned to a speeding view of stone walls and fields.

We'd booked into a hotel in the city – one that Sarah and John had stayed in many times. The fact that Michael had almost certainly been there too was a fine mist of annoyance around my head, though I said nothing.

I found the book Stephanie had given me, and opened it in my head. Galway. Lough Corrib like a horse with one leg placed before it, its mane tied into three neat sections, its hind legs missing. The names of towns like isolated notes from a slow air: Oranmore, Barna, Spiddal, Kilmaine, Athenry. The Partry Mountains rising over Lough Mask with their green height-lines casting shadows on a young man's imagination and longing. I saw Stephanie sitting forward on a bench at the train station, telling herself the story of how her father had drowned in Galway Bay.

I'd been thinking of her, and of Tina. Their names

arrived and I went with them into fragments of talk,
taste and touch. They were there, in each discussion of
love, and what love means. Although I'd told Sarah
about their lives, about how they had changed me,
several times during our late-night talks Sarah had asked
questions about them. I didn't mind. I wanted to tell
her what I could, but found it hard to respond. I fell
back on freeze-frames, on hand-held snapshots when the
light was failing. Their names placed borders around
what could be said. I offered brief sketches, fleeting
portraits of complex women, and Sarah took this to be
a sign of my unwillingness to open up about my life,
my history. She said that for us to know each other well,
we should be honest, to speak in detail about important
issues, especially about those we had loved. I took
exception to her use of the past tense, saying that I *still*
loved them. This prompted accusations of my not being
able to dwell in the present, that I was living with the
ghosts of love. I tried to explain. I said they can't be
defined by anecdote or a detail from a painting of the
past. Try, Sarah had said, but I floundered. One woman
missing, one dead, and now a woman beside me, casting
for news of what was held at the centre of my body,
caught there in the way I move and speak and live. I
became angry, and told her she was welcome to let her
past lovers enter our lives at any time; that she was lucky
to be able to speak so freely of them. She hadn't asked
me about Stephanie or Tina since, and I hadn't
mentioned the men she had known. They were there
though, and sometimes we saw them – men and women
with familiar names in the outlines of their bodies,
listening from the periphery, breathing quietly, waiting
for a chance to make flesh and blood from what
memory carves into the tongue.

If I'd told Sarah that I wanted to visit the grave of a woman I still loved, would she have objected? Would she see this as another binding of details from the past that I'd not attended to? Are the dead more accountable than the missing? Do they offer discretionary privileges to the curious heart? Are sympathy and acceptance the sole domain of those laid out in their terminals: plot or wall plaque, mud-ash on some beach? Can the missing lay claim to such territory, or are they spared these attentions because of the possibility they are still in the world? The missing are buried until their files are closed. They haunt the waking and sleeping of those in their long shadows. For some of these, no dog-walking line-search could locate them. They have gone beyond the range of forensics and ballistics to settle as the dust of memory. The dead are certifiably present. They are more durable than grief. The missing are a lifeline to sadness and black wonder. What is unresolved is another name for pain.

After checking into the hotel, I walked around slowly, taking photos and stopping for pints in old pubs with elaborate signs and emblems carved into their walls.

Late in the afternoon I called Finbar from a phone box. He said We held a mass for you. It was grand. You'd have loved it. We got legless and told Australian jokes. We filed past your open casket and recited poems. His tone changed, and he said Listen Jimmy, I'm sorry about that night up in Cork. We were drunk. Can we forget it now? I said I'd already forgotten it, and Finbar told me there had been no drama at work, that he was keeping the management informed of my recovery. He suggested I look up a friend of his – a woman who owned a florist in the city. I said I'd think about it, and took down the address. There was a long silence, and he asked how things were with Sarah. I told him we were married, with a child on the way, and that I wanted him to be the godfather. He said You're full of shit . . . aren't you? After I'd assured him of my capacity for holding faeces, he said You'll be going to the Aran Islands, of course?

Yes, tomorrow. The band are playing at a pub on Inishmore.

Right, I'm on my way, he said, and laughed. That's gorgeous country alright. Make sure you get a bike and wheel your way around the island. Unbelievable place.

A truck stopped nearby and men started unloading beer kegs from the back.

Sounds like you're gettin' a few beers ready for the evening. Then he said So tell me, is Sarah drinking much?

Yes. She's drinking all the time.

That's terrible, he said, and coughed. Well, you both take care now. And you'd better let me know if there's anything I can do, you know, when Sarah's time comes. A godfather. Jaysus, I'd better start calling the boys and gettin' things ready for the party. Don't suppose the little one will mind a bunch of standover men and assassins being there. He laughed loudly and said I'll see you, so.

I said goodbye as a keg crashed and settled.

I followed narrow backstreets lined with shops pressed together like book covers facing out from a dark, winding bookcase. Down past gutted warehouses where the fishmarket used to be. At the end of a street near the river I found the florist.

A woman was arranging flowers, pulling stems and shaping flowerheads. She stepped back to assess her work and asked if I needed help. I told her I'd spoken to

Finbar. She smiled and undid her apron. How is that wicked man?

As wicked as ever.

Come out back, I'll put the kettle on.

Irene took a sign with *Back in half an hour* written on it, and hung it inside the door.

I've different signs, she said. Depending on how long I need to go out or stay put and ignore people.

We sat at a table patterned with curls of ribbon, stem cuttings and petals. Her name was Irene Ryan. She'd known Finbar since high school. She told me about his wild nature, about how they'd almost been sweethearts. We drank tea, and then she brought out a bottle of Paddy. Several glasses later, looking out over the docks through a huge window, Irene said There's an Australian couple a few doors down. They've a bookshop. There's also a young Australian woman staying at Bryant's, a pub on Coughlin Road. She works at the pub and lives upstairs. A great girl. A writer. What's her name now? I've heard it alright. She's always carrying books when I see her round the town. She reads poems at the nights they have at a cafe. They're not too bad.

Irene put a decent band of amber into our glasses and said Are you staying long?

No, we leave for Inishmore in the morning.

Oh! You'll love it. In fact, the girl, the poet, goes out there. Stays at a place. Keeps to herself. The islanders must be wondering who she is. People talk.

Are you sure you can't remember her name?

Irene thought and said No, I'm sorry.

What does she do on the island? Did you say she stays on Inishmore?

I did. What does she do? Writes, I think. Takes photographs. She's very pretty.

What does she look like?

You're a curious article. She's slim, not so tall, long black hair. Very pretty.

How old would you say she is?

That's hard to tell. She looks different each time I see her, if you know what I mean. Some people are like that. Shape-changers. Irene looked out the window. I don't know.

Have you spoken to her?

I have. I said Where are you from, in Australia? Sydney, she said. I told her I've relatives there, in Petersham. Sydney's a big place of course, but I didn't push. I'm a firm believer in letting people give what they want, when they talk. So, she's from Sydney. From the city.

Irene paused for breath, poured more whiskey, raised her glass. Here's to you. Here's to Australia. Are you from Sydney?

Yes.

Where in Sydney?

The city.

Irene waited, glass poised, eyebrows raised. When no map of the suburbs of Sydney fanned open from my mouth, she said It's getting late. I really should take that sign down.

At the door she said I hope you have fun on Inishmore. Hire a bicycle. It's the best way to see the island.

In our room at the hotel that afternoon, after Sarah had played a lovely slow air on a penny whistle, we sat in high-backed wooden chairs at the window, cuddling and kissing. Then we sat watching the street, not talking.

I made some coffee, and then I told Sarah what the woman at the florist had said. I told her how I wanted to find out if Stephanie was on the island. To put her to rest, once and for all, I said, or to find out what had been happening since the day she left the antique shop.

Sarah sat quietly as I told her my thoughts and plans, chain-smoking, crossing and uncrossing her legs. I said Just imagine if she's really there, after all this time. What a story.

Sarah crushed out her cigarette and got up from the chair. She reached into her bag and lifted out a bottle of Bushmills and poured a large amount into one of the bar fridge glasses.

Here's to the ghost bitch, she said, and tossed it back.

She poured another. Tossed it back.

Could I have one of those?

Fuck you.

She placed the glass on the bed-head. She did not look at me. I'll be down at the bar, she said, and left the room.

I lay on the bed. Medication might have been keeping many things at arm's reach, but a complete loss of tact and respect weren't one of them. In the moment's heat I had let my thoughts go. Had I expected Sarah to be interested, to respond enthusiastically to this information? The thought that I might be acting cruelly hadn't occurred to me. I felt sleep approaching. It had serrated edges. As it claimed me, my legs kicked out and a surge of dull pain went through my chest.

I woke when Sarah got into bed. I asked her what time it was.

It's too late, she said, and shifted around, moving to the far side of the bed.

I woke again to the telephone ringing. I reached over where Sarah had been sleeping. She was gone. I knocked a glass from the bed-head and said hello.

A man asked if Sarah was there. I said Is there any

message? and he said No, I have to speak to her.

I hung up.

I heard splashing in the bathroom. James, was that the telephone?

I turned on the light. It was just after midnight. I said no, and sat on the edge of the bed. The phone ran again. I picked up the receiver and let it fall back to the cradle.

She came out dripping, clutching a towel. That *was* the telephone, she said. What's going on?

You're hearing things.

Who called, James? The Missing Persons unit? Have they some information for you?

Two people in a hotel room, staring at each other, not speaking. One dripping and shivering. One doing the same, on the inside.

The phone rang and Sarah moved quickly. She snatched the receiver up.

Hello?

There was a long silence. I looked at her exposed back. It was glowing red from the hot water, and bright lines traced her spine, catching in the loop of towel around her waist. Her hair was nibbed and dripping at the edges.

Yes, she said. Yes it was. No, it's not that.

Sarah moved from foot to foot. She looked over her shoulder, then turned back and said I can't talk now, alright? I don't know. I can't tell you that. Yes. I said I don't know. Alright, I will.

She replaced the receiver as if she were lowering a crucial link to a small, unstable freestanding structure, and said I'm going out for a while.

Who was that?

A friend.

What did he want?

Sarah didn't answer. She gathered some clothes from her bag and went into the bathroom. When she emerged, she said If you're lucky, there might be a fisherman down at the harbour who can take you over to Inishmore now. A couple of bottles might get you a ticket. Save you the agony of having to wait for tomorrow to get the boat to your darling.

After she'd left, I stared at the darkwood bed-head until it was asking to be reshaped. I obliged by putting my fist through the wood and splintering the knuckles of my right hand.

Morning came and I did not welcome it. The skin on my right hand was broken and still bleeding. My knuckles ached.

I'd been awake since Sarah left. It was rain-dark and miserable. Nine a.m. I went to the window and rolled a cigarette. Rainfans on the glass turned the street into a watercolour with vague shapes of blacked-out people and cars moving through it. The sound of tyres tearing through the slick. A woman stepped off the kerb below and wavered out over the road, coming and going as strips and flares of rain angled through her. Ahead of her, a brown shape moved quickly, as if her shadow had appeared, defying the need for sunlight to make it real. I lifted the window and cold wind burned my face. The woman was walking a large dog through a small park. It strained against its lead and stopped at trees, benches. Beyond them, on the other side of the park, the lights of shops were portside windows in some impossible, anchored liner.

Someone knocked on the door. I opened it to find Sean, who was eating a slice of toast, a coffee cup in his other hand. He looked past me into the room. Where's Sarah?

I don't know. She left early this morning. Said she was going out for a while.

Jesus Christ, Sean said. What have you done to your hand?

I said I hit the bed, and Sean shook his head.

You've been at it, haven't you. You maniacs. Did she say where she was going?

No. Someone called. A man. She said she was going out.

Right, he said. Not much we can do. At least for a while. Have you eaten?

No.

Come on then. Have a shower first, you look terrible. I'll tell the others. We'll be down in the dining room. Alright?

Sean turned to leave, then turned back. Don't worry, he said. She'll be alright.

Sean, do you think it was Michael?

I don't know. Do you?

I don't want to think about it.

Good idea. See you downstairs.

When I entered the dining room, John and Sean were heads together, talking. Padraigh was writing something on a napkin.

Coffee and toast, Jimmy boy? John said, easing away from Sean and sitting back in his chair, a line of smoke rising from his rested hand. I might have to feed you, from the look of your hand.

I was about to explain, when John raised his hand. No need. Sean's filled me in.

John took an audible breath. Right. Two things. Sarah might be a volatile woman, but she's solid. She'd never compromise the band. For anything. So she'll be back. Second. If it's Michael she's with, there's a good reason. It might even be for the best. If he's come all this way, and contacted her, and she's willingly gone to see him, they might be working things out, you know?

I felt a hot pressure in my head. Speaking was painful. If Michael's come all this way, I said, do you really think he's come to hold her hand? The pressure was behind my eyes now.

Padraigh lifted his head. Hold my hand, he said.

Sean said John's right. We know her. It's hard for you, but sit tight, James.

We have to be on that boat this afternoon. She'll be on it, John said. I know her.

I said some stupid things yesterday. I told Sarah that Stephanie, a woman I used to know in Sydney, might be living on Inishmore. She lost it. She was drinking heavily, down at the bar, wasn't she?

She was, said Padraigh.

She was, said John. Wouldn't talk, when I asked her what was wrong, like.

John patted his coat and trouser pockets. Have you any of that auld tobacco, James? I'm out.

I handed him the pouch and he said Sarah's told me about that woman, Stephanie. When she mentioned her she was a bit pissed off, but I thought nothing of it, if you know what I mean. A bit of harmless jealousy.

He struck a match, lit up and inhaled. You're sure there's not more to the picture? It's none of my business, of course. Tell me to shut the fuck up if you want to, but I guess you could say I'm concerned. I care about the both of youse.

There are some things. You know about some of them. You've seen us. There's the drink, and I've got

318

problems too. We've all got problems, haven't we?

You're right about that, Sean said. Anyone want more coffee?

Returning from a walk in light, steady rain, I saw Sarah coming up the road. Reaching the hotel, she leaned heavily on the wall and lowered her face to her hand, as if steadying herself before going through the door.

When I entered the room she was lying on the bed. I could hear her breathing from the doorway.

Please don't ask me any questions, James.

We've been worried sick about you, I said, and lay down beside her. I put my arm around her waist and she said Don't.

As we lay side by side, not touching or talking, the phone rang. It was for Sarah. The man's voice was slow and musical, not like Michael at all. Sarah nodded and lit a cigarette, then she started crying.

When I asked her who had called, she said The guards, and crushed out her cigarette. When I asked for more information, she said Not now, and lay down on the bed.

At the door I looked at her. She was lying on her side, strands of hair across her face, her left hand over her mouth as if she were trying to keep from saying something.

INISHMORE

S TANDING AT THE stern of the boat, Galway Harbour
thinning to dark shapes and lines, I gave in to
thoughts that had kept me awake all night. Sarah had
turned over and touched my face. She must have been
asleep, because suddenly she took her hand away. When
I touched her shoulder, she moved away even further.

I looked down into white wavelines pouring from
the side of the boat, and followed them as they fanned
out into the wake.

Sarah was sitting inside, between Sean and Padraigh.
She pulled a half-bottle from her coat pocket. She started
to unscrew the cap, paused, removed it and drank.

Sarah's voice came and went on the wind and the
droning surge of the boat's engines. Somewhere in the
midst of her anger I heard I don't suppose, and Maybe
you should, and then Your pathetic mystery girl.

The crossing took three hours. I stayed on deck. Sean
and Padraigh came out and stared at the wake. Sean said
Sarah's in a black mood. Padraigh, whose talking was
becoming faster and loaded with strange images, said
That's right, maudlin, begorrah. Then he laughed.

On Inishmore, as we walked along the jetty past fishing boats knocking at their moorings, Sarah strode off ahead, swinging her fiddle case. John fell in beside me.

That's a woman on a mission, he said.

Up the road past a long, slate-roofed pub angling out over the water, its foundations barnacled and strung with ribbons of weed. Small, low-roofed shops, their windows lit with handicrafts, the curtains drawn to the sides, tied with cloth and hanging like white sheaves of wheat. The houses in the main port town had either slate or iron roofs. There were none of the small, thatched-roof cottages I'd read about. I mentioned this to John, and he said They're here, but out of town, on the backroads. Out where the wind never stops.

The wind had been constant since we stepped from the boat. Miles of salty, skin-finding wind that came off the bay, raking the hair and stinging the eyes.

A blue van stopped. The driver got out and asked if we needed a ride. Sarah told him we'd not far to go, and he said I'll see you. He pointed to Sarah's fiddle case, and looked at the other boxes and cases.

You'd be the band then?

Padraigh said Lapwing.

The man smiled and said We've been waiting for you. Good job. It's tonight is it?

No, tomorrow night, Sarah said, and picked up her suitcase.

I'll be there, the man said. My cousin from Inishmaan is playing. He's a box player.

Right then, John said, and started walking.

Right then, the man said and climbed into his van.

We watched him go. Padraigh elbowed Sean gently in the ribs and smiled. A crow in a blue van wants the music, he said.

At the top of a steep hill, Sarah opened a gate to a large white house with field-facing windows and flowers burning in small window boxes. I stood aside as the others went into the house, and looked out over fields stone-covered and lined with low, bluestone fences. Cattle moved slowly through one, heads down into the wind. Clouds with dark blue undersides were massing on the horizon.

When I found Sarah she was unpacking her suitcase and arranging things on the bed.

Maybe we'd be better off in different rooms, she said, without looking at me.

I'd like to stay with you. To be here with you.

Are you going to ask me any questions?

I think you might owe me an explanation.

She looked at me. I know, she said. Can you give me a little more time?

I need a hug, I said, and moved to her.

Sarah moved away. I need some sleep, she said, sweeping clothes and toiletries from the bed.

I left her there. A different room. A similar scene. I was hollowed out and could hardly move.

The house had been extended to make room for tourists over the summer months. Sarah knew the owner, Mrs O'Flaherty. She was a big woman in a dark blue cardigan, which she buttoned to the neck. Her long black skirts swishing as she moved about the kitchen and sunroom, cooking and cleaning, arranging and rearranging furniture. Her heavy black boots could be heard all over the house. I guessed that this was the house Sarah and Michael used to stay in. The new section had a high ceiling and slate floor, with huge windows in the sunroom and a long table in the dining room, attended by high-backed wooden chairs. Our rooms were modern too, with clean, paint-smelling walls, carpeted floors and built-in wardrobes. Mrs O'Flaherty showed us around the old part of the house, where she lived. The fireplace had a wide, rough-worked whitestone border and an elaborate fire-grate with diamond shapes on the metal. Above the mantelpiece a framed Madonna kept watch, her eyebrows dark and thick, her hands together, fingers laced like white spiders mating, her heart a luminous red light in her chest. The wallpaper had tiny pale blue flowers repeating themselves from skirting board to ceiling. In one corner of the kitchen, a green panelled door. Above this, near where the roof sloped down, another green door – a copy of the other, though in miniature, set well above head-level. I wondered what kind of fabled guests this woman had entertained.

We were invited for tea and cakes in the sunroom, which was darkening quickly as the clouds I'd seen moved over the harbour.

Sarah's mood must have lightened, because she smiled when I pulled a chair up for her. When my hand lingered on the nape of her neck, she did not turn away.

Mrs O'Flaherty sat in a big wooden chair she'd carried in from the kitchen. She poured tea, cut the cake, and made sure that everyone was settled. She turned on a couple of reading lamps, which threw interlocking cones of dusty yellow light over the room. Then she began telling stories about the island. Sarah nodded and filled in some gaps, showing her knowledge. Mrs O'Flaherty warmed to Sarah's commentary, going off on new thoughts, touring the water and the land, hundreds of years, returning to emphasise some initial point, then moving off again. We went with her. More tea was made and poured, another cake brought out.

We heard of how Brendan Behan, on his second visit

to the island, had taken a small party of lads out to the southwest end, in the rain, each man with a bottle of something you'd never find in a shop. They climbed to the highest point, behind the last wall of Dun Aengus, the great fort, and sat on the edge, hundreds of feet above the sea. Behan started a story by shouting a sentence into the wind, and each man had to continue the tale, down the line. The story flowed back and forth, as did the poteen. Some men rose to go. Behan threatened them, saying if they wanted to taste the stirrings of immortality, then they must remain to finish the story. They stayed out there on that rain-lashed ledge for hours, the lads afraid to leave, completely legless, the story going God knows where.

Two of the boys finally said they'd had enough, and left. Brendan cursed their backs, and told them to expect trouble. The others stayed on, drinking and continuing the tale.

Mrs O'Flaherty passed Sarah her tea cup. So now there was a lovely man, Sean Mulkerrins. He was one who'd been out with Brendan Behan. He came down with the flu, and then got pneumonia and died. And John Muldoon, he was drowned a week later when a weighted rope uncoiling from the curragh's belly caught his ankle. He was pulled under. They were out at night, and when they dragged him back he was blue and gone.

Sarah said Is it true that Brendan Behan wrote his name with stones in one of the fields?

That's true enough, Mrs O'Flaherty said. But you know, there's cattle out there who don't know a famous writer from a wildflower, and they kicked the stones away. Some say it was the grieving friends and family of those poor boys who removed his name. I don't know.

Padraigh stood up. He took a deep breath and started quoting from *Borstal Boy*. John said Here we go now. Mrs O'Flaherty said Wait, and hurried off into the house. She came back with a dog-eared copy of the book, and she and Padraigh sat together, taking turns reading chapters for the next half-hour.

I'd heard Irish spoken before, in Cork, but only as examples of famous sayings or blessings. But here, in a harbourside, woodpanelled pub, with firelight glazing faces and pints, I heard a new language, watching the mouths of the men move to form the words. Sarah, John and Padraigh went deep into a long, animated discussion. John told us later that he never considered fishing to be a suitable subject for poetry, but that these men had spoken lyrically and indelibly about nets and ropes and traps. Padraigh made up a poem on the spot, in Irish, about fishing, and a whiskey was placed on his table.

Afterwards, Sarah and I were at the bar, drinking without speaking. Then she said James, the man who called was Michael. He wanted so much to talk to me. I didn't know what to do. I couldn't talk in the room. I felt I had to see him, to know, for good, that it's over.

But he fucking well near killed you in Cork.

Sarah touched her face, running her fingers over where Michael had hit her.

I went to him to find the truth.

And did you find it?

I think so. James, Michael was so sorry for hurting me. I met him at a pub near the river mouth. He looked ragged and thin. It was desperate. I've never seen him so thin. His beard had food and ash in it. We left the pub after a couple of drinks and walked for a while, mostly by the river. It was ... Sarah took a sip of whiskey. It was so intense. Then we walked back to his car and drove out to Fallon. We used to go there. It's a small place with lovely old stone houses by the water. There's an abandoned mill there, too, and that's where we parked. We got out and walked down to the water. We were standing near a broken fence, and Michael got onto his knees in the mud and told me he loved me. He held my hands and begged me to come back to him.

What did you say?

I told him I thought it was too late. That I was with you.

Jesus. What did he say?

He didn't say anything. He started crying.

When she lifted her glass, her hand was shaking violently.

So anyway, when I reached down to put my hands under his arms, to help him up, he said You're killing me, and twisted away.

What happened next?

It was already daylight by then. Some people had come down to the water. When they saw Michael kneeling there, they turned and walked away. I stepped away too. I said We'd best be getting back. Michael didn't move. He was sitting on his heels, shaking his head slowly. I went to the car and got in.

Driving back, I couldn't look at him. I was so scared of what he might say or do. When he stopped the car, a few blocks from the hotel, I did look at him. I saw a tiny blue beetle come out of his beard and crawl over his chin. As I was getting out of the car, he said You're going back to him, aren't you. I didn't answer him. I didn't know what to say. I was scared of telling him.

When I didn't speak, he reached over and opened the glove compartment. I opened the door and ran.

So have you come back? To me?

James, it was something I had to do. Please forgive me for being so reckless.

I wrapped her up and kissed her hair. I told her that I'd been awake all night, imagining them together in a bed somewhere. I did not repeat my question.

Padraigh, John and Sean were playing cards with some men at a table by the window. The room smelled of cigarettes and body odour and alcohol.

I'd already decided not to mention the drinking again to Sarah — at least not while we were on the island. Now it seemed even more appropriate to say nothing. I was about to kiss her, to draw her close and kiss her mouth, when someone started playing the fiddle. Sarah turned and said How wonderful, and the moment was lost.

The player was young, with long black hair and severe-looking black serge trousers and a black waistcoat. His dark blue shirt was buttoned at the neck. He stepped backwards and forwards, leaning and righting, his eyes closed, his sawing hand a black and white line of publight in the smoky air.

This feller's very good, Sarah said, smiling. I hope he'll be playing with us tomorrow.

He started into another reel, and Sarah asked if I wanted to dance. I said no. She jumped from her stool and stepped out onto the floor, weaving in and out of the music's tight lines, her head thrown back, her throat gleaming. A man joined her, and they worked the reel with a blur of feet and hands. Others joined them. The young player moved to the wall, giving the dancers room. A guitar appeared and was strummed furiously.

Then a melodeon breathed in and out, giving more substance to the dance. I was taken in by this raw spell, into which men and women stepped and laughed as others, at their tables or standing along the wall, clapped and stomped and yelled encouragement.

Time dissolved. The fire was fed. The music continued. I went out for air and found a wall of rain so heavy the masts of boats at the harbour were like broken lines of light seen through frosted glass.

As I was standing in the doorway, rubbing my hands, Sean came out and leaned in beside me.

You two are getting on then?

Perhaps.

Sean unwrapped a pack of cigarettes and offered me one. We lit up and looked out into the rain, at the shapes of boats and the dark wood of the jetty.

Have you been watching Paddy at all?

I said I hadn't, and Sean said When we go back in, watch what he does with his right hand. It's a weird thing altogether. He started doing it on the boat, on the way over. I thought he was just being Paddy, you know, one of his funny character traits, like. But now I'm worried. Let me know what you think.

Sarah was dancing again. I sat at the bar and looked over to where John and Padraigh were sitting. The other men had left the table. Padraigh was sitting up stiffly. John was watching Sarah dance. Sean was standing in the far corner of the pub, against the wall. Padraigh twisted quickly in his seat and his right hand shot into the air, then came down to rest in his lap. I looked over at Sean and his eyebrows were raised. When I looked at John, he was watching Padraigh intently. Sean joined me at the bar.

You saw it then?

Yes. Do you think it's a nervous reaction or something?

God knows, but it's very fucking weird. Thing is, how can you say anything? I mean, like, Paddy, why are you stickin' your hand into the air?

John saw us talking and came over.

Sean said Don't look at Paddy. He's watching us.

Jesus, John said. What's he doing now?

I lifted my pint and said Still watching us.

John said He's doing it more and more. Every few minutes.

Sarah pressed in between us and said Are you lads having a band meeting without me?

Sean told her what was happening, and not to look at him.

I glanced over and he was still staring at us. His right hand went into the air and came down. He just did it again, I said.

Sarah turned to the bar. He's coming over, she said, and called for a drink.

Padraigh stood beside Sean, his hands in his pockets, watching the fire.

How's it going, Paddy? Sean asked.

Padraigh's right shoulder jumped and settled. Are youse talking about me?

Not at all, Jaysus! John said. We were just about to call you over. We're trying to figure out if we can match the quality of this playing. They're very good, especially that fiddler.

Sarah turned back with her drink and said I know, he's got me worried.

Padraigh said Youse were talking about me, I can feel it.

You're way off the mark, Paddy boy, said John. If

we wanted to talk about you, we'd do it in front of you. I mean, we wouldn't want you to miss out.

Sean laughed, too loudly, then reached for his pint.

I guess we should be getting back to the house, Sarah said. It's late, and I want to sleep in. And I don't want a hangover. If I stay any longer I'll be sorry in the morning.

Good idea, said John. Let's all get some sleep. Are you coming, Paddy?

I'm not. His shoulder moved slightly and was still.

Sean said I'll stay for a while. You lot go. We'll be along later.

Right then. John got his coat.

Sarah said Will you be alright, Paddy?

And why wouldn't I be alright?

Just asking. I just asked James the same thing, didn't I, James?

You did.

I mean, why am I not alright? Padraigh pulled his coat around him and fingered the broad lapels.

It's okay, Paddy, Sarah said. No need to be cranky. I just care about you. I care about all my boys.

Sean said That's right. Grand. Okay, you lot get going then. He motioned with his head to the door.

I'm not cranky, Padraigh said.

We went to the door. The rain had stopped and the wind, though still strong, was coming in short bursts, sweeping papers up the road.

I'll be along in a little while, I said. I might go for a short walk around the harbour. I kissed Sarah. I won't be long.

John said Something wicked this way comes.

Sarah shivered. Promise you won't be long?

I promise.

They went up the road. I watched them go until they were lost to the crest of the hill, then I walked down to the harbour.

Most harbours with their docks, jetties or piers – large and small – take on a curious, melancholy aspect in the rain, especially at dusk or late at night, when you're the only person there, when the scrawling gulls have gone out like lights over the bay or river and the shopfront windows are black. The wood and the dripping chains can be sinister. The mast wires of boats can play a dirge and never finish it. The unseen slap and rush of pylon water can release phrases so old their origins are unknown.

I stood on the end of the jetty and looked for lights in the distance, out over Galway Bay. I saw black water, and something that could have been a large seabird surfacing.

A fishing boat creaked at its moorings. I went to it and climbed on deck to a smell of hauled netting and slime. Turning again to face the water, I thought of Mum and Dad, and what they might be doing. I'd not phoned or written for months. Mum still sent postcards. They filled a shoe box with domestic news, with details of life in the suburbs, with small print and talk of how she and Dad were getting on. They were doing things together – movies, playing bowls, the odd round of golf, having friends over for dinner. Between her lines I found a vein of sadness, though it might have been a view of my own life being returned to the cards as I read them. Dad's letters – there had been three – were thick with details from work and the front line of his new hobby: collecting shells. He found and bought and traded them. I'd promised to send him some razor shells – long, thin, twin-bladed things I'd found on the beach at Spanish Point, in Clare. I never sent them.

Then I stopped writing. So did Dad, though Mum's cards kept coming, and I felt sure that on my return to Cork I would find the latest instalments from her life. The longer my silence, the harder it was to make contact with Dad, even though Mum always spoke for him and signed his name on each card. She spoke for my sister as well. I knew they were thinking of me, though they never mentioned my tablets or the state of my head, bless their long-distance hearts.

I'd sent postcards to Harry during my first few months in Cork. I offered Guinness-distorted images of my walks home after the pubs had closed. I gave him shovel-by-wrench descriptions of gas piping and breaks in water mains. He responded with news of learning how to cut and shape stone, of his love for Jenny, of trying to make a baby.

He phoned one night. He'd been drinking. He said he and Jenny had *wasted the day arguing*, and that he wanted to talk. He said it wasn't serious. We often make faces at each other and say the wrong things, he said. When he asked if I'd found Stephanie, he filled the long silence he'd made by saying Listen, James, you know, I think about you often.

Our correspondence died out with those words.

Near the boat's wheelhouse I found a bottle. It was empty. I held it up to the wharf light and saw a globe of blurred amber. Setting the bottle down, I took a scrap of paper from my pocket, uncapped my pen, knelt and scribbled a short note on my knee. Then I rolled the paper into a cylinder and pushed it into the bottle's neck. Without a stopper, my plan was useless. It didn't matter. I hurled the bottle high. It cartwheeled and splashed down, gleaming where it bobbed on the oily tide. I'd said what I'd been keeping from Mum and Dad and Harry –

that I was happy, and completely in love, that my life was on an even keel. The bottle tipped and came up, tipped again. Then it sank. A tight-lipped sea burial for my lies.

Turning towards the pub, I saw a light. It appeared and went out, appeared again. I looked. Saw nothing. When it came again, I saw it clearly. I had to look inside myself. The light was red, now silver, with black lines forking though it. More lights joined it. They turned slowly, leaking a phosphorescent glow, and then they started spinning and throwing sparks. I closed my eyes and asked them to stop. I looked at the harbour. Something clicked on the water and dived, leaving a faint green line. The lights in my head went out, and suddenly I was very tired, and frightened. I walked back and forth. I stepped hard on the jetty wood. I said my name. When I didn't respond, I lit a cigarette and sat on the end of the jetty, exhausting each thought that arrived.

Entering the pub, I found Padraigh projecting his voice to the smoke-stained roof timbers, his right hand shooting up as if to emphasise a word, his coat tails flying. About twenty men and a woman were applauding each time he came to the end of a theatrical flourish of words. Sean was at the bar, looking gobsmacked.

He's into Beckett. Just before you arrived he was Estragon, before that Vladimir. He's lost it. These people think he's brilliant. Well he is, for fuck's sake, but look at him. Look at his *arm*.

Padraigh's arm was rocketing now, falling back to hang for a few seconds then hitting the air again.

A woman made her way from the back of the room to the bar. She said Someone should take this boy home, then she left. Someone else followed her.

Padraigh was speaking very quickly now, the words running into each other, sentences breaking off and reforming. A man shouted Turn it off! to much laughter. Padraigh's arm shot up. He started talking quickly. The terrible news will break and only the truly miserable will understand it, won't they, Paddy. I saw a woman gutting a fish by the river and I said Are you happy? She hooked out a slither of guts and said You know I am darling, as the gulls came down to clean her hands. Jesus be greatly honoured she was gorgeous. I said How's about a little sex, you miserable creature, and she swallowed me there, on the rivergrass, God almighty the woman knew how to use her tongue.

Padraigh mimed masturbation, and the barman said That's just about it now, and went to Padraigh, taking him by the arm. Padraigh's arm lifted away and he turned, glaring at the barman. Unhand me you fool there are people awaiting the end of this sentence. I challenge you to divest me of this flowerfall, you foul reject from a devil's gobhole.

The barman came to us. Get this man out of here now or I'm calling the guards.

Sean went to Padraigh and tried to speak to him. Padraigh twisted away and stood his ground, levelling a finger at Sean's chest. Sean looked around. People were on their feet, unsure of what to do.

And you! Padraigh shouted, glaring at Sean from under his eyebrows. You traitor of the badge of honour! You corrupt fucker in the head of reason! I told you my life in love stories and poems and you are shaking my heart. I will bless the rank denizens of Galway Bay with my spittle and take you down to death town where we'll drink and bleed in the trenches of mud. Fuck you and your kind forever!

When Padraigh turned, snapping his feet together as if to attention at some unheard command, Sean went to him and took him firmly by the arm. Padraigh swivelled around and punched him in the side of the head. Sean went down, overturning tables and chairs. He was helped to his feet by a couple of men who, when they saw that he was alright, went for Padraigh, one taking him high around the shoulders, the other going low, in a classic rugby tackle. Padraigh went down and stayed there, kicking against their desperate hold until someone else came and sat on his chest. He screamed and heaved against them. They bucked and swore and held onto him. When Padraigh had calmed down, breathing hard and fast, Sean knelt beside him. He said It's alright, Paddy, it's Sean. Padraigh breathed and shuddered. It's okay, you're fine. Do you think you can stand up now? I don't want to have to belt you. Can you stand up and behave yourself? Tell me you can do that now. For me. For yourself. Sean put his ear to Padraigh's mouth. I can't hear you, Paddy. Did you say something? He lowered his head again. You what? You can? You can stand up and not start swingin' at me? Do you promise? He lowered his head and listened. Nodded. Right then. I'm going to count to three, then these boys will let you go. You're not going to hit me again, are you, Paddy? Silence. Breathing. Right. Here we go now. Sean looked at the men who looked at each other. One, two, three. Slowly the men relaxed their grip. The man on Padraigh's chest lifted himself away carefully, as if trying not to wake a sleeping child. When the men had let him go, Padraigh slumped into the floor and breathed heavily – a slow, steady rasping sound – then he started crying. It was terrible. It came faintly at first, and then it grew, with high notes and low notes. It came from the back of his throat, and then from deep within, a wailing, broken line of weeping that filled the pub and made people turn away from this man on the floor, this stranger who had entertained them and had now reduced some of them to their own private tears.

Sean and I helped Padraigh to sit up. We held him. He sobbed and put his arms around Sean's shoulders, his face contorting with the effort. His body was puppet-like. The barman said I'm sorry, lads. A woman approached Padraigh and kissed him gently on the side of the head. God bless you, boy, she said, and touched his shoulder.

We went up the road, supporting Padraigh's weight. A few men came as far as the crest of the hill, where they said goodnight, and waited until we'd taken him inside.

After we'd undressed him and put him to bed, we went out to the sunroom. Sean's hands were shaking as he poured whiskey into our cups. He threw back his drink and poured another. I did the same. On the jetty I had seen what I thought had gone from my life. I felt awkward, vulnerable.

Have you ever seen anything like it, Sean said.

I said no, and drank my whiskey. Then I said There are some things the head can't explain.

Sean looked at me. What did you say?

I said nothing and then said nothing more as a light went on and my name was called into the morning.

MAZURKA

———

A<small>T BREAKFAST</small>, while Padraigh was still sleeping, Sean told John and Sarah what had happened. Sarah said We have to go home, right now. John agreed. Sarah said there was no way she was going to stay on the island to play a gig when Padraigh was so ill.

Mrs O'Flaherty, overhearing the conversation, suggested the band keep to their plan. I'll stay here with him, she said. I like the boy, there's no problem. I'll ask a couple of the lads to come over. We'll keep an eye on him. Sure, we'll feed him up and make sure he gets his rest. What instrument does Padraigh play now?

The flute, Sarah said.

No problem. I'll call Paul O'Leary. I think he's coming tonight all the same, but I'll call him. He's a fine man on the flute. He'll most likely know some of your tunes. It'd be such a shame to leave now. It's a bad time, yes, but go on. Padraigh's going to be alright.

Sean said I think he *will* be fine. Actually, I think that what happened might have been the end. You know? Like, he was a pressure-cooker and had to let off steam.

John said You might be right, Sean, but I tell you,

I'll not be goin' so far as to say it was good for him.

That's not what I'm saying, Sean said. I just mean he might be on the mend, now, after that's happened.

I'm not convinced, Sarah said. Let's wait until later this afternoon.

Sarah? John brushed her face with the back of his hand. It was the first time I'd seen him touch her. Come on, he said. Let's stay and play. Paddy will be fine.

Alright, I guess we should play. She was making fast, interlocking shapes with her fingers. I'm going to see if he's alright.

I'll come too, Mrs O'Flaherty said.

After they'd gone, John said This is fucking madness altogether.

Mrs O'Flaherty, who had only gone as far as the kitchen, said Well, John, I can agree with the madness altogether part.

Sarah and I went down to the pub. For a quiet one, she'd said, as we stood out front of the house wondering what to do.

Walking down to the harbour, we saw people arriving from the boat that had just come in. Some were carrying suitcases, others shouldered packs. A man wearing a big oxblood-coloured hat and sunglasses walked past, followed by two women, twins, their pale blue coats flapping in the wind.

In the pub, people were asking after Padraigh. We assured them he was fine. A man with a small black and white puppy in his arms said Did you know Brendan Behan came here once, to Inishmore? Terrible man. Told stories too. Had to be taken away by the guards.

We were drinking hot toddies when the barman asked about my accent.

You've got a bit of Cork in you, but what's under it? Australia.

Australia? Good man yourself. We get Australians here, don't we, lads? In summer you can pave the roads with them. He stopped wiping the inside of a pint glass and said We've an Australian girl here now, actually. She comes regular, like. Sarah sighed and said Yes, we know.

The barman said She's a fine girl. Keeps to herself mostly. He looked over at a group of men playing cards by the window. John, what's that girl's name? The one staying up at the old Callaghan place?

John placed his hand on the table. You know, I don't recall. Do you know, Paul? Paul said no.

It's the old place about five miles out, towards the fort, the barman said. You can't miss it. It's got red frames on the windows.

Why don't you just drive him up there? Sarah said, stepping down from her stool and putting her coat on. And while you're at it, why don't you make sure they're not disturbed for a few days. I'm sure they've loads of catching up to do. Jesus Christ!

The barman looked at me, and then at Sarah. Can you tell me what I've said, girlie? Have I offended ye? If so, I'm sorry, but that's no way to speak to me. I was trying to be helpful to your man here. No need for that tone with me.

Sarah went to the door and threw it open. Is this going to happen all over again? she asked as she went out.

I followed her. She was standing in the road, her arms folded.

Sarah –

Don't bother, James. Do you really think she's here on the island? You're pathetic. You've got this grand idea of yourself and you cut me out of the picture when it suits you. She looked up the road. Well, what are you waiting for? Fuck off and find her. Go and tell her how much you've missed her all these years, and when you find her, tell her there's no one else in your life, that you've been searching for her all over Ireland, on your own. Well, go on! She stepped over and shoved me in the chest. Go *on*! She pulled her coat around herself and walked off.

You don't need to worry, I said. It's alright.

Sarah went over the crest of the hill.

I followed her, but kept walking after I reached the guest house.

Narrow, wall-bordered roads winding past wall-bordered fields. A landscape of stones. An extension of the Burren, in Clare, that lunar plateau of limestone shelving and luminous rock. Here, from any high point on the island, a gridwork of drystone puzzles, wind-raked and perennially cold.

I'd been following the coast. Every few minutes, a headlight came on as the road passed under me. It was a faint red light, like the last sign of the afterburn a flashlight leaves in the eyes. The dreaded red death of terror, as my friend Glen at school used to call it. I worked hard on my breathing. Perhaps I worked too hard, as I could feel my hands going numb. I stopped and steadied myself, remembering how deliberate shifts in attention can be calming, or at least distracting, while panic looks for a good place to settle.

Where the end of the beach rose into the makings of a headland, I went down onto a narrow band of round shore stones. They clicked and rolled underfoot. They were either perfectly round or oval-shaped, and they sat in the palm with a lovely cool weight. Some had mauve flecks in a grey spiral, some were dark brown. I sat and picked up a large brown stone, its concentric rings gleaming with white swirls. I unzipped my day pack and lowered the stone into it.

The day was clear, the great bowl of sky cloudless and cerulean blue. I walked the length of the beach, my chest heavy, my pulse fluttering. I took the stone from the pack and held it tightly, rubbing its smooth grains with my thumb. It was like a centring force.

At the end of the beach I climbed back to the road and found a long section of wall draped with kelp-stalks, their rubbery skin fleshed with sun. They glowed like curious, malleable candles. A few cows in the field opposite had come to stand at the wall, leaning their dripping noses on the stone. When I went to them they did not move. Their eyes rolled back and they flattened their ears. They breathed my scent and chewed loudly, paused, chewed loudly.

The house was further than I'd imagined. I stopped outside a fence with large gaps where stones had fallen or been removed. There was a narrow, worn gravel path leading up to the front door. The roof was thatched, its small, four-paned windows set deep into a thick white wall. Around the edge of the roof thatching, wires with tiny wooden handles hung like tassels from a ragged hem.

I had that common, invasive sensation of being watched that people often experience when they're approaching a house. I forced myself to look at the glass. I saw a flash of sun, and then my shape folding into sections as I moved to the door.

The stone shifted in the backpack like a palpitation. Anxiety was performing intricate rope-tricks with the muscles and veins behind my ribs. I heard my breath peel away from the door wood. I knocked. My body listened for movement, for the scraping of a chair, anything. There was nothing but fast blooms of breath and a pulse in my neck that tapped out *Leave while you can*. I knocked again. Nothing. I went to the back of the house. Clothes had been pegged to a single strand of wire that ran from a bolt in the wall to a leaning wooden post. A red dress. A pair of jeans. A spencer. Two pairs of cotton briefs. Odd socks. I knocked on the back door. The dress fluttered over my shoulder. I caught the hem and held it to my face. It smelled of washing powder. What was I expecting? The scent of clovesmoke? The ghost of a whisky-spill? I went around to the front and looked through the windows. Made beds, a table set for dinner. A lit candle on a mantelpiece. Hoping no one was watching, I rapped on the glass. I heard the sound as if from inside, and it startled me. Taking a notebook and pen from the pack, I went to the fence and wrote quickly, then returned and slipped the note under the door.

> *When the day comes apart*
> *birds reel and go.*
> *The light is terrible.*
> *Hold the day together.*
> *You and the birds and the light.*
> *Hold on.*

A dark shape appeared on the road far below. I stopped and waited. As the shape came into focus, I saw an old man weaving from side to side, a straw bale strapped to his back. He stopped when the road began to rise steeply, got off his bike and walked. He paused to inspect something, then continued. When he reached me, he tipped his hat and said Will you be needing help at all? I thanked him and said no. He looked up at the house.

The soul knows the price of every harvest, he said, not looking at me. He gripped the handlebars and pushed away. I watched him go, the straw bale glowing like folded wings above his shoulders. And the harvest takes time, he said.

Instead of returning to the house I walked out to the fort.

Approaching it was awkward. Being uneven with slivers of sharp rock and loose stones, the ground was dangerous. As I neared the fort I could hear wind peeling off the walls in great sighs and lashings, and far below the constant working of the sea. The fort was a series of concentric, bluestone ramparts, at least thirteen feet thick and twenty feet high, forming a semi-circle with the two ends terminating at the cliff edge. These rings must have served as bastions or puzzlement, should the outer wall be breached. The wind came in at every angle, swirling. I went to the outer wall and followed it until I came to a narrow ledge. I sat down and dropped stones, counting out loud until they cracked and shot out of the cliff face into the dark boil of the sea, or knocked faintly at the base and were still. Stephanie entered every thought. Then Tina came off a length of wavelight and said something a knob-beaked, wind-riding fish-raider might give voice to before it dives. Stephanie. Tina. A headlight flickered over their faces and they were gone.

When I walked into the house I was undone. Sarah and Sean were dancing in the sunroom. John was playing guitar, and a man I'd not seen before was on fiddle. Mrs O'Flaherty sat in her big wooden chair, eyes closed, tapping in time with a book on her knee. Sarah saw me and turned in to take Sean's hand. Sean said How's it goin', Jimmy boy? Mrs O'Flaherty smiled and said So did you see the island? I sat down beside her and asked after Padraigh. She told me he'd been sleeping heavily.

When he wakes he asks for water, or a little tea, she said. He looks desperate, poor fella. I wouldn't have believed a man could lose weight in a day, but he's thin and getting thinner.

One more time! Sean called, and John and the man started into another waltz. Sarah looked at me this time, as she went around. There was nothing in her eyes.

I went in to see Padraigh. His pale, unshaven face was death-like above the blanket line. There was a sweat-stain on his pillow, and his left hand was a bone cradle at the side of his head. He looked different, as if another man had slipped into his body. It frightened me. Padraigh shifted in his sleep. His right hand moved under the blanket. He blew a line of sour-smelling breath and was still.

The waltz had ended. John put his guitar away and said You've missed the dancing. Sarah said He's been dancing alright, haven't you, James? Are you alone, or is she waiting out on the road like a poor, demure thing who can't tolerate company? Come on, don't be shy, bring her in.

Will you bring her in, James? Mrs O'Flaherty said, going to the window.

There was no one at the house, I said.

She must have seen you coming, Sarah said.

Will youse stop your bickering, for Christ's sake, said John. You think it's helping? I tell you, youse are like a couple of kids the way you taunt each other. He levelled a serious gaze at me. James, why don't you forget about this woman and concentrate on what's in front of you. I've been watching you. You've got someone right here who loves your guts, and you're off in your head, lookin' for bollocks.

Keep it down, you'll wake Padraigh, Sean said.

And you, John said, lowering his voice and turning to Sarah, You're puttin' your claws out at every opportunity. It's like you enjoy being angry. There's things in life worth gettin' furious about, and there's things that aren't. Yeah, your man here's been foolish, but you're behavin' the same. Get a grip. He poured a glass of water from a jug and drank it down. He wiped his mouth and said And you know somethin' else, I can't believe I'm actually sayin' this to youse. He looked over at Mrs O'Flaherty. You'll have pardon me for this, Mrs O'Flaherty, but you're both acting like shite. He went to Sarah. Give me your hand. He reached out to me. And you, bollocks, give me your hand as well. Now, here, take each other's hands. We did not move.

Come on, John said, and gripped our arms, drawing us together.

Sean said Do you two take each other to be eejits for as long as you argue?

Mrs O'Flaherty laughed and clapped.

We held hands.

Now kiss. Go on.

Not here, Sarah said.

Yes, here, in the church of friends.

We kissed.

Ah, Jaysus. John grabbed me by the shoulders and planted a huge, loud, wet kiss on my lips. He pushed me away, looked into my eyes, dragged me into his arms and kissed me again, this time on the forehead.

Sarah said If anyone kissed me like that I'd murder them.

John said Right, when you're ready, in your own time. But I tell you, if I hear any more hard words, I'm goin' to kiss youse until you beg for mercy.

Mercy! Padraigh shouted from his room, and we all went running.

LOVE NOTE

———•◦•———

A STORM BEGINS far out at sea, the isobars that define its passage like a raft of dispersing mutton birds. Or the storm stitches itself together inland with seams of dust and grass, windswirls of bark and seed husks. The air is alive with announcements of its arrival. An electric pulse goes into the skin, works deep into the scalp. Years of vigilance can't stop the storm's growth from a slight shift in the wind's intensity and direction to hours or days of wreckage.

I'd been keeping watch for years on a high, level place called Medication. Sometimes lightning came through the chemical wall I'd taken refuge behind, but I was grounded. A burn-mark on the nerves behind my eyes or a waning glow on my palm where I'd raised my hand involuntarily were the only signs I'd been troubled by the storm's advancing. But that evening, after I'd been out to the Callaghan house, a storm came in off Galway Bay and breached the wall. I was defenceless. Padraigh in bed, his own private storm sparking and blowing inside his head, while I was trying to hide the black weather that was raging the length of my arms and legs, its eye at the centre of my chest, its intensity so fierce it forced my hands and mouth open into voices I could not contain. I heard them and copied them. I sought my loves and found them. I looked down to where they were sleeping or hiding in the earth.

I crossed over the Bay of Dislocation into the Straits of Disembodiment. My head was scooting around in dusklight on a small island, telling its own story to the resident gulls. Having been quartered, my arms and legs opened or kicked in the doors of Irish-speaking lives who welcomed them in with Stay awhile do, ye poor sticks of the bloody migration will ye take your rest and flee?

One man in the warm cradle of exhaustion, sleeping. My body coming together in the smoky air above a crowded pub after being scattered the length and breadth of a stone-strewn wafer of land. When my body came together, the parts bruised or wet or rubbed with visions of orchids and rockroses and heath bedstraw, I staggered into a room lit with shark oil lamps and found an old woman keening over the body of her husband, a fisherman and teller of salty truths, laid out on a single, iron-frame bed, his cuffed hands together in a cold expression of holding the tail of a flexing fish, his skull trepanned with hawkspirals, his ears plugged with the ghost-burble from a wooden chest at the bed's end – unlikely outboard, light-stained vessel for religious things – and above this the slow parade of cloudshadow like a swan fleet on the wall caught in the lens an undertaker's apprentice was holding to the scene, a young man with a passion for amateur ornithology and photography, a man who has learned how to dress the dead as he would a prize game bird, drawing wet ropes of colour from the shell of a life and sewing the empty host of a bloodbeat with green fibre that a black serge suit or swathe of metallic feathers conceals appropriately, lovingly, until the walking or seated guard attends its passage through street or heath flowers to grave site or kitchen. When my body came together, I found myself standing beside a shawled griever, saying The breath of his life will be with you forever, and the woman responding with Hush now, fool, words are breakable. I said Words are all we have when prayer and belief go under. When my body came together I woke, clawing at the spell I'd not been able to shed like old skin. I found myself in a quiet, dark room.

Be still now and don't try to move, the woman said, leaning over me, her face losing the shapes of the years. She seemed younger than when she'd been deep in a throatsong for her dead husband. She said Two men missing, two men found, two men home to common ground. She said Paddy's come back to us, James, are you with him?

We are at the bar. I am trying to re-enter my body. I am terrified. The session in the Inishmore pub is in full swing. I could be staring at marionettes jigging under their wires in smoky light. Sarah is guiding me through the crazy weather my head has made. Highs and lows, hail and flickers of indigo light, steady, black and red rainlines. I am coming down. A pilot without instruments. A man who has been drinking heavily, with a bleak devotion to death and memorial. Sarah is describing the lie of the land. I'm coming in too low, but I'm desperate for contact with the earth. I look down and see people standing in the fog. They have made a fire. I circle back and lower my nose. Be careful, Sarah says. It's as if I can feel her hand on my arm as I breathe and fly, breathe and come in. That's it, you're doing well. Her voice is a wavering line of static over the storm. Then I see her. She is on the ground, waving, her hair lit with firelight. The runway rushes at me and I'm down, on one wing, ploughing a field to swing to rest with a glass of something black in one hand and a cigarette shivering like a white marker in the other.

As the smoke lifted, the harbour sounds and stone field sounds became the drone and sway of pipes and concertina. I chain-smoked and worked hard listening to Sarah and John, who were sitting either side of me, their mouths releasing equal measures of meaning and nonsense.

A panic attack can last a minute or a day. I had been away, in time, with no bearings. I had seen myself through an obsidian eye the puncture-wound of illusion leaves in the head. I had gone, oxygen-and-adrenalin-flooded, beyond myself into fenced-off fields and cropped roof thatchings to settle on a bar stool, watching people move and play and speak through the star of a prism in a beer puddle. My body had come together, but part of my head was missing. It could have been down at the beach, buried under a shift and click of round stones, or inside a house on a hill with small windows and a red dress cracking out the back. Most likely the missing piece of my head was years behind me, under the empty nightglass of a milk bottle after the coins had been removed, or on train tracks bloodied with a fall or a drop from life into the nightmares and headlights of those in attendance. I was back, but not complete. Sarah knew this. Although drinking heavily, she saw, whenever she turned to find me, a man with questions hanging from him – questions she had been asking herself: what are we doing? where are we going? what have we begun? I was too out of things to reassure her. I couldn't reassure myself. Holding her hand, I might as well have been palming a damp kelpsprig. My attention was outside myself, overhead. Projecting the hook of a racing thought into a crowd can slow the head to walking pace, so I let one fly – a thought that had the bloodplum eyes of cattle, a wet red triangle, and a crackling laugh inside it. The thought went out over the heads of the players and dancers and was caught somewhere in between. My head dropped anchor. I heard myself say Is it clear to starboard? I wanted to see sparks of reefwater as speed fell away to consideration. Instead, I sat with my hands around the wheelhouse of a pint of Guinness, my left leg shaking, the room grinding to a pace I could follow, Sarah going Clacketty clack the boys are back, John throwing shapes and whiskey, Padraigh shooting right-handed yelping to music, Mrs O'Flaherty at a table with old friends, clapping and laughing, her face lit up with whiskey and flameheat, Sean out there on the floor playing the melodeon with the needlepoint of a thought gleaming in the lapel of his coat.

Thoughts with highlights of order inside them were unreeling and forming. I could focus on the music, identify tunes and instruments. John's voice finally had sense behind it. Padraigh's hand went into the air and I laughed. John said Does this mean if I ask you a question you'll actually respond? I said Yes, and John said Jimmy, can you tell me about those tablets you've been taking?

The thought in Sean's lapel pulled free and whipped back into my mouth.

You see, I found a bottle on the floor when you were gone, he said, and I've this friend, a doctor in Dublin.

I called her and said What's the story with these tablets? So you see . . .

I sent another thought into the room but it got caught in John's hair as he lowered his head and said Why didn't you say something to us? To Sarah? We're your friends.

Sarah looked up from her glass. He's already told me, John. It's alright. I've known for a wee while.

Right, John said. I see. Anyway, feck all that shite about mental bloody illness. You're a sane man altogether, Jimmy boy. I've met some real crazies. You're not one of them.

It's not like that.

Paddy's the same, said John. Youse are both brilliant men. Youse have the dubious blessing of having fucked-up chemical bollocks. But you're fine. Just . . .

Running his fingers through his hair, John sighed and finished the breath with I just wish you could have told us earlier, that's all.

Sean came over and ordered a drink. Have you seen your man in the corner? The one with the mad hat? Unbelievable.

Four heads moved as one to better view this cornered curio. Having seen us leaning and looking, Padraigh did the same, the fingers of his right hand shooting out behind his bum like a starfish in a strobelight.

The man was wrapped in a huge dark coat, and his hat – dull and red and falling somewhere between an Australian digger's slouch hat and something Long John Silver might have worn – all but concealed his face. When he glanced up, the lenses of his sunglasses had flames in them.

There's one of the crazies I was tellin' you about, Jimmy boy, John said.

Sarah punched him in the arm. Leave him be, she said. I think he looks kind of interesting.

He must have heard us talking about him, Sean said.

I turned to find a long coat going out the door.

Maybe he just hates the music, Sarah said, watching the door as she drained her glass.

Padraigh opened the door and went out. When he returned, he strode to the bar and said Your man's a maniac. He was talking to himself going up the road.

The band played into the night and early morning. Padraigh sat out, but seemed to enjoy himself, sitting alone under the sea-facing window, drinking and moving in time. Mrs O'Flaherty came over with some friends and introduced them slowly, saying their names with lyrical authority, a little of their history, and loving every second of it. I haven't seen the dawn since I was wild and in love, she said. The man at her elbow said You mean the other evening? The small, crease-faced group erupted and went laughing back to their table.

I was exhausted. As Sarah and a young flute player entered the skin of an air, I caught her attention and waved goodnight, pointing up the road to bed and sleep. She smiled and lowered her chin to the fiddlewood.

At the house I found the door open. Stepping into a pale band of light at the hallway leading to our rooms, I heard a faint hollow sound and stopped. It came again, from the kitchen, the sound of someone dropping small coins into a glass. When I entered the kitchen and finally found the light switch, there was nothing but the blood-reminding lie of my shadow on the bench and floor. The pantry door was open. A few bottles clicked and rolled underfoot when I entered it. I looked up at the small green door above the pantry, but it was latched and silent.

When the bedroom light clicked on I saw wreckage. The beds were stripped. My notebooks were gutted, torn, the pens and pencils broken. Sarah's clothes were ripped and scattered. Then her pillow – a bloody mess with two deep slashes through the covering. Red pillow-filler clot-like on the mattress base. And looping out from one of the slashes, a gold chain, the links glazed with hardening red. I pulled it free and a ropeworked cross swung candied into my palm. Lovenote from the frenzied guardian of pain. Food colouring thrown into *Bleed to death my lovely, here, your necklace is returned with grief.*

I stood with a hammer in my chest going Stop this now. In the bathroom, with cold water fanning from my brow in deep porcelain light, I imagined a man wearing an oxblood hat and generous coat go weaving from the house with light dripping from his fingerends, down to a low, harbourside building where a woman was leaning into a swell of her own music. I waited for panic to come, but my breathing remained calm. When my pulse did not betray the faith I'd found to keep watch over myself, I went down the hill, unsure of how such news should be delivered, or if it should be delivered at all.

THE WALL OF DEATH

F OR MY TENTH birthday Dad took me to the Royal
Easter Show in Sydney. We walked around the
pavilions, stopping in shit and mud to watch the cattle,
then sitting in a grandstand while fat men in blue singlets
chopped the shit out of logs. We ate hot dogs and drank
too much lemonade. On the chairlift I dropped coins
into the ring while the bull-judging was on.

We heard it before we saw it – a high-pitched,
mechanical screaming. Dad said Chainsaws, but when
we got there, a man on a motorbike was riding around
the inside of a huge, circular wire cage. The wall of
death, Dad said, and I repeated the words. We moved
to where we could see the rider properly – a white,
helmeted streak of loud light going around and around,
criss-crossing upside down. I said The wall of death, and
Dad said Yes.

On the way home in the car, Dad said You can stop
saying it now, don't wear it out it's only words.

When I first saw the fort at the end of the island I said
The wall of death. As I walked out there it was grey

and blowing with sideways rain. I saw a line of men yelling words into the sea boom and passing bottles back and forth. I saw a man at the head of the line shouting encouragement as if to oarsmen in a stalled stone boat. The wall of death. What were the makers and keepers of this place protecting? Whose seaward or landward advance were they trying to stop? Walking into the rubble-littered layers of towerlight, no answers came at me. Did I say The wall of death? Did I repeat the words as I'd done in the car on the way home from the show? There was no one there to tell me, although I had a feeling that four words had gone into a loop and were being carried around and around on a sea-creaming wind.

FLASHLIGHTS AND VOICES

T HE NEWS WAS received with a shock of expressions
and responses that ended with a crowd running up
the hill to the house. The scene in the bedroom was
chaotic. Sarah vomited and shouted Michael's name
through the rooms. Mrs O'Flaherty sat in her chair,
attended by quiet-saying friends. A fisherman demanded
Michael's description. His friends came close and
repeated the details of his name and face and hair. I tried
to comfort Sarah, who was walking back and forth in the
sunroom, drinking from a bottle of Paddy, the red chain
and cross swinging from her fist. She spat and drank,
wailed and drank. John and Sean went into a huddle with
the fishermen, and when they broke ranks I heard We'll
need some flashlights, lads, and some rope. Let's meet out
front in twenty minutes, right so. Padraigh was in the
bedroom saying The fucker, the fucker.

When the fishermen returned with their wandering
lights and ropes coiled over their shoulders, Sarah went
to them and screamed I want you to kill that fucking
bastard and other words her sobs ruined before Sean
steered her back inside.

Four cars went out that morning, each in different directions into the lines of dawn, looking for Michael on backroads, the shell of a caravan by the headland, abandoned cottages with only two walls and a chimney standing, behind houses in the town, in the holds and wheelhouses of boats at the harbour.

Their trucks pulled up outside the house in sunlight, their ropes still coiled, their flashlights hanging like dud roman candles. They'd seen and found no sign of the man. They'd keep looking. Sarah was asleep in my arms on the floor, under a blanket Mrs O'Flaherty had put over us. John and Sean sat in silence at a table in the sunroom, smoking and looking out at the day. Padraigh had been gone for hours. As he was walking out, I'd said Where are you going, Paddy? It was the first time I'd used the abbreviation of his name. He stopped in the door frame.

My name is Padraigh, he said, and went out, swinging his arms and striding up the hill.

I woke to find Sarah gone. Mrs O'Flaherty was in the bedroom. The bed had been stripped and remade, the clothes and paper and pens cleared away.

Sarah's gone for a walk, she said, folding a sheet.

Before I could ask if she knew where she had gone, she said I think it's best if you leave her be for a while. She'll be back after.

When I asked if she'd seen Padraigh, she said no, and then she said That boy is a troubled soul.

The story Brendan Behan and his freezing, rain-blown line of captive men told from that lofty place was continued, embellished, late on the morning after Michael carved his presence into our room. Padraigh missing again, Sarah out walking.

One night shortly before we left Cork, up in my room, our bodies coming and going in stripes of red, faulty neon from a sign outside the window, Sarah had told me how she'd always wanted to play fiddle in the fort on Inishmore. She said Stone, Curved air, Wet acoustics. I said perhaps the band could organise a gig out there, make a day of it, a picnic, but she wanted to play alone, to know the sound of the stone spirals.

I could see, as she spoke, a woman at the centre of open-air ruins, moving to wind and bird cry, her red hair a flame on the stone.

It would have taken Sarah a couple of hours to walk out to the fort, more, most likely, as she was drunk and hadn't slept much. Her fiddle was in its case on the bed, so she hadn't gone for the music.

By midday it was raining hard, a flapping grey caul over the island, erasing detail, blurring the edges of landscape and thought.

I stood under the ringing eaves, trying to find shape and form beyond the road outside the house, the view-killing rain a wall of sound and sliding beads from the guttering.

Mrs O'Flaherty came to stand beside me. She was silent for some minutes, as if waiting for the rain and wind to make way for her voice. When they did not let up, she said That girl will catch her death. I tried to stop her. I said There's going to be rain, Sarah, stay put, I'll make some tea, but she walked out without a word.

John moved to stand behind us. He put his hand on my shoulder. This is a bad time, he said.

Mrs O'Flaherty continued. And poor Padraigh too. Jesus, Mary and Joseph. I've seen it a hundred times. It's simple. The boy needs love.

We watched in silence as rainlines swept over the fields. Mrs O'Flaherty smelled of lavender. A puddle at her feet blinked and shivered with each heavy drop from the guttering. I said Sarah wanted to play her fiddle out at the fort, and before I could say more, or Mrs O'Flaherty respond, a truck pulled up and two men got out.

We think your man left on a boat early this morning, the driver said, holding the door open. John Moore said he heard a boat leaving from the south end of town, around near Murphy's Wharf. He must have arranged with someone from Galway to meet him there. The bollocks.

The other man wound down his window and said But don't worry, there's already people over there lookin' for him. He'll be a sorry bastard when they've finished with him.

He leaned from the window. How's the lady? he asked softly. Is she, like, alright? Has she slept?

Mrs O'Flaherty walked to the gate and looked up the road. The rain misted her hair and quickly plastered it down. She stood getting soaked as the two men followed her gaze.

HORSES, WHITE AND
BREAKING

———•✦•———

T HIS STORY WILL BE told and heard in quiet places, in sleep, in the voices of those who were on the island and those who know variations of the story and request its true telling. It will become the echo of a shout or a cry on the wind, above and below the end of an island, at its highest point, where currentlines turn into horses, white and breaking.

Sarah walked through the fort, inward through its shell-spiral of rain-blackened stone. At the centre, she stopped when she heard a rock being dislodged, heard it clatter and settle, then she moved on, back out through a widening aperture of sweating stone to the cliff edge.

A boat was coming in, its prow punching through the swell before it nose-dived and came up again, its decks curtained with spillage. She could not see anyone on board. Five gulls painted the air above the dirty yellow glow of the wheelhouse. Sarah stepped back from the edge. The wind was unpredictable company there, on that rim of uneven stones and gravel, urging her forward, taking her by the arm. She took another step back and a stone rattled past her foot and shot over the edge. She leaned forward and watched it go, turning over and catching a sharp outcrop near the base of the cliff before it made a brief spark in black water. She stepped back again. Rain lashed the side of her face. A rock sheared off from the wall of the fort, angled close to her legs, and went over. She turned around and saw him. He was standing twenty or thirty yards away down the hill, legs apart and braced, a stone in his hand. The oxblood hat and sunglasses were gone, though the long dark coat swept out behind him, giving him a raven's countenance and poise. He tossed the rock from hand to hand. He looked around. When he spoke, he was not looking at her. It seemed he was addressing the outer wall of the fort.

I love you with my life, Sarah. Why are you doing this? He lifted the rock and let his hand fall slowly.

Sarah moved from the cliff edge, towards the fort. Michael threw the rock into her path. It shied and bucked, kicking sideways. He picked up another.

I would have done anything for you. You must know that.

Sarah spoke, the words hurting her neck. We're just no good for each other, Michael. We tried. Things change. We don't own people. We have no jurisdiction over their hearts. You said that.

Yes, but you shafted me. You fucking betrayed me. You took what I gave you and then you ran away. You laughed in my face.

Sarah took another step. Another stone cut into its path.

Are you going to hit me with those stones, Michael? Are you going to stand there and throw rocks at me? I want to go back to the house. Are you going to let me go?

No. I want you to stand there and listen to me. I've got some things to say. He moved a few steps closer and stopped.

The rain was now a vertical wall of broken ice. The surrounding fields and walls had gone, the sea a fog of gull and wavesound.

Michael dropped the rock. Hanging limply by his sides, his hands gleamed with runoff water. I would have continued, he shouted, his face rain-distorted and pale. I wanted us to be together again, but you spat in my face. You almost fucking killed me, Sarah.

You did it to yourself, Michael. You can't help it. You say terrible things to people and expect them to forgive you. You've done it for too long. People are tired of you.

And what about you? Have you got a bottle in your pocket? Your little amber helper? You can't step outside unless you're drunk.

Sarah wiped rain from her face and said I'm leaving here. Go home, Michael. Please. Leave me alone. Can't we just forgive each other and move on?

Watching Michael closely, Sarah skirted the cliff edge, walking away from the fort, down the hill.

Michael moved quickly. He cut off Sarah's downward path, weaving and crouching. Sarah stopped, chose another angle, and continued. Michael moved to stand ten yards below her. He reached into his coat pocket, took out a hip-flask of whiskey and drank deeply.

I guess you'd like some of this. No, of course not, you've got your own.

Are you going to let me past, Michael?

No.

We're going to get very sick if we don't get out of this cold rain and wind.

Poor baby. Do you want a hug?

Sarah pulled her coat tight and strode towards Michael, stepping to one side as she neared him. Fuck you, she said.

Michael grabbed Sarah by the collar and dragged her around. He tried to kiss her, but she twisted away. She slipped and fell. Michael was onto her. He lifted her and, using his weight, pushed and wrestled her back up the hill towards the fort, towards the edge of the cliff. When they were standing at the edge, she went limp in his arms and said I'm sorry. You're right. We can work things out. Michael said No, you're lying. They stood poised, arrested in a wet tangle of clothes and driving fear that forced their breath into fast, generous plumes of white that swirled away over their shoulders.

Please, Michael. Sarah tried to be calm, her voice blowing back into her face.

Michael wrapped her up and buried his face in her collar, in the dark ropes of her hair. He started sobbing. His cries came in loud, body-shaking bursts. I love you. Please, can you hear me?

Let her go, you fucker. A voice went over them. It seemed to come from the air below the cliff, flushed with rain and spray.

Michael turned, keeping a tight grip on Sarah. A man was standing against the wall of the fort. He was tearing at his hair, holding it out in black strings.

Fuck off, Paddy, Michael yelled at him. This has nothing to do with you.

You're wrong there. Let Sarah go and come here. I'll give you a hiding, fucker.

Padraigh moved from the wall. He took a couple of steps. Michael screamed at him to stay away. Padraigh kept coming. He veered sharply towards the edge, then stopped.

Sarah pleaded with him. Please, Padraigh, go away. Michael and I can sort this out.

You want to see violence? Padraigh spoke quietly, his head lowered. You want to see blood? He looked up and shook his head. I'm glad you're here, Michael. I am going to count to ten, and then we'll see who the hero is. You fuck. One. Are you ready for the pain, Michael? Two. Here it comes. Three. Four. Five. Six. Time moves quickly, doesn't it, when time is all you've got. Seven. Eight. Nine. Now take this grief and wear it well. Padraigh did not say ten, and he did not hesitate. He walked to the edge of the cliff and stepped over. He dropped like a bolt of black material, unravelling and trailing a rowdy hemline as he clipped an overhang and landed on his back on the rocks.

Sarah came apart and screamed a dead man's name as the man's blood fanned out beside his head. A fishing boat nosed through the fog. It slowed and hung off the booming shelf, rising and falling on the swell as Padraigh's blood went over the weedy edge in a red foam curtain.

Someone came on deck. Waved. Shouted. Went into the wheelhouse. The boat's engines roared and it surged away, back towards the harbour.

The ledge at the base of the cliffs below the fort is narrow – a winding band of stone, eight feet at its widest point. Washed by the slap and drag of a retreating tide, Padraigh's body was not recovered for several hours. A rescue boat went out for him – a stable vessel that, when seas permit, can approach the rocks. He was roped and pulled into the sea, then taken aboard. Weighted death with crab medallions falling from its winding sheet of tweed.

Michael went to a waiting group of islanders and police, his face bloody where a fist had said goodbye. He returned to Galway on a police boat with its extra passenger under wraps on the stern.

Padraigh's mother came from Cork to identify the body. John was there as well. He wanted to say goodbye, for all of us.

Two days of questions. Padraigh's suicide official. Michael unseen in the glare of a Galway morning as Sarah, Sean, John and I sat under the wide arc of a tree in a city park.

There was so much to say, though most of it went unsaid. There can be an awkwardness, even among good friends, when death moves into view. This was the case at first, that morning, in the park, but it didn't last long.

We spoke of Padraigh's life, his wonderful flute playing, his sense of humour, his caring nature. After a long silence, John stood up and said Enough of this now, come on. Do you think Paddy would want us to sit around here like the ugly shits we are and be black? The bollocks he would. Let's find a pub.

We drank and talked deep into the afternoon. There was laughter, tears and more laughter. He was a good man. He was. Remember when. I do. And then. Ah Jaysus. That's right, and when. Paddy boy. Who was it said. No, it was. He could play. Sometimes he would.

John reached into his bag and lifted out an envelope. It was stained with dark floral shapes, and the edges of the paper were torn.

I didn't know when to bring this out. I guess now is as good a time as any.

He opened the envelope carefully, peeling back the angular lip and withdrawing a folded sheet of paper. He held it up to the light. There are reasons for Paddy's death in here. It was found in the pocket of his coat. The police showed it to his mother while I was there, at the morgue.

He placed the letter on the table. After she read it, she just looked at me. God, it was bloody terrible. I didn't know what was going on. Neither did she. She asked me to read it, to explain.

So for fuck's sake, what is it? Sean was leaning forward, his eyes on the paper.

John sat back and rubbed his face. It's Paddy's description of a night at Blackmore House. He must have gone down into one of those rooms after we'd all gone to bed.

John tapped the letter. This gives some idea of how he felt, and what he saw, but I'm tellin' youse, we'll never really know the horror of what he found down there. In himself, like.

Would you read it please? Sarah was sitting stiffly, her hands in her lap. Read it now. I don't want to hear it, but go on.

John picked up the page and opened it. The spines of the words were visible under a ghost-print of ink.

PADRAIGH

I AM HERE in a room below this old house. My father's
room? It looks the same, at least, it looks the same
from the memory of what a young boy saw, one
afternoon, a few days after his father had gone out.
Forever. No windows. Dark walls. A large bed. A
marble washstand with a swing mirror. Floorboards.
Sarah and John and Sean and James above me, drinking
and laughing. Well, that's grand. Can they feel my
father's presence too? I am standing in front of the
mirror. There is a young boy inside me. I can hear him
breathing. He is there in the mirror. Where have you
been? Where is your father? I can't hear you. Gone?
Into the ground? Yes. The boy tried to get out. He
moved, and the man's body jumped. My mother told
me that while she was pregnant, lying in the bath, the
water would shiver when I kicked around. The mirror's
silver shivered when the boy moved and breathed. I said
It's alright, you can come out now. And so he did. The
man's body opened and the boy climbed out. He was
naked. He looked at himself. He said I know who you
are. The candleflame made his eyes look hollow. His

hands were shaking. He couldn't move. Behind him, the room was black, the air draining quickly. The boy said Look, I am dying. The mirror held him and held him. Wax folded over his small fist, and he started to grow. His bones creaked. As the flame tapered and fluttered, he saw himself fading in the mirror. He said I don't want to be here any longer, and the flame went out. The man and the boy, the mirror and the walls, the floor and the black air were gone. I am nowhere. I am waiting. To go out. Forever.

A SCATTERING OF
WINTER LIGHT

———

AT PADRAIGH'S FUNERAL in Cork, Sarah, John and
Sean played a couple of tunes. I read a poem. The
priest, who had been a good friend of his father, spoke
lovingly of a talented, generous man.

The wake was held at Padraigh's favourite pub, the
Western Star. It was a long, musical afternoon, where
all the stories we'd told on the road up the west coast
were continued, added to, repeated in song and words.
People came from all over the city.

Late that night, in Sarah's house, we made love in
silence. It was strange, because we were thick with grief,
and yet this seemed to make our lovemaking intense and
long. Upstairs, lying in the dark, we held each other tightly
and fell asleep that way. When we woke, at first light, we
were still in that position. We made love again, and we
cried, together, releasing the weight of sadness, collecting
the weight of the need to be together, and holding it in
the heat our bodies made, drinking each other's breath.

A Sunday morning. Sarah was standing at the window,
naked, brushing her hair. Summer coming through the

glass to panel the carpet with warmth and light. A line from a Leonard Cohen song arrived, and I quoted it — *I love to see you naked over there, especially from the back.*

Sarah stopped brushing her hair. She asked me what I thought Cohen meant.

I thought about the line, said it again.

Come on, James. What does he mean?

I think he's referring to sex, I said, but also how it's good to keep things mysterious, slightly hidden. That the obvious things are often the least erotic.

Sarah turned around slowly. She placed the brush on the table and said Yes, but what else?

There were tiny shadows under her breasts. I saw the blue forks of veins like contained stormlight radiating out from her nipples, her narrow waist, a thick red triangle of hair and the lips barely visible beneath it.

Do you think it's possible that he's saying it's good to see a woman's back? A woman who is leaving, that there's relief in the approach of someone's absence, in this case a woman's?

I said No, that can't be right. Why would a man find satisfaction in his lover leaving him?

Because sometimes we don't want to be reminded of permanence. I like the line. I love the song, actually, but I think there's a dark side to what he's saying.

Sarah picked up the brush. She turned back to the window. What do you see now? she asked.

Are you leaving me?

She looked down into the yard.

Have you noticed the flowers over by the fence, under the elm? They're beautiful. I planted that area with bulbs last year.

I said that I'd noticed them.

What colour are they?

Why are you asking me that?

Do you know what colour they are?

When I didn't answer, Sarah put her dressing gown on and went downstairs. I heard her open the door, and when I went to the window she was walking out across the yard.

She moved to the small garden plot beside the shed. She stood looking up into the branches of the elm, and then she knelt and passed her hand through a tight weave of flowerheads. She reached down. When she stood, she was holding a flower by the stem. She looked up at the window, as if expecting me to be there. Her mouth moved. I opened the window. She held the flower up over her head.

It's a hyacinth, and it's purple, she said.

I can see that, I said, and Sarah said Yes, but what colour is it at night, in the dark?

Before I could answer, she was moving over the sunlit yard, her hair blazing, her bare feet pale against the dark gravel on the path.

Sarah was late coming home from work one evening. I phoned the shop and was told she'd left early, around lunchtime. The woman I spoke to sounded hesitant. When I asked if she knew where Sarah had gone, or if she'd left a message, the woman took a long time to say that she was sorry, she had no idea.

I was led to the bedroom with fear in my head and hands as I opened the cupboard. Her clothes were gone. The drawers where she kept her underwear and socks contained woodgrains and shadows. Somewhere behind the scraping of a shovel, behind talk and laughter at morning smoko, as we laid pipes outside the city, Sarah had been hard at her own work inside the house. I sat on the bed. When I could move, I went looking for a note. There was nothing.

I entered and left pubs all night, a man hollowed out by absence and pain, scanning tables, bars and faces.

In the morning I phoned in sick and waited for the phone to ring. I moved about the house and yard. I made pots of tea and stood in the lounge room, staring at the telephone.

It rang in the afternoon, and I tackled it. It was Finbar. When I told him, he suggested we go for a pint.

I said no, I wanted to wait for Sarah to call.

You might be waiting a long time, he said.

Sarah's leaving was a slow dissolve. Scratchy dialogue bled over the stills that followed her into the world. I could hear her talking, faintly, in our room in Galway the night Michael had phoned her. I could hear my response, muffled by the pillow or the wind.

When I called them, John and Sean hadn't heard from her. Sean was effusive and full of suggestions, none of which held comfort or promise. John was quiet, and when I asked if there was anything he could tell me, he said he remembered Sarah saying something shortly after Padraigh's funeral.

She said she was tired of how love was such a bastard, or something like that. She said she was confused by her heart, and that she wanted to be calm for once in her life.

I wished he'd told me this before, and said so, and he responded with There are some things we need to keep our mouths shut about, James. Friends say things in confidence, and I believe Sarah's words to me fit that bill nicely. I'd like to think you agree with me on that one.

I said that I did, and it hurt to say the words. When I asked if he thought she had gone back to Michael,

John took a long breath and said It's possible. Anything's possible. Don't quote me. It's late. I have to. There are. You'll be. And then the receiver went dead in my hand.

Three days later the phone rang. It was late, around midnight. Sarah. She was calling from London.

What do people say, when time and distance have left the shapes of anger and pain in the air that divides them?

I'm sorry I haven't phoned, she said. How are you?

I could hear someone talking in the background. Sarah covered the mouthpiece. I heard the scratchy dialogue again, over a scene I tried not to follow.

I'm sorry, James, she said, as if from a great depth where sunlight dies.

What the fuck have you done? I did not say as I went to the end of my breath.

Sarah told me she was seeing Michael again. When I asked if *seeing* meant living together, she said yes, and then she said it was hard to talk.

So, you're singing and fiddling your way into a new life? Good for you.

James, I'm so sorry.

We spoke in broken sentences, over and under each other, half words and thoughts leaping into disconnections, my anger meshing with Sarah's attempts to explain what had happened.

From somewhere under the wreckage of our talk, we arrived at a place where Sarah said she'd come to collect what she'd left behind.

Two weeks later, a Saturday morning, Sarah called. She was at Blackmore House, staying with her sister. Could she come over? To talk? To get her things? I said she could get what she needed, but talk might be a problem, though I did not say how desperately I needed to speak with her.

I'd put her belongings into boxes and stacked them near the front door.

She arrived at two o'clock the next day. She'd cut her hair – a textured flame that followed the contours of her neck and head, her long green coat fanning the ends of her hair where it tapered off below her ears. She looked wonderful.

We sat on the edges of our chairs, finding amazement or sadness in the weave of the rug, the wall cracks over each other's heads.

I put the kettle on, thought better of it, opened a bottle and filled two shot glasses. Filled them again.

Thanks for packing my things, Sarah said, handing me her glass.

How will you get them to London?

I'm only taking what I need. I'll leave the rest with my sister. I'll be there until next weekend.

I arranged and lit a fire, and we sat before it.

When I asked if she was happy, Sarah touched the end of a burning peat brick with the toe of her boot and said No, not really. I don't think I've ever been completely happy.

I said I didn't think complete happiness was possible, and Sarah said that even being halfway there was something rare, something she ached for.

And when we made love? Were you happy then?

Mostly it made me sad. It was incredible, of course, but lovemaking always has a melancholy underside. Don't you think?

Yes. Did you love me?

I still love you.

Do you love Michael?

Yes. James, love can't be fenced off like that.

No, it's slamming the gate and running without word or warning.

Sarah told me about the nights when she left me sleeping, going down into the lounge room to cry and worry over the decision that was growing inside her. She went back to Galway, to the night Michael phoned at the hotel, to their meeting. She told me things she hadn't mentioned – how, despite his violence and what had happened to Padraigh, she still loved Michael, and that their love was unresolved. When I asked why she hadn't told me these things earlier, she didn't answer. Then she sat up. She said she believed it's possible to love two people, but that, when love is unfocused, as it surely must be in that situation, then something has to break.

Sarah reached into the pocket of her coat. When her hand surfaced, it contained a folded sheet of paper. She opened it, smoothed it on her knee, and began to read:

Did I speak enough? Have you heard my voice?

Would you like to hear it again? I love being with you.

It was the message I'd left beside her on that first morning, after the gig in Clonmel.

I took her hand. She let the sheet of paper fall. I pressed her Claddagh ring with my thumb. Her fingers closed around mine, and we kissed, lightly. When I put my arm around her waist and drew her close, she gave me her mouth and we lowered ourselves into an embrace that covered the floor with clothing. As I entered her, Sarah began to cry, silently at first, then with long, low syllables of hurt. I followed her, opening into loud weeping that was lost and found in the slow rhythm of our bodies. We kissed each other's eyes and let go, helplessly, in a darkening room flushed with a pulse of orange light.

Sarah phoned twice during the week. She'd been taking long walks, and was eating her sister's soup and soda bread *by the bucketful*. When I asked if she'd been thinking about me, she said Of course. When I asked if she'd thought about coming home, she said I did come home, last Sunday. We made love. I'm living with Michael. What does that say about me, James? I'm confused, and I hate myself for what happened. It wasn't fair.

It was wonderful.

Yes, it was, and it was selfish of me, and very bloody inappropriate.

I fought a sudden spasm in my chest and throat. Will you call before you leave?

Yes, of course. Will you be alright?

After we'd spoken I went outside. The night was clear and cold, indigo velvet, with stars pinned loosely into their designs. I rolled and smoked a cigarette, trying to see her face. She came to me, out of focus, her breath a plume behind her right shoulder.

I went inside and took out my box of slides. There was one I had to find, like an unfinished letter, curious and bright with expectancy, all the more intense for its incompletion – an image that could never be made final, although it seemed to crave closure.

The little light box flickered on. I lowered my eye to a cone of magnifying plastic. I saw a woman's face through the branches of a lichen-blistered cedar, where I had been sitting, watching her move through the grounds of a country estate. Her coat was the colour of the leaves, her eyes burnt sienna. Her features entered the texture of the bark. In a scattering of winter light, she was asking me to let go, to embrace the nature of my fear.

I turned away. The cut daffodil I'd placed into a scribble of thyme on the mantelpiece twisted once in a plume of heat and turned its light on. Behind me, the fire crackled quietly. On the table, a perspex rectangle glowed like a tray full of radium, a woman's face at its centre.

I sat down again and put my eye to that day. Her right hand was pressed flat against the tree trunk. I looked carefully at her Claddagh ring: two hands holding a golden heart. Friendship, loyalty and love. Friendship was never the issue. Love? It came with conditions and a drawerful of elaborate masks, but we loved each other. Painfully. Loyalty is what overspills from a guide-dog's eyes.

It seemed that any second she was going to look away from me, turn with a green flourish and walk through the ancient trees, her hair out behind her in the wind. I waited. I pressed my eye hard to the rim of the cone and moved it slowly across her face.

I turned the light table off and listened. Woodsmoke hung like rivermist under the roof beams. I saw a trout mouthing for air on a riverbank. I heard a woman's voice somewhere near. I felt fear like a hook in my mouth, and I swallowed hard. On the table, a woman's face, visible even in darkness.

BLOODFLOW

⸻

S OMEONE YOU KNOW dies, an acquaintance or colleague from work. Their absence is a burred edge on the days that follow their dying. You get caught as you move through the hours. You find yourself standing quietly, remembering a voice or smile as the office, the room or street moves around you. When someone you love leaves your life, another kind of death arrives. You stand remembering with a hole in your side. You are painfully aware of your body and how hard it can be to breathe.

When Sarah left, I ignored my tablets for a week. It was not an experiment. I knew the chemical equation for no medication plus deep focus on the head and heart. I'd been experiencing an irregular shock like a thin, hot wire lighting the centre of my chest when startled by something – even a gust of wind or sound could set it off. The profile of her face in silhouette on the Lapwing poster I'd pinned to the wall seemed to leer at me. I was broken by the memory-flash of her hair lighting the air as she played the fiddle at a party in Kinsale, the countless images of her smile framed in a face that came and went, looming and fading, sometimes reachable, sometimes a receding shape in the fog.

I found the lives of others in the spaces Sarah left, going down some sideroad of dream. Tina stepped out from behind a windbreak of pines and said The bookshop has gone to dust, are you coming? Stephanie opened the wingflaps of stained curtains. The door's open, she said, Mind your heart on the step. A current forked through my chest, and Death entered the room. I talked myself down from a high, windy place at the centre of my bedroom in the confines of my head. Stephanie and Tina left, although I didn't hear or see them go. When Death slipped away, I opened the bottle and shook a tablet into my palm. It was time to return to the slow, prescribed fixative of my time. I swallowed it with a sip of tea, then turned the desk lamp on and stared at a manuscript of poems. I waited. For what? For Sarah's face to float back into view? For Death to try my coat on?

I woke with my head on the desk. It was early morning. Overcast. Wind. Leaves scraping outside the front door. The wind died off, the leaves settled. I looked at the page my face had used in fitful sleep: black lines, arrows, circles, the private language of writing poetry. A saliva-bleed like a paisley petal blurring the words *unlikely predator* where my angled mouth had been.

Somewhere under the brief cover of tapping into the shell of a sentence, I heard the wind and leaves again, a dry sound, like an intake of breath measuring patience or a bloom of anger, like fingers and thumb rubbed together, papery and cool, beside the ear.

I went downstairs, moving in and out of my body under high ceilings beamed with smoke-stained timber, over floorboards warped and musical. In the living room I felt a flush of cold air. The front door was open, though I couldn't recall having opened it during the night. Outside, the path was leafless. Turning back into the house, the entrance like a drained aquarium, the coat-rack once again startled me into thinking I had a visitor. Then I heard the sound again, and as I entered the house I found a blackbird hanging from the curtains, watching me. When I moved towards it, it flew to the opposite wall, its wings scraping loudly against the plaster. My father entered the room and walked to stand beside me. He was wearing a sports coat with leather elbow patches. He smelled of Old Spice and cigarettes. He said Let me show you how to catch and hold a bird. He moved quickly. The bird hopped and settled and was taken into the cradle of his hands. It pecked at the joints of his thumbs, then relaxed, its underside rising and falling. Here, my father said, See how my fingers are laced, how the mounds below my thumbs make cushions for the wings? I took the bird and held it close. Its eyes were gold, the inside of its beak like a pomegranate seed. My father left the room. The room smelled of ash and a light quilting of mould.

I breathed slowly as I took the blackbird outside and let it go. It entered the spaces between branches of a fence-leaning tree, and was gone. I stood with my palms over my face, inhaling deeply, trying to locate something else beneath the smell of the bird, as if absence were olfactory, as if I were inhaling the scent of being unbelievably alone.

Despite the wave of depression that folded and broke over me, I was able to see through the vague shapes of my days, finding a curious, black comfort in my own company. To say that I was feeling strong in the wake of Sarah's leaving would be folly, yet I was aware of myself, and of what had to be done if I was to surface, whole and alive from the heart of the wave. I walked. In the evenings I saw Finbar regularly. At work I found relief in digging and sweating. I worked deep into the night on new poems.

Early one morning, unable to sleep, I lit a candle and carried it to my desk. Before placing it on the window sill, I saw myself in the glass, my face in a soft yellow light. I held my own gaze and I knew, when I looked away, that Sarah had not taken me with her when she left, that I was capable of moving on. I understood, finally, that fear and love are bloodflow, and I wanted to hear them with my life.

A TIME BEFORE WORDS

—•◦•—

SIX WEEKS AFTER Sarah had come over, I met Finbar at The Wide Valley. It was strange to be there, drinking under the room I once lived in.

Finbar was in a reflective mood, talking about his childhood in Clare. He offered me a room at his house, Until you're on your feet, he said, clapping me on the shoulder.

I said I needed to be alone, and Finbar fingered the bar wood, saying Solitude is the natural home for the death of love.

Someone started playing guitar. Someone else joined in on mandolin. Other instruments surfaced. A small table became a long one, with extensions of tables, chairs, pint glasses and legs.

During a break in the session, Finbar stood up and began to sing, unaccompanied. His voice was strong and fine, and when he finished he sat down and two pints appeared before him.

When the barman called last drinks, we were just hitting our stride. Finbar suggested we go to his place. The invitation was extended to the players.

As we ordered takeaways, Finbar touched me on the shoulder. I think you might be needed, Jim, he said.

I turned around. People were standing in small groups, putting coats on. Others were leaving.

Over there, Finbar said, pointing.

I looked and found Sarah standing in the doorway. Her hair was wet and dripping, her clothes dark and heavy with rain. She was pale and shivering. I went to her and put my coat around her shoulders. Her breath was all smoke and whiskey.

Finbar came over and I told him we were going home.

James, Sarah said, and touched my face. Her fingers were ice.

Down the path to the house, under a web of rain, the streetlamps up on the road throwing arcs of cold, familiar light, Sarah's weight on my shoulder and arm.

Up the stairs, pitching left and right, pausing on the landing for breath, not questions.

In the bedroom, Sarah sat down and looked at her hands or feet, or the carpet's frayed edge. She was swaying. I knelt and untied her boots, eased them off. She sighed and lay back on the bed, pulling the coat around her, shivering. I removed the coat, undid the buttons on her blouse, helped her to rise and be free of it. Her bra snapped and came loose, and it was hard to breathe as the straps slipped from her shoulders and arms. Her broad leather belt came away like the first wrap of a winding sheet. Her legs kicked away from the skirt.

Her face under the covers, she said something I didn't hear, and then she was asleep, holding herself. I sat beside her, looking from her face to a pane of rain-streaked glass. Then I went back, with small preparations, to a time before words. In the kitchen I found a wine bottle cork. In the cupboard, a length of fishing line. Attaching the line to the cork, I went upstairs and pulled down the covers to expose Sarah's belly. She moved slightly, rubbing her left shoulder. Moved again. Sighed. I kissed her forehead. Then I sat back and held the line between finger and thumb. The cork floated in the rain-dark light above her belly. I watched the rise and fall of her chest. I watched the hand that held the gleaming line. I could see, within the blur of a shadow on Sarah's neck, the silent, regular workings of her life. Then, as one who aches for a sign or the puzzle of some augury to present itself, I waited for the cork to move.